AMERICAN
MERMAID

AMERICAN MERMAID

A NOVEL

Julia Langbein

DOUBLEDAY

NEW YORK

This is a work of fiction. Names, characters, places, and incidents either are the product of the author's imagination or are used fictitiously. Any resemblance to actual persons, living or dead, events, or locales is entirely coincidental.

Copyright © 2023 by Julia Langbein

All rights reserved. Published in the United States by Doubleday, a division of Penguin Random House LLC, New York, and distributed in Canada by Penguin Random House Canada Limited, Toronto.

www.doubleday.com

DOUBLEDAY and the portrayal of an anchor with a dolphin are registered trademarks of Penguin Random House LLC.

Jacket images: (Los Angeles, CA) Sean Davey/Aurora Photos/Superstock; (sky) Dane Robertson/Shutterstock
Hand-lettering and illustration by Grace Han
Jacket design by Emily Mahon

LIBRARY OF CONGRESS CATALOGING-IN-PUBLICATION DATA
Names: Langbein, Julia (Art historian), author.
Title: American mermaid : a novel / Julia Langbein.
Description: First edition. | New York : Doubleday, [2023]
Identifiers: LCCN 2022021818 (print) | LCCN 2022021819 (ebook) | ISBN 9780385549677 (hardcover) | ISBN 9780593470145 (trade paperback) | ISBN 9780385549684 (ebook)
Subjects: LCGFT: Humorous fiction. | Novels.
Classification: LCC PS3612.A563 A84 2023 (print) | LCC PS3612.A563 (ebook) | DDC 813/.6—dc23/eng/20220725
LC record available at https://lccn.loc.gov/2022021818
LC ebook record available at https://lccn.loc.gov/2022021819

MANUFACTURED IN THE UNITED STATES OF AMERICA

First Edition

For all the mermaids out there

(you know who you are)

PART I

FINDING HER

CHAPTER 1

The novel that I wrote begins with a woman in a wheelchair falling into the sea.

It's not a comedy. I wrote it alone in a studio apartment in New Haven, Connecticut, at a table on a rug that looked like it had been digested rather than woven. For three years I came home from teaching English to teenagers at Holy Cross, a secular public high school on Holy Cross Avenue, and wrote in an exhausted, anxious daze. I remember the night I started. I had bought a bottle of terrible wine after work. I was writing in my diary, then I was lying to my diary, then I wrote her. I saw her, I felt her: she was not a broken woman but a mermaid after all. Her fear of drowning filled me, and then, buoyed up in drunkenness, I felt my legs twitch with a long-forgotten muscle memory of swimming.

I lie on the giant white raft of my super-king bed, twenty stories up in an executive apartment that I've rented for the summer in Los Angeles. I wasn't pretending to be an executive, and I'm embarrassed at being the wrong person for it. I have nothing but spare time here, as the time-efficient pod-coffee reminds me. I have nothing to scan on the scanner. This place was cheap because it's in Century City, the uncoolest part of LA. You can see my building with others of its kind: architecturally, they are big-boned admin women in gray pantsuits. Unless I've undergone some kind of retinal bleaching in the California sunshine, I think the wall-size windows are made of sunglasses glass, the pervert kind that dim. I feel like a pervert, that mix of irresponsible pleasure and occasional shrugging disgust. Pleasure because I left my teaching job and I have my days free, disgust because of what I'm out here to do. Sometimes I push my nose against the glass wall and look down from my death-defying diving board at the unwalked pavement below, the only part of LA that could just as easily be Stamford, Connecticut. If it weren't for the chilly stream of panic in my blood that runs on a loop like a corporate courtyard fountain, I'd forget where I was.

American Mermaid was published in December. I was a nobody—no babbling spectral internet persona, just a teacher—and I was told that I was lucky to get an advance of forty-five thousand. It seemed monumental, that sum, and I was grateful for the seventeen grand I pocketed after my agent nibbled and taxes chomped at it. Ten grand paid off my credit card debt. But even having seven thousand extra bucks was thrilling. Unallotted dollars not clothing me or housing me or drunk down inescapably on Friday at a bar three blocks from school.

I was thirty-three and even with my extra money my legs were hairy and my workplace was dirty and it was fine. Then suddenly it seemed the whole world might melt and recool in a smooth new shape.

In the spring, just a few months into the book's publication, *American Mermaid* appeared on the Instagram account of a professional internet presence named Stem Hollander, an athletic charmer in his midforties with floppy blond hair and ten cheeky grins, whose humpy Segway salsa dancing gets millions of likes between endorsements of fair-trade avocados and weed-lobby Democrats. After Hollander, the librarians picked it up. Then, to my surprise, some national treasure on the *Today* show open-throat screamed about it too early in the morning. Thanks to her it was packed up and palleted to Costco, where I've seen it myself on a chessboard of hardbacks, a rook's jump away from *Dieting for Joint Health*. I did a gimmicky magazine interview where I met a male journalist my age in a leather jacket in Atlantic City at a bar with live mermaid shows. Women with big naturals, their legs bound in plastic tail fins, pretended not to need to breathe, writhing on the other side of a scratched pane while we drank rum runners as if the Garden State Parkway weren't five miles away. I cried and the journalist described it, which I think got me foreign sales in thirty-six countries.

But Stem Hollander got it all started. He Instagrammed a picture of *American Mermaid* on his reclaimed marble nightstand. It was sandwiched between *Balderdash*, a book your uncle definitely read, about a Great Dane in the British Army who changed the course of World War II, and *Shots Shots Shots*, a memoir by a twenty-four-year-old fashion model that's been taken as a polemic against recovery. I remember thinking, proud and bewildered, *I wonder if this is what it's like to see your kid walk at graduation, in the lineup between a jock and a twat. I know her so well, but who is my daughter in the world?*

She could be a movie star, they told me: immediately after Hollander's endorsement in April, the film agents came calling. *American Mermaid* was an action film waiting to happen. With your gift for *female-driven* action, you play right into Hollywood's new hunger for ladyplots (I paraphrase, but barely). You could make a *mint*. When they told me I could be rich, I felt stupid for being so happy with seven thousand dollars, like an adult hugging a teddy bear. But my whole idea of myself was that I would never make any money. I had only gone from less remunerated to lesser remunerated, from funded doctoral student to academic to public school teacher. My other professional fantasies all put my cup yet further from the gushing falls of Mammon: poet, ceramicist, elder-carer. *Someone* has to set up the internet cemeteries; it might as well be me.

It was therefore completely believable to me when the book

began to sell into the tens and then twenties and thirties, and eventually hundreds of thousands, that my cup still rattled hollow. The earnings from the first royalty period paid back the publisher's advance. The second royalty period, which would begin in July, would last six months, and then the payment would not come for another six to nine months after. When I heard about the success of the book, I often felt like someone else had written it, someone wearing fresh lipstick and signing a deed, while I sat in my familiar studio, drinking coffee that tasted like plastic because my coffee machine is so cheap, it melts itself.

On May 1—International Workers' Day, whoops—I told my principal, Pamela, a nice lady with a nut-brown pelt helmet, that I was leaving Holy Cross and moving to LA. I was surprised at how sad she seemed about it—not merely annoyed about the hassle of replacing me, but disheartened.

"You've been such a gift to our students. They just love you." She shook her tufted head and looked down at her desk, a bombed city of paper towers.

"No, they don't," I said, imagining for a split second the slack-faced, self-absorbed teenagers I spent my days with tearing their shirts and sobbing over my grave. A tiny laugh contracted in my throat. I quickly turned it into a cough. The principal leaned to the side of her desk and pulled the plastic tab on a bulbous blue water-cooler. *Glub, glub, glub.* Over my stage cough, the office resonated with a sound like a blue whale burping from its forehead at forty thousand leagues. She handed me a cup of water.

"They *do* love you, Penny, and I'm sorry you don't see that. I hear them talk. And they talk about the books in your class. I get the feeling you crack these books and something of them leaks into real life. I don't know how you do it, but I hear them talking about characters from these stories like they're alive and doing things in this world. I've been here seventeen years and I've never seen anything like it."

I thought all teenagers were like that: borderless blood sacks where everything intermixes—sex, self-regard, anger, hunger, fiction, feelings.

"I know I can't keep you here with any kind of financial incentive. I used to teach math, you know—had to trade it in for this to send my own kids to school." She half waved her hand across her desk before dropping it onto a pile of paper, like a magician at the end of a trick that didn't work. Her forty-five coffee mugs—Fat Albert, Meryl's Bat Mitzvah—made Pam seem like she came from another time, a time before Starbucks.

"I figured you just liked . . . power."

"That's ridiculous, Penny. I'm the principal of an underfunded state educational institution. I'm not King Lear."

"King Lear just didn't want to die."

"I don't know. Mister Gatsby. Pip."

"They all just wanted money."

"And status," she said. The watercooler released an autonomous belch. We faced each other over her desk.

"You should have taught English, Pam."

I quit my job and moved to LA because I want money, too. I want money not to be something I can count like stones. The $1,540 I bring home every two weeks fritters away visibly, in chunks. A forty-dollar bar tab is a tenth of the slab of what I've got left after rent. I want money to be a substance that can't be counted, a vast pool I can float on, dip a hand down into without knowing where I am in it.

Last night I was floating around a party, because there are always parties and it's my job to go to them. "Wow, your dad is Wallace Stevens?" is something I heard.

I woke up the next morning and tried to figure out how someone at a party's dad could be Wallace Stevens. Wikipedia: Wallace Stevens had one daughter, Holly Stevens, born 1924. Could she have been there? No, everyone at that party was thirty-three. As I squinted at my phone screen in the dark, it illuminated a message on stationery ("Mountain Plaza Residence") on the nightstand. It said, in unfamiliar handwriting, "Derek Leary called several times." I must have fallen into my bed with the note in my hand blissfully drunk. But I woke up alarmed and found a series of unread texts from Derek on my phone: "I'M COMING TO LA." "I'M STAYING WITH YOU." "COOL?" "OBVIOUSLY COOL, RIGHT?"

Why is Derek coming?
Is this some sort of intervention?
Who gave me a paper phone message?

Derek and I had been teaching together at Holy Cross for only a couple of months when he began driving me to the pier at Long Wharf after school. We'd sit and talk in his car. Once we were sitting on the pier, looking at the Sound, and a large yacht appeared to be coming at us with surprising speed. Out of the silence I said, nodding at the boat, "You'll walk the plank. They'll ransom me."

Derek finished sucking on a cigarette, and without moving his head, his eyes rolled toward me slowly in their lizard sockets.

"Don't flatter yourself."

I love Derek, but I hope this man is not coming to save me.

On the way out of the apartment I stop at the security desk, where an attractive thirtysomething woman in a blazer stares at her smartphone.

"Hi," I say. She looks up with raised eyebrows. "Did you give me a note last night? On my way in?"

"It must have been the night guard."

"Okay. I'm sorry, I don't even understand how my friend managed to call the security desk here."

"Oh, that's simple. If someone calls the apartment's landline number, it comes to us and we transfer it to the room. The night guard must have taken a message for you when you weren't in."

"So, like a hotel."

"Nnno."

I walk a few steps toward the door and then pivot back to her with an apologetic gasp. "Oh! There's no laundry machine up there. What do I do about laundry?"

"You'll find a bag marked 'laundry' in the closet; throw what you need washed in there, call downstairs, and someone will collect it. You'll get it back in a day."

"Great. So, like a hotel."

"No."

I don't understand anything.

CHAPTER 2

I am at another party.

"Oh my god, you wrote *American Mermaid*?"

"That's so cool!"

One of these people does music for movies and the other is a screenwriter. These two people are the only people who don't look like members of a superrace. Everyone else at this party has taut skin and shimmering cheeks and hard, white, plastic teeth. I become self-aware of my bone teeth. Lightly smoked bone. My teeth look like antiques compared to all the teeth here, like valuable scrimshaw.

"I think it's so genius that you put your superhero in a wheelchair," the composer says.

I ask him, "Do you actually call yourself a composer? Or is that just for Tchaikovskys?"

"It's for everyone." I keep saying things that would have sounded conventional or even nice in Connecticut but pick up spite as they zip through desert air. Anyway, the dig slips off his smile like studio rain off a silly hat.

We are in the "Hollywood Hills," which is only words to me. I'm sure it connotes more to someone else: Porn? Wind? I am letting myself be taken places. Mostly I'm taken places by my film agent, Danielle MacAleese, who is my age, fun, and mean. She is at the same firm as my literary agent, who is old, sober, and nice. The first time Danielle and I met, at the Union League Cafe in New Haven, a waitress dropped one French fry on the black satin lapel of the business jumpsuit that encased Danielle's softened athletic frame. She looked at the fry skidding onto the table as if it were a severed finger. She jerked her face upward, cocked her head to the side, and squinted at the waitress.

"No, I mean, honestly, is this you trying to fuck with me?" she said to the woman. I wouldn't have used any of those words in that situation. Not one. How did she even know to start with "No"? We have different sets of words, I realized, which seems a good enough reason to hire someone.

That night we had a conversation where all my smoldering rocks of anxiety were doused by Danielle's cold confidence. I said things out loud, things I'd never even said to Derek—how afraid I was of being poor the rest of my life if I stayed a teacher. Danielle nodded, encouraging me along but skimming the details until I hit the cancer part of the story. If I had been a streaming movie, she would have been on her phone until this part.

My mom was diagnosed with breast cancer during my second year of teaching at Holy Cross, and her oncologist said I should do the BRCA1 and 2 tests. My parents paid for the tests, which cost over three thousand dollars. They were going through such an ordeal with my mother, they wanted to make sure my sister, Susie, and I were safe.

Susie tested negative, and I tested positive, which was strange, because Susie always seemed more like my mom—sporty, likable—and now a test showed that I was my mother's true heir. I have a mutation that will, with a 75 percent degree of certainty, develop into cancer in my breasts, and P.S., it's probs lurking in my ovaries, but that's for the sequel.

When I got the results, I started to have anxiety about everything. Suddenly death seemed imminent. I imagined my bicycle crunched by buses, nothing left of me but a blood-soaked flannel shirt. I was carrying a curse. I had to get rid of it—any smart person would, why else did they create the genetic test? So that when the doctors detect a lump in years to come, you can say, real chill, "Yup, there she is"? But salary-wise, I took home just over thirty-seven thousand dollars a year after taxes. A preventive double mastectomy will cost seventeen thousand out of pocket, and reconstruction using saline implants would be another seven thousand. My usually solid health insurance hadn't caught up with the science of genetic testing and deemed it all too speculative and cosmetic. My parents offered to pay. And I wanted to have the thing done, desperately. But I couldn't handle the idea that, like a third wife, like a hopeful actress, like a hottie bimbo, I was going to charge a boob job to my daddy.

It's a weird enough concept, elective mastectomy followed by reconstruction. A little bag of salt water, a pristine ocean in a pod, will live inside you, and your nipples will be fully decorative like the knobs on a Travelodge nightstand. You'll feel compunction explaining this to people, as if by having one surgery to stay alive and another to look exactly as you always have you've been a privileged narcissist.

But the weirdest part was that I couldn't see my life the same way, economically. I had considered myself financially independent until all this. I thought I was self-sufficient, self-supporting. My life involved no great luxuries and the crush of teaching sometimes overwhelmed me, cumulatively. All those early mornings and then finishing grading and class prep pretty late and feeling a bit resentful for doing lawyer hours for babysitter money. But nevertheless, I thought I was on my own until I realized I was a complete joke, an adorable diorama about folk independence in the king's museum. I make enough money to rent lodging, eat food, and finger the sale rack at J. Crew with some performance of intent. But if I need a dental crown I have to call my dad.

I know I sounded like a greasy teen in the leather booth across from Danielle at the Union League Cafe, whining about financial dependence instead of being grateful I've got someone to depend on. The conclusion of the story should have been "They're willing to save my life" and not "They're willing to save my life, the fuckers. I need to fill my bank account like a brewer's vat so that if I encounter difficulties"—here one of my ovaries winks at me—"I can face them on my own."

Danielle nodded earnestly, her head dipping over and over, eyes closing occasionally like she was listening to a soaring aria. I believed she wanted to help me and would and could. At one point, Danielle took a phone call that ended with her saying, "Great. I'll have my assistant send you that juicy, juicy check." I imagined a juicy, juicy check so wet with money you'd have to handle it gently or it'd rip like pear skin.

"Great." "Great." "Great" was what Danielle gave me, with little ducks of the head for each of my anxieties. "Great, you don't want to be poor, I get it."

When I got into the stuff with my dad's politics, she lost patience. "Fuck your baggage, Penny. Look: Come out to LA. Be a boss bitch. Join us. Join us women who don't have to borrow money from our dads when we want a nice pair of shoes." Or a safe pair of boobs. "Join us." Danielle loves, I've since learned, characterizing "boss bitch" life: We wear fur sandals. We ski alone. We pay people to pay people.

But she's right. It's not my *fault* that it's not feasible to have a middle-class job anymore. All I want is to be a teacher. Can't I just be a teacher? I don't want to drive Uber when I've finished grading in the evenings if I hope to buy property or see Japan or avoid cancer or treat cancer or have a child. I can't even drive—I'm incapable of staying within the lines; my driving teacher once breathalyzed me. Danielle seemed so right: the only way for me to become my own boss was to leave teaching, go to Hollywood, assume my place among the other educated "creatives," and make bank.

I ordered the soup-and-salad combo because it was the cheapest thing on the menu. Plus, it seemed like a lot to me: two things!

But when I ordered it, Danielle said, "Soup and salad? You sure that's enough? It's a pee and a fart. Get something substantial." It seemed like she knew more about my real hungers than I did, and that I should trust her knowledge of what would nourish me. "I'm getting the cassoulet," she said. "This has to get me back to New York." As if she'd be hoofing it alongside the Metro-North tracks on the metabolized steam of bean and duck. This you could imagine easily. One day, if I came to LA and hired Danielle and became a boss bitch, I might know that what I deserved and needed was the Frenchest stews I could find and I, too, might power myself to places on rare proteins.

My confession to Danielle—panic about money, hatred for a world in which you couldn't do something as basic as teach, hatred for my dad and all the waxy-headed dad-faced assholes who thought anyone struggling financially had opted out of success— seemed like something she'd heard before. Or else she saw the profit in me and didn't care. Danielle signed the check, and I watched her do the math for a 20 percent tip, and I thought, *See? She's one of the good ones.* Did a little part of me feel something sour in my jaw occasionally during this conversation, feel a little curdling in my stomach? Of course. But I told myself this: I freed a mermaid in a book, and now she's freeing me.

Tonight, we met at Danielle's stucco castle in Silver Lake. While she got ready, she gave me a goblet of chardonnay and put me in front of a reality TV show about a five-hundred-pound teenager who gets gastric bypass surgery. The laparoscopic camera tunneled through soft floes of yellow fat, searching for the teen's stomach. Danielle zapped off the TV on a shot of his body, naked, looking like the cushions of a beige leather sofa piled on a metal table.

"I've seen this one," said Danielle. "He ends up *hot*." Her eyebrows danced up and down for a moment, and we laughed together.

"You should track him down," I said, rolling with her suggestiveness.

"They did a reunion show. He's dead. Pop the wine in the fridge, let's scoot."

Danielle drove us to an angular house, like a bony person itself, full of bony people.

The way I make the most cash, Danielle said, is to write the adaptation myself. To option the book with myself attached. But since I have no track record of making movies, she paired me up with two experienced male screenwriters. Still, I'm being invited into an expanding, self-aware category of demanding, creative women. We'll laugh at the same things, me and powerful women like Danielle. We'll share tips on where to find the shiniest jumpsuits. Maybe I'll get a plaster castle, too!

Later, in the car, my mind drifting on the subject of plaster, I mentioned a Turkish artist I knew who made papier-mâché casts of political asylum seekers' bodies and shipped them all over the world to unsuspecting government addresses.

Driving, scanning the horizon, Danielle said, "Weird. Why?" And suddenly I had no idea.

CHAPTER 3

EXCERPT FROM *AMERICAN MERMAID*

"I'm going out, darling." Eleanor Granger paused again for a response as she wrapped a scarf around her head. It was 1985. June, the first of three months that she and her husband would spend in a small, waterlogged cabin on the southernmost tip of Vágar. To protect the coastline, buildings close to the sea couldn't be more than shacks, so that's what they had: drywall that never dried, a bedroom with windows on three sides opening onto watery skies or the crashing coast. Eleanor often woke up believing she was a teenager at summer camp in Maine, with just a canvas tent between her and the surf.

"All right, hon, I'll stay here," said Dean, leaning over some maps on the kitchen table.

As the wooden A-frame receded behind her, Eleanor's boots slipped on the damp igneous rock. *This rock was born yesterday*—she made herself laugh—*compared to the granite in Maine.* She imagined she could feel the difference in her soles; the soft, wet rock of Vágar, barely cooled lava, giving way just a little, whereas the granite floor of her childhood shot through her bones with each step. Tanker-like clouds moved slowly ahead but let some light ripple across the yellow-green fields of the island's interior. She thought about her father, whom she would follow along the mossy forest trails in Maine. He would take a knife to the roots of chanterelles and meadow mushrooms, leaving them toppled. "Remember the spot, Nellie. We'll send your mother back out with a bucket."

Unthinking—or thinking about Dean, absently, about his new habits of seclusion, his obsessive reading—she took a left down toward the water instead of up toward the village. A dirt path descended to a beach of black pebbles, freshly darkened with each lick of the sea from her left and each dribble of moisture down the cliff from the grassy slopes to her right. She scanned the pebbles for life, for hermit crabs or starfish. There were gulls swirling and crying in the air not far ahead, so something must have washed up. As a gray-speckled mound came into view on the pebbles, she thought, with great sadness, that it must be a baby pilot whale. The Faroese had been doing ritual hunts recently, where they shuttled whole pods into a coastal bay for slaughter. Sometimes one or two would escape the corral, but they'd die anyway, drifting off course, confused. There had been reports in the paper about locals getting sick from the whale meat, and they'd forbidden the eating of it. Maybe this was related, some surfeit of toxicity in the animal's blood. She'd bring it up with Dean, she thought, suddenly hungry for an interesting conversation with her brilliant husband; he knew everything about the natural world.

Dean Granger rummaged through a box of tins they'd brought from America and pulled out some olives. Vágar was a promising site for research into renewable energy, but it didn't exactly have a robust consumer economy. One could tire of preserved fish. Granger drew a heavy breath. It didn't make sense, his melancholy: he was a superstar. He had been the first engineer to make natural gas economically viable. Granger's method of blasting down not with fire but with chemically treated water was the only way to chase the gas out of East Texas shale and it was making him millions. Now he was again on the verge of a technical breakthrough. They called it EGS, enhanced geothermal systems: the possibility of fueling not a couple of Icelandic villages with heat from mere meters deep but the whole goddamn globe with energy pulled directly from the core of the earth. Whoever cracked this, people said, would solve the energy crisis for good.

And yet over the past few years, he had started to feel a fatigue that no sleep could heal, a kind of infinite tax on his consciousness. What was he *doing* here? What was the point of trying to develop newer, safer energy? Let's say he figured out EGS and made a template for an extraction process anyone could use. What about the coal and gas interests? What about the endless desire for plastics? Would idiot teenagers and pudgy sugar addicts suddenly slurp their Mountain Dew from oiled canvas pouches? And what of the ten-story heaps of plastic already choking Chinese estuaries, floating in the Pacific like a bloated corpse? Granger was the smartest guy on the planet giving sustainable energy the biggest shot it had. From this pinnacle of hope, he surveyed the future and saw that it would not be enough.

Nell ended most days cheerful, having solved problems—*local* problems. She'd done a planned burn or she'd mapped the extent of a protected species. They'd met in graduate school, in a geology course, and they had always shared a connection to the earth, a way of seeing the ground they walked on as productive and alive. But Nell didn't see the big picture. They had followed the boom in literature on climate change in the 1970s. After the first World Climate Conference in Geneva six years ago, acronyms were spawned (WCIP) and declarations made (". . . it is now urgently necessary . . . for the nations of the world to foresee and prevent man-made changes . . .")—and nothing changed. The climate had become something for schoolchildren to sing about. He puffed a sad laugh out his nose. *Children.* Typical of childless couples to need a cause. Maybe that's all their ecological consciousness was. A pathetic attempt to sustain life for others, since they'd been unable to create it themselves.

He finished cranking the can opener, and as he went to tip the lip open, he felt a sharp pain in his index finger.

"Goddammit!" A bead of blood appeared on his finger and grew until it burst into a crooked trickle down his wrist. He grabbed a kitchen towel with his opposite hand and wrapped it tightly around his finger. He picked up the offending can to read the label. "Pawcett Food Co., Red Bluff, CA." *Well, guess what, Pawcett Foods? In about a hundred years, you'll be swallowed by the sea.*

He put the cut to his lips. He hated blood, the penny taste of it, how it was always a surprise, bluer or blacker than you'd imagined. He preferred a geological body. You cut the earth open and it just breathed at you, a hot, salable breath. He paused to let a vision rush in: a bunch of hippies in Red Bluff, CA, standing waist-deep in water, not in 2085 but now. Tomorrow. He saw himself on the high ground, a wounded earth bearing him up.

He imagined siding with the hard truth, even if it meant that a great silent crack would separate him, unseen, from his wife. He would have to rescue her from her own impulses. (He pictured her heaving a sandbag onto her back to the ratty coastline of a poor town.) He would have to deceive her along with everyone else as he laid the groundwork for his plan, but in the end, when she was safe and insulated from the horrors of the final catastrophe, he knew she would stay by his side.

He grabbed for the kitchen sponge in the sink on the island to wipe up the brine and blood that seeped into the unvarnished pine table, but a chef's knife, the blade matte where it had run through a block of cheese, was lying on top of it. He lifted the knife. Just then, he heard the door slam. His wife was inside, shoes on, her jacket removed and wrapped around something in her arms. She looked strange, somehow. Dazed. She usually came back hale and chatty after her walks, but she was frozen and white. "What?" said Dean. "D'ja bring back dinner?"

Eleanor approached the table and laid down her bundle. She

unfurled the windbreaker partway to reveal a living thing: a baby, green-eyed, red-cheeked, holding two fists up toward Eleanor. Dean was alarmed but felt this kind of thing was his strong suit. He wiped his hands, put down the knife. "Jesus Christ. Where did you find him? *Jesus Christ.* I'll call the cops." He was about to turn toward the wall-mounted telephone. "You want a tea, Nell? Or a drink?" Then Eleanor, that same dazed face, pulled away the rest of the windbreaker. Just where the baby's belly button should be the soft skin transitioned into scales in glinting, untarnished silver, like a tray of new dimes.

"It's not a boy, Dean."

To the same rhythm with which the little creature opened and closed her fat fists, she lifted up and clapped down the bifurcated, ribbed, translucent fins of an unmistakable tail.

CHAPTER 4

In my book, Sylvia is twenty-four when she falls into the sea. Her parents have kept her from the water all her life. She assumes that this is to protect her, because when water touches her shriveled gray skin from the waist down it causes burning pain, and her weak, deformed legs would never keep her afloat. When she falls into the sea, a suicide, her wheelchair peels off her and sinks quickly to the bottom. She is scared and believes she is about to die, here, in Boston Harbor. But suddenly, submerged, the pain subsides and her scarred, fragile legs, which unbeknownst to her are the vestiges of a powerful tail, begin to pulse.

I spend much of my day responding to an email thread with Murphy Dicek and Randolph Reynolds. They are the two components of a writing partnership. They did a high-grossing film together about a Black female bank robber for Universal, so Danielle thought with their help, we would turn my book into a killer feminist action movie and sell it to a major studio. Two weeks ago, the two of them went to a pitch meeting and sold the idea to the studio—Danielle said it was a slam dunk, having me on board, the female writer of the hit feminist book, and they called back to say yes before Randy and Murphy had even pulled out of the parking lot past the giant billboard of a robot with machine guns for hands and Tom Cruise for a face.

Variety reported it in early June: Universal buys rights to *American Mermaid*; Randy Reynolds and Murphy Dicek to pen script with *American Mermaid* author Penelope Schleeman. I signed a contract at Danielle's house, where she used a lot of enthusiastic language about the future ("great together," "feel so great about this," "amazing team"), and filled out some paperwork, and then a few days later I went to an ATM outside in the sunshine and my balance showed fifty-two thousand dollars and I had to put my hands up on the screen, on either side of my head, and go in close to see it clearly. I felt like there was a bird warbling in my throat, and I couldn't stop laughing at things like babies walking and buttons on the elevator, I was so happy. My surgery was now within reach, but I couldn't just drop everything and head to the hospital. We had only eight weeks to turn in this script to the studio, and anyway, the last thing I felt like doing was booking it. Instead I walked past fast-food windows, saw the price for a four-pack of nuggets, and thought, *I could buy 416,000 nuggets!* Me and a handful of hacker anarchists and some clever children: very good at math, still can't make money.

Or couldn't, until now.

This is how I'll get the castle and join Danielle's feminist wine club ("Dude, we drink Ridge with a *straw*." High five). There are moments still when I remember my old life in New Haven as perfectly satisfying (cheap oysters on the blue linoleum bar at Steve & Eddy's between the highway and the Sound; local radio top-ten-at-ten DJ'd by a lovable penis; that box wine with the rabbit on it and grading and putting my forehead on the table alone because a fifteen-year-old with a thesaurus has called Edith Wharton a "panjandrum"). I don't especially want to be intubated with expensive cabernet, but I know when I'm falling asleep, dreaming of big paper checks *juicy* with money, that I'm smiling because I won't be an expensive asset of my father's. I'll own myself.

Murphy and Randy are heterosexual adult men who act like the best teenage daughters you could ever want. They are best friends who gossip while they pee together, they have butts made of COR-TEN ship-building steel, and they are nice to everyone. These two reek of competence, and they seem to have no doubt that in the six weeks that remain until the end of July, as is contractually stipulated, we'll deliver a bang-up final script. These email conversations happen regularly from about nine to twelve, and three to seven every day, reliably, like a tide.

Randy:

What we're saying, Penny, is that it doesn't change all this to make her 18.
　　We want to make it prom. Like your classic cinematic Under the Sea prom, and she's there in her wheelchair and the boat sinks.

Murphy:

You have to think CINEMATICALLY. In your book, she's suicidal, which is cool for a book. But think about how it will LOOK when a ferryboat full of teenagers in party dresses goes underwater: paper fish, paper streamers, glitter, pom-poms, all of the prom décor goes under!!!! You have a *Titanic/Carrie* sequence but instead of killing everyone, Sylvia has her A-HA moment and starts SAVING PEOPLE.

It's not an "A-HA" moment. She doesn't realize that yogurt gives her gas. She kills herself and lives.

Randy:

Go to Netflix right now—I want you to see what Nils Matheson did in *Category Five*—it's a scene where a resort in Bali gets sport-fucked by a cyclone. I think it'll give you a sense of what this prom disaster sequence could look like. You need to give yourself permission to imagine huge-scale effects.

I write back:

Okay, I understand that a party is more visually interesting than a single woman on a pier. But eighteen? Nobody gives a fuck about eighteen-year-olds.

Murphy and Randy go silent for three hours in a way that suggests that many people give many fucks about eighteen-year-olds.

I reply again:

She needs to have been through college, I'm sorry. It doesn't make any sense for her to be an effective eco-warrior later if she's never trained as a scientist.

Randy:

Isn't it technically awesomer to just know stuff without being taught it? What if she just KNOWS science?

You can't know stuff without being taught, I think to myself but do not write, and my thought comes with an image attached, and it's Derek with his khakis hanging off his ass, his hands on his hips, at the front of his classroom in Connecticut surrounded by sixteen-year-olds. I imagine Derek saying something like "Okay, what kind of invisible is the Invisible Man?"

CHAPTER 5

There are parties every night. I go to the parties because otherwise Danielle will make me do more "generals." "Generals" are meetings—you could have ten a day—in identical prop-strewn bungalows owned by producers where a mechanically breezy intern says, "So tell me about yourself. What, like, movies do you like?" You get a bottle of water. Sometimes they ask, "What are your ideas? Anything you want to write about?" But Danielle told me never to answer this question.

"Because we don't want them stealing my ideas?"

"No, because it's boring."

Danielle's only other instruction for the general was a text telling me to "dress SUPER CASUAL." A follow-up text read "LIKE WEAR NOTHING." Once at a general, I was tired and something about being in a bungalow full of toys made me feel like a child at a social worker's office and I melted into myself and said I wasn't sure I'd ever write again. For five silent minutes, the intern propped her smile up like a primitive bridge.

So now Danielle directs me to attend parties, where there are usually specific targets for me to meet: producers and studio executives to appetize with the hot ham of my next idea or who might bring me on to scripts in development; showrunners on female-driven projects who might hire me as a staff writer; influencers like Stem Hollander who capriciously gift the attention of millions to the books and albums and sweat-wicking yoga thongs of the few.

So far, I've smoked weed with two part-time caterers.

At the last party, as I waded past an open fridge the size of a classroom blackboard, I bumped into a guy and said, "I'm sorry," and he said, "It's coal."

It's coal. Everybody's snake jaws; everybody's vowels tumbling out unworked like big, dusty rocks.

Derek didn't want me to leave Holy Cross. We had a good thing together at the school. We talked about the kids we both taught, we talked about the books we were teaching and the conversations we'd had in class about them. That was a rare pleasure, we both knew. Looking back, it's as if teaching happened in a drunken blackout—I can barely remember what we said, but I remember currents of hilarity and anxiety and a kind of embalming, communal boredom. At moments, talking with fifteen-year-olds about *House of Mirth* was a holy heaven. Because nobody can win. Because everybody's a bit ridiculous. Because some kids are gay and don't know it, wide open and don't know it, smart and don't know it. They'll all have a way, someday, of talking at parties and at work. They'll become used to being dominating or ironic, they'll play their lexicon like a keyboard and they'll have their familiar chords and modulations. But now they're atonal, so dumb they're avant-garde. Wild, without self-interest, around a table set with no food at a meeting with no purpose other than to talk about a story there's almost no chance they perfectly understood alone.

"Bortha Dorset is a psycho and it's her fault the main lady kills herself," says a fifteen-year-old boy in a stiff Giants hat about Edith Wharton's women. (I don't make them take their hats off—the hat thing is a battleground for the older male teachers. I never got it.)

"Her name is Bertha Dorset," I interject, "and the 'main lady' is called Lily Bart. Why do you say that it's Bertha's fault?"

(Another student:) "I don't think it's Berfa's fault at all. Lily Bort was greedy and she shouldn't have been such a snob."

"Bertha," I correct them, *"Bertha Dorset."*

(Another student, a pretty smart one:) "I think we're supposed to see Barta as part of, like, a bigger problem that Lily Whatever can't escape from where she's been raised to, like, please men and that's her only skill. So Barfa USES that and makes people think she's a slut but she's NOT. So when no one will like her anymore, DUH, she takes a thousand Tylenol."

"*Bertha*. It's *Bertha*," I insist. It's amazing how preternaturally deep they are; they dive immediately to the very deepest levels. At the same time, they cut through the surface so fast as to completely miss it. They never get anyone's name. No one seems to catch that the story took place in the Gilded Age, or ancient Greece, or Tsarist Russia. But they fully take the body hits of pain delivered by one character to another, as if everyone were a sophomore at Holy Cross.

Derek, who fought the currents along which educated, upper-middle-class men drift into positions of power and prestige, knew that heaven, too. He had come to know what I knew of those classroom hours, the immediate access to the deepest parts of things that these idiot children had, hours that earthly measures valued low and that made our shared love of it that much more binding. We appreciated it in the same way, although I'd stumbled on it almost by accident (I had a PhD in literature and no job), while he'd come from lifelong Catholic do-gooder doctors who, through exposure to their well-lived lives, had made it impossible to just show up at Deutsche Bank with the password of his pert, perfect, pan-white face and ask to trade currencies.

That's the other thing about Derek, the thing you never know how to factor in: his face. He's so accidentally, uselessly handsome. I sometimes wonder whether all his choices have been to thwart the determinism of his leading-man face, the slightly hooded blue-gray eyes, the wide, smooth forehead, narrowish full lips that almost look pursed at rest. A few freckles to make him more perfect in imperfection. And the real fireworks happen when he talks or smiles or laughs. Some people's mouths are as simple as the slot in an alms box, but Derek's has a whole complicated machinery that goes into gear when he smiles. There are ropes and pulleys in his jaw, under the skin, and his cheekbones sharpen and a dimple emerges, and the world sighs.

His whole life, everyone has wanted to be affectionate with Derek, so that he'll smile and they can see more aspects of his beauty as it moves. Even I have to remind myself not to want to talk to him just to see his mouth move; I want to see more of his interesting teeth when his lips draw back, like a pervert angling to see more leg. I wonder if this has given him the room to be contrarian and still loved. Plus, he can be a cigarette-stinking low-earner in a Holy Cross fleece who always gets laid.

Derek couldn't believe I would leave it. "I can always come back," I told him, although Principal Pam had explicitly not given me that assurance—they would have to line up a replacement over the summer. But he felt my departure was a symptom of something else. If you loved to teach, you were crazy. Those classroom hours mattered to no one. The kids went through them as a routine and then forgot them in adulthood, and the state salaries were a form of condescending smile, particularly for English and history, although Lord knows the sheer socioeconomic leprosy of the art or music teacher. (At Holy Cross, our arts teachers were paid so little as to be essentially volunteers. They compensated for this by being unapologetically beyond any administrative control. Karla, the music teacher, had once been a chorus girl. Now in her mid-fifties but still beautiful and vain, she kicked herself around the school backward in a wheely office chair, swearing that this alone prevented varicose veins. Karla was not paid enough, in her mind, to obey Holy Cross's health and safety rules and did not care when her chair, which was not designed for transportation, toppled over a minor bump or barrier and tossed her to the ground. Karla often had flowers in her hair, sometimes because she was a kooky old hippie and sometimes because she'd just been extracted from an herbaceous border.)

Once it made sense to you, once teaching made any sense to you, then logically it was impossible for much of the outside world to make any sense. If I abandoned Derek and Holy Cross, I would abandon an unspoken resistance to a rational, market-based, mappable world, one in which our peers, emitting strange signs of what we read as insanity—Christmas cards: for weeks we puzzled over one that said "HAPPY HAPPY from the Danlers"—would surely no longer get us. Karla started to make sense. "It's for her veins," we'd say if someone new showed up to campus and boggled at the sight of a middle-aged woman rolling down a hill backward on an office chair and flipping over into the flower beds.

Derek and I had this conversation over and over again, especially after the book came out and an exit door opened for me from the shabby, righteous warehouse where we held each other hostage. I remember a time in his Band-Aid-colored Toyota, in the parking lot of the organic food co-op, when he was crunching through a slavery-free chocolate bar and I was smoking.

"What if I want a family?" I asked. "How can I have a family, how can I be a grown-up, on thirty thousand dollars a year? I don't want to have to take my dad's inventively undertaxed money forever." And Derek said, breathlessly, like a romantic exhortation, "*Don't have a family*. What more could you need?" He would never support anyone, he said. And always on the tip of my tongue was this question: How could we be readers, how could we be lovers of the impossible and the imagined, and not want to swell up with a new character, pull it onto land from a sea we made, and trick it by disappearing behind our hands? But I couldn't say this to Derek, because while he can comfortably turn to me from the driver's seat and ask me to Google "penis tingle when I wear a winter hat," I found it humiliating to admit my maternal impulses.

"Why does everyone need so goddamn much *money*?" This was

one of Derek's staple rants. "Just *don't* get a Vitamix. Just *don't* go to Tuscany. It's not that hard. You can take home seven hundred and fifty bucks a week and live like a queen," he said. He hoisted up a dusty brown lump of chocolate: "A queen!" I hadn't told him about the genetic test—I knew from the minute I got the results that it was going to spoil our paradise of parsimony and routine. I knew it would spoil the illusion of freedom we felt as we sat with our dirty sneakers on the dashboard, working chocolate and sucking the last from our KeepCups and queuing up cigarettes for a light before returning to a job we loved. A thing that was our deepest joy. I once told him he had bad breath and he said, "P, we always have the same breath."

CHAPTER 6

EXCERPT FROM *AMERICAN MERMAID*

The breathing was so slow and deep you almost couldn't see it. Her lips were dry and white. No one needed to say aloud what they were all thinking: she looked dead. Eleanor avoided looking at the baby's hand, where the cannula entered under a strip of tape that puckered her soft skin. Eleanor ran her fingertips down the length of the infant's tail. Where the tail broke into two diaphanous petals, she lifted her hand and started at her stomach again, not wishing to go against the grain of the little creature's tight, tiny scales.

Dean Granger was across the room with the doctor. He heard Eleanor sniffling and came over to her. He sat down and wrapped an arm around his wife.

"Eleanor, we have no choice. If we put her back, she'll be alone. She'll be defenseless." He invoked the baby whales, adrift and devoured.

"We don't know for certain that she'd die if we returned her—mermaids aren't whales. If they have comparable brain size to us, comparable emotional and intellectual capacities—they will want her back."

"What are we supposed to do, how are we going to arrange a pickup? Eleanor, think about it, there's no way that returning her to the sea is doing her any good. We can assume that these creatures have existed, unknown by man, for millennia, right? But we have mapped the oceans, we know what's *not* there—railroads, skyscrapers, universities, museums"—here he spun around, gesturing at the banks of equipment in the operating theater—"*hospitals!*"

Eleanor looked at the girl's baby skin, dark like a walnut shell, so soft that it gave at her touch like just-risen dough. No one would believe she and Dean had produced her. But all their friends would believe an adoption—they'd be relieved. She could hear them now: "Finally, they've stopped trying. Thank god."

"Eleanor, do you know what we're going to give her? Humanity. We're going to make her a person. She can have a name, she can learn about things. Newton, Brahms, the Hoover Dam! She'll walk the halls of knowledge."

"I don't think she'll ever walk, Dean," said a young man in scrubs, black hair jutting out of his blue operating cap, sitting on a stool with his legs crossed, his forehead resting on his palm.

Dean looked up at Masahiro Harada, annoyed, and back at his wife. "Nell, Masahiro and I have run test after test." The doctor shook his head almost imperceptibly. "We're not taking anything away from her. She doesn't have superpowers, she doesn't have superstrength, she can't lift a car, she can't even see in the dark! She's a person that evolution lost in a pocket somewhere, forgot to finish evolving. Let's lift her up to join us here on dry land. That's what we're doing."

"We *are* taking something away from her. She won't be herself. She won't swim."

"No, she won't swim," said Dean. He shrugged. "It's true, that's one thing she's *very* good at. And we'll take that away. She'll never win the Olympic gold in freestyle."

Masahiro started to say something, but Dean interrupted. "I'll tell you what we'll give her." Now he held the sides of his wife's face and looked her right in the eye. "The best mom in the world."

Eleanor Granger felt her body flood with a feeling of warmth, as if her borders were breaking and everything in her would spill onto the cold floor of the operating theater. She would give all of it to the little person, she would fill the world to the brim with herself, and the girl would swim in that and float and always be protected, and maybe even play and thrive. Eleanor would be her sea if she had to.

"Don't worry, Eleanor. We've got money. We can care for her. She will be our daughter and we'll give her a beautiful life—I can see it play out already."

CHAPTER 7

An email from Murphy to Randy and me:

Hey guys, attached find a skeleton outline for the whole shebang. It's all basically empty except for MAJOR plot points, ie

- MERMAID's suicide etc
- Flashback to MERMAID being found by ADOPTIVE PARENTS (EVIL SCIENTIST DAD/NICE MOM)
- MERMAID reconnects with DOCTOR (Masahiro) after suicide
- DOCTOR training MERMAID; planning for confrontation with EVIL SCIENTIST DAD
- Final showdown with EVIL SCIENTIST DAD (incl. MERMAID'S ULTIMATE DEATH)

These posts can be moved around a little but I've got them laid out pretty perfstein timing-wise for a script coming in at 100 pp, yerrrr welcome. Sylvia, I think you should hammer away at the early years stuff. You know what's most evocative in the teen years, so pick a scene from the book and suck the fat out of it and get us something that tells us everything about her in literally three pages. Randy, you and I are taking a first stab NO PUN INTENDED at the suicide scene (I know, she drowns) and we'll circulate everything for edits Thurs.

> Love you guys just kidding.
> Murphy

An email from Murphy, sent seconds after.

> LOL whoops Penny I called you Sylvia. Hot Cycle melts my brain!!!!

I read these emails on my phone at a CVS that I almost died crossing a highway to reach. I am in the shampoo aisle, deciding between gem-colored gels that will all do the same thing to my hair, i.e., leave it matte like sawn wood. I flare up with alarm at how much they cost—$8.99, $11.99, and then the same again for conditioner. That's a *lot* of money. I know there are tens of thousands of dollars in my bank account now, but I haven't gotten used to it, don't quite believe it, and have kept my old habits because of a superstition that I'll buy salon shampoo thrice and my new coins, my fantastical digital zeros, will be gone. It was all a test of my virtue, like a fairy tale. I was given magic beans and I mustn't simply eat them like they're Old El Paso frijoles pintos; I have to plant them on a propitious night, I have to give them to a passing beggar lady, I have to throw them over my husband's shoulder under a full moon.

I've been in the shampoo aisle for thirty-five minutes.

I'm a little scared to go home—"home"—to my shelf of a fifty-shelved glass coffin in Century City—because I will have to respond to Murphy, and I want to seem amenable, gracious, an integrated component of a successful team. How do I say no already?

But here's the thing: Sylvia doesn't die in the book. "MERMAID'S ULTIMATE DEATH"? Who decided that? *Why?* Why kill her? She's incredible. She's fast, brilliant, and powerful. You just *try* to kill her, Murphy. You'll see. I know Sylvia better than they do. She came out of my voice and I'll have to use that voice now, somehow, to protect her. I have to play it smart.

Now I'm going to make a short-term savings by buying a travel-size bottle of expensive shampoo and then, distracted by my own regret, be flattened by a Kia Sorento on Santa Monica Boulevard.

CHAPTER 8

EXCERPT FROM *AMERICAN MERMAID*

"Let's get you up here safe and sound," said Mr. Howard, sandy-haired, sleeves rolled up. He pointed at one of the elevated stools at the classroom lab bench. "Jeff, give me a hand." Mr. Howard wanted to get Sylvia out of her wheelchair so that she could sit at the table with the rest of the class. Sylvia longed to work at the lab table.

Jeff was a football player from the shoreline that Sylvia knew only from a distance. She looked over at him, and he seemed happy to be asked to do anything other than chem. The other students sniffed some chance of interpersonal drama in the air—Jeff was going to take Sylvia in his arms—and fifteen pairs of beady adolescent eyes fixated on him.

"Sure," said Jeff, aware that suddenly he was being monitored by the cruel collective of his peers.

Mr. Howard taught chem but was the soccer coach, too, fortyish and fit. He leaned down, and Jeff joined him. They gave each other instructions:

"Yeah—good—around the—"

"Got it."

"Sylvia, can you grab our shoulders?" Mr. Howard smelled like clean laundry and Jeff smelled like dirty laundry. Or was it the reverse? (Later, analyzing every microsecond of the experience, Sylvia would wonder who was doting and fastidious, Mr. Howard's wife or Jeff's mom?) Her chair wheeled back behind her and up she floated, her flannel shirt and her corduroys clinging to her backside. Her legs dragged behind her as the two men hoisted her forward. With Sylvia's arms around his neck and shoulder, Jeff swept his right arm under her legs, gently shifting her into a sitting position, and she was lifted up onto the lab stool. The stool dropped down an inch or two, and the ripped black vinyl seat cushion wheezed a little as she sunk into it, and she was there.

"Great," said Mr. Howard, who, sensing the eyes of all the little wolves around him hungry for some humiliation, decided to be very normal. "Does everybody have a chlorine vial?" Clinks and clanks, as pairs of hands began to play with their lab equipment, the moment over. But Jeff stayed there, with one hand hovering behind Sylvia's back, and another under her legs, five seconds, ten seconds. Fifteen seconds. Sylvia looked into his eyes for the first time—brown, heavy-lidded—and saw something she didn't recognize or know what to do with. *Store this picture,* she thought, *figure it out.* Finally, Jeff dipped out and away and loped back to his lab partner, a zitty, mouthy kid named Chuck, who held a dropper over a plastic bottle and said, "Yo, dude, I poisoned your Gatorade." They both howled.

Sylvia and her lab partner, Claire, began the experiment according to the instructions on a handout on the cold slab table. Claire had blow-dried her hair that morning. It was a shiny slope with an S-wave around her face.

"Okay, do you wanna do the dripper and I'll do the mixing?" Claire lowered her voice, curled her mouth up at one end, and leaned in. "By the way, what was that? Jeff must, like, *love* you."

It happened near the end of the class period. Forty blissful minutes had passed too quickly for Sylvia. She would remember it in images: The blue drop of acid, heavier than the water into which it had been dropped, sinking like a solid body and then hitting the beaker bottom and unfurling upward into artful plumes. Mr. Howard's worksheet, overflowing with Sylvia's indigo script—she had noted the chemical properties of each acid. Claire's face, or rather her two faces, the slack one that Sylvia saw when Claire pretended to participate in the experiment and the vivid, alert one she turned toward the boys at the next table over. Mr. Howard, with his hands on his hips in the middle of the room, pleased with the hum of activity around him. And then it happened.

All at once, Sylvia screamed without knowing she was screaming. It was a pain that lit up her spine from the nape of her neck and zipped through the arches of her feet, firing every millimeter along the way. It changed her mental map of her own body, the picture of herself in her head: her spine wasn't like a popsicle stick, giving structure, but a barbed wire, strung through rotten, pulsating matter. The pain came from her spine, but she would never have described it as back pain because it was so deep and sharp and loud inside her that it made her piercing heart feel like a plausible source, her searing stomach, her unbearable brain, her eyes that suddenly transmitted nothing but yellow flashing light.

When Sylvia woke up, she felt the cold stone lab table from Mr. Howard's classroom under her back. *They're doing an experiment on me,* she thought, irrationally embarrassed and flattered. And then Masahiro was there, holding her hand, and she knew she was in his office at the hospital and that there would be more surgeries.

Jeff's shoulders, his brown eyes, the feel of a strong arm bracing her with real caring—the smell of him. There was a pop song everywhere that winter, twangy and dancy but all in a minor chord, with a starlet singing, "Get inside my eyes, baby, get inside my mind, I'll get inside your backpack and we'll leave all this behind." To Sylvia, it had always seemed absurd, even desperate: "I'll get inside your backpack, you don't even have to murder me first; no, no, I'll dump *myself* in a quarry." But all the kids in school sang it, sexily, doing a dance where they hoisted their backpacks up and popped their chests out. Sylvia had noticed Claire's chem notebook was filled with dress designs for prom, designs in which Claire's body was a stick figure with huge boobs, overlaid with dresses slit to the hip. She was embarrassed for Claire that she had such notions of herself inside her head, baffled that she'd let them pour out onto notebooks that anyone might see. Was Claire, a short, cello-playing teen from Rye, not embarrassed to harbor this burning, desired image of herself as a—what? A swimsuit model? A kind of teetering IV-drip with breasts for bags? Sylvia closed her eyes and tried to think of Jeff, to feel the minor bass line that was all over the school, the pulsating maybes that electrified the space between boys and girls. She started to cry. The sadness of her deep secret began to expand in the emptiness created by painkillers: she had never felt any of it, only watched and waited on the outside of the sexual charge that seemed to have her whole school caught in a hot net.

She felt Masahiro's hand slip around hers. She opened her eyes: Masahiro had kept the lights dim so as not to wake her, but she saw his face, his always alert eyes fixed on her, his head slightly tilted.

"Why?" she asked him. "Why aren't I normal?" Was it just the drugs? Was it a dream or did Masahiro put his head in his hands and cry?

CHAPTER 9

A text thread between me and Murphy and Randy.

Murphy: Randy and I really love this aspect of Sylvia, that she doesn't feel sexual attraction for anyone
Murphy: She's like, anatomically female but her gender identity is FISH or whatever
Randy: But we also need to find a way around this
Randy: For example, Murph and I were toying with the idea of Masahiro administering her some kind of a sexual hormone
Murphy: In a compassionate way, to help her be like other teenagers
Randy: We know that he has tried to be super ethical because his family was A-Bombed etc etc, so this was something he was really resisting
Murphy: Exactly, like, we love love love the atomic-bomb backstory
Murphy: That's staying
Murphy: And it's a really important part of his character that he's gentle, he doesn't want to do harm
Murphy: But R and I have been banging our heads against a wall about this and we don't see any way out of it. We need her at some point to have sexual feelings
Penelope: But do u guys not see it as a violation that Masahiro sliced her tail in half and made her pass as a human without her knowing
Penelope: That *was* harm

Randy: Well we didn't see it like that and we're pretty sure audiences won't

Murphy: It's complicated, right? The point is, you need some DRIVE

Penelope: The whole point, the whole pathos of her among humans, is that she's totally outside all circuits of human sexuality

Randy: Sure, but PATHOS is for books. Movies are made of MINUTES

Murphy: Minutes need to moooooooove

Murphy: Mermaids don't have vadges

Murphy: We get that! And we love that

Murphy: But we need something here

Murphy: If Masahiro doesn't give her some kind of sex hormone, she needs to just feel something, a little something, on her own

Murphy: Otherwise

Randy: You have to think CINEMATICALLY

Murphy: Yeah otherwise imagine camera comes in close on the face of Amanda Seyfried and she's staring into the middle distance—without a MOTIVE, what does the audience think is going on inside her mind?

Murphy: Literally nothing

Murphy: The audience needs to know her desires

Randy: And those desires need to be important

Randy: Trust us as people who've done a lot of screenwriting, characters need DRIVE

Penelope: Yeah but her drive is to save the world's oceans from becoming a toilet

Murphy: We don't see a conflict between doing that and being sexy

Randy: Yeah, it doesn't stop

Randy: It doesn't stop

Randy: Well I can't think of any sexy environmentalists right this second

Murphy: Some of the Sioux at Standing Rock were cool looking

Randy: For SURE

Randy: Hmmmm, I mean, why can't she just have a secret vagina?

Murphy: Only the three of us will know about it, Penny! Just a tiny fish's vagina?
Murphy: And that way she will share something with the people trying to empathize with her
Randy: Fish MUST have vaginas you know?
Randy: Just like, a divot
Murphy: Just the tiny thumb in an inside-out oven mitt
Randy: Yeah, the front pocket in a doll's jeans
Murphy: Penny, we're joking, but we're serious
Randy: I'm actually not joking at all
Randy: I'm looking around for an oven mitt to help me think this through
Randy: I have an idea
Randy: Let's meet at Oyyi in the Grove for sushi
Randy: We can work through a rough arc of act I and then we can "do research" on fish anatomy
Randy: We can look at a whole tuna and get a sashimi boat and write it off as business
Penelope: FINE

"Write it off as business"? No one told me I could do that. Proudly, I think, *I do need that scanner.*

I concocted the begrudging tone out of sheer pride. I'm thrilled R&M want to meet. The truth is, I could use the company. When I was teaching back in New Haven, I was at school by seven thirty and doing mostly stupid things like Xeroxing packets or speed-reading "My Last Duchess" in the teacher's lounge on a sectional sofa wet with tobacco juice spat by Marco, the wrestling coach. He brought in tins of homemade biscotti and everyone forgave his filthy habit. I liked Marco, I liked his dry, lumpen, cherry-scented biscotti, and it seemed like a decent trade to wear his brown drool on my ass.

This is why I need Danielle.

I need to leave the unwonted softness and idiot-faced empathies of the teaching life. I need someone to pull me up from a spit-wet sofa and take me by the hand to the agora and teach me what a good trade looks like.

I don't drive, so I keep going for walks, accidentally finding myself approaching a highway and turning around hoping no one has seen me almost walk onto an access ramp to the 405. In LA, anywhere I can get myself without help is somewhere no one should be.

Murphy, Randy, and I meet within hours at Oyyi, a sushi restaurant attached to a fish market attached to a Crate & Barrel. When I was first partnered with Randy and Murphy and we started meeting back in early June, they seemed totally identical, but with each meeting, I acquire slightly more of the differentiating eye of the mother of twins. For example, they're both wearing shorts, sunglasses, and backpacks, but Randy's wearing socks in his New Balances, while Murphy is barefoot in Vans. Murphy is more vain.

You would think it might alarm a sushi chef that three strangers arrive and ask to inspect his kitchen, but Murphy sidles up to the man with an easy intimacy. Murphy is slightly hotter in the face than Randy (Murphy used to be an actor) and more confident with strangers, so he's the one to put his hand on this Japanese man's shoulder and whisper like his personal attorney, "Chef Kenji, we knew we'd see the best stuff here." A note of self-deprecation seals the deal ("just a couple of writers who don't know the first thing"), and a sighing Chef Kenji soon leads us into a pass between the market and the kitchen galley where one of his apprentices, a twentysomething white guy, is breaking down a yellowtail amberjack. The fish is literally yellow-tailed and about sixteen inches long, shiny, metallic, and taut, as if it were filled to bursting, like a party balloon.

The apprentice starts by taking a thin blade and inserting it in a pinpoint perforation at the base of one of two fins on the belly. He cuts up the belly, and as the walls of the fish's gut pull apart, a pink mousse oozes out. "Aw, man, lucky you," says the apprentice, "you got a lady." He pulls out the roe, which look like two long, pink peapods. They come out surprisingly intact, and he lays them on the cutting board. Then he inserts a hand and scoops out the guts—cords and beads of pastel goo that look individually shrink-wrapped. He tosses them. The rest is just sort of reverse carpentry. Very pleasing to see. The blade cuddling up along the spine, the little pivot at the gills, the quick incision behind the collar that unlocks the two fillet slabs from either side of the animal.

A few minutes later, the three of us sit around a large platter of pink and white tiles of fish flesh, taking turns with our chopsticks. We have a whole, unviolated mackerel next to us, ruler straight, its back iridescent and tiger-striped.

Randy and Murphy ask what I've been up to. I say I've been working on a new book, which is a lie. (I know I don't have another book in me.)

I tell them my friend Derek is coming soon to stay with me.

"Is he your boyfriend?" asks one of them.

"No, he's kind of a mess."

"You can date a mess," says Murphy. He swings his chopsticks toward Randy. "Randy's girlfriend sells conch jewelry on Venice Beach. She literally sells seashells by the seashore."

"She's not my girlfriend. It's just a physical connection." Randy says this calmly, with exaggerated respect.

"You guys bang," says Murphy.

Randy looks irritated. "There's something gross about *banging* a nursery rhyme. You wouldn't want to"—he pauses, swallows—"*blow* Jack Horner or *fuck* Miss Muffet."

"'She sells seashells' isn't a nursery rhyme. It's an elocution game. We did it in acting class." Murphy sits straight up and starts moving his lips wildly: "HE THRUSTS HIS FISTS AGAINST THE POSTS AND STILL INSTISTS—*fuck!*"

The hostess at her podium turns around to glance at us with alarm. Murphy smiles at her and makes a small, seated bow with hands in sudden prayer at his chest. At first I wonder whether this is racist, but the waitress smiles back, so I guess he pulled it off. I imagine myself bowing at a Japanese American waitress after screaming an obscenity; she would and should hate me. Murphy and Randy turn back to the conversation, certain Murphy has applied his charm like a balm. But my eyes linger on the motionless back of her, wondering what we've set simmering.

"So what's Derek's deal? He's staying *with you*? Like in your hotel room?"

"Yeah, he's—he's a teacher like I am—used to be—so he doesn't have a lot of money." Murphy and Randy nod sympathetically, as if I've revealed that Derek lives with a rare blood disorder. "Plus it's nice to spend time together. We taught together at the same high school."

There's a pause. Nobody wants to talk about my old job. It's like we've all gone on one of my doomed walks to the highway: silently, we turn around.

Randy, moving a pearly sliver of super white tuna around in his mouth: "So what have we learned from this whole . . . fish experiment?"

"I couldn't watch," says Murphy. "But I think the fish dude's name is Gabe. He went to Portola High with me. A real sweet guy. I thought he became a teacher or something."

"Jesus," I moan. He's a me. "We'll be extinct soon."

Randy, again, in responsible mode: "So there *was* some kind of hole after the last fin."

"It's a butthole," I say, sighing. "Fish don't have external *genitals*. How many times do I have to tell you, if you insist that Sylvia have a sexual charge, you're going to have to communicate that some other way than through her *fucking* someone physically."

Randy, calming: "Listen, this is a PG movie and nobody was ever going to show anybody *fucking*, as you say." *As you say*—he's put on a slight lawyerliness, but it doesn't work for him. He seems to be performing it for Murphy. Now his hands have formed little paddles, like Murphy's do when he's serious. Randy chops the black lacquer tabletop in front of him to mark important words in his speech. "We just want to understand"—chop—"how this character's body works"—chop—"so we can understand her mind, you know?"

"Mermaids have been super sexy throughout history," Murphy says by way of defending his and Randy's angle here.

"Mythology," I say.

"Whatever," Murphy says. "We're not the first people to try to understand how mermaids appeal to men. To people."

I've made the point before to these two that there is a whole Harlequin subcategory of mermaid romance fiction, mermaid YA fiction, mermaid fantasy—*Sirens, Ocean's Call, The Deep*—most of it about teenagers with big boobs that are tuna from the waist down and sacrifice themselves for the human man they love. (I also found a porn called *Coral Pleasure*, which agreed that mermaids have no genitals; under the circumstances, the film made lemons into lemonade.)

The mermaids in these YA and erotic novels are full of sexual desire that kills them. But before it does, the reader gets to spend a lot of time imagining breasts, pert the way only waterborne breasts can be, nuzzling out of an insufficient mollusk bra. It's about coming of age, of course, the unself-aware girl suddenly wanting sex, wanting to be split, wanting a vagina magically hammered into her by a witch. In the end, the mermaid is punished for entertaining the thought of her own sexual satisfaction. She ends up dying—or else having to be saved by her rich sea-daddy—for trying to *be* with the man, while the reader re-buttons his or her pants and thinks, *Poor sexy dead fish lady. Well, that was fun.*

I never thought about this body of fiction when I started my book. All I knew was the Sylvia that came to me at night while I was writing in my studio in New Haven: long-bodied but always folded up, seated, land-bound; unaware of the operation that had given her legs as an infant; intelligent, alert, ashamed, adopted, desperate for joy, easy to laugh, often in pain. She sees her parents as a benevolent unit, people who have tried only to make life easier for a girl born half broken, immobile. She has no idea that there's a whole different way of being, an easy automatic power she would possess if she only found her way to the water. The water, the comically infinite lapping buckets of it that lie just miles from her home. Hans Christian Andersen's little mermaid and all her descendants are always trying to leave the place where they're powerful, mobile, and knowledgeable, bargaining away *even their voice* in return for a place where they are ignorant and adorable. Disney's Ariel shoving a fork in her head: "*Dinglehoof!*" You dumb idiot.

Sylvia, on the other hand, started on land and discovered the sea.

"I want this movie to work. I want you to like her, I want audiences to like her," I say, "but she's going to have to win your interest some other way than by being sexy like a woman . . . *penetrable*. Look at this thing!" I jab at the mackerel, formal and disapproving with his straight back and his closed-mouth frown. "It's a bullet! It's sealed and sleek and there's no, there's just no way to sexualize a fish."

A discreet waitress has been refilling our tea. "It's for a movie," Randy tells her. She does not make eye contact.

"What if we just . . ." Murphy blows out a puff of air. "People don't research this stuff. We can get away with it."

"Naw, Penny's right." Randy rubs his temples. "If a mermaid can have sex, then we've created a world where your goldfish would have to be dragging his dick along the bottom of the fish tank."

"If that's how you have to think about it, I guess." The New England Protestant in me wakes irritably as I survey our luxurious massacre. "You guys could have Googled this," I say, stabbing a chopstick-pincered piece of salmon at both of them. My focus shifts from their tan, groomed faces to the salmon itself. There's a little triangle of broken glass poking out of the pink morsel, like a shark's tooth. Neither of them has noticed.

"You know what, Penny? Sometimes you have to get off the page and go experience things in real life," says Murphy. He pauses chewing to flash that almost-actor smile.

CHAPTER 10

I am sitting in a glass-walled room full of craning metal arms with microphone hands. The two women with me have faces wasted on podcasting. Michelle Ng and Nico Graves, hot, game, and fast-talking, have a show called *The Vagina Dialogues*. They wrote a best-selling parody of dating books called *This Blow Job's Gonna Cost You a Steak*.

"So, do you want to drink during this?" asks Nico, in ship-wrecked jean shorts and an oversize white T-shirt with ropes of gold necklaces that scoop between her breasts.

"Will you guys?" I ask.

"We usually do, unless we're drying out. Mich?"

"Dude, I have such a gut right now?" She lifts her fast-fashion Pendleton-patterned poncho and shows me a surprising belt of fat. "But fine." Nico opens a minifridge under the table.

The interview starts with them asking if my parents are married and ends with them asking if my parents are alive. In between we don't talk about my book, except to drop its name a couple of times, which will please my publisher just fine, but we drink a few margaritas each. Nico's mug is a small porcelain toilet.

I have a bottle of water that I don't touch.

. . .

After the interview, we are on lounge chairs around the pool of a fancy hotel.

A hostess put us next to a row of three guys on lounge chairs, who give us cool nods and go back to their conversation.

Nico, Michelle, and I are drinking Coronas and Nico tells a story about how her friend went to Mexico to drink ayahuasca and Michelle hears "Hiawatha" and then one of us goes, "Wait, who *was* Hiawatha?"

"Was Hiawatha like a sexy little Indian boy?"

"Yeah, was he supposed to be a hot—like a hot Indian teen?"

"No, eww, no, he was a *child,* he was friends with a *bear.*"

"No, that's *The Jungle Book.*"

"Wait, was Hiawatha a girl?"

"Why do we know Hiawatha if there was no Disney movie about her?"

"I think our moms must have read us a book?"

"Our moms! YO, MOMS!" This has set off Nico, who can't stop saying "YO, MOMS."

"I call my mom 'Moms.' But only when I'm wearing my baseball cap to the side."

"Yeah, only when she's getting snacks for my street hockey team."

Two of us are looking up Hiawatha on our phones and one of us is just saying "Yo, MOMS! What's for SNACKS!" and then one of the guys next to us tells us in a French accent that Hiawatha (which he pronounces *Ayawassa*) was a historical figure, a precolonial leader of the Onondaga people and a founder of the Iroquois Confederacy but we probably know the nineteenth-century poem by Longfellow about Hiawatha's youth in the forest, later popularized in a lavishly illustrated children's book.

We are stunned by the sudden intrusion of benevolent and sincere aid. We know that he's made himself vulnerable, taking this professorial tone and using absurd words like "nineteenth-century," and that with one roll of the eye and a "Thanks, asshole," we could make him feel small, but we *don't,* we don't! On the contrary, we have to wrap him in blankets of our affection so that he doesn't get socially sick from exposure after such an exertion of sincerity in this irony environment, such a delivery of real information.

"Where are you from?" and "Yeah, what's the accent?" and "That's *amazing*" pour from us wasted women all at once.

His name is Franck, which is pronounced *Fronck,* and he's Swiss, and his two friends flanking him on lounge chairs, bare-chested and dozing, are American. We all shake hands. Franck quickly sheds the image of the know-it-all. Shrugging, he claims everyone in Switzerland is obsessed with the American West, but we have all started to notice his lovely little-boy side part, and he is still being accidentally articulate in the way of nonnative speakers ("A Gallic fascination with cowboys . . ."). He is a hero, leaping up on long, lean legs to get a round of margaritas, leaving us to meet his two American colleagues, and we don't even mind that these guys all work for a Swiss bank. Here at this low, flat, art-deco hotel, the four p.m. light snaking around on top of the blue pool, the margarita salt begging for the next margarita, "Swiss" to us means goats on snowcaps and real good chocolate, not tax opacity and Nazi gold.

Nico and Michelle sit upright now, and the lounge chairs have moved into a semicircle. A complete stranger, a squat, heavily muscled man with his shirt off, pulls a chair up and joins us. He has a preposterously low voice and his tiny nipples remind me of the buttons on my childhood TV remote. We are shocked and feel instantaneous scorn and delight. He drops a two-ton "WHAT'S UP" at our feet. "HOW DO YOU GUYS KNOW EACH OTHER?" He beckons to a waitress with a whistle that he makes with his meaty fingers in his meaty mouth, and it is so loud, like his talking voice, that we have every reason to believe he is being broadcast. He is an excised or waylaid scrap of a Hollywood studio's colorful product. A bike cop on TBS, an extra gladiator, a bachelor for a Bachelorette.

"We all went to high school together, actually," says one of the bankers, a midwestern-seeming floppy blond.

The TV man, scream-talking: "OH NO WAY. WHERE?"

"Switzerland," I say.

"WHAAAAAAT THAT IS CRAZEEY. SWITZERLAND?"

"It was an international boarding school in the Alps," Franck interjects.

"OHHHHH COOL." As if this explanation solves an outstanding mystery.

The false memories come fast. We'd all gone to senior formal together, he and Mich had dated—that was all complicated, who had slept with whom, and people's memories were vague at this point. The other banker asks, "Mich, didn't we make out in the van with the Junior Orchestra on the drive back from Bern?"

I jump on the line: "Naw, that was me."

"You don't remember that?" Franck seems worked up. "That made me so angry. We were together at the time." He looks at me with real possessiveness in his dark brown eyes and I look at him with the fond nostalgia of a woman formerly possessed.

Every few minutes someone calls, "Schwitzer Academy Goats!" and the rest of us respond "Goats Forever!" or "Goat Fever!" or "Fear the Goat!" One of the bankers starts bleating periodically.

"Dude!" says Nico, staring at her iPhone. "The podcast went up like twenty minutes ago and it's already been downloaded sixty thousand times."

"How is it up already?" I ask. "Don't you need to do things to it?"

"Our whole thing is, we don't edit," says Michelle, unrepentant. She rattles the ice in her empty margarita.

I'm pleased at this interjection. I don't care about the numbers—in fact, I know alcohol is deferring an anxiety I will later feel because I don't remember what we said in the interview—but I want Franck to know that I became something after Schwitzer Academy, that I am a writer, a lady writer. I want him to imagine the dignity that probably envelops me when I'm at my desk, under a flexible Bauhaus lamp like a mechanic, retooling my manuscripts. Because he, I imagine, is a Swiss financial genius who spends his evenings reading Longfellow and is obviously the most worthy gentleman that I could ever come across. I hope something will alert him to the fact that I am the woman God has molded for him, to understand the literary references in the wry remarks he'll make under his breath at the glittering dinner parties and on the hyperoxygenated pine trails of the exurban Geneva of our married life.

"You wrote a book, Penelope?" says Franck in a gentle voice. "I always knew you would." He takes my hand.

The meathead's name is Gil, a fact he has slammed into each of our palms with a hot handshake, and he manifests great pleasure, in his gaping smile and his knee-slapping laugh, at the group storytelling that slowly seals him off from us entirely. It seems to me that eventually he will have to throw up his hands and shout-say, "WELL YOU GUYS ENJOY CATCHING UP," and go back into a television somewhere. It shows how little I know LA, and the priority that LA makes of keeping the party alive. When you exist to be hot and striving and maybe meet J. J. Abrams on a rooftop bed at a cocktail lounge, partying is not indulgent aberration, not the tomorrow-sabotaging idiocy it is everywhere else. Gil doesn't need to go home and sit on a protein shake. He's met drunk, agitated strangers: he's on the job.

He says, "SO WHERE'S THE PARTY NOW," and starts bobbing his head back and forth to communicate great anticipation of THE PARTY.

We dive into the street, leap into cars; we tangle and slap arms. Nico yelps at one point, and I see one of the bankers pick her up off the ground. We are inseparable; we always have been, we always will be. We are all so obviously of the same species, we are a school of fish, and Gil is some dumb diver, foreign here, trying to breathe in a world in which we move inventively, make dazzling catches of quick tosses of wild words. We tolerate Gil's motionlessness amid our elegant underwater play.

CHAPTER 11

The electronic fairy tinkle of my cell phone wakes me up. It's been in my dreams for some time, this sound. What were my dreams about? They were some continuation of last night's antics—seamless, to go from drunk to dream. I had dreamed more about the Swiss bankers and me and the podcast girls leaping through the night. Weightless, the room-temperature air of downtown LA, the temperature of a dream.

"SUSIE" appears on my phone's screen. I moan a deep "Hiiii" into the phone. I expect my exaggerated croak to launch a funny account of my wild night to my sister.

Her tone is immediately one of wartime seriousness.

"What the HELL, Penelope. Mommy's been crying all morning."

"What? What happened?"

"What happened? Your selfish mouth happened."

"What are you talking about?" I ask, sounding more baffled than I am. I knew yesterday after the interview that I had been drinking and gunning for laughs with Nico and Michelle on the podcast. I hadn't exactly had my family's reputation at the front of my mind. My family. Most of the time they are to me like characters from a much-loved book. My mother, a former forest warden, spinning the combo lock on her gun safe, on the phone about a "planned burn." My dad making jokes about how he married an arsonist: "Family pet? How 'bout we keep a tort lawyer in the backyard?!!"

He roars his laughs. It's something you like about him despite yourself, the way a murderous gangster looks great in his hat. But nobody's a caricature. If you asked him, he'd say the most important thing in his life was his family. He'd say we're the reason he left a government job to become a corporate litigator when I was thirteen. More space, more security, and he could pick up the check for the four years of light beer, Chaucer, and a cappella that certified his kids for the good life. He'd point to the frames parked on his desk: Susie holding flowers, the D-1 rowing champ; my dad and my mom dressed up at Susie's wedding, arms behind each other's backs; me in a graduation cap, smiling blankly.

"You literally called Daddy an asshole on national radio."

"No, I did not. It's just a *podcast*."

"Yeah, WORSE. People actually listen to it."

"I never called Daddy an asshole."

"Sorry, you're right. You called him—and I quote—'EVIL, evil like the bad guy in a movie. Evil like the dad of the kid who dies in *Dead Poets Society*. Evil like all the dads in the TOWN OF FOOTLOOSE,' WHICH ISN'T EVEN A TOWN."

I remember now. Hearing it back, it makes sense to me. I do feel that way. Or I felt that way, so securely, in the booth with Nico and Michelle, or when I'm looking into the eyes of people of my generation, and sometimes at night when I'm falling asleep and I'm angry at my effortful parents for things I can't explain.

"Well, I never called him an asshole," I protest.

"No, you just said that he and his entire generation should be shoved off a cliff in their Dockers. You called him racist, too."

"Well, he is."

"Dude, he *voted for Obama*. You know what? Daddy's a Republican. Get over it. He's not MOOMAHAR GADDAFI."

I close my eyes.

"Jesus Christ," she continues. "Daddy's such a bad guy? He paid for us to go to private school. He puts money into a pension savings account for you. He does all kinds of shit that you don't even stop and thank him for. He paid for our genetic tests. He paid for your stupid Brooklyn Sex Camp!"

She means my undergraduate degree from NYU.

"Do you know what he was doing before he had to come home and take care of Mommy because she is so upset about how you publicly trashed our family? He had taken the car and driven to some gay resort town in upstate New York to visit an antiques shop that was going to sell him a three-hundred-year-old Dutch salt-cellar in the shape of a motherfucking frog because Mommy loves FROGS and SALT. No, but let's BURN HIM AT THE STAKE because he calls Black people THE BLACKS."

"I—I wish you could see how I see things."

"You think you're the catcher in the rye. But you're not. You're just the asshole in the Marriott."

"It's not a Marriott. It's not a hotel, actually."

"You're an asshole. A female asshole. A FE! MALE! DICK!" She's screaming now. "YOU ARE THE EVIL ONE. YOU ARE A FORCE OF EVIL."

"I'll call Mom and explain it was all metaphors, all just jokes and metaphors."

"All just metaphors?" From maximally upset, she suddenly speaks very calmly. "Wow. Okay, HENRY LONGSMITH WORD-FELLOW. You're a psycho." She hangs up.

CHAPTER 12

An email from Murphy:

> Hey Penelope,
> Saw you'd made some changes in the master script last night super late. Totally know what it's like when you have a great idea but from here on out just make notes on your own draft and then when we work on that section together, circulate the draft and we can all confirm. Otherwise, people just inserting stuff, we'll get lost. Especially if you're going to cut big sections. I know that must be super frustrating for a novelist used to just frolicking naked alone in a field of words, but this is like a community garden and we have to stick to our plots or bitches get killed.
> SORRY can't stop thinking about this story, have you guys seen it? latimes.com/hermanocanyon899004feat.com

Murphy's link leads to an article about a guy who was obsessed with his community garden plot and killed an old lady who encroached on it. He composted her body and used it to fertilize lush heirloom tomatoes and mile-high corn, which were photographed for the article with their watertight sheen like the centerfold of *Gourmet*.

When I've finished reading the grisly story of the Hermano Canyon Garden Murder ("'Honestly, I won't miss her. Everybody thought that lady was annoying,' said a fellow gardener"),

I'm pulled into the suspended trance of the internet for a while—Twitter? *Daily Mail*?—but something snaps me out. I didn't write anything in the master script last night. I shake my head a little, as if to loosen memories from the coils of my brain. I was pretty drunk. But I have no recollection, none, of going to my computer. *What did I cut?* I wonder. How do I find out without alerting my co-authors to the fact that I blacked-out vandalized our million-dollar sports car?

I call Murphy.
"Hey, Murph. Sorry about last night."
"No worries, it happens."
"You reverted the master script, right?"
"Yup."
"Great, can you just remind me what I cut for my own draft?"
"Ha."
"What?"
"Finding late-night inspiration in the bottle?"
"I'm so sorry, man," I say, actually shifting my stance into a cool poolside contrapposto, imaginary wineglass in hand. "It was a party with some—media people."
Murder me murder me cut me up and feed me to the feet of your beefsteak tomatoes lest I ever speak again.
"No prob."
"But are you sure it was me? Last night?"
"It wasn't Randy and it wasn't me. Had to be you. No one else has the password."
"Right."
Murphy sends me the deleted text:

INT. MASAHIRO'S OFFICE, SYLVIA ON EXAMINATION TABLE

SYLVIA
Why? Why aren't I normal?

MASAHIRO
You're better than normal, Sylvia.

SYLVIA
I just want to be like the other girls. I want to have boyfriends and go to prom! I want . . . I want to have sex!

MASAHIRO *turns away, seemingly embarrassed.*

MASAHIRO
I'm sorry but . . . that kind of intimacy won't be possible for you, however much desire you feel.

SYLVIA
I feel so much desire!

Woof, I hate this passage. Sylvia hotted up and huffy. I'm impressed at the stranger in me who did this, who had the guts to go in and slash something—like one of Danielle's crew of unapologetic women.

Now, in the light of day, I have to apologize. What did the brave, drunk Penelope of the night gain? Murphy put the text back in the script: "I want to have boyfriends and go to prom!" The sad yelp of this line reminds me, despite myself, how badly *I* wanted these things in high school, when I wasn't sure whether I was a woman yet and needed a local bozo's clumsy desire to confirm it. Somehow dreams of impossibly romantic scenarios—stolen kisses behind barn doors, secret meetings in meadows—animated my mind at night. But my partner in these fantasies was always disposable, unlikely, the older brother of a friend, glimpsed once, a knock-kneed pile of sinews you'd never heard speak.

I haven't progressed much. I've found a way to keep sex in the drunken circuit of fantasies but excise it completely from my life. I don't know where the sex is in me, but it's not in the smart part. It's the element that involuntarily warms and bends toward the pleasure and comfort of strangers, thrilled to interest men in Panthers jerseys at airport bars. It's the part of me that's proud to have earned the condescending caresses of the older history teacher at Holy Cross. The part of me that lights up to tangle with bankers at poolsides. One of Sylvia's great powers, which she knows only as a weakness, is her immunity to sexual desire. When alcohol had shut my functions down to a few blinking lights in my animal brain, I must have leaped to protect her from the humiliations of desire.

CHAPTER 13

EXCERPT FROM *AMERICAN MERMAID*

I must control my fantasies, thought Sylvia, lying in bed the night before her sixteenth birthday. *They will kill me.* Fantasies of rhythmic motion, her whole body bending and curving, without resistance, resonating with long, unbroken currents of pleasure.

Swimming.

She imagined herself drawing a bath, something she'd never once done—she could almost hear the *squeak squeak* of the metal tap turning in her hands.

She knew she'd feel pain, but the fantasy poured into her mind and filled it anyway. *What if the pain burns off?* The images of water, shimmering like magic, dispelled the fear.

Visions of her body in the water made her salivate, made her tongue feel cold. Once, her school had gone to an art museum. She had lingered at the courtyard pond, leaned over and put her hand in among the lily pads. Her whole body had pleaded for more. She kept her icy hand still in the water until the fat-bellied goldfish forgot she was there, and then she snatched at them with a flip of the wrist. Her class had turned back, almost in unison, at the sound of a splash. Below the cement rim of the pond, she released a panicked goldfish, then wiped the slime of its thumping body on her jeans reluctantly, like the memory of a lover.

. . .

Every few evenings, Sylvia's mother washed her hair. Sylvia reclined against a specially designed basin, large and low with a little cushioned lip on which she laid her neck. She wore a plastic protective gown over her legs. (They washed the fine, shriveled skin of her legs as you would a silk, with powders.) It was a ritual they both loved, without ever saying as much.

Today was Sylvia's sixteenth birthday—unbeknownst to Sylvia, it was the June day she had washed up three thousand miles away from Westchester on a slate gray beach—and as Eleanor held her hands at the girl's temples, keeping soap from her eyes, she thought how remarkable it was that Sylvia had really become their daughter, beloved, interesting, kind. Her mind drifted to tomorrow's party.

"Oh, that reminds me," said Eleanor all of a sudden. "I forgot to call the caterer back." Eleanor hung up the hand shower, wrapped her daughter's hair in a towel, and cranked the cushioned seat up. "I'll be right back." She rushed out with a finger in the air.

Sylvia smiled at her mother's investment in throwing her a good party. As she hoisted herself up on her elbows, ready for her mother to move her to the wheelchair, her eyes fell on the tub just next to her. The hand shower was within reach. *You have to master your fantasies,* came the thought again. What was this, some kind of death wish? All she knew for sure was that the water would burn her.

But maybe it would be okay. She'd burned a thousand times before. There were plenty of triggers for her pain: damp days, chemical particulate. Sometimes she didn't even know what had caused an episode. It was a terror that she lived with, never knowing when it would erupt, shatter her mind, engulf her nerves. But she always survived.

She grabbed the hand shower.

When Eleanor Granger heard the screaming, she dropped the phone and leaped three steps at a time up to the bathroom. She pulled her daughter out of the tub and held her, both of them panting, on a rag rug on the bathroom floor.

They were still, breathing for several minutes, Eleanor letting out heavy sighs of relief that her daughter was okay.

"What were you thinking?" Eleanor asked gently, not to punish her. The girl was already suffering enough—tears streamed down her blotched and twisted face. But Eleanor was shocked nevertheless, glancing over the rim of the half-filled tub. She'd been protecting her daughter her whole life, from environmental dangers and human cruelty, but she never thought she'd have to contend with her daughter's own instincts. "Oh, sweetheart. Please don't do that again." They would talk later. For now, just calm. "Let's have dinner. It's just you and me, Daddy's at the office."

"No, he's not. He's—he's in our house."

"What do you mean?"

"Daddy's here." Sylvia held her head in her hands, a confused look on her face. "He's in the basement." Her words came out weak but clear. "He's got a fish tank, a giant fish tank, and there's something in it, swimming and screaming."

"Daddy's not here, honey," said Eleanor Granger. *It must be some kind of memory,* she thought, guilt turning in her stomach. *A memory of the surgery, kicked up by trauma.* "It must be the pain, doing funny things to your senses." Eleanor gave her a squeeze. "I *wish* we had a fish tank in the basement. It would be better than that stupid billiard table no one uses."

Sylvia managed a small smile, because she knew her mother was trying to dispel a feeling of fear and panic, and she appreciated the effort. But the fear swirled in her still, fear of her own desires (*could she have drowned?*) and fear of this new feeling, nothing she'd ever felt before: like knowledge but physical, a scene impressing itself on her mind, whole and complete. And most terrifying of all was the picture it gave her: her father was in this house, and someone was suffering at his hands.

CHAPTER 14

Greg Kinnear
Gene Hackman
Mark Wahlberg
The Swedish guy
The Danish guy
Fucking KevCos
Fucking Mickey Rourke
Too bad Kevin Spacey's outta bounds
[Weeping emoticon]
Hugh Laurie?
Hugh Bonneville?
Hugh GRANT?
Gerard Butler
Too horny
What do you mean
He just has a horny mouth, too horny for a dad
I trust you man
Stanley Tucci
Not horny ENOUGH
No
MATT DAMON
OOOOOFF that's good
MATT DAMON as Dean Granger AND as Masahiro
WAIT

So good, right?
WAIT
You are a genius
We are a genius
Matthew Damon as both Granger and Masahiro is so good
Can we make that happen?
Let's reach out

I watch this conversation type itself out in front of me. Murphy says that the studio wants to "aim high" for the role of Dean Granger, that the studio feels there will be huge demand to play this man, who accelerates the final blow of irreversible climate catastrophe and saws his daughter in half.

Fine.

But Stanley Tucci *not horny enough*?

I wrote in pen—useless, wet, mute pen—on a pad as I watched them type: STANLEY TUCCI = IF A PENIS WERE KIND, but I couldn't type it because I can't cause rifts midproject. But now I know their eyes don't register the heat in the same places mine do, i.e., rippling blanket-warm off Tucci's dome wherever his small feet take him, at a gentle trot, now passing by the version of my dreams that men make.

CHAPTER 15

EXCERPT FROM *AMERICAN MERMAID*

Dinner was over and Sylvia was curled up against her mother on the sofa in the living room of their Westchester home watching a rental movie called *Annie*. In the movie, the lady who runs the orphanage banged around drunk, but Sylvia didn't know what drunkenness was. She thought the character was disabled, clumsy from a birth defect and slow-talking from related damage. With dread, it dawned on her that this howling, injured woman was irredeemable, ugly. Worse: a joke.

Eleanor Granger had a wide alpaca blanket around both of them. It was Sunday night. They were happily tired from yesterday's birthday party, a gathering of ten nerdy girls, karaoke rental, and sparkling cider. Daddy Warbucks was just negotiating for Annie when Eleanor remembered something.

"Did you need me to sign that permission slip? Let's do that now so we don't forget." She gently propped her daughter up on the sofa, got up, and walked into the kitchen. She was back a moment later, a crookedly Xeroxed school form in her hand. "Here, I've signed. They want Daddy's signature, too."

At the mention of her father, Sylvia clenched up. She could feel her heart knocking. She tried to keep her gaze steady on her mother, to breathe normally. But Sylvia still did not understand what had happened the night of her birthday, when she foolishly tried to swim. She felt a confusing mix of shame and guilt, an acute memory of physical pain, and then—this image of her father in the basement, cruelly looking on as someone suffered. Perhaps like the lady in the movie, Sylvia's physical deformity was also a moral one. She must be a terrible person to entertain such a vision.

Sylvia hadn't been able to look her father in the eye since. He was in his office now, down a long hallway from the den where Sylvia and her mother had been watching the movie.

"Why don't we take a break?" Eleanor paused the film. "You go take this note to your father for a signature, I'll do the dishes, and then we'll finish the movie." Eleanor rubbed her daughter's arm and gently ushered her into her wheelchair, which was just next to the sofa.

The wood creaked under Sylvia's chair as she pushed her way to her father's office door. She took a deep breath, her heart racing, although she couldn't quite explain why. Their family had gone from wealthy to superrich over the course of her childhood, and this house had marked that transition—custom built by her father, four stories with an elevator. Her father's office was an isolated annex. Unlike their clean, modern home, the office was dark and full of things—old rifles, topographic maps, dead animals—that must have meant something to her father alone, but which he never decoded for her. She knocked.

"Come in," came the familiar voice. "Sylvia," he said, looking up from his computer, which illuminated his tired face with a blue-white glare that contrasted with the dark wood of his office. "How nice to see you, my love."

"I have this note for you to sign, if you don't mind." She found herself on alert, scanning her father's tone minutely. *How nice to see you, my love* had been almost too warm. Or was she just being crazy? All this suspicion because of a—what—an *intuitional spasm* the night before?

"Of course I don't mind. Where are you headed?" Sylvia noticed the rings around his eyes, the way he hunched in his office chair.

"We're going to Bournemouth Colony. It's a fake pilgrim settlement. They have actors and stuff."

"Ah, immersive history. An outing tailored for weaker students without the discipline to sit down and read. Where is it?"

"I don't know." She swallowed. "Peekskill?"

Dean Granger pushed his chair back, stood up, and stretched. He walked around his desk, took the slip from her, and signed it messily in the air.

"What have you and Mommy been up to? I'm sorry I've been so busy," he said.

Something told Sylvia to push. The spasm she'd had the night before—that feeling of pressure on her skin, blazing a picture into her mind—she had to know whether this was just another symptom of her disability, of her falling apart yet further. "Were you at work two nights ago?"

"Yeah, I've been meaning to apologize to you and Mommy," he said. "I've been at work so much recently." He handed her the slip and smiled. "What movie were you two watching?" Sylvia registered that her father at least checked in on them via the closed-circuit security cameras. But she didn't care about that right now. She needed to be sure. In the knowledge that had come to her the night before, she felt that her father had hurt someone, that her father had been responsible. She believed that if she asked, he would tell her. He had taught her to admit to wrongdoing. He was square-jawed and gray-haired and lived in a castle like a just king. He would tell her if she pushed.

"Was someone hurt?" she asked.

"Hurt?" Dean Granger held his daughter's gaze for a moment. "Hurt—how?"

"I don't know—hurt."

"Oh, honey." He pulled a stool alongside her, a giant tortoise shell mounted on black wooden legs, and slid onto it, so their eyes were level. He put his hands on his daughter's shoulders. "You have a lot to learn about boardrooms. You can have all kinds of arguments, but they're not allowed to hurt you."

"Can you hurt other people?"

Dean Granger laughed. "Nope, that's not in the rules either. But you can be a real *son of a bitch*." These last words he had said in a conspiratorial whisper, permitting himself this little vulgarity in front of his daughter in an intimate moment of apprenticeship, a whiff of the whiskey men poured each other. "But you're very sweet to worry about me," he said, running a hand down the back of her head, across the very spot where just the night before she had received an image of someone writhing in pain under the cold gaze of Dean Granger. "Go finish your movie," he said. "I'll be out in a bit."

He held the door for her and she spun herself around, pushing one wheel and pulling the other, knocking against the domed back of the mounted tortoise. Sylvia's mind was a muddle. Her father had been so convincing. She was sure her wires had been crossed. With dread she realized some other part of her was broken, not just her bones and her skin but her mind, her imagination. She had been needlessly mean and suspicious: she pictured her mouth growing crooked over time, like the leering Miss Hannigan.

"Oh, by the way." Dean Granger held Sylvia's chair back a moment. "Are you feeling better? Your mother mentioned you'd had some sort of episode last night. You thought I was in the house or something?"

"It was just a cramp."

"What did you think I was up to?" Her father laughed, although there was nothing funny about the question.

"It was just a mistake. Sometimes the pain—it makes sounds."

"What did you hear?"

"I told you, nothing."

Dean Granger drummed the fingers of one hand on the armrest of Sylvia's chair. "Right."

Something was up now for sure, but Sylvia couldn't think about it here in her father's suffocating office. She felt an overwhelming need to escape, to go back to the airy den where her mother waited for her, where she could settle back into herself and think. She was desperate to smell the dish soap on her mother's hands, to be wrapped alongside her in musty alpaca.

"Well, in any event, I've got guys coming in here tomorrow to remove the tub. And the basin. We're getting a professional nurse in here to wash you, even your hair, with a dry powder. Seems like that whole setup is a risk for you." He stared at his daughter's unmoving face. "Anyway, one less thing for your mother to do."

"Great," Sylvia finally said. Holding the permission slip in the air, she said, "Thanks," and rolled back down the hallway, tears spilling down her cheeks.

She was a child, a "special-needs child," a person who'd had no exposure to the wide world outside school, her Westchester home, or the Upper Manhattan doctor's office where Masahiro healed her. The everyday life for which she was physically inadequate broke her, serially, in painful parts. It was often hard for her to think about the world objectively—to see it eagle-eyed, as maps, as networks—because pain focused her inward, narrowed existence to the shock of the specific moment, clouded her eyes. But in this moment, as the hallway creaked beneath her, as she gripped the metal rims of her wheelchair, she knew with complete certainty that she had just discovered something about her father, and that he had just punished her for it.

CHAPTER 16

An email from Randy:

> Guys, I think we found her. We should all be feeling very excited about Jellica Nye. Her manager says she is super interested and I have a phone meeting with her agent later today to talk up the part. Penny, obviously you are less familiar with the casting process, so let me warn you, get ready to have *very little say* in this. But I think if we can get Jellica horny for this, that's great for us. Murph and I have a vision board up in our office plastered with actresses' faces and Jellica has been BREAKING through the crowd. Face is STUNNING. (Bodies don't matter, these people are all stupidly hot-bodied and directors can double anything they don't like.) Let's chat this afternoon!

Google told me there was only one taco place within walking distance of Mountain Plaza, my corporate residence in Century City, and so I walked there. It was a chain called Pink Taco, which made me want to grow a beard and live in an Airstream and punch my tin door open every morning to a desert where no one's genital-shaming corporate cantina could find me. The whole time I was walking, all I could think of was the grotesque vision of a vagina conjured by "Pink Taco," bubble-gum-colored, shiny with crema. I scowled, but I wanted a big salty lunch, so, feeling unprincipled,

I went along, checking on the map as the dot that represented me moved closer to my ethical compromise between greed and guilt.

Is this funny and am I a prude? I wondered. Back at Holy Cross, the students had started calling me Miss Hymen. My last name is pronounced "SchlAY-man," so it was a bad half rhyme at best. One of my students burst out laughing during a non-hilarious discussion of *Macbeth* and I grabbed his phone. Another student had texted him "Say HY to Miss HYMEN (()) FOR ME LOL." I held on to the phone. I shrugged and stayed frozen in my shrug with my arms up and asked squeakily and sincerely if this was really how they wanted to make use of sex ed. In the end, I queried, had any of them "properly learned" what a hymen was or did? ("It is made of Saran wrap," said Martin Babic, a very earnest translucent Slavic boy with reluctant hormones who had misunderstood the gym teacher's use of simile.)

I gave them a whole talk about how stupid they would feel years later for thinking "hymen" or "smegma" was the funniest thing in the world, but they were deep into the thinking and couldn't see out of it. This is one of the dangers of their ineluctable depth: they live the poetry, the true value of the way words resonate and not their dictionary meanings or conventional uses. It's why teenage mouths are the hotbeds of slang, and its most natural environment. Some years only sounds would erupt: everyone saying "WOMP" to each other, because they liked the way it moved in their heads and echoed in their ears, big and rubbery and round.

For something like the same respect for poetry, I had to stand firm on Ms. Hymen: "It doesn't even rhyme," I told them. "It's not even a pun! If anything, call me Miss Gay Man, you know? Something that actually works." But I regretted it right away because I didn't want Anthony the librarian, for example, thinking I was somehow trying to steal some part of him. But Miss Gay Man was a crown I had to bear since I'd put it on my own head, and I apologized to Anthony, who only laughed, because he, too, knew the unavoidable glue of poetry that held the title fast to me and did for the next two and a half years, until I left. With their sneaky, collective power, they hadn't simply nicknamed me; they had convinced me to rename myself.

Whoever decorated Pink Taco has obviously never been inside a vagina. It's full of fish hooks and hard corners. I shouldn't have given them any of my money. I should not have walked along the sunbaked slabs but rather stayed in, eaten a yogurt in the cool, worked. Embarrassed to be seen making an order at Pink Taco *by the person taking my order at Pink Taco*, I became very quiet and defensive: "Give me a Tecate," no eye contact.

Now I am depleted, back in my non-hotel, lying on a hard "modernist" sofa, empty takeout taco paper and a beer can on the floor within arm's reach. Computer on my chest. The tinted floor-to-ceiling glass wall has gone deep amber, protecting me from the searing, high midday sun. The sun is beaming an extreme laser heat, like hate, and my tinted wall is some kind of corporate mediator, telling me "The sun has complicated energies that have nothing to do with you."

Is that what's made me complacent recently? My Xanax of a non-hotel? I've been letting R&M's emails go by. I've been saying yes. To be fair, they're very good at their jobs. They can convey complex action scenes with an amazing thrift of words, the pace never dropping, something I don't know how to do. They want Masahiro a little younger. That didn't seem worth a fight. I bought a cropped white-silk shell today for $185 at a boutique on Rodeo Drive (my superstitions about money are no match for growing insecurities about being writer-ugly in a sea of actor beauty). I'm savoring the idea of wearing it to a party tonight at the beach where no one will know I eat vulgar vagina jokes for lunch and talk to glass walls.

My eyelids are half down, my hand dangling off the sofa, when suddenly my computer rings. Murphy wants to FaceTime. I spring up, put the computer on the coffee table, wipe grease from my face.

"Penny, what's up."

"What's up," I say, as if I really don't have much spare time. When, in fact, I've been daydreaming like an adolescent, picturing my body a paper doll for purchased things, seeing my silhouette trail a cigarette at the end of my long arm by a cool pool, radioactive desires implanted in me by 1980s billboards, slow to break down.

"Just not getting much of a steer here on casting," says Murphy.

"But I thought casting's not up to us anyway."

"Well, you know we have this table read scheduled right after the script delivery."

"Two weeks from Wednesday." I've never missed a deadline in my life.

"So," Murphy continues, "someone has to read that part, and whatever actress we bring in to read that script for the producers—who knows—might fall in love with the part. It's just a chance to get someone we like interested. So do you have any input here?"

"Yeah," I say, flashing back to the classroom, to days when I was hungover or underprepared, when I'd do my laziest move of reading aloud to the class and then asking others to continue the reading. It was a move I learned from Derek, who was a completely captivating reader: Derek's face on display, his mouth in motion, the gears and ropes and pulleys all ticking along without your contriving to keep him in conversation. You could study his jaw, the way his two front teeth crossed each other slightly, although, as with truly beautiful people, you could never study enough.

When I read aloud, I could expect to hear yawning, the sound of foreheads hitting desks as I broadcast the story from my unremarkable perforated griddlecake of a face. When I handed the performance off to another student in the class, the anxiety usually woke people up, but the price to pay was that rather than make the time pass, it often elongated it excruciatingly. One minute expanded to contain the mortification of hours and days as we all watched some poor kid stumble over simple words like a drunken horse breaking shins on low hurdles, just begging to get shot. ("That's enough, Martin, thanks." "You're welcome, Miss Gay Man.")

"Get someone who can fucking read," I tell Murphy.

"They may not be Ph*D*s, Penny, but they can all read."

Dammit. Somehow Murphy's made himself seem a champion of female intelligence while I'm the kind of person who treats starlets like red meat. I hear a mumbling off-camera. Murphy turns his head. "Mm-hmm. Okay. You—you want to tell her?" Randy pops onscreen.

"Hey, Penny!" Randy is extra warm. Maybe he knows it's weird that the two are working together without me, even though officially it isn't. They are writing partners, after all. "So here's the thing. Pretend you're an actress."

"Uh-huh." I burp Tecate with my mouth closed.

"Actually, never mind." He searches for language. "Actresses are like hunters. No, like murderers. No, wait. Actresses are like—crazyyyy—beautifulllll—no, wait. What I'm trying to say is, they need *roles*."

"I know what an actress *is*, Randy. Just a starving person who acts."

"What I'm getting at is that there are only so many roles in a given season, and they turn down certain roles for other ones. What makes them choose one role over another?"

"I don't know, their abusive managers or something?"

"No. Managers are rarely abusive, Penny."

Murphy, from offscreen: "That's directors!"

"Actresses choose one role over another," says Randy, "because it has the biggest potential to make them a star."

"Don't we just call everyone 'actors' now anyway?" Aha! Now who's a champion of women?

"Sure, sure, on their tax returns and to their faces. But we're talking about them as a species here." Randy's hand floats up and traces a wavelet in front of his face. "Look, Penny." Randy glances offscreen and back. "If we're going to get someone really good here, *really* good—the mermaid has to die. I know you pushed back on this earlier, but coming into production, it's obvious this is the best way. Murphy really sold me on it."

Murphy is the "structure" guy, I've learned: he's the discipline, the hard choices, always reminding us that it's got to come in under one hundred pages. Like a fiscal austerity wonk, he blames the numbers when he takes away Granny's dialysis. Randy, in contrast, started out in sitcoms and rom-coms. He's hyphenated half-funny.

"Sylvia *sleeps wit' da fishes*," he says, because he's the guy who quotes the best of other movies; an avid diner, but not a chef.

It's early afternoon now, and the sun is brighter than ever. The tinted glass has darkened in reaction, as if keeping me from a report of worsening news.

I feel suddenly exhausted. I need to nap before tonight's party. I need to be fresh. We'll be by the water, at some rich guy's house. There I am, by the pool, all in white, smoke trailing from my extended arm.

"You want her to die permanently?" I ask.

"Yeah," says Randy. "Murphy has it all sketched out."

"How does she die?" I ask about the person I created, the woman whose heartbeat I sometimes felt as I wrote her pulsating bodily expeditions into the cold, electric sea. *How does she die?* I hear myself ask a bro and a failed actor I met six weeks ago who might help me get rich.

"Well, you have a choice," says Randy's face from a box on my computer screen. "Grilled, fried, or Cajun blackened."

CHAPTER 17

EXCERPT FROM *AMERICAN MERMAID*

The day that Sylvia killed herself began with a surprise phone call from her mother at work.

"I'm in Boston. Let me take you to dinner."

"What's going on?"

"I'll come get you."

At 7:15 p.m., Sylvia took the elevator down from the Devon Energy offices on the eleventh floor of an unmemorable green-glass tower in downtown Boston. She rode the elevator with a colleague, a combustion specialist in her forties, brassy and well-liked, who checked her watch and winced.

"Late to pick up my son. Not a good look," said the woman, shaking her head. "Oh my god, get this. You've met my son Lucas, right? He's eight now. He has a *girlfriend*."

"Awwww," obliged Sylvia.

"It's *so cute*. We were at the supermarket the other day and I put some strawberries in the cart and he goes, 'Can we get some for Rosie?' They hold hands and stuff. *What a little Romeo!*"

"Cute," said Sylvia.

"I'm like, *Are you using protection?*"

Sylvia was repulsed but tried to guess what someone without her deficiencies might say: "Adorable."

The doors opened with a ding. The colleague quickly offered to push Sylvia's chair, but she declined with gentle thanks. They said good-bye and Sylvia caught sight of her mother outside the security turnstile. Her mother's was the most familiar silhouette in the world to her, but jarring to see at Sylvia's office.

"Oh, darling," said Eleanor as she dropped to one knee next to Sylvia's wheelchair. Eleanor was solidly built and elegant, and as Sylvia embraced her, her hands registered the muscles on either side of her mother's straight spine.

"What's going on?"

Eleanor Granger's gin and tonic had been ordered but not delivered when she looked Sylvia in the eye and said, "Masahiro is dead."

The words made no sense to Sylvia. She had seen the doctor just a few weeks ago, at his office as usual. She had told him about breaking up with her boyfriend—the first and only one she'd ever had. She wasn't heartbroken at all, and Masahiro had been strangely silent. But he had seemed healthy. Masahiro, dead?

"How?"

"He had an aneurysm."

"An *aneurysm*?"

"Just like that, honey."

"But—"

"He was visiting family in Japan. They say there's very little pain with an aneurysm."

"But—he's *dead*?"

"You never know with these things," said Eleanor, now taking her daughter's hand into her own. "I think about this all the time with Daddy, or me. This was just his genetic narrative. This was always waiting to happen to him." A teenage waitress asked if they'd had a chance to look at the menu. Sylvia looked away from the waitress, toward the wall, as tears filled her eyes. His *genetic narrative?* But what kind of a narrative just stops in the middle?

They didn't stay long at the restaurant. Sylvia toyed with her fork, couldn't eat, looked lost. Her mother paid and they left.

In the taxi home, Sylvia's gaze slipped over gray-brown Boston, but her mind was in Masahiro's brightly lit office in Washington Heights. For some reason, this was the memory that came first and most clearly: Sylvia remembered being sixteen years old, with her eyes closed, on her side, while Masahiro examined her spine.

Masahiro was quizzing her. "A cubical block of metal weighs six pounds. How much will a cube of the same metal weigh if its sides are twice as long?"

"Can I write this down?"

"No, no, picture it!"

"I can't picture it."

"Draw it on your skin, on your hand." Sylvia traced the two cubes with a finger across the chaotic map of shallow wrinkles and blue veins on her palm.

"It's not just doubled, and it's not just squared," she began.

"Good! You saw through that!"

This was old hat for them. Since Sylvia's earliest school days, she had been driven to Masahiro's office after the bell rang, when other kids went to soccer or ballet. Masahiro would swing a metal surgical lamp over to the paper-covered table where Sylvia sat so that she could see her homework. Masahiro would look over her shoulder, cover a US state on the map, and make her guess the capital before returning to a reflex test or preparing a steroid injection. If she was there late, Masahiro would duck into the hallway and return with KitKat or Snickers bars from the vending machine. There was so much energy in Masahiro's face, his quick smile and dark, leaping eyes, that even the white streaks in his black hair couldn't age him, only capped him with incongruous dazzle.

When Sylvia's SAT scores came back a few months later, Masahiro jumped in the air in his doctor's coat, his orthopedic sneakers squeaking on the linoleum floor. She had a perfect score in math and nearly perfect in verbal.

"Verbal logic is overrated anyway," said Masahiro. "Words, words. When you're a doctor, words are the crazy part. 'Gurney'! 'Salve'! 'Proctalgia fugax'!" Sylvia giggled. (They had a long-running joke about proctalgia fugax—there was a ridiculous pamphlet about it in the waiting room with a picture of an old man in coveralls clutching his rear and pouting theatrically. On particularly tough days, when Sylvia was in pain or felt low, Masahiro would make a very serious face at her, hand her the pamphlet, and say, "Read this carefully." It always made her laugh.)

"But you can trust science," she said.

"*No.*" His smile dropped momentarily. "Not science." He turned away from Sylvia and fiddled with something on his desk. "But you can trust numbers," he continued. "More or less."

Masahiro had let her look through her first microscope, he had let her prepare her first slide. In her bouts of excruciating pain, he had sat beside her and held her hand, sometimes fixing her eyes with his until it passed. He knew her. Bursting with tears, she came back to her aching body in the taxicab in Boston, and at twenty-four years old, she suddenly realized that *he was the only one who really knew her.* And he was—dead.

The college catalogues had come pouring in during the spring that she was just remembering, the spring of her junior year of high school, and with every flare-up of spinal pain, or with every recalibration of her fragile joints, Sylvia would be sent to Masahiro's office and he would help her imagine her future in ways no one else did.

"Do you see yourself secluded in the woods? Or would you want to skip class and wander an art museum? Would you be scared or excited by people-watching in a subway?" She said she wanted to study science but also economics and literature and music—everything, she said breathlessly. She dreamed of somewhere sunny, full of kids who wanted to be up at the lab bench as badly as she did.

. . .

"Stanford," Sylvia had told her father. Dean Granger had leaned back in his leather office chair and chewed the inside of his lip.

"Stanford?"

Sylvia remembered pushing her wheelchair up to her father's desk and handing him the Stanford brochure. All the brochures that came that spring contained pictures of beaming college kids, loaded with books, on green velvety lawns. Stanford's catalogue showed beach volleyball players leaping up in front of a crashing surf. The one spiking the ball wore a cut-off maroon T-shirt bearing just the top of the Stanford S.

Dean Granger had taken a heavy breath. "It's a great school. I just don't think you'd fit in there," he had said, pointedly holding the brochure so that the beautiful-bodied athletes faced his chair-bound daughter. Blood had filled Sylvia's ears, muffling what her father said next—some dismissive words about "California culture."

Then his tone shifted. "You know, there's nothing more interesting than the very ground we stand on. How do you think I got all this?" Dean Granger's arms floated up, and he looked at the walls of his office, pinned with exotic artifacts—a Renaissance platter, a Mayan pot. "All this," he implied, meant not just his knickknacks but the world itself. "MIT is *the* place for fracture mechanics. Learn how to break into the earth and take what people need. It's exciting stuff."

"But Masahiro went to Stanford," Sylvia had protested.

Her father darkened. "Stanford isn't what made Masahiro. Besides," her father said, smiling the smile of a man pretending he had not spent the vast majority of his daughter's upbringing locked in his office, "we couldn't bear the thought of you so far away from us. Anyway, you won't be able to see Masahiro anymore if you're in California. Stay close, and he can still treat you for us."

She had attended MIT, double majoring in geology and mechanical engineering.

. . .

The taxi stopped in front of Sylvia's apartment. In seconds, her mother was opening her door and unfolding Sylvia's wheelchair. Sylvia caught the cabdriver stretching upward so that he could see, in his rearview mirror, what precisely was wrong with this girl.

Her mother undressed her as if she were a child, with almost no words. She held the pajama shirt wide open. Sylvia threaded her arms and poked her head through. Her mother offered to wash her hair for the first time in eight years, but Sylvia shook her head no. Eleanor Granger lifted Sylvia into her bed and pulled the covers up to her chin. She smoothed her daughter's hair. She did not know that it would be the last time.

"I'll be sleeping in the spare room if you need anything," Eleanor Granger whispered to her daughter, and the door closed with a click.

Sylvia's body shook with sobs, which activated the pain centers in her lower back, down her thighs, knees, and shins. The physical pain—sometimes like needles but sometimes mounting into sudden acid stabs deep in her marrow—felt utterly of a piece with the blackness of her heart. *Bereft.* "Bereft" was the word that came to her mind. Something ripped from her. She pictured her chest cavity and saw only suffocating lungs that couldn't cry hard enough, and a black, unbeating heart suspended in a pool of mute black ink. She was empty of life. There was no way of believing that on the other side of this pain would be regeneration, recovery. Nothing had really ever diminished her body's capacity for pain besides, momentarily, Masahiro's presence.

Pain had been there her whole life, a constant, while fear had started one day with a little observation and since grown rampant. It was the fear she first voiced in Masahiro's office after her tenth-grade seizure at the lab bench. She'd realized that day that Jeff, who had stared into her eyes searching for some connection, had a crush on her. Any other girl in that situation would have felt excited, thrilled, some fluorescent teenage version of attraction—maybe even love. She had felt nothing. She had never felt anything. Was she cursed to always be alone, sexless, loveless?

Brian, a decent and compassionate nerd she'd met at work—her "boyfriend" for a couple of months—had been so duped by her. She had caressed his face, she had laughed in his car. She'd done things that she saw other women do. But when they kissed, it was like eating food she wasn't hungry for. Rather than deliver herself to instinct, she retreated into her mind, where she calculated every rotation of her tongue, every deployment of her hand, just hoping that he liked it. She felt shame now at the thought of it. When he wanted to go further, she was too scared, not of pleasure but of pain, that his touch might trigger something. And then—the fear that what he found would disgust him, that she was too different, too weird.

The only thing that truly transported her, that made her heart race and face flush, was the fantasy of moving not toward a lover but of moving at all, of moving freely, of swimming. But those very fantasies, her irrepressible fantasies of pushing rhythmically through matter, she understood to be just another facet of a failure to live on this earth, of a desire to die.

Decisions happen sometimes without being made precisely. Sylvia never decided to kill herself. Like an aneurysm, this decision was simply an event in her brain, the appearance of the knowledge that she would die at her hands, and soon. When she did eventually find herself very slowly pushing her wheelchair through the lobby in pajamas and a parka, having the concierge call her a cab to the Tide Street pier, she did so without sorrow or elation, but with a sense of will, of drive. Of executive competence. The only person who really knew her, the only human connection she would ever have, was gone. The absence of sexual desire in her life made her see its overwhelming presence everywhere else. It wasn't simply that she would never have a husband named Brian; she didn't know how to dress, where to look—how to be a person. Some string that connected everyone didn't thread through her, and it made sense that she would tumble like an errant bead off a table.

Her mother would suffer—she didn't want to think about that. Her father would be embarrassed, that was certain. *Good,* she thought. *He needs something to go wrong in his life if he's ever going to be saved.* Saved from being someone who's bought insulation from the real world, saved from feeling godlike in his dominion of EarthSource and his wife and all the people who did what he said because it was their livelihood. *By killing myself, I'll help my father: I'll make him human,* Sylvia thought as the cabdriver helped her into her wheelchair at the pier.

"You gonna be okay?" the guy asked.

"Yeah, I'm fine," Sylvia reassured him. She flexed her biceps and smiled at him. He didn't seem convinced. "My boyfriend's meeting me here any minute."

"All righty. You have a good night," he said, slammed the passenger door, and loped back around to the driver's side.

It took about forty minutes to wend her way along the pier, past Houlihan's, Blacktop Eddie's, Marina Eatery, and Legal Sea Foods, a beckoning, red-lit corporate fantasy of timeless port life. Eventually the working boats began to appear in greater numbers, the choppy Atlantic water slapping against their hulls.

She found herself at an abandoned dock. She wheeled herself to the end. It was after midnight, early June, and it was dark except for the reflections of the distant red lights on the prickly and kinetic surface of the sea. Hers was an exceptional mind, by all accounts. Was this reason to live? Could she apply her skills to environmental protection, or retrain and devote herself to vaccines, malnutrition, gene therapy?

No. *A person with no will to live can't be a lifesaver,* she thought.

Finally, her mind went to Masahiro. The only glimpse of a wider world of human connection, of a happiness earned by her in her own life, had been with Masahiro—ironically, she realized, in the peaks of pain. *The pain.* To be finally released from this *terrorist* of a body, this threat of constant, random crisis in her nerve center. *Oh god, yes.* She looked down one last time at her legs, at their withered attenuation under her thin pajama pants; down from her flat thighs, to the limp planks of her shins, to her grotesque, swollen ankles, to the twisted stubs she hid in lying prop shoes, shoes that never bore any weight, that never touched the ground. She spoke silently to an unnamed spiritual power: *Whatever you made, it didn't work. My "genetic narrative" wasn't tenable. I was bungled by you, I was fatally incomplete. They tried to save me, to fix me, but I can't be fixed. I was born broken and I want to die.*

The sea slapped loud enough against the work boats and the pylons and the dock that no one heard the sound of a wheelchair hitting the choppy surface of the water on the south side of Boston's Tide Street pier that night, or saw its frame tip slowly forward so that the inflated rubber wheels, which finally stopped spinning, were swallowed last.

CHAPTER 18

We are speeding toward the water, Danielle at the wheel, and I hear only one out of every three words she says, because the windows are open, and whipping down the freeway toward the beach is so relaxing I've shut down most of my sensory functions. But I gather that Dick Babbot is a big deal. Dick Babbot is a legend. Dick Babbot is the best. He started writing for sitcoms in the 1980s. He created *Jasper's World* and *Growing Up* and *Open Season* and he should be a jillionaire except he kept getting taken advantage of by women.

Now I ask to roll up the windows. I want to hear this.

"He's had like four wives. They're not gold diggers, they're just weird bohemians. They'll have three kids and open a yogurt shop that goes bankrupt, or they'll save a goat."

I take a moment to ponder goat-saving. What are the risks to goats? I start to imagine a goat in four red thigh-high boots on a street corner, but I don't think Danielle would enjoy this image, and I don't want her to know what a psycho junk shop my brain is, because, after all, I'm someone she's bet on. We are in business.

"Are there going to be goats at the party?" Cool Business Question, Business Person.

"No. He has a house in Upstate New York basically for his ex-wives' animals. Anyway, he's a genius, but his kids are *super nice* nothings, like they don't do *anything* but chill out, and sometimes they'll be extras or PAs on his shows."

"Isn't it okay to chill out if you're children?" I ask.

"No!" she says with that Danielle speed, whipping her blue eyes, squashed in a quizzical-mean squint, toward me and then back to the road. "They're between fourteen and thirty but they all act like babies. He has to do things just to make jobs for them—like he literally *handwrites* his scripts so that one of his kids can type them up for him." She pouted at me as if we'd just seen a video of a puppy running into a mirror.

"And then he has a set of legit toddlers and babies, too. I don't know who'll be there."

Danielle flips on the turn signal, takes a slow turn. She drives like she talks like she works: with unperformed confidence.

"Yeah. Babbot loves to make shows, and loves to make people," she continues. "He doesn't really care about money, he's a dreamer. You should see his tweets, they'll just say, like, '*Bridget Jones's Butthole.*'"

"I don't get it."

"Yeah, not yet. But you will in five years when it's a hit series on HBO."

"Could you make a series called *Bridget Jones's Butthole* without Helen Fielding's permission?"

"Look at you, mini-agent!" She puts up a hand for me to slap. "Get hungry, you boss bitch!"

I've never been prouder of anything in my life. How hard am I beaming? I feel like my Lexus seat warmers just went on. To my relief, she continues.

"You get my point. He *would* do something like that, something very meta, a parody or something. He's deep. And yet, people love him. He's been massively successful. He's someone you should be pitching projects to. He should live in a house made of Cristal bottles stacked like Lincoln Logs and instead he's got this shambolic life and fritters it all away on his hippie family."

"I like him already."

"Everybody does. Everybody loves him. He's like an earth dog."

"What's an earth dog?"

"Sorry, I was focusing." She shakes her head a little, keeps her eyes on the road. "I meant earth god."

"What's an earth god?"

"I mean he's a powerful guy who's not even trying. Anyway, if you meet someone and they're not a writer or producer, they're probably a wife or child. So just keep it cute."

Earth god. What the fuck was that? If you hypnotized Danielle, like the highway just had, would you find secret poetry?

Dick Babbot is bad at money, but not that bad. We park, pull our cooler of rosé out of the trunk, throw some towels over our shoulders, and walk up through an alley crowded with Teslas and Range Rovers. All the houses in Malibu have the same priorities—perfunctory little back doors, grand façades facing the sea. Dick's house, three stories, gray blue, wearing a long bib of a porch, belongs somewhere in Maine. To one side is a house from the future, aluminum-looking with rounded towers, and to the other side is a house from Miami, pink stucco, agape with big open windows. We go find Dick first. He's got shorts hanging off his flat old ass and a half-unbuttoned checkered shirt on, trying to get a grill going out beyond the porch. He hugs Danielle and says her name with loud, unbridled joy, hugs me and welcomes me and raises his voice with excitement when Danielle tells him I'm adapting a novel I wrote about a mermaid.

"Sweet, you can do some research, then," he says, tossing an arm out toward the water. "Tanner's already way out there." He squints up at one of his sons, a golden-skinned kid in surf shorts flopped on a boogie board fifty yards out. I am distracted by the fact that Dick Babbot does not talk like adult men I know on the East Coast; he says "like" and "way" and his hard *R*s are the only thing curbing his formless vowels. Men in authority want seawater voices, old and briny, but this guy's is pool water, room temp and chemical and welcoming.

"You girls get a drink. Marly made a killer sangria. I'll have burgers up in, like, a day and a half." We laugh and head back to the porch, kicking sand.

"He seems cool," I tell Danielle. She's gratified.

"Isn't he the best? You should talk to him about *American Mermaid*. I bet he'd have a million ideas."

We're on piles of pillows on wooden wraparound benches and I'm remembering nobody's name. Some weirdly sensitive woman, who looks about thirty, with a pretty, sun-damaged face and a pink sarong she rewraps constantly, gets wild-eyed and wants to talk to me urgently when I mention in the course of a self-deprecating joke that I got a PhD. I realize with embarrassment that the fact that she wants to do a PhD makes her one of Dick Babbot's Damaged Kids. It is the sign of being lost, unmoored, insubstantial. She wants to do a PhD in literature and food studies "looking at, like, language and systems, and how it is that when you say 'bread' you can be not talking about bread at all."

"The poetry of 'Wonderbread,'" I say in agreement, and briefly check to make sure no one else heard me. You can tell who the writers and producers and agents are, and all of them know and are very kind to Dick Babbot's Damaged Kids. "Marly!" shouts a guy in a white button-down shirt holding two bags of upscale Belgian beers. He drops them and up goes Unmoored Damaged Sarong Daughter into his arms. I end up in a conversation with that guy, a writer, later. The conversation surprises me in its seriousness. He really wants to get into it with me about teaching, about how important teaching is and how we can get bright people to do it. He wants to diagnose why I left Holy Cross.

In this moment of meaningless, temporary social contact, with this guy whose name I haven't retained and who writes for a flashy procedural I never watch, I find surprising shelter for sincere reflection.

"It's honestly the most fun you'll ever have, teaching. I don't know why everyone doesn't want to do it."

"I want to do it!"

"You should."

"Too late." He looks at his beer, as if he's one beer too late to do something no one does because it doesn't pay.

"It's also hard in a crazy-making way," I admit. "I had to come home every night and drink a box of wine to unwind from having to deal with all of these *unformed* people. Conversations with forty-five people a day who are all in a state of *becoming*. You see too much. Too much minor humiliation. Too much effort. Just one preteen girl with puppy fat and visible nipples—I'm devastated."

There is a long pause. I tip back a plastic Lakers freebie cup of juicy sangria. Fruit hits my face. When I'm done drying my nose with my shirt, he's still trying to imagine what it is like to have your day crushed and bruised by the sight of swollen nipples.

"Yeah, I guess with boobs, you want them fully formed or not at all." A gull shrieks.

We get burgers and you can almost forget it's a showbiz home. Some messy four-year-old in water wings bumps into my legs as I'm scooping up a white, creamy pasta salad. The surfers have come in and are famished, don't want to talk; they spear burgers with forks, collect cold beers under their arms. I'm gently drunk but nothing crazy. The sangria's full of juice, and suddenly I have to pee, badly. I ask a teenage girl, no doubt a Damaged Kid, very at home in her string bikini in the living room, where the bathrooms are and she says, "Oh, there's like nine."

I start on the ground floor. There's a baby being changed. I move to the other ground-floor bathroom, a small toilet by the laundry. There's an older baby on a plastic potty on the normal toilet. I go upstairs. There's a mom sitting on a stool by the tub and two babies in the tub, swimsuits on the floor. I check in a couple of bedrooms.

One bathroom locked. I go up another flight of stairs. There are two ten-year-olds playing in a girl's bedroom. "Hey, do you guys have a toilet in here?"

"Jenny's on the toilet."

Are there more toilets up here? They shake their heads.

Back down, still busy, back down again. I go out to the porch, report to Danielle I couldn't find a toilet. She's midconversation. I drink more, cross my legs tight, sit, pretending to be part of Danielle's conversation with a bunch of writers, but I'm monitoring the stabbing pain in my abdomen. "Just give it a minute," Danielle says.

I try again, and there is a slightly different assortment of babies in and on all the tubs and toilets. I knock on doors and listen to busy babble. I open doors and am met by the floating, curious gaze of fat children sitting in toy-littered baths and smaller fat children standing, crying, naked, being rubbed red with towels. I burst into the last possible toilet on the top floor and I ask if Jenny could possibly be done yet, and they tell me, laughing, singsong, "Jenny broke the toiiiilet." They point to water creeping into the blue carpet from the tiled bathroom floor, so I go back to the first toilet and I ask two mom-like people who are grappling with two babies in two swimsuits if please could they get out for *one* minute so I could take a quick pee, I've tried all the other bathrooms.

Their faces go from attentive and amused to hard and angry.

They stare at me, and what I understand suddenly is that I've insulted them—not just for being moms, for being trampled, hardworking moms underappreciated by society at large—but for being Dick Babbot's ex-wives or wives or sisters or eldest daughters, the women who are the closest, in his home life, to Dick Babbot. They demand a high tariff of flattery and indulgence from the writers who want to do business within the city of love and money that is Dick Babbot and that they protect, all the while knowing they will never occupy the rank of "creatives" and are seen as ragged, unnecessary impediments to Dick Babbot's singular genius. For some new trader fresh to Babbot City to march into the bathroom and ask the women to *leave*, to *remove Dick Babbot's pudgy seed from its plastic potty and erase ourselves so that some Harvard twat can pee out Marly's Sangria and Tweet about it*—I had done something terrible. I was fooled by the familiarity—the familiality—of plastic plates and pasta salad and the sheer presence of children into thinking we were in some egalitarian utopia, naked babies and flashy producers padding around together barefoot. But anxiety and insecurity were odorless gases, and I've ignited them.

"Who *are you?*" comes the response from one of the messy mothers' mouths and both of their eyes. As if to say, *You're not even in the inner circle, are you? How dare you command* us wives and women? The viciousness in their faces is terrifying, eyes narrow, lips curling.

The babies freeze.

"I'm really sorry, I'll just wait," I say, and sprint away to the porch. I stand next to Danielle, who calmly talks to one of Babbot's kids about staffing jobs on TV shows, but I glance over my shoulder after a couple of minutes and see one of the moms whispering to someone and pointing at me. What is she saying? Will they kick me out?

She's some friend of Danielle's.

Well, they both have to leave.

I'm squeezing my crotch muscles and slightly tilting forward to dull the stabbing pain in my bladder. My eyes, with sudden relief, meet the sea.

"I'm going in," I tell Danielle. I peel off my jeans and my cotton top. No space in my mind for the usual body anxiety as I look down at my pale inner thighs, pillowy against my black one-piece as I bend down. I march toward the water, pass Dick at the grill. He's impressed I'm going in: "THATTA GIRL." (He doesn't yet know to hate me; the women haven't told him.) It's freezing. The minute the water hits my toes, I start to pee. I walk with my legs together, like my ankles are tied, until my crotch is wet. I let go. It goes forever. Still peeing. Still peeing. Still peeing.

Now I am done. Oh shit, I am so grateful. But suddenly I wonder: Is it weird to get into the water up to your *vagina lips* and then turn around? Will everyone know I've used Dick Babbot's private sea—Dick Babbot's sons' playground—for a toilet? I can't turn back now. It will be obvious I just peed publicly in front of fifty people enjoying Chardonnay and pesto. The sea is a gorgeous and endlessly changing tableau for the lazy drinkers on the porch. Everyone watches: pretty, near-naked bodies in the foreground, the sporting action of the middle distance, the far-off kites and sails. I turn around for a moment. Danielle waves. I recognize White Shirt Writer Guy and Damaged Sarong Daughter in beach chairs, facing me. I paddle into the water a little more. My skin prickles, but I'm adjusting to the cold and now it feels nice.

The waves have the force of muscles suddenly expanding and contracting with capricious will. I keep my eyes on the waves that are coming. I paddle out a little more to be at the crest of a big one. I'm lofted high up, my heart floating in me, and brought gently down. Memories of other places I've done this come back, overlapping: Jones Beach in college; Florida as a kid; Cape Cod, sometime—or was that just Sylvia in the book? I get into a rhythm of this, surging upward, delivered gently down. At one point, I let out something of a "whoopeeee" or a "yeee." I can almost forget the mommies, the towering, bluish wooden lodge where a militia of Babbots is forming to meet me when I emerge. "Generous" and "healing" are words that occur to me about the sea as kelp slaps my ankles and my palate adjusts to the pungent salt that I lick off my lips.

I time the next wave wrong and get pummeled as it crests, but it's harmless. I ball up and plug my nose and wait through the tumble to rise. I get to the air and turn toward the shore and I'm a ways away, I realize. Another wave comes. I try to ride its momentum toward the beach, paddling with it, but when it crests and dissolves into froth finally, my toes can't claw into the sand, the water's still too deep, and I'm sucked back out.

Now, very calmly, and with the appearance of great competence to those on shore, I am going to swim like a *motherfucker* and get out of this grip and back to shore. I count to three. I go as horizontal as possible. I put my head under, I take long strokes. I kick hard, not just from the knees but with the length of my strong legs. I work hard for thirty seconds or more (it feels great), my torso twisting the way it should so that each stroke can extend fully. I must be swimming beautifully. I wonder if anyone notices. I am a good swimmer, I know, tall and trained, with smooth strokes and no stupid tics. When I stop and rub the water from my eyes, I am out of breath, but I am only a stroke or two from shore. There's a red plastic kiddie shovel so close I can see its cheap frayed edges. Surely in a moment my feet will hit the sand. *Thank god.* I paddle forward with what energy I have. I will get back.

Then some muscle in the current contracts. Some band of water tightens around me and pulls. This one feels distinct, like a monstrous snake or a giant's curling fist. It yanks me back, and then down the beach. I sense I am moving toward Dick's neighbor's house, the one that looks like it's from the future. I'm not moving myself. I'm an object, being moved. Danielle holds her hand over her eyes like a visor. Dick looks up from his grill.

For a split second I imagine the mothers have done this: they gathered in the laundry bathroom and chanted some hex, stirring the potty together. *We and our throbbing, productive wombs call upon the sea to swallow this woman, or rather, this self-interested, word-spitting, sea-peeing she-thing.*

And it does.

"What the fuck happened?" Danielle is coming toward me, at the head of a crowd of Dick Babbot's chatty, speculating guests on the beach. Another crowd of guests looks down from the porch, pushing against the railing as if it will keep them safe. They bring their drinks. I can see the mothers lurking in the back, safe and smug, holding their bundled children to their hips.

"It was a riptide," says the lifeguard, panting. He's tall and bronze, but I can't see his face because from where I'm lying the sun is right behind it. I look up at him, amazed at the intimate contact we've just had. I think at one point he held my crotch and my shoulder like someone in oven mitts holds the sides of a casserole. It strikes me as modern and sad that now he'll walk away.

"Are you okay?" asks Danielle. She is legitimately concerned, but also playing the role of Super Agent before the assembled partygoers. She puts her hands on my face, like a lover.

"I'm completely fine," I say. In truth, I haven't checked in with my body yet, but I'm desperate to be completely fine. I haven't registered how hard I was slammed on my back when the lifeguard pulled me out of the water.

"This happened to some fat comedian last week," offers one of Dick Babbot's Damaged Children.

Dick Babbot pushes himself through the crowd. "Oh my god," he says, laughing. He takes me from the lifeguard's care, pulls me into his tan, naked, hairy chest, and holds me tightly. The smell of propane coming off the white pubes on his dark chest is suffocating. "It's the *mermaid*." I feel the laughter pumping through his warm body. "It's *our mermaid*," he repeats. "What a great story. I've gotta write this."

CHAPTER 19

The ceilings are so high in the Soho House's cement-walled, ivy-draped, communal work space that the pop music, played from speakers far up, doesn't reverberate like it would in some two-bit coffee shop. It flaps and hovers high above our heads, like a distant, colorful bird of paradise. We want to dance with somebody who loves us, we sing, as Whitney Houston's lush vibrato pours down into the bad coffee of our voices like heavy cream.

We are agreeing on plenty today, the twins and I: the flashback structure that reveals to the audience, although not to Sylvia, Masahiro's treachery. We already knew that Masahiro, owned by Granger for some dark reason, performed the surgery that split Sylvia as an infant, and, before that, he helped Granger run a series of tests on the baby. Those tests showed that aside from cutaneous respiration—like other amphibians, she could take in oxygen underwater through the living veil of her beautiful skin—she had no superhuman strength, her vision was normal, her brain size and cognition tracked with humans.

But after Sylvia's sixteenth birthday, when, submerged in water, she experienced a new kind of vision, Granger demanded that Masahiro report to him on changes in her body, in her moods, new feelings, growing powers. Granger needed to know what his tests had missed. I had seen this at school a thousand times, the "underperforming" students who had secret abilities that tests never measured—the nonnative English speakers who looked at your whole face as you talked because they'd learned to read minds, to skip language and go right to thought.

We are working on the scene where Masahiro confesses his spying to Sylvia, but also confesses to her what nobody knows, not Dean, not Eleanor: that he executed Dean Granger's wishes in splitting her tail, but he made it all reversible. If she ever made it to the water, her legs would lock together, her skin would bond, tail unfurl; she would be a mermaid again. He built Sylvia a secret door to a future of her choosing.

This is why, for the twins, Masahiro is "basically cool although he did some uncool shit." They are so good at cutting through complexity, I have imagined letting them loose on major political conflicts. They show up in Israel: "You guys give these guys one chunk west of the Jordan River and everyone chill." The soft rattle of arms laid down in sand; the angelic gasp of flavored seltzer opened and shared by Jew and Arab.

Randy reads, "Interior. Dean Granger's office. Masahiro in his midforties sits on leather sofa facing the camera, delivering his reports to Granger. Same room, same position, but Masahiro is now forty-eight, fifty, fifty-two. With each cut, his hair whitening, he looks more glum and self-loathing. Cut to Dean Granger, facing camera, elbows on his desk, listening, occasionally making a note.

"Cut to Masahiro at the last session with Granger." He looks to Murphy. "Masahiro speaks."

Murphy nods and starts reading: "Uhhhh, Mistahhh Granjah, I berrrieve Syrrrvia—"

My mouth starts talking midsip of coffee with a dribbling "No nono nonono." I slurp and wipe my chin, head still going back and forth, back and forth. "No no nononono."

Murphy and Randy laugh.

"Just kidding!" says Randy, putting a hand on my wrist. "Come on. We're having fun."

The mere idea. "No no no no."

"Pe-ne-ro-pee. Do not-ahh be mad at me," says Murphy, his terrible accent taking on now even more damage and license.

"Murphy, seriously." I look around. We're blessedly alone.

"Penny, relax, we're having fun. We got tunes." Randy points to the speakers in the ceiling. "We got a script. It's all good." He looks me in the eye, smiling, tilting his head like a reassuring nurse.

"Okay. We've had our fun. So much fun."

Randy continues in this "caring" vein. "Yo, I heard you had a pretty bad scare at Babbot's house this weekend."

"You heard about that?" The fact that I've been discussed pleasantly confirms that I exist in Los Angeles. "How did you hear about it?"

"I don't remember," says Randy. "Someone told me."

There's a pause. Murphy starts poring over his script intently. Randy bobs his head to Toto's "Africa."

"Do you have *that many* conversations?" I ask. "You don't remember who reported to you that your cowriter almost died at a barbecue?"

"We know Dick," Murphy offers. "We have a lot of friends in common."

"Uh-huh." I roll this around in my mouth a minute. Tastes like a lie. "You guys, I worked with teenagers. I'm very experienced with lying." To be fair, the students didn't often lie to me. But I heard them lie to each other a lot, reporting things their friends never said, referring to strange moneys earned, claiming to have blown and been blown. They were livers of fiction and believed their lies and lied excellently. But when you hear a cherubic, smart fourteen-year-old say that she saw someone butt-fuck on a bus at robotics camp in Bridgeport, your knowledge of the world is simply too much for their nevertheless slickly delivered fictions.

"Actually, we talked to Dick Babbot," says Murphy. He and Randy exchange a quick glance. "He's really supportive of this mermaid project."

"He is?" I ask. Babbot didn't know I existed until a day ago.

Randy brightens up and reaches over the faux-graffitied wooden banquet table and pats my back. "We're just glad you're okay."

I'm not sure I am okay. I've been massaging myself a bit, twisting to try to address a throbbing ache in my lower back. "I felt like I owed the lifeguard my body afterward. Like in *Jane Eyre* when she saves Rochester from the fire and they're standing in their nightgowns and he makes her shake his hand."

"Hot," says Murphy.

"If only you could write your own life," says Randy.

Murphy mimes me typing on a laptop. *"Penelope, a pale size-ten writer, gently caressed the lifeguard's rippling bronze abs as their lips drew together."*

Randy jumps in. "Cut to them fucking."

It was a bit of an embarrassing admission, and I'm half glad the twins have spun it into a joke. Because it's real, the deep-down insane way I feel I owe every man on land, so that when a male person does me a kind turn—in this case his job—I think I ought to invite him to the inside of my body.

I turn to the unfinished business on the open page before me: "Look, Masahiro was born in Cleveland. He's a completely native English speaker. Okay? Is this something we're going to have to fight about?"

Randy shakes his head. "No way."

"That said," says Murphy, "we've had interest from some Japanese-born actors. I think we should at least look into them. They're super-talented guys and we don't want to be discriminatory."

"But that's not—that's not the character."

"Okay, but why can't he just be Japanese?"

"Because he's American."

"Then why Japanese at all?"

"Because—because he just is. His mother immigrated."

"What do you mean, he just is? We're rewriting this right now."

"He's American, born to a Japanese mother."

"Okay, so he can just be Japanese. It's not that different."

My pulse is racing now. I close my eyes, and slowly, to the canopy-descending rain of "Lady in Red," put what tastes like a cashew and horsehair protein ball in my mouth and throw my whole body into chewing it. It is satisfyingly distracting to attempt to move this shit around my mouth like a damp anthill. Is this what these balls are supposed to do, shut you up to defray "creative differences"? The annoyance I tried to swallow surges back at double strength and I go to spit into a napkin, but it's like the protein ball expanded in my mouth and I'm disgorging a complete sandcastle—Randy's and Murphy's faces disgusted—as I say:

"That's NOT who he IS!"

Suddenly the pop music cuts out, and there's an electric squeal, higher and harder than any alarm. Our hands go to our ears, and we duck as if this noise is an ax swinging from the mezzanine. Murphy mouths something and runs off. The pitch shifts, climbs higher in barbed half steps. I see someone on the other side of the room clutch his head and crawl under a table. We have to leave. This sound will kill us.

It goes on for what feels like minutes. We reel around. The staff have disappeared. It's just me and Randy.

Suddenly, it stops. My ears are still ringing, my mind electrocuted.

We shake out our ears. We swear. The speaker fizzes again with synthesizer harmony as if nothing had ever happened. Murphy returns, muttering about how many people will be fired for this. I can't think anymore, but Randy gets us sparkling water from an urn, sits down, gets back to business. He reaches across the table and puts a hand on my wrist. "Masahiro's a great character, Penny. I understand why you feel protective."

My ears are still screaming. My brain sloshes in my head. What are we talking about? A person, a real person we both know. Masahiro. *We have a lot of friends in common.*

The twins, I realize, are getting easier and easier to tell apart. Murphy is smart, but Randy is caring. And they're both assholes.

CHAPTER 20

"Your mother tells me you called me a—an *asshole* on the radio." My dad hates swearing and stopped using slang in the late 1950s. I can tell by the all-absorbing silence behind him that Harold Schleeman is in his upholstered office in midtown Manhattan, a symphony of shit colors in leather and wood, with some incongruous accents like a glass award clock from the American Trial Lawyers Association and an antique bronze of a Bavarian peasant girl at a water pump. My dad likes to invoke our regional ancestors and their crossing in the 1850s, helpfully escorting the connotations of our brazen German name away from the Holocaust and toward a festooned weinstübe.

"I didn't call you an asshole."

"Bad-mouthing your own family is disgraceful. It's baby stuff. Grow up."

"You're taking this wrong."

"Your mother tells me you're out there trying to get some kind of a Hollywood career off the ground. I think it's just folly. Leaving behind a salary and a pension."

"Well, I have an agent who knows what she's talking about."

"Bull manure. She'll string you along—what's she got to lose on you? You make money, she makes money. You ruin your life, she's fine."

Sure, if you don't understand that I'm entering a close coterie of boss bitch creatives who make each other wet piles of she-money as a gesture of caring, then yes, technically he's right.

"Just say 'bullshit.' I promise, it's less gross."

"Penelope, you're so smart, but you can't seem to *use it*. You got a problem with the world? Fine, go join *Greeeeenpeace*. Go join the Red Cross. What kind of a stand are you taking getting on some potty-mouthed radio show and telling a bunch of people your dad's a *bum*hole."

I feel the entire surface of my skin ripple with disgust. "Just say 'asshole.'"

"Don't tell me how to talk, Penelope. Your mother played me a minute of your radio show."

"It's not my show."

"Two drunk girls getting another to crap-talk her family. Just disgraceful. You all sounded like a bunch of teenagers. You have a PhD! You have students that look up to you! Or *looked* up to you. Can you imagine if they heard that?"

"I didn't call you an asshole. I called you evil."

"You want to go around crap-talking your family because—what? Because we disagree on abstract concepts like regulation? Like redistribution? Penelope, I'm your *father*. I love you. I have always had great hopes for you."

Abstract concepts. Maybe I am my father's daughter: it's all jokes and metaphors! But his made him rich.

"I don't want to fulfill your hopes."

"Is that what this is? You're committing career suicide just to spite me? Boy, that's dummy stuff. That's real teenager stuff. And I suppose you're out there racking up credit card debt."

"Actually I got a *juicy, juicy* check a few weeks ago."

"Okay, and you've put aside half for taxes? And paid your hangers-on? And amortized it over the period until your next paycheck? And have you scheduled your surgery yet?"

"You're such a bummer."

"Don't use that disgusting language with me."

"Do you not know what 'bummer' means?"

"Penelope, you can make me out to be the bad guy here, but the fact remains, I want you to *live,* and live well. I don't want you in poverty. Poverty isn't a joke. And when you make a fool of yourself because you have *no idea* what you're doing in *Hollywooooood"*—he gives this word the same elastic derision he gave "Greenpeace"— "what's going to happen? Who's going to pay the bills?"

"I can pay all my own bills now! I could go to a dentist and you wouldn't even know!"

"Good! Go!"

"My writing partners are *amazing.* My agent's top-notch. I'm working *really hard* here, making tons of connections. I have meetings like every day with important people. You don't know the first thing about this world. Those drunk girls—they're very successful drunk girls."

"They sounded like idiots."

"Your generation got to be drunk at work HUMPING a deregulated market to riches. WHY CAN'T WE be drunk in the fucking shambles you left us?"

"Don't you use that language. And your economic history is a *fairy tale*! Where's your self-respect, Penelope? You've got no gravity."

I look around my hotel room, its many shades of white, its evanescent glass surfaces echoing back sweetly, *no gravity.*

"This is the *opposite* of career suicide," I say to my dad, as always almost shocked at how badly I put my case, how quickly I play into his description of me as an impractical and vulgar fantasist. Maybe that's why I keep Derek around; he's even more impractical and vulgar. When I feel myself fitting too well my dad's image of me, I think of Derek, who got a police citation recently when he was so stoned that he threw the TV remote instead of a cigarette butt out the window because he got his hands confused.

My dad has to go. We exchange perfunctory good-byes. He reminds me softly that the surgery is important, that it's a matter of time, that he'll pay. He says, "Think of your mother." He means "think of her anesthetized, lasers needling through her chest." But instead I think about the way she listens when I swear, never scolding but letting vulgarity lead her to the hot vent in my mind that sent up the "fuck" like a flare.

I throw myself back onto my bed. My hands go into rigor mortis as I scream in frustration. I'm trying to make money, out of myself. Self-profit! For him, surely that is the opposite of self-killing. I try to think what the opposite of suicide is. Of course, I see Sylvia: suspended in blackness, ready to be gone, and then alive for the first time.

CHAPTER 21

EXCERPT FROM *AMERICAN MERMAID*

Sylvia reemerged, wet, panting, blissful, just before dawn. She lay on the dock, her hands clasped between her breasts in gratitude. She flexed; her tail curled up. She saw the new dawn light filtered through the membrane of her fin. As her tail rose, her spine—source, always, of potential alarm—pressed into the wooden beams of the pier, whole and unbothered, somehow in lockstep with the rest of her finally. But as she watched her tail fin dry, she noticed it begin to wilt at the edges. Her scales glinted in the dawn light but soon dulled, and as the beads of water evaporated, leaving behind little feline footprints of salt, her skin began to shrivel and shrink. Her body from the waist down started to feel tight, squeezed, even crushed by its own skin, until the pain began again, this time where her tail fin had just been but where two stumps now wriggled. She threw her head back, straightened her tail, and tried to shake off the pain, loosen this feeling of crushing tightness.

And then it was over. She was exhausted and her head ached. She put her hands to her temples, which felt as thin as the top of a drum and beaten from inside. In a fetal position, she opened her eyes and saw two knees, the two shapeless gray slabs that she had always known as her doomed and useless legs.

She had no way to get home. But what was her home? Where

did she belong? The immobility and disadvantage that had characterized her life until now was associated with the very air between things in this dry, built world. She had found her home. Her home was water, ocean: everything maps left blank. She slapped her palms down by her sides, digging into the moldy boards of the pier. From there to the crooked parking meters in the lot to the exhausted and extinguished harbor bars and the jagged silhouette of the financial district behind them, all she saw was a rickety game of chutes and ladders. Only the lush, contiguous force of the sea below was real. She pushed through her hands, lifted her naked torso, turned her face to the sliver of morning sun leaking its lemony light onto the surface of the sea. This was a game, she thought, collapsing on the dock, that she would have to play carefully.

It was only a few minutes before a young fisherman came upon her—must have noticed her from a distance. Ran up with "My god, are you—" She took his silence as a sign that he'd noticed her shriveled, shapeless legs. Emergency services were called. More harbor crew were hailed over, blankets were thrown on top of her, and soon she was in an ambulance, bumping along to Mass General. Strapped onto a gurney, rattling on the thin cot mattress as the ambulance sped to the trauma center, Sylvia saw the concern in the paramedic's eyes.

"Was this a suicide?" she asked.

"Mmm," replied Sylvia, somehow in love, remembering the sharp turns and quick thrusts of her night in the sea.

"With your disability, it's a miracle you didn't die." The paramedic, stout-bodied and in early middle age, probably had her own children. She spoke to Sylvia with the stern caring of a mother, of a person who wanted her to live. But everything was different now for Sylvia. She'd sprung from the sea that morning with the knowledge that she was something else, something *other* than human; and that made all these people *other* to her. Kind as she wanted to be, even the paramedic presented an unnameable threat to Sylvia in that moment.

"Who was it?" asked the paramedic. "Was it that nice fisherman?" Sylvia looked confused. "Some kind of hero must've pulled you out of there." Aware of the medic's gaze, she was careful not to smile. But she knew heroes were no longer required.

Sylvia was frantically eyeing the supply closet in her room at the Mass General Trauma Center when a nurse came in and told her she was being discharged into the care of her guardian. But how? How had her mother found her? She hadn't given them any information about her identity. Eleanor must have called around to all the hospitals. Her *mother*—what did that mean now? All those years of caring, of washing and dressing. But until Sylvia knew more, she felt a conflicted instinct to flee Eleanor Granger. She would have to find a wheelchair somehow, find some way to crawl out of here, even to a neighboring room. She rolled off the bed, her legs flopping first. She tried to hold on to the bed rails, but she found that her usually strong arms were exhausted, trembling—she must have exerted herself enormously in the sea—and they collapsed under her. She fell to the floor and whacked her head on hard linoleum. The door opened with a heavy click. Sylvia heard the nurse yelp, "Oh my god," and as she bent down, she was joined not by Eleanor Granger but by Masahiro, who wrapped his familiar hand around the back of Sylvia's head and looked into her eyes.

"Yes, this is my patient. Her name is Sarah."

"Mas—"

"Shhh." He pressed a finger to her lips. "Stay calm. We'll get you home soon."

The two helped a listless Sylvia up and into a wheelchair. She tried to hold her head straight, but her vision was blurred. She thought she heard the nurse say something like "Good luck, Dr. Wong." Then she blacked out.

. . .

When Sylvia came to, the past day had dissolved into a dream, and she was certain she was at Masahiro's office in Washington Heights, after school. But it wasn't his office. Not the brightly lit consulting surgeon's room, but a living room, a few ugly brown pieces of furniture here and there, a stained carpet, tinny blinds.

Masahiro sat at a desk, facing away from her, in the dark. His arm was moving. Maybe he was writing, or drinking. It came back to her suddenly, the news her mother had delivered, the weight of the grief that had followed. But now, here—Masahiro, alive?

"Dr. *Wong*?" Sylvia said.

Masahiro whipped around, a scalpel in his right hand. His eyes were wide with surprise and concern, but he quickly started laughing.

"Wong is *Chinese*," said Sylvia.

Masahiro shrugged. "If you're going to bother lying to a nice nurse, *really lie*." A grin spread across his face. He got up, moved to the sofa, and wrapped his arms around Sylvia. They both had tears in their eyes and sputtered with joy and laughter.

Sylvia didn't know where to begin, she had so many questions. She wanted to say to him, "Doc, I'm a *mermaid*," but she had the sense that he already knew. He was, she realized, not shocked. Not shocked that damaged Sylvia had been pulled from the sea, giddy and determined. Masahiro stood up, crossed the dark room, and looked back at Sylvia, his expression steely. She saw why he had a scalpel in his hands: on the desk there were identity photos, carefully sliced and ready to be pasted into a pair of passports.

"Sylvia. Your father is not who you think he is."

CHAPTER 22

"I don't understand how you could talk that way about Daddy."

I am in my executive apartment, lying on my back on a bed with sheets that were freshly changed this morning by a maid, for whose benefit I chewed on my lips to connote "business thinking" while arranging unnecessary receipts for shame tacos and shit shampoo on a glass-topped table. (I felt my dignity was already shot, but I could salvage hers.) Earbuds pipe my mother's sobs into my ears. My eyes are closed, but I imagine my mother is in her bedroom, at her desk. When she was an ecologist she would pick us up from school covered in bramble scratches, a wood louse inching out of her cuff after working in some Jersey or Connecticut forest. But when I was in middle school and my dad moved from the DA's office to a law firm and our family suddenly had money, the rapidity with which she took to manicures and luncheons was head-spinning. She still had the muscles and the build of an outdoorswoman, and she could never soften her sculptor's hands, but she wore pink lipstick and tennis whites, like a Working Group dog groomed for the Toys. I imagine her at her desk, shoved into the corner of her bedroom as if it were a dirty secret that she ever worked, with a big desktop computer on it (why update her equipment?), a screensaver of me and Susie playing in the yard as kids. A boreal forests wall calendar is the only hint of her training.

I know what she will say. *Your father has a professional reputation. You are reckless and selfish, you need to think of him.* Maybe she's more of a guard dog than anything: you can't say a word about my dad without offending her deeply. I told my mom he needed to stop wearing wire aviator bifocals because he looked like a serial killer, and she gasped, stopped the cart at Target, and gripped my arm. "Your father would never kill a single person, *much less many. In a row.*"

"It's *fashion* feedback," I said, storming off into a tall hedgerow of sweatpants, alarmed at how tightly she was suctioned to him. It isn't fair how the things I say never make a dent in him but slice her to the bone.

Now I've committed a real offense and she is hysterically wounded. Hearing her moan on the telephone and ask how I could be "cruel" between choked sobs is too much for me. A deep, strategic fold in my brain starts to activate without my willing it. I'm sinking into a chemical bath of my mother's pain, and it's changing me. When she starts to talk, I groan a little.

"Sorry, I hurt my back, go on."

She pauses, still sniffling. "You hurt your back?"

"Yeah, I almost drowned at a party on the beach. It was a riptide. Same thing almost killed a comedy friend of my agent out there last week." *Almost killed*—this kind of language is an opiate I'm releasing into the waters my mother and I share, pumping through the umbilical line between us.

My mother and I know something about shared poison, since I tested positive for BRCA. Our bodies are similarly coded. The same fragment of text is written into our DNA, into our biological stories, as if the same character appeared in hers and mine. Hers has been defeated, driven out temporarily, although he looms and the city quivers as it goes about its business. The villain hasn't appeared yet in my story, but he's scripted into the future—same hat, same cape, same amoral intent, leaping between her blood and mine.

"I had to be saved, it was"—I sigh a long, reflective sigh—"really scary." I hear a clonk and rustle; she's sitting up, she's put the tissues down, she's worried. "I was slammed down pretty hard right on my tailbone."

"Can you walk?"

I sound weak. "Yeah, with help."

"Oh, my baby." (*Baaaay-beee,* the first note lofting up and the second plunging down, like the swelling waves at Dick Babbot's beach.) She offers to come to California to help me. She offers to pay for a ticket home for me. I say I'll be okay. I top up the opiate, describing things about my executive apartment I know she will like ("double sinks," "lobby porter"), and before I go, I reassure her that I never meant any harm, that the listeners were like me, young women who spoke ironically, in coded ways, and that no harm would come to Daddy.

I tell her I'm sorry. I do feel sorry, I feel sorry that she came to me with specific points ready to deliver, and that I, knowing her chemical makeup as a mother, paralyzed her. I did what my father does to her: I disabled her intellectually and activated her caretaking impulses. She has no defenses; it's like plucking salmon out of the crowded shallows where they are driven shaggy and incautious by a need to spawn. But what were my options? Let her cry at me? Let her defend my father, whom she helplessly loves? Agree with her? *Mom, Susie's right: I'm a female dick.*

I lurch to get out of bed and am thrown back into my stack of luxury-cotton-coated white pillows, surprised by a slim, shooting pain that runs up from my tailbone to my left shoulder blade, where it sinks in like the tines of a fork. I wait a few minutes and try to lift myself up again, but the pain explodes.

Oh my god: I can't move.

CHAPTER 23

EXCERPT FROM *AMERICAN MERMAID*

"Where the hell did Rob go?" The door thwacked in its ill-fitting frame behind him as Captain Horgan lumbered out from the little office shack onto the sliver of the dock where his crew—twenty ragged men between eighteen and thirty leaning on each other, made intimate by shared exhaustion—looked up. They squinted up at him through the rain. Horgan was pissed off at their blank, screwed-up faces. He looked past them at the hundreds of house-size cargo containers, orange, red, blue, and yellow, stacked up neatly as far as the eye could see.

Horgan's trawler was heading out in an hour, and he was furious.

He repeated, "Where the *fuck* is Rob? I can't push off a man down."

Silence.

"You guys aren't supposed to leave. When was the last time you saw Rob?"

"He was just here," said one of the men. They were all young but bore themselves like old men after weeks on the trawler, universally drained and hunched, moving minimally to lift a can of soda or a cigarette. Most had had only a few hours' rest, but you couldn't tell the new arrivals apart from the guys in the middle of a twenty-seven-day shift. The new ones were prefatigued by the knowledge of what they were in for, the stench, the repetition, the deafening thrum of the conveyors and the power washers, a blood-soaked floating factory that they endured with the singular objective of a three-thousand-pound check at the end.

Horgan threw up his hands and stormed back into the office, the thin oiled-canvas-and-metal membrane that ensured the captain's status.

No one was looking at him. Their hooded heads were bowed, bored or looking at a cell phone. A few texts, a last gasp of contact with a girlfriend or a parent before the *Amanda* plowed into the North Atlantic—most of them hardly knew where. It all looked the same, and the only thing that marked one part of the sea from another was whether they hit a hot spot, and then it was a blessing and a curse. A big haul meant a bonus, split among the sorters and the gutters. But the nonstop scanning and slicing and picking and chucking could last six or eight hours without a break.

Another had gone missing before Rob, but it was hardly surprising. Everyone was always talking about quitting, about fucking off at the next unloading. No one talked about their families or their lives. It was too loud by the belts, and on deck their words were snatched from their lips by the kind of winds no one on land could imagine.

"I think Rob went home," ventured someone. "I think he had enough."

But how? boggled Horgan. How would Rob leave the industrial port at Killybegs without getting his passport and his things from Horgan's office? No wallet, nothing but his gut-stained work clothes and coveralls, he would spend seven days on foot getting to Shannon, waltz into the airport, and say, "One ticket to Cardiff, please!" *Yeah, right.* And what about the week of work he'd already done? Would a nineteen-year-old dropout with no prospects walk away from three grand in the bank?

The stink of fish had sunk deeply into their skin and hair. They ate rehydrated pack-noodle soups out of paper cups to the tinny incessant hammering of rain on the high bluffs of containers, rivers now gushing and pouring off the docks between them. The cargo boats were immobile in their immensity, but the fishing trawler moaned as it pitched fore and aft, a monster hungry for meat, rattling its chain.

Leaning on his neighbor, a young man slowly stood up and stretched. He was in his early twenties. He had just finished his first monthlong sortie, and now he knew he'd been duped by his training week in a warehouse in Liverpool, where he had figured it wasn't so bad. The camaraderie there had been okay, and there was no seasickness, and you could talk to people and take breaks. Out on the water, it had been almost impossible. There had been moments, nearly eight hours into exposure to the deafening thrum of the processing track, he'd thought the smartest thing to do was go over the side.

At this moment, his mind was a dull buzz of fatigue and a vague dread of the future.

"Gonna take a piss," he said. One or two faces glanced up and nodded.

"You better come back!" he heard Horgan shout behind him as he left.

He walked through the corridor of containers, stacked so high they seemed to meet one another in the sky above his head. Amid echoes of rainfall and footsteps, the young man looked for signs pointing to the port toilets. He'd piss into the sea just as easily if he could even find it in this maze of dark corridors, flush with runoff.

Suddenly, he heard the sound of someone singing. A child? A phone or a radio, surely. But it wasn't coming from a phone or a radio. It wasn't distant or canned. It was immediate, almost in his head. It was hard to judge distance.

Humming. Playful humming, up and down, meandering.

The young man became curious, turned right and left and left again—took every turn so that the music became louder, until finally he burst out at the end of one pier of containers abutting a small line-fishing vessel. It was coming from the boat. The young man looked around. There was no one watching, no activity in that part of the port. He leaped onto the fishing boat. The singing now was unmistakable. It was a song being hummed—giggled sometimes?—by a female voice. He walked around the side of the boat, around the steering cabin to the aft deck. Nothing. No one. It was getting louder. He looked over the edge.

The face of a beautiful young woman, half-submerged in the water, stared up at him from just beside the hull.

"Come, come down here," she said to him, laughing like an ingenue at a cocktail party wanting to gossip behind a curtain.

The young man was alarmed. He put himself in a lifeboat roped to the side of the vessel, lowered it down.

She put her arms over the edge of the lifeboat, reached up to him. She looked up at him with wonder and awe.

This far-flung man had been reduced to a brutal nothingness over weeks at sea. His body had been only an endless generator of repeat motions, allowed short bursts of desperately reparative sleep. The eyes he had met had been only the eyes of other men—if "men" was the right word; the eyes attached to working bodies. eyes that were dull and bloodshot. Now this face: dark, glistening, with large black irises, rimmed in wet lashes. She peered up at him as if he were interesting, beautiful himself. *You found me. You heard me.*

"Are you okay?" he asked.

She nodded, slowly, pushed herself up on wet arms, her face meeting his. She simply breathed in by his ear, sighed a little, and asked, "What's your name?"

"Are you okay?" he persisted, but she shook off his question and leaned in so that her lips brushed the folds of his ear.

"What's *your name*?"

He told her his name, and she repeated it and he repeated it. His name was the means by which she could frame this murder as an honor—she would retain it and bestow it on her daughter. Therefore, the young man's whisper was the final precondition of his death, although the moment he uttered it, he felt as if the infernal stink of the gut-soaked basement of the trawler evaporated and he was himself again, whole and admired. The kiss was unexpected. As she floated up to him on long arms perched on the lifeboat's rim, her breasts and ribs and a curious vial on a cord around her neck now in view, he pushed himself toward her, eager to meet her, eager for her to stay. The kiss was long. The man's hands relayed to his aching mind everything they touched with disbelief and total pleasure. His eyes stayed closed, her lips on his, as her hand moved between his legs, faster and faster—just a few seconds—until he came, shivering, nearly unconscious.

Then, as suddenly as a startled frog, into the water she flipped, taking the man with her. The empty lifeboat teetered a moment in the rippling water but soon stood still.

Beneath the surface, the mermaid held the man by the hands. There was no need for choke holds, for violence. She was grateful to him. He tried to jerk away. Once or twice he freed his hand and tried to turn up toward the surface, but she quickly swam above him and with two hands on his chest gently pushed him down. He could see nothing in the pitch black even though he held his eyes wide open in the cold salt water. But she saw everything. She found his hands again, kept pulling, until the last few spasms had worked themselves out and he was still. She kept going down, down, down, holding the man by one hand, his limbs out as if he were soaring through the stars in a children's story. She arrived at a pile of rocks, moved them aside, and pulled a knife from underneath them. She released the man's hand and moved herself down his body to his hamstring. Knowing well that he was dead, she inserted her blade into his femoral artery, first just opening it, and then slitting along the thick tube a few inches. It was a matter of only a minute or two before the exquisite calligraphy of the man's blood, as it leaked into the water in a hot line, quickened the dogfish and cat sharks out from their silent vicinity. Finally, after the crabs and rag worms worked over the body for hours, there was nothing left of him.

Yes, there were other mermaids.

CHAPTER 24

Murphy: We need to do something about the fact that a very important aspect of your whole mermaid mythology is
Randy: Hand jobs
Murphy: HAND JOBS
Randy: Penny
Randy: Be reasonable
Randy: Hand jobs
Penny: What?
Penny: It works in the book
Randy: Yeah but
Randy: HAND JOBS
Murphy: I actually think we need to cut the whole "HARVESTING" thing
Murphy: We can keep the wild mermaids but I really don't think we need the SEMEN HARVEST
Murphy: Just
Murphy: Penny
Murphy: I'm going to email you a draft of that section as R and I have it now
Murphy: It's like end of ACT II and you still meet this mysterious, badass mermaid but you don't have to watch her give a HAND JOB.
Murphy: Plus if we cut harvesting then we can also get rid of the whole patronymic thing
Murphy: I cannot handle hot mermaids named KEVIN

Randy: I don't even think there is hand job porn
Murphy: Of COURSE there is
Murphy: There's Ritz Cracker porn
Randy: Still
Randy: It's like cinematically impossible
Randy: Obviously you see this, Penny
Randy: The marketing department will give you a point-blank no
Penny: But they let people have sex all the time
Randy: I mean you can't have SELENA GOMEZ GIVE A HAND JOB
Penny: Have you asked her?
Murphy: She's just an example
Murphy: Jellica Nye
Murphy: Shorshay Ronan
Murphy: Sursshay?
Randy: Soaiuersse
Murphy: Soahouereshï
Penny: Guys
Penny: It's really important
Penny: It's not something you can just do away with—otherwise how are there mermaids? How do they reproduce?
Murphy: Here we go
Murphy: How do fish reproduce, Penny?
Randy: Let's go back to Oyyi and bang the mackerel together at the crotch like Barbies, I'm starving.
Murphy: I'm free until haircut at 7
Penny: THEY SPAWN
Penny: By the way, it's the MOST cinematic thing
Penny: Against the indigo blackout of the sea at night, this woman tossing the glittering harvest of semen on her waiting eggs?
Penny: Its milkiness catching the surface light that drifts down as the substance dissipates into a pearlescent haze and the magical eggs become activated by the warm, biological emissions of a recently murdered man?
Murphy: Honestly sounds more like Ina Garten making tapas

Randy: Oh Ina Garten has killed
Randy: Dude she worked for the Clintons
Penny: The semen-harvesting also explains their genetic diversity
Murphy: YAWN
Penny: Murphy this is important
Penny: For centuries they've been snatching poor and marginal men, pirates, dock workers, merchant marines. Over time they've incorporated a huge range of phenotypes
Murphy: Oh that IS a good point! Amazeballs for casting! She could be black, she could be white
Penny: She's CLEARLY mixed
Randy: I feel gross thinking about all that semen soup
Randy: I'm just glad nobody has said "cum" yet
Penny: MURPHY
Penny: WHY ARE YOU GETTING YOUR HAIR CUT AT 7PM?
Murphy: Whoa relax it's a salon-cum-concert venue OOOOPPS SORRY [devil emoticon]
Murphy: Penny I don't think you understand how much has to get cut to fit a 350-page novel into a 100-page script, with lots of major action
Randy: You need to get cool with killing your babies
Murphy: An R rating cuts your audience in half
Murphy: And you don't want to alienate all those little girls
Randy: Need those little girls
Murphy: You don't want to be showing little girls hand jobs
Randy: Yeah even pearly semen tapas
Randy: Too much for little girls
Murphy: Not happening
Penny: So why are they killing men, then?
Penny: Why mess with them at all if they don't need their seed?
Murphy: Well isn't that even awesomer now?
Randy: Yeah now they're just murdering.
Murphy: Which is way cooler.
Randy: And CLEARER

Murphy: Cleaner. LADYMURDERFISH COMIN FOR YOU
Randy: Not cummin' for you
Murphy: To be clear
Randy: Just out for murder
Penny: That really changes our understanding of the wild mermaids, then
Randy: Changes into awesome
Randy: P, I'm sending you some pages later today
Randy: You'll see
Randy: The audience won't question it
Randy: It makes sense ladies would want to kill men, right? Isn't that the whole point of feminism?
Penny: Depends on the wave, but no
Murphy: Oh my god
Murphy: I just got the best idea
Murphy: For the trailer. Giant text. FIRST. WAVE. FEMINISM. And mermaid leaps out of a bright blue wave and stabs a sailor in the heart
Penny: *That's* PG?

PART II

HIGH AND DRY

CHAPTER 25

I have been immobile in my bed for five hours, looking at my phone and debating whether to call Danielle or to lie here longer, trying to prompt a recovery with occasional, awkward stretches. But is it unprofessional to ask your agent to help you out of bed? Shouldn't I make her some more money first? I move to call her when the phone rings and the receptionist announces Derek.

"Oh thank god. Let him up. And can you give him a key card?"

The first things out of his mouth are "WHAT THE FUUUUHCK IS THIS PLACE?" and "WHERE DO YOU PARK YOUR TESLA?" I'm screaming with laughter but also pain as he drops his backpack and climbs on top of me like a dog and gives me a hug with his big greasy head burrowing between my shoulder and my ear.

"Derek, I'm *hurt*," I scream, and, "Thank god you got here when you did, I had some sort of spasm and I can't move."

"Oh, sweet," he says, leaping up and jogging backward to the other side of the room. "So you can't stop me smoking weed in here."

"DON'T!" I say. "It's a nonsmoking non-hotel."

"So it's a smoking hotel, perfect." He's already laughing at the story he's about to tell me. "Dude, I made the *sweetest* deal." He explains he got dropped off in front of an unappealing pizzeria on my lifeless corporate corner, and he went in and saw that they had a million pizzas and were closing in a few hours. "I go, 'What are you going to do with all that leftover pizza?' The guy goes, 'Throw it out.' So I go, 'I'll take whatever you haven't sold at the end of the day and give it to a shelter.' So now *every night* I get free pizza *and* I feed the homeless."

Derek loves free things and frissons of social democracy.

"Do you know any shelters?"

Derek ignores me. "On the way out, the guy goes, 'See you later, Pizza Hood.'" He doubles over laughing. "PIZZA HOOD."

"Derek."

"What?"

"Did you hear nothing I said?" I say. "I'm hurt."

And with that, suddenly, I burst into tears.

Derek wipes the laugh off his face. He comes over to the bed, sits down sidesaddle, facing me, with a look of pity. "I told you not to do this."

CHAPTER 26

EXCERPT FROM *AMERICAN MERMAID*

"I was so sure I was dying. I had given up. On everything. I felt pain, but it didn't matter. I knew it would be for the last time."

Sylvia sat on the coarse sofa where she had woken up disheveled but thrilled. Masahiro, in an armchair pulled near her, was completely absorbed by her description. He marveled at her energy—she still hadn't eaten much since waking at the motel, although he'd put a stash of convenience-store snacks on the oval coffee table in front of them.

"And then something happened." She closed her eyes and swayed side to side on the sofa, remembering. "I just . . . the pain subsided and I thought, *This is death. It's heaven. Not clouds, but cold water. Not god, but little creatures. Tiny fish.* And when I ran my hands down my body, I wasn't dead. But I wasn't me anymore."

"No."

The dreaminess fell away from her face, and she zeroed in on Masahiro. "What am I? It almost seemed like a . . ."

"Ichthyogyn."

"A . . . mermaid?"

Masahiro nodded.

He told her the story of Eleanor's fateful walk on the Faroese pebbles twenty-four years earlier. Sylvia listened in wonder, but her eyes traveled the room until they landed on her legs, sticking out before her in filthy jeans.

"*What happened to me?*"

"I said your father isn't who you think he is—that's true. But I suppose I'm not either." Masahiro looked away from Sylvia, and when he turned his face to her again it was tight, stricken. "I've been healing you all these years. But I also broke you—not because I wanted to. After they found you, Dean brought you to me and ordered me to—to split you." Masahiro stood up and began to pace. His back was to her, but he heard her murmuring.

". . . split me?"

"They said they were saving you. But the truth is, they wanted you desperately. They'd wanted a child for *so* long. And nothing had worked. They had spent years trying, sticking Eleanor with hormones and implanting embryos, watching her swell up with hope only to bleed out in tears. Eleanor had just turned forty-two; they were giving up. When they found you, it wasn't 'The Little Mermaid,' it was 'Thumbelina.' The earth gave them a magical baby, this barren couple. It gave them a child. Granger will say that he wanted to give you humanity—to evolve you, invite you to the species that created, I don't know, the *Vitruvian Man*, calculus, béchamel." He snuffled a little laugh. "But the desire for a child, an heir to everything he'd made, this worked on Dean as well as Eleanor. It was, in many ways, against his own interests to turn you into a girl. He couldn't study you or use you as a mermaid. It didn't matter—he desired a child, and by a miracle, he got one."

". . . Turn me into a girl?"

"Split your tail. Give you legs. Eleanor thought they should return you to the sea, but Dean convinced her it would mean certain death—how would they contact your family? A baby seal or a whale without its mother will die in short order—why would you be any different? Then Eleanor wanted to keep you as a mermaid, in a tank."

Keep me as a mermaid? Sylvia imagined herself in an aquarium in her parents' living room. It was preposterous. But somehow, preposterously kind—that her mother would be willing to love something she couldn't fully possess. "You did live in a tank for nearly a year anyway. It took me that long to prep the surgery. I was thirty years old. My training was in radiation trauma, which often involved surgery. But for this I consulted with dozens of specialists, orthopedic surgeons, prosthetics people. I worked off models of your bones. I practiced over and over. We didn't have 3D printing then, so I had to employ a medical model-maker in Long Island using drawings I made from your X-rays. He couldn't believe I wanted a mermaid skeleton—I had to tell him it was for a movie. He was tickled."

Sylvia's mind raced to keep pace with the story, a story she couldn't believe was hers. She shook her head. "But—*all this pain.*"

He stopped pacing, returned to the love seat, and fixed her gaze with his as intensely as he ever had. "Listen to me. The pain was for a purpose. You transformed into a mermaid last night because I made your surgery reversible. I gave you a choice. Your joints below the tailbone—each one splits into an intricately carved pair, like two little netsuke, which interlock along the femur and tibia. Your original tail was covered in very fine, sharp scales, just like fish scales. Made of enamel and dentine."

"*Dentine?*"

"Mmm." He tapped his front tooth. "Fish scales are like little teeth. Made of the same stuff. Yours were thinner and harder than any I've ever seen. But I had to replace them with an artificial bio-responsive metallic mail that I developed from my experience with postradiation skin grafting. It's like very fine wire when dry, but when fully saturated with water, the interlocking fibers activate around your bonded flesh, tighten, and become unbreakable, flexible, responsive."

Sylvia tried to speak, but the questions in her mind were too big for words.

"Your pain—at least some of it—is my fault. As it transitions, the dry, microscopically fine barbed wire that covers your legs twists and digs into you before it becomes your miraculous metal skin."

Sylvia looked down at her flat, lifeless legs, source of so much shame. Just hearing them described made an itch swarm across them. The memory, then, rushed back: the morning sun on that harbor pier licking her tail; watching it sparkle like a polished weapon. *Miraculous metal skin.*

"God, I'm so relieved, Sylvia." Masahiro put his head in his hands for a moment, and when he lifted his face again, it was streaked with tears and his voice was choked. "It was a huge risk. What if you'd gone through all this pain for nothing? But last night proved it—it wasn't for nothing. I'm sorry. I'm so, so sorry. For all the pain, for the not knowing."

"But why didn't you just tell me? Do you know how much easier it would have been to suffer if I'd known? How could you look at me writhing in pain and confusion for decades and never say a word?"

"Money, for one thing. I wanted to tell you so many times but—"

"Money?"

"It costs your father more than a million dollars a year to treat you. I need the lab, I need the equipment and supplies."

"But I wouldn't have needed all that treatment if you'd just returned me to the sea!"

"I've been waiting for the right moment! You were at college, you were learning so much, you seemed—"

"Yeah, when I wasn't on a gurney! When I wasn't missing class because I was here getting Sensorcaine injected in my fake fucking thighs!"

"I didn't want to choose for you."

"You wanted to wait until I'd had enough? Until my desperation was so bad that I was willing to die? Was that the sign that I was ready?"

Masahiro couldn't make eye contact. He rose again and turned away—Sylvia thought he might be sick—and steadied himself with a hand on the desk for a moment. Then he turned back toward her.

"Maybe I was afraid it wouldn't work, that the joints wouldn't lock, the tail wouldn't hold—they'd never been tested. But it *did* work. You found your way to the water."

"Because you died and I was distraught!"

"I was coming to get you! I had to fake my own death to get away from your father!" Now he descended to the love seat again and took Sylvia's hands in his own. "Sylvia, I know this is an impossible new reality to take in. And I'll stay by your side, tell you anything I can, help you physically adjust. But your private pain—this family story—is just one piece of something much bigger. Please, *please* forgive me. Because I need you now. We need to work together to stop Granger."

Sylvia met Masahiro's sudden urgency with a hardened, wary face. It would be all too easy to make her father the bad guy. But her father hadn't wielded the scalpel.

"Your father is not the green billionaire everyone thinks he is. Worse: he's going to melt the world, on purpose."

"*Melt* the world? What are you talking about?"

"Your dad is a fraud." Masahiro explained how Dean Granger had made his first millions in the 1980s by developing the technology behind fracking. This much was true. So it made sense to everyone that the same pioneering scientist had finally cracked enhanced geothermal systems, EGS. This was the holy grail of green energy, a way to tap the six-thousand-degree liquid furnace at the heart of the planet, a well of infinitely sustainable power. EGS was what put him on the cover of *Time* in 1998, holding a long drinking straw that pierced into the earth, pictured as a juicy orange.

"But it was all a lie," Masahiro said.

"His power plants supply half the voltage of the Western and Texas grids. You can't fake that."

"The *green* part is a lie. He claims his plants are geothermal, but they're not, they're just fracking. It's just gas, flushed out so sloppily and quickly, with so much leaking methane, it might as well be coal. He never really made the leap to EGS."

Sylvia considered the possibility of this ecological conspiracy at her father's hands. "That makes no sense. Sure, my dad wants to be on the cover of *Time*. But not enough to risk his whole career on fraudulent claims of virtue. If anyone figured this out, he'd be bankrupt, criminally liable."

"Aha, so what's really going on?" For a split second, Sylvia caught a twinkle in Masahiro's eye, as if they were back in his office doing trigonometry. "Where does he do all his EGS research?"

"The Faroes."

"Right. The North Atlantic. He has a big team up there sounding the ocean beds, carrying out major exploration. It makes perfect sense, that's where geothermal heat is most accessible; he can tell everyone he's carrying out R and D. But it's all a cover for what he's really doing: hunting mermaids."

"Mermaids," repeated Sylvia, the thrilling plural of it hitting her for the first time. There were people out there—no, not *people*—animals like her. It was a thought she stored away to savor later.

"Human evolution split off hundreds of thousands of years ago. We knew this happened with Neanderthals and Denisovans, but no one suspected it happened in the sea. When dinosaur bones were first discovered in the ocean, people explained it away with myths and stories—these were sea monsters, Jonah's whale. We did the same with mermaids—we explained away a scientific truth with myths and stories. Your father, in discovering you, could have taken credit for a giant leap in knowledge—he could have been our era's Darwin."

It was a strange thought. If her father was Darwin, what was she, some sort of turtle?

"But that's not what he wants," Masahiro continued. A toxic mix of cynicism and greed had infected Dean Granger as he had come to understand the climate crisis in the 1980s. He saw its scale, saw that no one would commit to stopping what had already begun: a calamity was coming. "That's why I had to kill myself."

"To escape climate change?"

"No, Sylvia, to *prevent* it! Your father has announced something called CleanBeam."

"CleanBeam? That's been his obsession for years—he's found a way to extract limitless clean energy from the arctic seabed."

"He doesn't want to solve the crisis. He wants to speed it up. The machines he's built, they're not for energy capture. They dig past the mantle to release geothermal heat. In temperate zones they'll simply puncture the seabed and let the heat leak out like a poisonous gas. And in the arctic, the geothermal units will power lasers into the underbelly of glaciers and ice caps. Instead of a decades- or century-long process, Granger will make the Great Flood, the final warming, happen in days. What I call your father's cynicism and greed, he calls economic rationality. He has a once-in-a-geological-era opportunity to hold all the wealth and power in the world."

"But what do the mermaids have to do with CleanBeam? What does he want with them?"

"Until eight years ago, maybe he was just hunting them, maybe he wanted to collect them, play the biologist. But since that night . . ."

"Eight years ago . . ."

"Do you remember? Your sixteenth birthday? When Eleanor was washing your hair."

Usually, when she thought of that night, she was filled with shame at her foolish adolescent impulse to fill the tub and swim. But now the shame evaporated: she had been *right* to seek the water, to dream of it, to need it.

"You were right, Sylvia."

"I wanted to swim . . ."

"No, you were right about your *dad*. Well, you were off by one floor. Your father wasn't in the basement that night, like you thought. He was in a secret lab one flight below it. You envisioned a tank and your father hurting someone in the tank. That *someone* was a dolphin. He was testing a tracking gun, shooting chips over and over into the animal's skin, practicing until she bled out."

"That's whose screams I sensed?"

Masahiro nodded.

The idea of a deeply feeling creature trapped and tortured three floors below while she had eaten birthday cake and done karaoke filled her with sadness.

"But from that night on, your father knew he'd missed something. You weren't just a girl with a tail. You had some kind of—"

"Knowledge." That feeling—Sylvia closed her eyes and felt again that sensation of events conveyed to her by a cold pressure on her mind.

"Yes. A telepathy. From then on, Granger demanded I report on you regularly. I was a spy, an informer." He rushed to add, "You don't understand how afraid I was of your father. I couldn't say no."

Sylvia felt suddenly fatigued by this revelation, by a sense that she would have to do everything alone, that no one could be trusted. But she couldn't get back to the sea by herself. She needed Masahiro still. She looked at him, in this ugly room, his face tight with worry, his kind eyes searching hers. He had come back for her. He was here.

"I'm sorry. I reported just enough to keep him satisfied. But I never told them about your mutable skin, your bondable joints. And I lied to them about your emotions. I never reported on your . . . your 'immunity' is what I called it in my notes." He cleared his throat and looked down a moment, more a father in his awkwardness than Dean Granger had ever seemed to Sylvia in his sweeping confidence. He didn't have to say it: Immunity to sex. Men. Desire. "I don't know why I kept that from Granger—I guess I figured it was connected to your mermaid powers."

Masahiro pulled himself together and spoke energetically. "Please don't lose faith in me. If I hadn't been reporting on you to Granger,

I never would have discovered CleanBeam, or his plan for the mermaids. Just a week ago, you were having those horrible spasms, and I needed access to some X-rays I'd passed to your father. Dean was in Vágar, it was the middle of the night there, so I convinced Eleanor to let me into his office in Westchester. When I was getting up to go, I tripped on the leg of that horrible stuffed tortoise and banged into the wall. A wooden panel popped open—a secret compartment full of documents, maps, blueprints. All the CleanBeam diagrams, the timeline, the damage projections.

"Dean Granger has had me under his thumb for thirty years. And I knew he was a megalomaniac—nice people don't rack up billions of dollars. But once I understood the scale of this crime he was planning—of CleanBeam—I had no choice. I staged my death, packed a bag, and I was coming to get you."

"Why do you need me?"

"No one else can find the mermaids, Sylvia. They survived for hundreds of thousands of years, glimpsed but never caught. They've outsmarted your father for two decades. But twenty-four years ago, they lost a baby. Maybe, all this time, they've been looking for *you*."

"Someone's been thinking of me? Missing me?"

"Desperately, I suspect. And these mermaids—your family—if Granger finds them, he'll ruin them. He'll enslave them."

"So ever since he discovered my—what you call telepathy—he's wanted the mermaids for CleanBeam?"

"Imagine for a moment you want to boil the sea. You've got the drills parked all over the world, lasers idle under the ice caps. You just need to turn them on and let them rip."

She pictured the metal drills siphoning the earth's gut heat. She saw the hulking machines, unmanned.

"He needs workers."

"Global infrastructure will fail. Mermaids are mobile underwater, cognitively sophisticated, and they can communicate telepathically across vast distances. When the radios fail and the robots can't be recharged, mermaids will be pressed into service. Threatened, forced. He'll take so much pleasure in it, too. His hunt has become personal now. When I was in his office, looking through his files—he *doodles* them in chains, Sylvia. He's furious. The whole world shows up double-time at Dean Granger's call; these creatures have told him to *fuck off.*"

Sylvia beamed, proud of these mysterious things, slipping smartly through a treacherous sea.

"We have to get to Vágar. Did you socialize last night?"

"What do you mean?"

"Did you meet other mermaids in Boston Harbor—or, I don't know, did you get out to Massachusetts Bay?"

"No, no one."

"I think Granger's figured this out already. They must have a very niche habitat. That would track with sightings—in old maritime history and in mythology. Always up in the North Atlantic."

Sylvia felt her skin in that moment like a thirst. She was desperate to cure the prickling dryness that sapped her power and held her down on this dull world's lumbering, flat paths. She was dying to swim.

"We have to get you in the water," said Masahiro, as if reading her mind. "If we're searching for mermaids, we have to start with you." Sylvia gave him a steely look, weighing in her mind whether this was still the friend whose death had made the world unbearable for her.

He picked up a packet of Skittles off the coffee table in front of them, ripped it open, and poured a few into his palm. "Do you think there are some vitamins in the green ones?"

Sylvia shook her head no. She could see him trying to get back to normal, trying to make her laugh like he used to, but she wouldn't give it to him yet.

"Then maybe we should get some real food." Masahiro dumped the candy on the table, wiped his sticky palm on his jeans, and held out his hand. She looked up at him from the sofa, then back down at the legs he had carved for her. He hadn't told her everything—how, for example, her father had controlled him—but she believed what he *had* told her. Her very body was the proof.

Her body: Masahiro was no longer just a doctor managing his best with a strange case. She had lost the innocent and unexamined trust she had always placed in him, but she had gained the knowledge and insight of a man who'd half created her. She wanted to ask, *What was I like before the split? What did the tests tell you when I was a baby?* But always when she turned inward to run her fingers over the mystery script of her biology and what it might spell for a chance at happiness, the same question arose, terrifying and unanswerable: *Am I immune to love?*

CHAPTER 27

I'm on a date. Next to us, two young parents, tattooed in intricate indigos and teals from their fingertips to their jawlines, take turns feeding their fat baby. The baby's blank skin between them, to my eyes, wants tattooing. The parents are dazed, dragged inward by their own fatigue. They dig silently into their bowls of black grains and unusual greens. All three, the parents and baby, feel uncompelled to speak. They each seem completely alone while completely together. I become self-conscious about how hard I am working to try to talk to Franck.

To say his name is to suggest some kind of continuity—Franck the Swiss guy from the other night, by the pool—but we seem to be in a world that is totally incommensurate with that one. If we are here now, the other night never happened. Or, if the other night was real—the weightlessness, the intimacy of a shared past—then we can't be here now, in metal chairs that scrape the asphalt.

After we agreed to meet for lunch, Franck suggested this restaurant via a curt but enthusiastic text: "WE MUST TRY DANTES!" The place is a faux Teutonic Tudor hut set back from the road. It looks like something Hitler built for Donald Duck, which is also true of Switzerland. This is an example of a thought I can't say to Franck but am thinking.

I took an Uber here and wasn't really paying attention to anything, transfixed by the sheer unanimously dusted variety of shop fronts and parched plants, until we stopped, and I was startled. The

Uber driver double-checked his windshield-mounted cell phone: "Yeah, this is it." I realized all the people on the sidewalk were in a line. A little stupid and shocked, I got out of the car—wincing, pressing my tailbone with my palm—and joined the end of the line, like the newest dead person in heaven.

I was nervous, not knowing if I'd recognize Franck, not knowing if it was unwise to dredge this perfect relationship up from drunken memory and expose it to air. The group, all of us strangers who suddenly fell into a deep connection, a real connection. We all loved each other that night, and Franck and I enjoyed a particular silent, knowing intimacy amid the jubilance of the group. It was a connection that felt honed by time, and deep, as if no two people understood more while saying less than the two of us. At one point in the night, the tequila was starting to feel too acidic in my mouth, and I looked up at the bar at the after-hours place where we all squeezed onto a messy arc of black leather couches. Franck looked back over his shoulder at me, smiling, while a bartender with a stretched grip delivered four frosty pints of lager, exactly what I didn't know that I knew that I wanted. *This is how we do things*, I thought, superficially, like a woman married sixty years, confident then that our instantly time-tested love owed nothing to the hyperconductivity of the drink-filled night.

I had been standing in line at Dante's for only a few minutes, totally preoccupied with the terrifying possibility that I would have to stand for a long time with my back aching, when Franck popped up out of nowhere, arms wide like a showman: "This is it, enh?" And then he draped himself loosely on me in a hug. I think I heard a kiss. The hug pushed the expanding fumes of his cologne up into my nose and mouth, left me feeling like I'd just spit out a flower and a mint.

"I'm so sorry," I told him (a bit relieved, in fact, to have an overriding urgency we could both turn to), "but I'm in terrible pain and I need to sit down."

Was this what people felt like when their spouses came back from war, or from one of those bachelor parties in Lithuania? When you almost can't remember anything about a person until they are in front of you and everything rushes back all at once? The way he had kind of a long jug-shaped head, and the way his nose had a knuckle in the middle, and the different browns in his eye. He had been wearing a suit at the pool, and I had, without thinking about it, expected him to show up in a suit today, but of course he was in a posh windbreaker and jeans and Adidas. Different clothes made him more dimensional, embarrassingly real, and more of a stranger.

"Sit down? Why? Are you okay?" His minky brown eyebrows zipped toward each other as he scanned my body for the problem.

"I had an accident. I almost drowned." This made me seem like a baby. "I'm actually a really good swimmer," I added. "It was a riptide."

"A tide hurt your back? Like that?!" He swooshed his arms through the air at me in a karate chop. "Wow," he said, but he pronounced it "Oooooauoooo." His attempt at a hard *w* to flank the *o* was just more *o*, a butter knife made of butter.

"No, it was the lifeguard."

"Ooooauooo," he said again.

"In the saving part."

"You had to be saved?"

"Riptides are really powerful."

"Oh my god." His eyes were satisfyingly wide. "I don't know anything about riptides," he said. "Tell me." I think I remember knowing this about him, when we were people who knew each other: he likes to learn.

"You wouldn't have them in your lakes."

"In my— No, no." He laughed, then got grave. "You need to sit. Hold on."

Franck interrupted conversations at several tables with empty chairs. I saw people shake their heads at him. He darted about, a bit crazy-seeming, trying to get chairs out from under people at a restaurant with a pressing, hour-long queue; tan, hungry, artist-looking would-be diners, intimidating in short-short overalls and wide-brim felt hats, glaring down at seated diners. The diners, themselves beautiful and deserving of their long-awaited seats, luxuriated in their seatedness, lightly toasting their smiling faces as they tilted their caged metal chairs to the sun. Into this taut, silent war of passive aggression, Franck dove with voluble sincerity. Hunched over the most beautiful couple I've ever seen (everyone here recognized it and stole glances; a cotton slip dress barely reached the top of her thighs, glowing birch bannisters), he pointed their attention at me and I saw him say ". . . very severely broken."

We progressed through the queue, me seated in a chair Franck had wheeled out from under a beautiful butt and Franck standing next to me, helping to scrape my chair forward inch by inch as the line moved. If he caught a stranger's eye he pointed to me and whispered, in a false aside, "My great-great-aunt."

Now we are both seated and his attention darts between my dish and his and the three others he has ordered to taste. He looks lustily at my oyster liquor and chia orzotto with something something, which I'd been forgetting to admire while it had been filling my mouth with the taste of original Pringles and jizz.

"Try it," I say, aiming for upbeat. *I am so sorry. I am so sorry that I am not the easy, joyful, pleasing woman I was when we held each other under a margarita waterfall, humming the same tunes.*

He has taken a bite of my black rice and moves it around in his mouth. "Uh-huh, hmmm," he says, as if the food has said something interesting. I am jealous of my rice. When he begins to talk, there are purple stains around his front teeth from the black rice. He motions at the room around us. "At first this was a jam shop," Franck explains.

"What the fuck is a jam shop?" Fuck. I don't think I swore when we were married in our minds in the drunken night. I was serene and accomplished.

Franck snorts. "Touché." He says it not in English but in French, the *t* a little spongy and the vowels a glimpse of a world of fast, fluid continuity, a wet whirlpool of a world where he is mobile. He's so good at English you forget that at some point early on he was, and maybe still sometimes is, stranded or stuck in this language, this blocky maze of guttural stops, prepositions left around like chairs in a hallway.

"It was a shop where they sold jams."

I find I have nothing to say to this. If his teeth are purple, are mine? I swish some water around.

"You know," he continues, "jam." I don't think I *do* know jam. "*Confiture*," he says, the word emerging self-contained in French wetness.

"Confiture?" I do not even try to imitate Franck's sounds. I say in unaccented English, "Con-fitt-chure . . . Sounds like something much more serious than jam: a contract of some kind."

Franck, eager to help: "We also say '*marmelade.*'"

"Yeah, that sounds more like 'marmalade.' Which I understand to be jam." I'm being a schoolmarm about marmalade. I must seem both fastidious and boring. ("We say 'marmalade.'" "Oh, you say 'marmalade'?" Is this what it's come to? So soon? As if, when the booze left us, it took everything, more than had been there to start. We are dry rags, the stuff of flags on legislatures.)

"But it was a big hit? When it was a jam shop?" I say.

"Enormous."

"Wow. That doesn't make any sense. Jam is, like, pretty stupid, right?"

It would be the easiest and most expedient thing for a person on a date with a woman with a spinal injury in the desert, over strange foods coveted by people with recording contracts and long femurs, to simply agree that jam is stupid. But Franck is a gentleman. I have always known this. I saw it when we were underwater and I was an easy, charming woman from whom joy and accomplishment rippled. I was the natural partner for a gentleman. I had written a novel, for all he knew, sober under a nice lamp. And because he has integrity, it seems as though Franck does not want to call jam stupid.

He puffs his cheeks out, raises his eyebrows, lets his head fall to one side in rueful contemplation. Oh god, he's got to be remembering the wild currants he collected for his *maman* on green, flowering slopes of their hillside farm, and the candy smell of the currants boiling away while he caressed a young Bernese and waited for his first taste of the new season's glorious lacquer-like *confiture*. That's ridiculous: I edit the puppy from my fantasy and leave him sitting at a stocky wooden table, dressed like Pinocchio and licking his lips. None of this helps me not feel like a bad person for calling jam stupid. What's next? Is Beatrix Potter a dumb muff? Are dollhouses for shitheads?

"Hello?"

"What?"

"Are you okay?" he asks. I've been spacing out.

I text Derek on my way home and meet him at a bad sports bar. I can barely walk by the time I get to him. I go from table to table supporting myself, as if shot, until I reach his booth at the far back and collapse. He asks what's wrong with me.

"My back, remember?"

He orders four beers, one each for us and our future selves. We drink. I feel myself lifting off the seat with relief, first inches then feet, as we drink and talk: *To be in a world that feels like home*, I think at one point, not listening to him talk but watching him as if I were. The Dodgers game is on in the bar and he's lecturing me about how people think baseball is statistical but basketball is equally a statistician's sport but nobody sees that because everyone's racist. The irritated passion in his voice transports me to our grubby life in New Haven so securely I can smell the bready felt of his car seats. (Now he's doing an impression of a *New Yorker* poem: "My Beagle, Bailey, knows nothing of drones . . .") I pretend to listen just enough to convince Derek that we're watching the screen together. Great big mouthfuls of beer in this un-Californian dark brown bar are filling me from the inside, but it feels as if something were flowing in around me, lifting me slowly off the ground so that at one point I find myself no longer in pain, dancing to a commercial jingle for a vacuum cleaner while Derek feigns embarrassment.

"This guy's a right-wing extremist," he says, tipping his pint at the screen where a pencil-necked dweeb with dead eyes pushing a cordless vac says, "Our cleanest clean yet."

"Go bleach your asshole!" Derek shouts at the TV. I fear we've been inappropriate and prepare apologies as the bartender cruises toward us with leveled, intense eyes from the other side of the bar. I should have known nothing could sink this beautiful man: the barman gives Derek a surfer's high five and Derek's mouth swells toward his cheekbones in a smile, finding a dimple like a wave finds an eddy.

When we get back to my non-hotel past midnight, carrying eleven boxes of pizza that should have gone to the homeless, there is a bored man at the front desk where the bored woman usually sits. I announce my room number and show him an ID pass, and he says, "Oh, I've got your laundry right here, it's charged to the room."

"Why won't you just call yourselves a hotel?" Derek needles.

I've never seen Derek's sense of the world's lying, inverted value system as anything but a concept. Until now, we were rarely outside of Holy Cross, or we were hunched together in the diving bell of our conversation, in a movie theater or on a sidewalk, feeling the outside as a form of pressure. I've been so deeply confused about why this isn't just a hotel. But I am embarrassed to see Derek's sense of injustice leap into action at a helpful man in a name tag that says "Larry" who sits for a living.

"I don't call it anything, I just work here."

"Embassy Suites is a hotel that's an apartment and it admits it's a hotel. Why can't you?" I've had this same thought.

"Look, I'm just the night guard."

"Guard! Where's your guard equipment? Where's your shield and your hat?" The guy looks tired. I laugh to show the guard that it is supposed to be funny, but maybe it isn't, maybe Derek has made the man feel small for not having a hat, or for working for an amoebic corporate "residence concept" that is nothing more than a hotel that refuses to title people receptionists and concierges and pay them union wages.

I pull Derek into the elevator, and as we shoot up, the floor pressing into our soles, my ears popping, all the things I've been escaping come back into view. I close my eyes, run my hands over my face, moan.

"The other writers," I say. "They want to kill the mermaid."

"Whoa," Derek says. "Does she die in the book?"

"Excuse me?"

CHAPTER 28

EXCERPT FROM *AMERICAN MERMAID*

Dean Granger had not read the details. He was sure that, as usual, the offers his investors had made were more than enough. He had just been on the phone with some of them. There was almost nothing he loved more than these kinds of pep talks. It gave him a feeling of plenty, as if he were walking downhill to an orchard all his own in high summer, when he heard their unwavering deep voices say things like "Dean, if it's anything like your last project," and "I think we've all got complete confidence . . ." He would say the word and their cash would flood in—an apt metaphor this time.

Granger kept the TV or the radio on during the day while he worked—sports games, the news and traffic. Sometimes he liked to listen to the classical station, the prickly little harpsichord notes racing along with the rapid firing of his calculating mind. Long before he'd started work on CleanBeam, he had thought of his mind as a powerful beam of light, which, for some tasks, worked best at medium or low, so that it could be used to, say, illuminate something instead of incinerating it.

That was the case now, as Granger examined a strange new problem.

Sylvia was alive. Sylvia could, more importantly, swim. Sylvia—imagine! Still a mermaid. How? What mechanisms had made his daughter into a miraculous convertible? He would find out soon.

Masahiro, my friend, you have done me a huge favor. Sylvia being a mermaid was the keystone to his plan. There was only one missing piece now: the other mermaids. Nothing worked without them. He spit a loud "Goddammit" into his empty office, banging a fist on the desk. Still the mermaids, always the mermaids. He had such plans for them, if only he could find them.

Granger's fixer, a former cop named Lawrence, had found Masahiro and Sylvia easily. The disabled woman who threw herself into the harbor channel wasn't something the paramedics forgot easily. Lawrence now tailed the two of them at a distance, waiting for Granger's orders. But Granger didn't yet know how to shape his pitch to Sylvia. Who was Sylvia anymore? Irrational animal or trained scientist?

He would appeal to the latter. Without Granger's intervention, in twenty years the world would be a war zone—half a billion climate refugees, radicalism, and disease. *With* his intervention, the world would be merely a flood. He would accelerate global warming past the slow social and political grind toward nightmare and directly into biblical parable. The people who would eventually die would simply die sooner. The waters would surge up and swallow them, but quickly. Granger's pontoons would be readily available to the rich, much of Europe and North America, and of course the Russians, Chinese, Indians with deep enough pockets. EarthSource would ensure survival to those who remained, at great cost.

What he would offer his daughter was no less than a chance to be, after his death, the most powerful person in the world. He felt a shiver of excitement at how close this scenario was, how urgently he could make his case to Sylvia. She was smart enough, he believed, to see this clearly, to stay on the side of the survivors and not to throw in with the doomed poor.

He didn't think Nell needed to know about Sylvia. Nell with her noblesse oblige projects, who, along with a phone tree of well-intentioned wives, said, "It's not too late to *do something* about climate change." As the cells of fish in Fiji rattled with plastic particulate, the heroic women of Westchester organized a Harvest Festival. They lobbied the supermarket to use less packaging, in one vendor in one state in one country of a sweating, rotting planet. He told his wife he was part of the solution, but he had long ago realized any hope of a solution was a cozy liberal's naive fantasy, the fantasy of people for whom things had always worked out. Dean Granger remembered a kid at his school whose dad died young of a heart attack. He remembered watching the kid's mother and sisters move out of their house in the neighborhood—the way they crowded, all three kids, in the doorframe until the very last second, as if clinging to a piece of high ground, waiting for a lifeboat. Well, no one came to save them. They had moved to a poorer part of town, with dirtier kids and worse schools. Things didn't always work out. The worst was coming, and some people were going to be screwed.

Dean Granger flipped the TV to the national news and buzzed the housekeeper for a drink. A dad in a Ford commercial checked the rearview mirror. His pretty children giggled at a cartoon playing on a TV embedded in the back of Dad's seat. *That's right,* thought Granger, *sit in your giant car, sedating your kids while you poison their world.* Granger had loved Sylvia, of course he had. Other people had dumb chubby replicas of their mediocre selves: his child was a miracle, a gift from a sea that had chosen Nell and him. His throat tightened as he remembered Sylvia in the earliest years, when she was so small and defenseless, and Masahiro was forever inserting a drip in her hand. The reparative surgeries, the moments when her back would spasm and her skin would burn. In this great project of remaking the earth as it fell apart, of controlling a new ratio of land and sea, Granger still believed that Sylvia, who had paid a terrible price to join him on high ground, would be his greatest ally.

She had been a beautiful girl; all his friends said so, particularly after her disappearance, in this period of tentative mourning that made Granger profoundly uncomfortable. Not because he knew she wasn't dead, but because so public a—not a failure, but a *negative*—a loss—was embarrassing to him, something off-color in an otherwise harmonious biography. Dashiell MacFarlane, a hedge fund guy and a rival of his in terms of net worth, had bumped into him at the Oak Bar last week. MacFarlane had had the nerve to give him *sympathy*. "How are you holding up?" he'd said, tapping him on the arm gently. It was too much to bear. He felt like leaning in and saying to MacFarlane, "I'm holding up fine. *I'm about to decimate your net worth*. I wonder how *you'll* be holding up."

The housekeeper knocked sheepishly and delivered the drink. He thanked her and brought the glass directly to his lips to minimize eye contact with the woman before plonking it down on a coaster. The door clicked shut behind her, and Granger whirled around in his office chair to face his main computer monitor. The screen blinked awake, and Granger, lazing back into his plush leather chair, began to click through his inbox.

The newscaster's level voice emanated from the TV. ". . . This is only the most recent video to surface of anonymous workers undergoing injury or possibly death while working on these ships. According to a recent report from the USLC, a watchdog group for international labor conditions, as many as 24,000 workers, often undocumented young men, die every year while working on fishing and shipping vessels in international waters where protocol for reporting is ambiguous." *Poor bastards,* thought Granger. No one's going to figure out a way to regulate this—pressure's too high, profits too good, and if you kill a little Filipino boy in the non-place between continents, it doesn't make a sound.

"Some ship captains have pushed back," continued the reporter.

"I'm sure they have," mumbled Granger, remembering his own conflicts with the cabalistic psychos in the merchant marines and shipping.

". . . saying they're doing their best to keep their men safe when faced with dangerous and unpredictable conditions. The head of one major shipping company blamed global warming for the increasing danger. Others have said the figures are inflated and the videos are hoaxes."

Granger was just drafting an order to one of his Pacific team engineers when the newscaster's voice, coming to the end of her segment, shifted into an ironic key: "One captain is telling everyone who'll listen that it's not labor conditions killing these men—it's *mermaids*."

Granger froze. The email he was writing, everything in the room, became a blank except for the words coming from the television. His chair squealed as he rotated toward the screen. Granger seized on the name of Captain Ross Horgan, of the trawler *Amanda*. Horgan was disheveled, sandy-haired, his eyes red and small, his gullet swollen and stippled with gray: "I know how it sounds, but listen to me: Mermaids are killing our men. *Mermaids*. I've seen it with my own eyes."

The report ended. The news anchor responded with a stiff acknowledgment of the segment's whimsical conclusion ("... no matter *who* is responsible ... serious issue ... thank you, Maryanne"), and that was all from them, good night. Granger muted a frenzied, red-lit Pizza Hut commercial.

He wrapped his fingers around the perspiring glass cylinder of his drink, but he did not lift it. No, no, no. No time for distraction now. It was time to turn the laser beam to high; it was time to think.

It was around eleven p.m. when Granger picked up the phone.
"I need you to bring Sylvia to me."

CHAPTER 29

The electronic chime of my phone interrupts a dream. I'm so sad it was just a dream; I would never tell Derek this, but in my dream I was wealthy. I had a warm, self-satisfied feeling that everything would always be okay, because I had millions. I wore a fur coat and I kept buying things for people, movie tickets for the whole line. I'm so sad I've been pulled out of it. I beat flat the puffy duvet around me to try to find my phone, which must have fallen into bed with drunk me last night. As I wake, I remember the lunch with Franck and I feel guilty that he must not have enjoyed me, guilty about my childish need to run after Derek and get drunk. And there was something else.

The cold phone is in my hand. It's my sister, Susie.

"Hey, what's up?" I say.

"Oh my god, nothing," she says. "I wanted to tell you about something I learned at work."

"Okay."

"Penny, I think I know what your diagnosis is."

"I think I know, too. Slipped disc."

"No, no, no. I mean your mental diagnosis." Susie works in fund-raising for a major consortium of hospitals. She has no medical expertise.

"What do you mean?"

"Well . . ." A consistent low-level static sound tells me she's in the car. "Wait, hold on. I'm doing drive-through, stay with me."

I hear a voice say, "That'll be eight eighty-two, ma'am," and Susie says, "Thank you," in that weird dialect white women reserve for the service sector (*thinkyiaowwww*).

I am pleased she called. I realize I have a hangover. I'm not yet sure of its magnitude, and I like training my attention on Susie: imagining her car, an Audi, her keys attached to a pink fur ball with a Coach logo, an array of heels on the mud mats in the back.

"Did you have to call right in the middle of a transaction with someone else?" She knows this drives me crazy. "I mean, you've got miles of road alone to call me."

"Well, I *happened* to remember I wanted to talk to you."

"It just seems rude to the drive-through lady."

"Oh my god, Mahat Magandi, I would applaud you right now, but I'd drive off the road and plunge to my death and *then* who's the saint? So listen, since I manage several people now, I had to go to a G-E-T away day."

"What's that?"

"Oh my god, you don't know what G-E-T is? That school you worked in was a fucking joke. Gender and equality training. Everyone has to do it."

"Maybe they trusted that we would be sensitive to gender because we read literature." That was it, that was the other thing: *Derek hadn't read my book.* The other wound that I woke with.

"Are. You. Joking? You live in such a bubble. You think fifty percent of the world's population is Jewish and ninety percent have vibrators. *Literature?* If anything, that just makes you weirder and more likely to make assumptions about gender. *Literature.* You teach teenagers to worship John Steinbeck's magnificent salty shaft and you think you understand QUOTE UNQUOTE gender politics."

"All I'm saying is, we *talk* about these things in class, you know, gender, power."

"Well, maybe." She pauses to take a sip of something. "Ugh, that's disgusting."

"What's disgusting?"

"Starbucks."

"What did you get?"

"Chicken Tetrazzini. I got a fucking coffee."

"What was eight dollars?"

"Oh my god, you're such a SPY. Why are you OBSESSED WITH HOW MUCH MONEY I SPEND? Wait, let me finish my story."

"*You* called *me* right as you were paying."

"So I have to do this G-E-T training, which involves this lady coming in for a half day with a bunch of posters. Nobody has to work, everyone gets sushi, it's perfect. You learn about unconscious bias. So, for example, when I say 'Doctor,' you picture a man, which is sexist. Like how in your book the doctor's a man. Why wasn't it a woman? Get it?"

"The doctor—"

"Just listen. So she showed us a poster with definitions of different kinds of sexualities on it, explaining all the parts of LGBTQIA— like what's 'Questioning' and 'Intersex.' "

"Uh-huh."

"And you are DEFINITELY ASEXUAL! You check every box." Susie gasps. "Wait, it makes so much sense now, that's how you were able to write a book! You don't waste time thinking about sex like normal people."

"There's no such thing as 'normal'! And that's *not* what asexuality is—"

"Okay, this is great, you're opening up."

"No, this isn't about me, I've just read stuff."

"Oh, good, yeah, find a pamphlet. I think the point is, most of human culture revolves around sexual relations, and if you can't get that, then it makes sense that you'd be sort of, you know, unsympathetic."

I see Derek stirring on the sofa, and I lower my voice. "I'm not unsympathetic."

"Why are you talking so low?"

"I'm tired."

"From fucking?"

"Ew, gross."

"See? Penny, I think you need to embrace this. The minute I realized it, I was so relieved for you. There's like a whole community out there. You guys can go and do jigsaw puzzles and eat soup and no one will judge you."

I think about the parties here in LA, bloodthirsty comedians and groups of stoned close friends whispering. Soup with asexuals sounds nice.

"I just feel I can finally understand you. Like, remember when I told you I was getting married and you didn't care?" I do remember that.

"That's crazy, of course I cared." Maybe I should get out of this conversation. I'm meeting with R&M in a couple of hours at their office. The table read of the final script is in two weeks. Things are getting intense. I start to mutter about having to go, but Susie pours forth with purpose.

"It's okay, I forgive you. They taught us how to deal with this at the G-E-T training. You have a *condition*. You're *broken*. I accept you."

"They told you to tell your coworkers they're *broken*?"

"No, no, that's my own thing, but they told us to accept people who are different."

"I'm not a different *species* because I don't prioritize sex. And by the way, I went on a date yesterday."

"You *are* a different species. I can finally appreciate that. Although I guess you guys will be extinct soon. And definitely don't date, that's *so sad*. That's the saddest thought. Did you go into it being like, *Oh, maybe we'll fall in love and eventually I'll have the sex with the nice man,* and then you had a panic attack and ran away?"

"No." One hundred percent. "Look, I have to go to a meeting."

"Good! Have meetings! Throw yourself into work. How's it

going, by the way? I've been telling everyone my sister's a big-time screenwriter now."

"It's going great. A lot is changing." These words, like a magic spell, release a swarm of anxiety in me.

"That's crazy that you're letting these people change your book."

"What do you mean?"

"I don't know." A long, sharp slurp through a disposable lid. "Nobody could even ask you about that book when you were writing it. It's so . . . It was so private. I still wonder, looking at your basic-ass life sometimes, *Where did this story about mermaids come from?* I know you better than anyone, but this stuff comes from a protected part of you. Some nature reserve where no one's allowed to bring their stupid shitty dog. And now you're letting people in to drill a pipeline." She huffs a little laugh into the receiver. "I'm almost jealous." Derek is awake now and plods into my bed. "Who's that?" Susie asks.

"Derek." Derek gestures at the phone. "Susie," I whisper.

"What the fuck is Hot Marx doing in LA?"

The two don't really get along. Susie represents Consumers Who Brunch to Derek, and Derek represents Activists Who Smell to Susie.

"He's keeping me company."

"WHY?"

"Well, he drives, for one thing."

"You know, he was the one guy I was like, *maybe* she's going to finally be in a relationship. I mean, *I* think he's an Occupy tent turd, but you seem to get along." Derek smells himself, twists his face, and points to the shower. I nod for him to go ahead.

"Yeah, no."

"Okay, I'm at work. Have a great day in your no-stakes emotional world of sexless love, WHICH I ACCEPT. I love you."

I love her, too.

CHAPTER 30

EXCERPT FROM *AMERICAN MERMAID*

After a long, quiet stretch of highway, Masahiro asked Sylvia what it had been like down there.

When Sylvia went to tell him, she realized she saw it all in flashes. Moments. She remembered at one point running her hand along a hard, curved surface, rounded like a snout, and realizing that it was the front of an old VW Bug, long sunk. Her memory of her night in the sea didn't unfold in time, but was like a sea itself, a dark depth out of which things might buoy up. That feeling of amorphous darkness, like liquid, was capable of carrying an infinitely fast charge. A place that severed the downward tethers of gravity and reoriented motion so that the first gesture wasn't a fight to lift up. The first gesture was motion itself, was to choose, with a ripple of the hip and a tilt of the shoulder, which among infinite vectors to pursue. If walking is progress—one foot before the other, drawing in a line—then swimming is play, scribbling through matter with the spine. A current would brush her ear, and she would turn, curl under herself, and bring her tail around to feel the same current, the way a cat works his jaw and then his haunch against an outstretched hand.

Masahiro saw Sylvia searching her memory for answers. He didn't want to push her—she had the right to be guarded after what she'd just learned. At the same time, he was dying to know. "How long did the transition last? Was it quick, when you were fully submerged? It should have been much quicker than with partial saturation." She didn't respond, only nodded vaguely. Masahiro sighed and faced the road. "I understand if you don't want to tell me."

"No, that's not it." She wanted to talk about it, to relive it. "It's just that . . ."

"How did you see?" asked Masahiro. "Could you see everything? Do you think your pupils dilated fully? Or were you sensing objects another way?" Masahiro looked at her. "Do you have radar? When's the next McDonald's?"

"I don't know . . ." Sylvia said, almost inaudibly. "I can't remember."

"You can't remember?"

"I remember the very beginning, when I thought I was dying. And I know what it was like, but I don't know what happened, or when, or even for how long I was under. I know it was the happiest I've ever been."

As they sped along I-84 in the beige Camry, the radio station played its ID clip—"The hits of the eighties, the nineties, and today" in a robotic male voice—which fizzled and gave way to "Backpack," a hit from eight years earlier. "Get inside my eyes, baby, get inside my mind, I'll get inside your backpack and we'll leave all this behind." Sylvia remembered the year that song had been everywhere. She remembered lying on Masahiro's examination table after her spasm in chemistry class. She remembered the smell of Jeff Johnson, the football player, as he hoisted her up to the lab bench and then held her too gently for too long. Jeff's tenderness that day had opened up some line of inquiry in her mind that ultimately led her to plunge, lonely and desperate, into Boston Harbor.

"If you'd split me completely, without the possibility of becoming a mermaid again, would I have been . . . a typical girl?"

"You wouldn't have been able to walk. But you would have had less pain."

"No, I mean—would I have felt attraction, desire?"

"Ah—this question." Masahiro, focusing on the road, put on his most doctorly tone. "I can't perform a control experiment; I don't know whether it's endogenous or—"

She twisted in her seat and faced Masahiro, assessing him as if he were an outfit on a mannequin. "If I were just a human, would I have fallen in love with *you*?"

"Ha." The doctorliness fell away, and his face softened into a lopsided smile. "No. I don't think so. You would have had more friends. You would have been really obsessed with your friends, that's how teenagers are. You would have hung out with someone named Mandy to get to someone named Luke that you really wanted to kiss."

"Sounds terrible."

"It's tough."

Sylvia squinted, as if staring extra hard at the doctor would reveal something she'd missed, some romantic substance coming off him in purple vapors.

Nothing. "What about you? Are you immune to love?"

"No, I'm not."

"Are you in love with me?" She asked this with the seriousness of a dogged scientist.

"No." He smiled with his eyes on the road and repeated, "No."

"Have you ever been in love?"

"Not the way you mean. I've been very disciplined in some ways. I had different priorities."

"Are you sad about that? Do you want to be in love? Doesn't it seem cool? Or important?"

Masahiro thought for a moment. "I don't know . . . it's too late for me. I can't imagine it anymore. Although I would have liked to have kids. I would have *loved* that." Masahiro's attention drifted for a moment, but he snapped out of it with sudden vigor. "You know, that makes me think: maybe your immunity to desire can *tell* us something about mermaids. It must have to do with mermaid evolution, patterns of sociability over thousands of years. They—you—must not have evolved to rely on pair bonds the way *homo sapiens* did. Maybe it points to group child-rearing, matrilineage."

"I wish I remembered more from that night. I have a good memory," Sylvia said, shaking her head.

"You have an extraordinary mind, Sylvia. Keep thinking. Maybe if you try to tell me about it, you'll trigger something." She wanted to cry, suddenly, because it was exactly as it had been in Masahiro's office when she was a kid. Always training her, always helping her think. *Say the problem out loud. Recite the capitals. Tell me the formula for a sphere.* In this moment, she didn't care about his loyalty to her father, the darkness she sensed when he spoke about his partnership with him. She had almost lost Masahiro. All she cared about now was that he was here. As Sylvia found herself overcome with gratitude for Masahiro, she watched the man jerk the wheel to one side as they approached a rest stop with a gas station and a Burger King.

"Time for a Whopper."

"No, thanks," muttered Sylvia.

"I'm talking about the toilets."

"Gross." But this time Sylvia let herself laugh, and Doc caught it.

"Gross," Masahiro agreed, distracted with delight as he curved off the highway.

"I remember finding a car. I remember—"

"Did you eat something?"

"Did I *eat* something? Doc, relax, you're getting your burger."

"No, no, this is important. You say you went down to the pier around one a.m. When you came up, it was dawn. You weren't sleeping for those five hours—minimum—you were swimming. You say you remember a feeling of positively flying through the water. That takes an enormous amount of energy."

"I was ravenous in the hospital afterward."

"But you didn't faint. They gave you Vicodin in the ambulance. If you'd had an empty stomach, you would have been sick. You would have been hypoglycemic." Sylvia stared at Masahiro as he slid into a parking spot outside the rest stop. The car stopped, and Masahiro sat perfectly still for a moment, left hand hooked to the steering wheel, right hand resting on the gear shift. "You must have eaten down there. Think. Did they have a Burger King?" He flashed a sympathetic smirk and hopped out of the car.

Sylvia didn't understand. She didn't remember anything but playing, the dense, infinite, liquid sport of it. She tried hard to remember anything else—what had led her to the VW? What had come before, after? Masahiro slammed the door, walked around to the trunk, and extracted a wheelchair. He opened it up on the sidewalk in front of the car and came around to the passenger door to get Sylvia. He pulled her legs to the side, and she twisted her torso along with them so that she was dangling out of the car, and then she wrapped her right arm around Masahiro's neck. He lifted her up and carried her to the sidewalk, kicking the car door shut behind him. As he was bending over the chair, about to place her in it, Sylvia gasped.

"What? Are you okay?" Masahiro, practiced at this, searched her face for a sign—was it her spine? The joints in her feet? Her skin? But she wasn't wincing in pain. Her jaw hung open and her wide eyes were fixed on her right hand, which clutched Masahiro's shoulder. Masahiro followed her gaze to her hand, which released Masahiro from its grip. She held her fingers out straight, like a woman showing off a new diamond ring. A tremor shot through the hand, but Sylvia and Masahiro could still see the blood under her fingernails, the little reddish brown arcs that, if you didn't know better, might speak of pottery class or a vegetable garden.

Sylvia retracted her fingers, made two tight fists.

"Who did you run into down there?" Masahiro asked, a gentle prompt, already moving toward forgiveness of whatever had happened.

Sylvia flipped her hands over and looked at her palms. "What did I do?"

CHAPTER 31

I am at a party at the home of a filmmaker married to a chef. I never clock names, but I clocked "Finola and Guy" when Danielle said their names in the car on the way over.

"Finola?" I repeated.

"Yeah, it's Irish. Not that she's Irish."

No, of course not.

I don't know what I was expecting, but the exceptional beauty of this home has me reeling, frantically sad that none of it is mine. I am supposed to be meeting Stem Hollander here, the guy who liked my book and put it on the internet and greased the wheels of my good fortune. I was thinking how comfortable it would be walking into a party ready to slide into a warm, one-person pocket of admiration. But now I am miles from feeling admired, sitting on a sofa thinking that it used to seem obvious to me, as a person with relatively little income, that what you do is dictated by what you can afford. ("Hey, you can go to Mexico, ten days, four hundred bucks, all in!")

But things in Guy and Finola's house have been dictated by their surface qualities, by how much someone loves walnut, by someone's exposure to the tilework of Moroccan riads, by a bodily experience of intimate spaces in the little cafés under the Bridge of Sighs. Rich to me means hard surfaces, large, shiny refrigerators, and the talons of little dogs tapping in marble foyers. But I'm learning rich can be soft, infuriatingly soft; rich can be small; rich can be perfect rags.

These rich people aren't defined by being rich, but obviously things are densely beautiful with their own expense—the dark, interesting polished wood of the floor and the wide boards framing the broad windows that give onto a middle ground of wilderness, before the beaming lights of the city.

The house is low and wide—fuck you, square houses of the poor and the towering towers of the vulgar!—with navy walls and a bright Mexican carpet and somehow a beautiful brown velvet sofa. It's probably not called velvet, it's probably something new and environmentally sustainable called "Shylex" or something new and environmentally sustainable and French called "Chailesse." But it absorbs everything, it absorbs your question about how much it cost as you sit under an asymmetrical lamp made of ropes and next to a squeaky, self-involved rubber plant. The filmmaker, Finola, is in a low leather strap chair stroking a white wolf in the corner, her thin neck stretched as she stares up at a yammering man in black, short stovepipe pants. It looks like we are on a 1920s ocean liner and he's the coal-stained stevedore who knows his place and she's the captain's wife. The wolf watches the husband toss corn-flour-dusted soft-shell crabs in a pan of hot oil. The smell of toasting, salty corn makes everyone a little hungry, and we pull extra-long sips of our cold drinks.

The back wall of the kitchen is a large wood-framed glass panel that Guy tilts open into the cactus garden behind, which, if you weren't such a basic and forgettable liver of life, you would have considered for your home instead of that rattling tin extraction fan. At one point, I catch the filmmaker's eyes across the room and I wonder if my eyeballs just scream envy, so I pretend that my gawping is a refined interest in design by pointing like a child learning new words and saying, "I like your navy walls."

"Bowery Blue," she says, lifting her hand off the wolf to make air quotes. Finola has it all—she is rich enough to own opposites. She lives in a big cocoon of brand-new ancient-Roman jewel tones with a kind wolf, comfortable in her luxury and sardonic about its labels. I find the following thought not as a string of words but as an instantaneous hard feeling, fully conceived, like palpating a lump: *I fucked up.* If I'd known it was possible to feel ethical and live like this, I would have tried to be rich. What a failure of vision. I thought I was superior to people when I was poor and teaching, because, with my thirty-seven grand doled out in semimonthly paychecks of seventeen hundred dollars, I was somehow clinging to an experience of the real—real people, real things. I was better than rich dicks in Range Rovers, people who drove army vehicles to return blouses. Rich dicks sucked money in and spat it out like ranks of blind oysters lining the seabed, thoughtless bivalve conduits for capital that would compound into a fossil record of the economy without ever really living. I was better than any of those people. But here, in Finola's dark home, a place deeply pigmented in what feels like huge, careful intelligence, she, too, is also better than those people.

I'm afraid to talk to her anymore or she will know that I want to push her down the stairs and wear her hair and call myself Finola, and also it seems right that "Bowery Blue" should hang in the air like the last notes of a piano recital, so I nod and slip away.

I am sitting in the garden behind the ocean liner of a house, dark and horizontal, Christmas-lit by the city below, aware I should be looking for Hollander, should be holding out my hand until I find his. But I'm stuck looking out over the city from this mountainside I never knew Los Angeles had. There's no moisture in the air here, but the lights, little and big, blinking and blaring, bleed into a gauzy atmosphere of dust or pollution. There are people studded about under a trellis roped through with pretty vines (*Are they grapes? I suddenly think. Do they fucking make wine?*), but there is one guy sitting in a chair, silently staring at the trellis and holding a gun. I don't know guns, but it's long and has a long, straight spout. *Spout*, I think. *That can't be right. It's not a teapot for bullets.*

The man holding it is not wearing a shirt, only jeans. One leg is crossed over the other, ankle at the knee, gun resting on his thigh.

I share an ashtray with him. He notices me staring. His eyes dart over to me and back to the trellis. He says, squinting like a cowboy over the smoke from his cigarette, "Rats."

"Rats," I say. "'Rats' like 'goddammit'?"

"No, rats like rats."

I do not give any sign of understanding. I light another cigarette. There is an open bottle of sweating white wine nearby and I splash some of its contents into my tumbler. I look around again. People, mostly beautiful, standing or draped on artful garden furniture (a thick, fallen tree trunk sanded flat on top). An alien-beautiful woman in a tangerine shift. A guy fidgeting with a fire pit, some people smoking weed. But it seems obvious to me that the most interesting thing at this party is the half naked man with the gun.

I want him to sense that I am settling in near him for a while.

He goes on: "The roof rat. *Rattus rattus*. It's a big problem around here. They come in from the fields and the forest in a drought." He exhales a long, tired sigh, looks at me hard for the first time. "They're absolutely fearless. Come and nibble your neckerchief right off."

I do not know if Half Naked Man is mean-spirited or not, but nevertheless I now feel like a real loser for having worn a silk scarf to a cool party: "neckerchief." When I graduated college, my parents got me this scarf from Hermes for something like four hundred dollars. It's melon-colored and Russian bears dance around its border, pawing at Cyrillic letters that mean nothing to me but I assume are a comforting fairy tale for oligarchs about three bears who ate porridge while ninety-seven bears got none. I thought that it made me look moneyed, but now that he's called it a neckerchief, I feel like a United Airlines stewardess, prim and uncool, and I start tugging it down off my neck.

"You're going to shoot them?" I venture.

His eyes stay fixed on the trellis: "No, I'm going to shoot myself and then I'll see if they come running to cry over my corpse. Then you bag 'em, okay?"

So he *is* mean-spirited. But he's made me part of his team. I am ready to bag the mice at his corpse.

Maybe he senses this. He edges back in his seat, becomes expansive. "Rats. Monsters. They fatten on wild fruit."

Fatten? This man talks like Deuteronomy. He is some biblical hero, Samson, greasy, with his big mounds of pecs and the divots between each of his stomach muscles catching the light from the city as he curls forward. The violence in his fingertips is ready to be kindled, and my name is Penny and I will be serving you today in United Airlines Platinum Premier Class.

I want his grease on me.

"How do you know Guy and Finola?" I say, immediately ashamed at my shitty wedding chat.

Half Naked Man suddenly jerks up in his chair, brings the rifle to his shoulder, and traces the tip of it from his far left to his far right as the plants on the trellis shiver.

"Fuck. Fast little fucker." He takes a swig from a bottle of Sol. He barely turns his head, but his arm swings out toward me, bearing the beer. "Ice this for me?"

Sure that's no problem, sir, I can go ahead and do that, I think as I silently plunk his Sol into the ice bucket with the sweating wine. Suddenly he sits up straight-backed, tracks his gun across the trellis, and—*pop! Pop pop!*

"What about all these people?" I ask. *Safety first, here at United Airlines.*

"It's only an air rifle. I couldn't kill you," he says.

"I'm not worried about me." *It's the other passengers, sir.*

"I mean, if I held the barrel to your head, maybe I could kill you."

I wince. *I am going to have to call security, sir.*

"Relax," he says. "I know what I'm doing."

I shrug permissively. *If you say so, sir, but you will have to store your firearm for takeoff and landing.*

"But you missed?" I venture.

"They're lightning fast. They're travelers. As a species, they're used to traveling miles and miles in search of food, evading prey. These assholes—these *specific* assholes—gave Europe the plague, killed fifty million people."

"So we're like Argentinian Nazi-hunters." I pull that comment out of my mouth like a party clown pulls a fluorescent handkerchief: confused at what my face produced, pretending I had nothing to do with it. I look at the wine bottle, empty, or near empty. I should slow down, but what the hell, this is war.

"I'm going to get some more wine," I say. "You want another beer?" *Coffee? Tea? Me?*

"Yeah, bring over a couple," he says.

Right away, sir.

When I come back, bottles clinking in my arms, he springs up, stretches—his stomach muscles rearrange for a moment, expand, flatten, and then come back together into their egg crate. He holds out the gun to me. "Want to try?"

I am the flight attendant, standing in the aisle in my too-tight skirt suit with my silk scarf, ever the powdery-skinned face of company compliance and customer comfort, when suddenly the heat-packing criminal on my flight is asking me to join him.

"Do you know how to shoot a gun?" he asks, his voice level.

We'll run away, we'll rob things that deserve to be robbed.

He's holding out his weapon to me with one arm, eyebrows raised, expectant. I'm scared of guns, but I don't want to be a stewardess forever. I'm humiliated by my politeness and servitude and by my satin cowl, which I'm shoving in the back pocket of my jeans as I shake my head no, I've never shot a gun, but I'd love to try.

Now he's wrapped around me from behind, digging the rifle

into my shoulder, tilting my elbow upward. It falls a little, he taps it back up like a ballroom instructor. Aim here, push here. I glance around to see if we're making a spectacle, but the party is carrying on around the terrace—the fire pit's been lit farther out, and it seems to pull ambient attention more than Half Naked Man and United Platinum Plus. We trade places, he's standing now, lighting a cigarette, tapping the water off his Sol, alert next to me. Now I'm doing exactly like he did, sitting in the chair, the gun resting on my knees, scanning the trellis.

"Will I see them?" I ask.

"You'll hear them."

"I go by sound?"

"You go by gut."

He wants me to succeed, to learn. I want to please him. I want him to be proud of me, to let me join him on all of his hunts, to tug at his elbow outside of all the places he serves as sentinel, asking if I can bring him water, ice his beer. Asking to know what he knows about animals and how they fatten and the millions that died in times before. He'll do crunches in the hut that we share, and I'll watch him, holding my knees, glad that he's getting even readier to contract his midsection if needed in the course of protecting everyone, while I lose the memory, day by day, of the scarf I once wore when I was salaried and civilized.

The trellis is still, and now it's me who extends my hand and makes demands.

"Can I get another wine?" I say, no-nonsense, like I'm asking for a cartridge.

"Yeap," he says, as if for the thousandth time in one of the long chains of rote moves we perform at our post.

There is a long silence. I hear him suck on cigarettes. I hear him adjust his position, putting feet on the table, taking them off. But there's nothing awkward, no one feels the need to fill the silence. At one point, some lady in high-waisted jeans and a dumb bun stomps up, rams the table, sets the bottles rattling, blurts, "Has Toby left, you guys?" We both look at her with such molten, unfiltered hostility that she backs off slowly with a "Jesus, never mind."

We settle in like this. Each gulp of wine is a performance of our solidarity, so I don't feel them accumulating, but the wine bottle has been replaced a few times. His empty Sols line the table. This is the way it goes, on the watch.

Suddenly, there is a rustle. Half Naked Man sits up, cranes his neck.

"You got one coming in," he says in a low whisper. No screaming, no hysterics. This is what we've waited for. I pick up the gun. I nestle it into my shoulder. I look up. The sky is completely dark. When the leaves move, their shiny edges glint with the light from the city. The rat has stopped. Do I hear him sniffing? *Go by gut*, said the man. I can feel this fucker up above me to the left, paused. Suddenly again, the rustle, he's making a break for it. In a fraction of a second, I've made some deep-brained calculation about speed, distance, and time, and I've picked my spot just ahead of where the fucker paused, and now I'm pulling the trigger.

Pop. Pop.

Thud.

The next morning, stinking of woodsmoke and cigarettes, insect bitten, dry in the throat, and throbbing with a headache across my forehead and down my temples, it came back to me. First, the moment the rat fell down through the trellis, when the *pop* was still echoing in our ears. It dropped the eight or so feet onto the table with the kind of thud you hear around construction sites. It fell onto the center of the table between me and Half Naked Man, sending all the empty glass beer and wine bottles crashing. Bottles were shot clear across the patio. They rang and skidded on the flagstones for what felt like minutes.

Half Naked Man held his hands up to his brow until the commotion stopped, and he said, "Holy shit," and there was real pride in his muck-colored eyes, his tan face crinkled on one side by a satisfied twist of a smile. But then we both came in to look, in horror, at the thing. Its fur was black, and anywhere you could see it, the skin was brownish pink. The rat's eyes were little glossy black beads. Its tail was endless, kinked and cracking, thick at the base and thin at the tip like the dry, searching root of a big, moldering tuber. It lay plumb on its back, black rubber nose pointing toward the house, one bullet wound visible in its neck—like I'd stabbed it with a pen. The other wound must have been hidden by fur. Its pink hands were oddly human, and between its legs was some horrible fur-obscured genital mass, pendulous labia or a furry pair of balls.

My adrenaline was coursing from the shot, from the hit, from the sound. But it changed temperature in my body, from hot to cold, from a feeling in my veins to a thumping in my ears, when I saw the blood start to pool on the beautiful, thick-slabbed, worn wooden table, fill its grooves. Rat blood. I became aware of the crowd gathering around us. News was spreading ("Wait, *what?*"), heads were snapping over toward us from farther and farther away. Beautiful people were leaving the fire pit.

"Go." He reached for the gun. *"Go,"* he loud-whispered. "Let me deal with it." I looked to my right, toward the house and the huge movie-screen-size horizontal glass window where I saw Finola, her wide white crepe pants billowing forward with each step, like nursery curtains in a breeze. She could not care less about the commotion, but the white wolf was whimpering at the door to be let out. He smelled something.

I wanted to run, but when I stepped hard into my heels to spring up from my chair, my tailbone sizzled like a thing dropped in hot oil, and the hot lashing went all the way up to the nape of my neck. I fell back into the seat. Bodies were all coming to encircle us at the table, at various paces, but all of them coming. Danielle would be among them. "Sorry," she'd say. "Sorry my client painted your deck in pest blood. Is anyone staffing right now?"

He slipped a T-shirt on over his head, a V-neck so deep I had to imagine him commissioning it from a seamstress, her nodding no, him nodding yes. When I saw it on him, I knew I had once again squandered the imagination I came here to sell. Half Naked Man was no warm if reluctant hero, no partner, but a callous handsome man who would not look at me again.

Our hostess floated her way to us on the heels of her wolf.

I could sense Half Naked Man was about to claim the kill. I would have let him if I could have dashed for a cab. It wasn't exactly a federal courthouse, but I still didn't like the idea of sitting there performing an obvious lie, even to rich strangers, many of whom—actors, agents, lawyers—lied for a living and may well have leaped into an operatic chorus of nodding assent: "Of course! The Man! The Man has killed the rat! The hunchback lady drank and watched! The Man killed the rat!"

I reached over and took the gun from him. Finola had parted the crowd and arrived at the tableside, stood there like King Arthur, if King Arthur had used top-flight Korean facial acid and hit the lamplight like milk glass.

"I'm so sorry," I said, looking her in the eyes sincerely, since I had nowhere to run. "I had no idea I was a good shot."

CHAPTER 32

EXCERPT FROM *AMERICAN MERMAID*

"We need to understand what you're capable of." The road streamed quietly by. Rhythmic barriers pinned back a shadowy forest.

"You made me, didn't you?" She said this with resignation, staring into the woods, but it came out spiked with blame.

"I didn't *make* you. You're not . . . Pinocchio."

They both paused, weighing wordlessly whether they were, in fact, like a childless craftsman and a remarkably self-conscious doll.

"You're a species we know little about," said Masahiro, so gently and humbly that Sylvia regretted her last comment. "I've watched you grow up. I've been here your whole life—and even I don't know what you're capable of."

"Are you scared of me?"

Masahiro thought a moment. "No. I probably should be." At this, Sylvia felt a flash of power, just a little pump of some thrilling confidence run a quick circuit through her veins. It surprised her. "What I'm scared of is billions of people drowning. For your survival, and for theirs, we need to know more."

"You don't have access to your lab anymore?"

"No. I'm dead. I'm—who am I today?"

Masahiro checked a driver's license he'd made with a surgical scalpel, a laminating machine, and some ninety-nine-cent nail polish from Walgreens. "I'm Freddy Noguchi."

"Who am I?"

"You're Jacquelyn Prendergast."

"Doc, you have to let me do the names."

"I like Jacquelyn Prendergast!"

"It sounds like a soap character."

"I give you a nice, ladylike name, and what do I get? Complaints. Fine. Next time you're—you're—Doris Chunk."

Sylvia couldn't repress a laugh, and Masahiro glanced at her, happy. Then they were silent for a while, each staring at the road in contemplation.

"We don't need my lab," said Masahiro. "But I think, before we go overseas, we need to figure some things out. What we need is a pool."

"My parents' place in Westchester has a huge indoor pool. I never even saw it, but I know it's there."

"Too dangerous."

"They're always traveling."

"Your father had that house purpose-built for his own experiments. It's full of surveillance and secret spaces."

It is? thought Sylvia. *The literal foundations of my childhood were some kind of conspiracy.* She couldn't square that idea with memories of the comfort she'd felt at her mother's side.

"What about my mom? If we talk to her, surely she'll join us, help us. She's a good person, I know she is. We could reach out to her without my dad knowing."

"I'm sorry. We can't trust her. She's too . . ." He looked at Sylvia.

"She's too good a wife."

"There was a Holiday Inn a couple exits back advertising a pool."

"Who goes swimming at a Holiday Inn on I-84?"

"Exactly."

Sylvia and Masahiro had both fallen asleep lying atop the mauve floral covers on their separate double beds at the Holiday Inn

Express Sturbridge. Now Sylvia woke up to find herself alone. She looked at the red-scripted digital clock in the darkness. 6:13 a.m.

Suddenly the door lurched open, and she saw the silhouette of her friend, backlit against the bright white hallway, holding scissors and something else. Masahiro moved a reading light from the side table onto the floor beside him and flipped it on. He rummaged around, pulled something out, and, crouching in the light, began to work away. She heard Masahiro's little noises of concentration and satisfaction—*mm-hp*.

Finally, she asked, "What are you doing?"

"Oh, you're awake," he said. "Good."

He stood up and flicked on the room lights. Sylvia covered her eyes for a second with her hand, and when they'd adjusted to the brightness, she saw Masahiro, hoisting two pairs of his underwear, cut in half and resewn into a makeshift bikini top. He held it up to his chest.

"You ready to go swimming, *baby*?" The *baby* was exaggerated, mock sexy, and it came with a swish of the aging doctor's hips, a bit stiff from a day on the road. "Don't worry," he added, "they were unused! And it's just for today. We'll stop at a sports store on the highway and get you a real top." It was typical of Masahiro, thought Sylvia, to imagine in advance how her dignity might be threatened, how she might be exposed, and to do his very best to protect her, even if his very best was a bandeau bikini of briefs.

On the way to the pool, Masahiro returned the scissors and the sewing kit to a large lady with metallic red hair at the front desk. She had her arms up, two bobby pins in her mouth as she struggled to wind the fragile strands into a chignon.

She now saw him push a young woman in a wheelchair and seemed to have inferred that he was just about the nicest man in the world.

"You get that button back on?" she asked, the bobby pins still in her teeth.

"Button? Oh, yeah, button—thank you, yes."

She spat the bobby pins out into her palm and dropped her hands, which left her frazzled hair standing upright like a red furry dollop. "A man that can sew, phew, you're a lucky lady." She winked, and Masahiro pushed Sylvia past the desk to a separate elevator that opened onto a small underground pool. As the door closed behind them the lady could be heard muttering, "I need me a mirror."

The relationship between Sylvia and Masahiro had, until this strange recent turn of events—until their untimely deaths—developed almost entirely in seclusion. It had been grown in a lab, in Masahiro's sterile yet somehow warm hospital office (all the funny pamphlets he kept around, the knickknacks and netsuke on his desk). And now this friendship was out in the environment for the first time, and she saw other people seeing the two of them. What did they think of this duo, a middle-aged Japanese American man in baggy jeans and Converse, and a young mixed-race woman in a wheelchair? Was he her carer, her doctor, in their eyes? Her *lover*?

She shuddered. What did the receptionist mean by "lucky lady"? Lucky to have such a nice father? Ha. She'd been told her whole life she was lucky; lucky, with her disability, to have been adopted by the Grangers, with their infinite resources. Masahiro himself was, she realized, a kind of luxury gift offered to her and paid for by her wealthy parents. Now she and Masahiro had been unlocked from this system of patriarchy and patronage, so who were they? The best answer she could give was two ghosts trying to figure out if they could engineer a haunting.

Masahiro sat in a plastic armchair in the small, dank basement pool room of the Holiday Inn Express off Exit 3A on I-84 outside

Sturbridge, Massachusetts, and watched a mermaid do laps. She wore her new one-of-a-kind designer swimsuit. Masahiro's eyes stung from the chlorine in the air and he perched nervously on the edge of the flimsy chair, worried that Sylvia's sensitive skin would be porous to the chlorine, that she would somehow experience pain or poisoning. Suddenly he laughed, noticing how Sylvia, who could breathe underwater through her skin, stopped at each end of the pool, popped her head up, turned around, and continued. It was some concession to the human need to take a breath before kicking off in the other direction. She paused, resting her arms on the grimy plastic ledge of the pool, and looked at the doctor.

"Why are you laughing?"

"Why are you coming up for breath?"

She hadn't even noticed she was doing it. "I've never been in a pool before." She started laughing herself. "I've only seen, like, the Olympics on TV. I'm still—culturally—human."

"You don't have to be." He shooed her with both hands. "Be a mermaid."

Masahiro's observation sunk into her mind and suddenly a question rebounded back: *What else,* Sylvia wondered, *am I doing because I still think I'm only human, because it's the only culture I've known? What powers do I have that I've simply* never used *because I've never seen them used, never been told I have them?* She dipped back into the water. Her tail, undulating minimally and with almost no effort, took her from one end of the pool to the other in the blink of an eye, so she began to trace a circle as big as possible, whirling around gently, her arms behind her, stirring up crud and stray hairs from the ugly tan tile below. Sometimes she twisted around underwater and faced upward, looking at the bare caged bulbs that studded the ceiling. The water transformed the stark lights into undulating golden planets. *What could she do?*

It struck her that maybe the only way to know, to truly know, what she was capable of was to find other mermaids. Like whale dialect or birdsong, perhaps new ways of talking and thinking would have to be taught to her.

"Sylvia." Masahiro's voice, muffled by the water, interrupted her thoughts. Still moving backward and facing up, her head emerged from the surface. "You promise you're not feeling any pain? Let me know as soon as you feel anything." He gestured toward his kit, full of steroids, analgesics, numbing agents. Sylvia looked down at herself, lifted her iridescent fan out of the water, examined it, and smacked it back down on the surface. The sound it made—like concrete cracking, loud enough to shake the walls—frightened them both. Feeding on the awesome energy of that huge noise, she lurched forward, pulled her tail under her and felt herself moving large volumes of water back and forth as her torso rose up into the air. She looked superhuman, floating vertically, flanked by sloshing wakes at either end of the pool.

"No." She grinned. "No pain."

Masahiro couldn't stay seated. He kept popping up nervously, trying to assess her. "Because it's a respiratory organ, your skin has always been sensitive to airborne pollutants. I was afraid this bleached water would somehow hurt you. But—" Sylvia wasn't listening anymore. She'd gone back under.

Sylvia relaxed, slowly sinking to the bottom of the pool. Her back was flat against the slick, tepid tiles of the floor and her tail swished above her, up and down, an action that she had no idea she used to do as a baby, lying on the black pebbled bed of the dark straits and still lagoons of her infancy in the North Atlantic. She fell into a kind of trance while oxygen seeped into her skin and carbon dioxide left her in little strings of bubbles from her nose. Her mind became a kind of proxy for the water itself, empty and cold but gently swaying. Into this blankness, figures suddenly emerged. First shapes: lines dashing in square circuits, flowing around. Pooling into orbs and bulbs before slithering away again into linear circuits. The more she relaxed, the more she saw an expanded, complete pattern, meltingly crisscrossed like pilled plaid.

She stayed like this for some time, until the pattern was not something she held in her mind's eye, but something in which she was fully immersed. Then, suddenly, they emerged: the unmistakable silhouettes of people. Two people coming together and embracing, shimmering silhouettes against a field of black. Someone bending down, as if tying a shoe. A stout female figure, reaching up with both hands above her head, as if fixing her—

Sylvia gasped like a human, suddenly taking a mouthful of water into her windpipe. She burst above the surface of the water, coughing. Masahiro jumped up from his seat and came to the edge of the pool, which she now gripped, facedown. He saw Sylvia's back, imprinted with a grid from the tiled floor, the makeshift brassiere twisted about her as she convulsed at his feet.

Masahiro sat on the ledge and then slipped into the water, which was up to his waist, so that he could see Sylvia's face and reach her chest and back, but he was helpless to do anything. When she finally stopped coughing, she lifted her head to find Masahiro's eyes, panicked, searching her for clues.

"What *happened*?" he asked.

"I gasped," she said, and started laughing. "I gasped like a stupid human."

"You *gasped*? That's it?" he said.

"That's it."

"You're not hurt?"

"No, I'm not hurt."

Sylvia had recognized the silhouette of the woman with her hands up. It was the lady at the desk upstairs, still fixing her hair. It wasn't a memory or a dream. It was a real-time transmission. First she had traced the water moving through the pipes of the Holiday Inn, bursting into showers and swirling through toilets, kettles, an industrial dishwasher, several boilers.

But then, somehow, she had been able, with increasingly clarity, to "see" bodies within a certain range. She felt their volume, their distance from her; she felt them move, sweat, vibrate with sound.

Water. She could sense water, and people were mostly water, each one a jagged, hurtling lake. This was what had begun to happen on her sixteenth birthday, only she hadn't stayed submerged long enough to realize that it was more than an intuition or a dream. It was a kind of vision, a sounding of water.

"Doc," she said, "I have a new trick."

CHAPTER 33

"Okay, so she can see toilets. ANYWHERE."

"That's her superpower."

"She's like, I can see ANY TOILET within forty feet."

"And she can tell you if it's a number one or a number two."

They pause their laughing to gasp.

"Penny, we're not making fun of you. I'll tell you right now what you're about to say: *Read the book, see how it works in the book!*"

"And we get it, it did work, because you could describe her thoughts."

"But imagine it onscreen. Are we gonna have a blank screen for her inner thoughts, then some squiggly blue lines that all meet to form cartoon toilets and washing machines? It'll look like a commercial for 2000 Flushes."

"And washing machines!"

"SHE SEES KETTLES."

"I know where your kettles are. Be afraid."

"I'm a superhero. I sit outside your house in a wheelchair imagining your dishwasher. Have a great day."

Randy and Murphy laugh, and I fake laugh, but I also try to interrupt them. I'm making a mom face, which I hate doing—I'm *so deliberately* not a mom! What have I skipped all that sex for? I've done everything to avoid this performance!—but I need to show the mix of acceptance-in-disapproval that moms, functional and forbearing, have to wear so often in the face of abominable bullshit.

Grade school brothers punching each other in the nuts at the bank gave rise to this face, and I have to borrow it now, eyebrows low and flat like two stone lintels, head at the conventional tilt of maternal compassion.

Randy and Murphy and I are at their office, which, I've now learned, is also their home, because they are housemates. I don't know why this surprised me. I suppose because they're in their thirties and they have enough money to have separate houses. It explains why they are always working together, one whispering in the wings when I call the other. When I asked about it, they said that they work so much, this is the best way. They can wake up and work. I asked if people think they're in a relationship. One of them said, enthusiastic, "Oh, gayness definitely made this possible."

Their laughter peters out. I talk slowly and clearly.

"She has sonar," I say. "Like a dolphin. It's pretty fucking cool."

"Like a dolphin," says Murphy. "So dolphins know where all the toilets are?" At the same time, Randy says, "Do dolphins have Toilet Sense?" They point to each other, the chuckles rolling again.

Danielle lives in a castle; these boys live in a fort. It has crenellated walls. I think it's called Spanish Mission or something. You walk in to a double-height entrance foyer with a view to a loft upstairs bordered by a low wall and a wooden railing. It's something a cowboy would fall over after getting punched in the face in one of those all-saloon brawls. Yes, this is a place for stunt violence: there are vases around to shatter on heads, pool cues to crack over a knee, a long table downstairs you could grab a guy by his vest and bowl him down. I imagine a suave interior decorator saying, "I call it Rancho Diablo Posse Pit." Randy and Murphy turn to each other in slightly differentiated very-short shorts: *"Perf!"*

Or maybe this is just Spanish Mission and I'm starting to feel embattled.

After all, we are physically very comfortable. Turning right off the foyer is a polished-wood living room with a hearth built into a stone wall facing a U of couches. Randy and Murphy recline on the arms of the U, and I am at the center, or the bottom, depending how you look at it. We all have papers around us. Randy descended from the balcony office this morning with a freshly printed story outline, impressively coded with fluorescent tabs for things we need to go back to, things that need to be decided. I adapted the road scenes; they were all dialogue anyway. Randy and Murphy wanted to do Sylvia's first test swim in the sea after reuniting with Masahiro, because it's a scene full of violence and they're good at that.

They're real professionals.

"Can you stop focusing on the toilets?" I ask. "She can send out incredibly powerful sound waves that come back to her and tell her the shape of water. When she's in the water, she uses sonar—inaudible sound, think about that; a scream no man can hear—to see." The twins aren't listening. "Sure, she figures it out in a Holiday Inn, but doesn't Spider-Man discover his *ejaculate rope*—because that's so dignified—by shooting it around his teenage bedroom?"

Murphy is still recovering from his laugh, but Randy sees that I'm dangerously earnest. Randy puts his papers down and holds his hands up low, like the sheriff's pulled a pistol on him.

"No, you're right, you're right. It *is* cool. And we're pumped about how to make it cinematic, right, Murph?"

The grade school brothers have stopped punching each other's nuts at the bank, sensing Mom will take something away. How did I get into this role? I see *myself* as a nut-punching brother! They have tricked me into dry superiority, where I don't belong. There is a place—most places, in fact—where I am playful. At Holy Cross, any little silliness on my part made a huge ripple on the still pond of teacherly authority, giggles spreading around me in circles.

A classroom memory comes to me in a flash of one of my eager front-row girls last year saying, "Lily doesn't want to marry what's-his-face Dorset, so why is she always trying to hang with him?"

"How else am I going to pay for my ball gowns?" I twirled around, bumping into my desk chair.

"Oh, so you're a prostitute?" someone fired back.

"Well, am I a prostitute? If I have to trade my affection for survival?"

Even the most disconnected kid checked in: "Miss Gay Man's a prostitute?"

It wasn't a useful laugh that erupted in the classroom, not a laugh used to charm or to belong or to look informed. It was a laugh none of them could help: Miss Schleeman, a bad actress and a willing embarrassment to herself, had gathered her mimed skirts and backed into the corner of the room, a Gilded Age beauty in bad jeggings whom these teenagers could mortify and distress with their modern mouths.

A desire to be back in the classroom comes to me as pure sense memory: the rubbery smell of the room, the peripheral sight of Eamon the wrestler predictably asleep, how hungry I always am in there—a few minutes into class, no matter what I've eaten, ravenous.

In other places, with other people, I am easy. Why can't I be that way here with Randy and Murphy? Some game of musical chairs started without my knowing, and they grabbed the chairs and I'm standing up like a fool. Now it seems I've always been a schoolmarm. *That sounds like marmalade, by which I mean jam.* A person who cuts definitions precisely, leaving a little pile of sawdust behind that she blows with a quick puff, claps her hands clean, proceeds. This isn't me.

"Do you understand how important water is? How it facilitates everything?" I say.

There is a pause.

"You fucking will when it swallows you," I say, looking at neither of them, eyes on the fire grate.

"I knew it," says Murphy, picking up his script and flipping through it madly. "Where is it, where is it?"

"What?" I ask. Randy looks equally confused.

"Penny, once is one thing. But please, there's a process here," says

Murphy, a little anger knocking the practiced chord of his "caring" tone out of tune.

"What?"

Murphy reads: "Interior. Pool room, Holiday Inn. Masahiro: 'They're trying to take your powers away from you, make you sexier and more helpless. They want to kill your sonar before they kill you.'

"Sylvia: 'I don't get it. Why would they want to do that? Aren't my powers amazing? Isn't it something to watch me discover them?'

"Masahiro: 'They don't understand how important water is, how it facilitates everything.'

"Sylvia: 'They fucking will when it swallows them.'"

I am frozen, confused.

"Sorry, you found this in the master script?" I ask.

"Are you serious? You're going to pretend you didn't do this?" says Murphy.

"Do what?"

"Penelope, you've inserted a little threat."

"I didn't do that."

"You just used the same expression! Of course it was you!"

Randy's face has been scrunched up since Murphy started reading.

"I don't get it. What—who's the 'they' there? That was added to the pool scene? Where she figures out her radar?"

Murphy nods at Randy.

"Sonar," I say.

"It's us. We're the 'they.' Cute, huh? *They're* trying to take your powers away, *they're* trying to kill you."

"I didn't do this."

"Yes, you did. You did it drunk."

Did I? The night at Finola's—who was I then, the night I killed something? Did she—I—a sharpshooter high on wine, have the guts to do this?

"And what kind of a threat is this anyway?" Murphy continues. "Sylvia's gonna drown us? *You* are? Maybe this is how high school works, but it's not how Hollywood works."

Randy is still struggling to follow. "Wait. Who's really the 'they'? '*They're* trying to take your powers away'?" He looks from me to Murphy in genuine confusion. "Granger? Or just like, the patriarchy?"

I shrug. Murphy levels a steely gaze at me.

"Holy shit. You can't mean—" Randy points to Murphy and then swings his finger back around and jams it in his own sternum, eyes wide. "*Us?* Me and Murph?" Randy tilts his head back and cackles. "This isn't that kind of movie, Penny. Although, actually, *Deadpool* breaks the fourth wall a lot and it's a nice comic touch."

"I didn't do it!"

Murphy gets up and walks away. We hear the tiny fresh click and sizzle as he opens a can of seltzer. Murphy reappears. He looks from me to Randy and back. "We have to trust each other here. Penny, I will have you removed from this project if you do this again, okay?" He wants the "okay?" to be cool, but it wobbles with anger. He sails back into the kitchen.

"Relax, Murph," Randy calls out. He turns to me, grandpaternal, hand on a Navajo blanket on the back of the big leather sofa: "Now, Penny. Don't drink and write. Anyway, the booze is giving you ESP." He puts his hands to his temples and pops his eyes wide. Murphy steps quickly back in from the kitchen, staring at Randy, who doesn't see him. "We hadn't even told you about the sonar thing yet," Randy continues.

"The truth is, Penny," Murphy says, hands chopping down, "the studio people already gave us notes on this; it's a production thing. You can't FILM sonar. So she's just going to have great vision. Which is still *extremely cool*."

"It's a *minor* technical difference," says Randy, squinting. "She'll see with her eyes instead of her forehead. Think about it, cinema's a visual medium. Makes sense. We can't film the feeling of knowing something's happening."

"Gotta see it." Murphy points at his eyes.

You can't film knowing something in your body. Here in the Rancho Diablo Posse Pit, I know something has happened that I never saw. I was drunk last Friday, but shooting the rat sobered me up. I remember coming home in the Uber with a driver named Jorge, who didn't believe I'd shot a rat and told me all the dead things his cat brings him. I remember telling Derek about the shooting, and him saying it made sense because I was nasty at House of the Dead 2 at the arcade in North Haven. I ate hard old pizza and tumbled into my bed.

Here is what I don't know: Who is changing the script?

Rising up from the deepest, wordless part of me comes the contour of my suspect, thrashing her tail, training her mind.

CHAPTER 34

EXCERPT FROM *AMERICAN MERMAID*

Sylvia had been gone now for some time. Masahiro, solitary and still, sat on a towel on the sand and waited for his friend to come out of a cold and empty bay.

They chose World's End, a marshy, meandering nature preserve forty minutes south of Boston. They knew that, after dusk, in one of the park's many little coves, Masahiro could lift a woman in her underwear from a wheelchair and dump her into the sea unseen. They had strapped a GoPro camera onto Sylvia—she looked ridiculous, but the two couldn't come up with another way to see what Sylvia was seeing down there, what she was doing.

As Masahiro sat, listening to the hissing of wind in the reeds, watching the sun sink slowly past a pink horizon on the water, he played out their next moves. They would fly through Copenhagen to the Faroes. Masahiro imagined lifting Sylvia into the water at one of the little coastal villages near Granger's R&D station—just as he had done a moment ago, watching as her skin snapped taut under his very eyes, glinting as she kicked off against him. Her face, so often twitching, eyes darting in concert with her anxious mind, went completely still, like a believer baptized, as it sunk beneath the surface. Or like a plumber baptized, with the GoPro beaming from her forehead.

Masahiro, with a hand under her back, had watched her hold

steady through the pain of transition—ten, fifteen seconds. She had fixed him with her eyes during the worst of it and even managed a little smile, anticipating the pleasure of her imminent dive.

They had found trust again after Masahiro's revelations. So it was with growing dread that Masahiro saw he had to tell Sylvia the rest. Otherwise Granger would twist the story himself, use it to his advantage. Masahiro would tell her how he and Granger really met—and about his own mother, and the radiation burns that he watched her suffer her whole life, and how it all justified what he'd done. Once she knew the whole truth, would she ever see him the same way? Would it finally eclipse her ability to forgive?

He practiced the words he would use to explain and soon the words disappeared and his eyes were closed and he was living it again—the detergent smell of his mother's dresses as he followed her around the house, both of them like children, equally dependent on the doctor who was supposedly curing his mother. A wave of nausea rose in his stomach as he remembered the sound of her retching, either from the sickness or, he suspected in retrospect, the pregnancies she had suffered at the doctor's hands. Sylvia would understand that what Masahiro had done was right. The doctor had deserved it. You can't just steal people from the world and make them yours, even if you've convinced yourself you're helping them. His own righteous judgment of the older doctor echoed back at him as a rebuke. *Knowing all this, you stole Sylvia and made her the Grangers'*. But, of course, if Masahiro told the whole story, all the way to the bloody end, Sylvia would understand that Granger owned him completely, that Masahiro never had a choice; that he was trapped, blackmailed.

A subtle shift in the sound of the reeds pulled Masahiro from his reverie. Something was punctuating the shushing of the papery stalks. His heart pounded as his peripheral vision registered a figure standing only a few feet behind him.

When Masahiro jumped to his feet and turned around, he recognized Lawrence right away. Squat and humorless, Lawrence was

Dean's fixer, a cop who'd left the force under suspicion of corruption and landed the gig of his life, paid exorbitantly to do almost nothing but stay on call for Dean Granger. Lawrence faced Masahiro, hands in the pockets of a thick blue New York Mets bomber jacket.

"Doctor." Lawrence wasn't an actor. He looked at Masahiro with lead eyes, unfriendly and unfeeling.

"Hello, Lawrence." Lawrence's gaze moved from Masahiro to the towel on the sand, Masahiro's laptop, a small duffel bag, and the wheelchair. Lawrence stepped back and rubbed his jaw. Something about this scene had thrown him.

"Lawrence—"

"What the fuck? Where's Sylvia?" Usually unflappable, Lawrence kicked the sand, pissed off at having to improvise.

"She's in the water," said Masahiro. "Granger hasn't told you everything."

Lawrence surveyed the scene, calculating. His head rolled back, and his chapped lips curled into a pout.

"I was told to bring Sylvia in."

"Can we just have a talk?" The doctor softened his tone to sound reasonable, but it came out conspiratorial, an amateur criminal trying to broker a deal.

"What did you do with the girl? Did you bury her?"

"Bury her?" Masahiro's face felt hot. Granger had given this violent dope a misleading set of facts. As a safe exit from this scenario became more and more difficult for Masahiro to imagine, he saw another facet of Granger's looming power: that even to tell the *truth* would only make Masahiro look like a kidnapper and a killer, while Granger came out the loving dad of a special-needs daughter.

"Lawrence, if I tell you what happened, you won't believe me."

"You don't have to tell me. I get it. Did you fall in love with her, Doctor? Not supposed to do that, you know. 'Gainst the rules. Then maybe she didn't love you back, maybe you got angry. It's the oldest story in the book, isn't it?"

"That's not what happened." Masahiro pointed out at the sea. "She's in the water."

"Goddammit, Doctor M, you're a sick fuck." Lawrence shook his head, hands on hips. "This is *not* what I came here to do." He pulled out his phone, fiddled with it a moment, and jammed it back into his pocket, sighing loudly. "No service."

"This is a misunderstanding, Lawrence. If you'll just wait here—Sylvia is supposed to come back any minute now. You'll see."

"Wow, you really think I'm stupid, huh? It could not be clearer that you think I'm a *dumb fucking idiot*." Lawrence boiled with real anger now, and Masahiro sensed that he'd hit a trip wire with Lawrence, activated some resentment that had been produced by the two men orbiting Granger at vastly different angles: Masahiro the valued doctor and Lawrence the expedient thug. Masahiro had always been consulted; Lawrence had been given precise instructions, like a kid sent to the corner store.

"Lawrence, please, *please* just wait." His mind was shrieking with fear; he could barely swallow. "She'll be back, she'll explain."

"Your bullshit isn't working on me, you fucking creep." He smiled at the evident panic on Masahiro's face. "That's right, no one here to protect you now. Just you and me."

Lawrence's eyes narrowed, and he crouched low. Then he lunged at Masahiro with an object in his hand. Masahiro darted aside, but Lawrence grabbed his jacket with his other hand and pulled Masahiro to the ground, where they rolled in the soft grass. Masahiro was shot through with adrenaline, feeling Lawrence's sheer bulk on top of him, his dense muscles. Lawrence brought a six-inch blade down onto Masahiro's chest but Masahiro threw both hands up and pushed with everything he had against Lawrence's arm. Masahiro caught a glimpse of Lawrence's face, always so still, now twisted into a purple scowl of rage.

Masahiro shoved Lawrence off him long enough to get up and start running. He had no idea how fast Lawrence was, or how close behind—there was nothing in that moment but pure, blinding fear. He felt as if his legs barely touched the ground. He was halfway down the dirt path that led to a forested trail to the exit—maybe fifty meters from where they'd scuffled—and Masahiro realized that he was alone. Lawrence was nowhere near him. He bent over to catch his breath, his chest heaving. But he felt little relief. He needed to get Sylvia and get back to civilization, to cars and witnesses and safety.

Facing the shore now, Masahiro was surprised to find that Lawrence had abandoned pursuit of the doctor and was walking toward the water, straight through the grass—he was now maybe ten, fifteen meters from shore. To his horror, he knew that Lawrence must have a new target: he must have spied Sylvia at the shoreline, and he was headed toward her. *Oh god,* he prayed, *Sylvia, stay in the water, stay in the water*. Could she have hoisted herself out before realizing the danger she was in? Within moments of leaving the ocean, she would be alone and confused, paralyzed by pain as she split again into a woman. She would be helpless when she realized the figure approaching her was Lawrence, not Masahiro.

It was only now that Masahiro noticed his hand stinging and looked down to see blood pouring from a gash through his palm, across his wrist and forearm. He would need to stanch the blood or he'd pass out soon, but he couldn't stop to tend to himself now. He had to protect Sylvia. He started toward the beach, his mind filled with fear, until it was interrupted by a sound. Incongruous, unbelievable, in the thick, dry-throated chemical horror of Masahiro's panic, to hear the languid, casual, pleased and pleasing trill of a girl's song. It was made of words but none were recognizable yet all made sense. It was in a language, it seemed, Masahiro had invented. His own heart's native tongue, the rhythms of his deepest, loneliest hopes; the shapes he saw when he fell asleep. Made easy, made real, matched and teased out by this floating melody, which both filled the air like a chorus and hit him like a kiss, like the whole sea whooshing in a shell by his ear as he stumbled toward the beach.

He saw Lawrence lumbering slowly and methodically toward the water. Masahiro couldn't think straight, couldn't think at all with this music. He tried to plug his ears, but he couldn't control his mangled hand, and when he brought it up to his face, he felt the warm blood from the jagged gash swipe across his cheek. At one point, he noticed his white canvas shoes were fully coated in red.

Sylvia. Sylvia. Lawrence would kill her or capture her. He would have no obstacles.

Masahiro couldn't see where the water met the land. The grasses between him and the shore obscured his vision. But right where Masahiro had released Sylvia into the water earlier, he saw something dark emerge. The world was slightly spinning now, but Masahiro tried to focus, lurching, spilling blood, slop, slop, like a messy cook, one step after another. He could see Lawrence was getting closer to her.

But then the strangest thing happened: Lawrence walked through the grass, over the sandy shore, and straight into the water. Masahiro saw Lawrence's stocky square frame in its shiny blue coat, step by step, disappear below the grass line. He simply walked into the sea. There was no sign of him or of Sylvia, or of any contact between them.

Masahiro tried to pin his eyes to the spot where Lawrence had disappeared. Dizzy, he passed the marks in the sand made by his scuffle with Lawrence, then reached the wheelchair and the towel. It was dead calm except for the same reeds, hushing like a nanny after a nightmare. He stood there in shock until his legs, which had carried him halfway across the park like a rocket, buckled under him, and he fell to his knees. His head hit the damp sand, and he saw black.

. . .

When Masahiro came to, it was nearly dark. The wind had died down, and there was just the distant sound of water lapping at the shoreline. His eyes opened to a muddy, empty stretch of the coast and the sky going navy above it. He propped himself up, turned around, and saw Sylvia, dark against a darker sky, sitting in the wheelchair, clothed but shivering. He knew Sylvia's body well: she was never cold. She wasn't shivering. She was trembling.

She and Masahiro had slipped between Granger's fingers, but not for long. They would have to recover and get back on the road. Lawrence was nowhere to be seen, and Masahiro was relieved: Sylvia had killed a man. Now he knew he could tell her his story.

CHAPTER 35

"I heard you shot someone," Danielle says casually, tilting a bottle of zinfandel toward her oversize wineglass.

"It was a rat." Does this undermine my suitability for boss bitch life? I'm not sure whether to nod like I fucked a sailor or wince like I broke a vase.

"So. Gross," she says. I wince. "Can't you get rabies from rats?"

"Rabies isn't that bad actually," says her friend Felicia, a costume supervisor. She leans on the medieval arch that separates Danielle's kitchen from the living room. Felicia is very warm and never seems to have a care in the world. She is bored with normal clothes, and always wears something like a fortune-teller's satin helmet or a Girl Scouts sash. I can imagine it's relaxing to be always almost in costume. Today she wears the green visor of a midcentury bookie. "Rabies is basically coke," she says, lifting a discreet vape pen to her lips and waving away rabies with her other hand.

"I was just helping this guy," I say. "He was trying to kill the rats. They come in from the fields and the forest." *They come in from the fields* . . . I'm repeating what the guy said, hoping his authoritative language will remain persuasive in the melon-fresh air of Danielle's stucco castle. "I thought it was just a game. I had no idea I would actually hit one."

"That guy was hot," says Felicia, who was at the party.

"Who was he?" I ask.

"I don't know. A nobody," says Felicia.

"A nobody?"

"Yeah, someone's family."

"Whose?" asks Danielle. "John Rambo's?"

"Dunno," says Felicia.

"Am I a nobody?" I ask, to my surprise, out loud. I remember being at the party, looking up to this man. Wanting to leave my life and append it to his, wholly. In the dark, drunk night, he was a leader, a hero, a partner. I should now feel embarrassed at my drunk worship of a nobody hick I can barely remember on a bug-bitten patio, but the attachment was so powerful that it's stayed in me and I retain a residue of loyalty. I hate to think of him begging for a job, being snubbed, living somewhere small and dirty that isn't a reconnaissance tent I helped him pitch.

"You're a somebody"—Danielle leans in, holding her bulbous wineglass up between us—"in a *different world*."

"Ooooooh, that's fun," says Felicia, leaking steam from her mouth.

"You mean the world of my imagination?" I ask.

"No, in *book world*," says Danielle. "Now you're becoming somebody in the real world. That's all."

The question of my reality, while very interesting to me, seems lamely, damply philosophical in this dazzling home, with sunspots dancing on the wood floors, filtered through the lemon trees outside the open windows. Somewhere there's a party setting up to feed and slake the thirst of the people we'll know and meet and impress, we beautiful, creative women. Felicia in her visor, unfazeable; Danielle, like a pharaoh, both arms on the armrests.

I scan the room for a return to the superficial. "Is that a Dorothea Tanning?" I ask, pointing to a painting pegged to the wall over a sideboard at the far end of the room.

"Yeah," says Danielle. "I only collect women." It's an allover brown-gray picture of a woman in a white shift dress and heels, sitting at a table laid with food. Next to her is a man three times her size in a gray suit. A doll-size servant woman stands as tall as the girl's knee. Everybody drawn to a different scale. Anywhere else, I would have seen it as a domestic, female dialect of surrealist weirdness, but here, in Danielle's home, through Danielle's eyes, it is a diagram of differential status at a Hollywood party. Tanning's Dutch browns become dust bowl dirt, blown west onto the woman's white dress and the curtain-size lapels of the exec whom she needs to impress at her table.

"I mean, it's not *the real thing*. The painting itself can't be displayed. It's in a vault. Too valuable. The insurers had that made."

"By whom?" I ask.

"Dorothea Tanning."

"WHAT?"

"Yeah. I had her make another one."

My eyes go wild with disbelief.

"Just kidding, she's dead." Danielle throws her head back in a noiseless laugh. "It's a digital print."

Felicia oozes over to the painting, puckers out her painted lips, and blows a brief screen of white vapor across the surface. She turns and gives me a religious smile, like nothing good could ever come to harm.

I think I belong in book world.

CHAPTER 36

I am standing at a podium facing rows of about a hundred chairs in a brightly lit chain bookstore. The woman who does the programming for this particular store—a lady in a turquoise turtleneck who laughs really hard but then finds herself stranded and confused the minute her laugh ends—has ushered me to the podium, saying, "I bet you're an old hand at podiums." I don't get it. "Because you were a teacher," she says. "You stood at podiums?"

I finally understand what she's saying, but I have no response. "It's *podia*," I say, dropping my voice with exaggerated erudition.

"Oh, sorry, podia," she says, taking the correction seriously.

"I'm just kidding," I offer quickly.

She laughs maniacally and then is bereft. The class of women who facilitate cultural events is easy to humiliate, and I have humiliated her. But I didn't do it on purpose, I was just looking for a joke. We got rocked out of kilter because she overdignified me, and then when I was trying to rock us back by insulting myself, I threw her overboard.

The seats are all taken, and there are people behind the seats, standing. Almost all of them are women. I know from my publisher that my readers are mostly women between twenty-five and forty, but I know from TikTok and Instagram that I have an intense fan base of teenage girls.

I had no experience of teenagers when I started teaching. At first

I was scared of them. I still am. I love them, too, how bad they are at all the normally easy things of life like saying your name to a stranger or drinking a drink without making noise or remembering to bring even a single piece of paper to a class that needs paper every day. How the child is still there, in their idle doodles of puppies, or in the way, for a few of them still, "my mom" is a consistent, neutral service provider.

But as they change, they give off something, beyond the literal odors that they can't control, the black pepper smell of their BO. They have no firm borders; their very contours are wobbling and disintegrating so that the heat of human blood and the cycles of sleep and wake, hunger and thirst, are too close to the surface and seeping out. You can tell, talking to one of them, that they're thirsty, that they're warm, that they're bored. Everything's available to view, to sense, like the organs of a fetal animal pumping away beneath a veil of tissue.

The thing you realize after you've worked with teenagers for a while is that, by some long-honed evolutionary process, they are fine-tuned sensors of the vulnerabilities of others. They may be pink-skinned, hearts fluttering on the surface, hormones swishing visibly around in them like laundromat suds, but they will find a way to thin *your* skin, send *your* hormones crashing. When the first spongy-nippled teenager crawled out of the primordial mud and found herself facing a predator, she felt the breeze on her spleen and said, "You're older than my mom, right?" or "Do you get pants at normal stores?" or "Do you want me to introduce you to my uncle Diego? He owns his own car."

So now I am at a podium in a bookstore lit like an airport, and I can see that the first three rows are stacked with teenagers. I can tell, because suddenly I am self-conscious about my own looks—am I greasy, do I look like a secretary in this blazer that I thought was cool this morning in the context of my executive suite? They have all read my book, they stained their minds for hours with the wet fantasy of a hurting woman's return to the sea. They cried and twitched their ankles when I described Sylvia's dark, dreamlike dives. And now they come to meet the sea witch who made this potion, and it's a woman with a bad back, hobbling, in Janet Yellen's conference wear.

Who are we kidding? None of these bitches knows who Janet Yellen is. What does Janet Yellen have to do with the crashing endocrine surf where these creatures play?

I'm looking at this concentration of teenagers with their one hundred percent stupid outfits that they care so much about. Look at them, all of their shoulders bared, peplums and pleather trims, for some reason a lot of prints that include pineapples, bright pineapples, capitalism flexing its silent biceps, showing it can make the world's most self-conscious people uniformly dress like uncles who get DUIs.

Among these teenagers, like a wooden eggcup on a shelf of costume jewelry, I see a girl. She wears a navy wool sweater that is slightly too big but not fashionably baggy. It looks like the kind of thing people wore in postwar Europe: something warm and durable that owes its existence to necessity and inflation. Every other garment in this audience owes its existence to the desire for nanosecond-newness, driving choice into the arbitrary and insane: a shirt with no shoulders? A shirt that says SHIRT on it?? This single girl wears a sweater because part of her is cold; the others wear their sweaters because part of them is empty. My focus clings to her. She doesn't notice, because she's reading. Eventually, things settle, turtleneck lady introduces me, and I, too, read.

I read from Sylvia's search for the wild mermaids. Afterward there is a Q and A. The woman in the turtleneck passes around a handheld microphone. A woman sitting next to her teenage daughter asks, "How did you decide to make Sylvia disabled, and did it come from your own experience?" No, I respond. I tell her that it started as a metaphor for being trapped, immobile. "But the more I wrote her, the more I felt not her disability but her power, even on land, where she can't use it. But isn't that true of everyone? When we come out into the dry marketplace to do business we have to wear these signs around our necks—but aren't you someone else entirely in the deepest parts of you?"

The teenage girl looks mortified that her mother may be about to answer a question publicly about her "deepest parts." Now I pin the daughter with my eyes.

"Sylvia, wise, powerful, protean Sylvia, has been convinced that she's broken as an entry fee to a civilization that wants to define achievement as masculine, dominating, individual, straight, rich. I don't know, does that sound like an experience *you* can relate to?"

Simultaneously, the teenage daughter says, "Not really," and her mother chokes on a sob.

Turtleneck moderator woman pulls the microphone from the mother's two-handed, white-knuckled grip and incants, "Metaphors *are* maaaaaagic. Okay, next question."

This one comes from an older woman: "I'm wondering if you've read any of the other literature surrounding mermaids currently being published? I'm thinking *Sirens* and *Call of the Deep*?"

I say I haven't read them, but that it seems to me that a lot of them are more in the genre of erotic fiction, which corresponds to the traditional myth of the mermaid but not "to their existence today." I realize "their existence today" doesn't make sense, so with a little eye roll, I add, "Well, I say that as if they existed." I shrug as if to say, *What a silly dreamer I am,* and there is a tremor of sympathetic laughter in the audience.

Last question?

The girl in the sweater looks up from her book, which she is reading again, and maybe was reading during my reading.

"Hi," she says. "I actually didn't really like your book."

"Okay," I say.

"Actually, I liked Masahiro's backstory. Seemed vaguely interesting."

Uh-huh. The dropping of the atom bomb is "vaguely interesting." Teenager alert.

"But I wanted to ask about one of your choices in particular that I didn't like."

"Sure."

"Why does she have to be unconscious when she goes underwater? Why don't we get access to that? Can't a woman retain her clearheadedness even when she's doing battle?"

"Well, she undergoes such powerful physiolo—"

"I think that your choice? Plays into masculinist stereotypes? About female hysteria? And muddy thinking. I would like her to go underwater and get *clearer,* report back to us readers even more clearly and vividly what it's like to dismantle EarthSource's geothermal infrastructure or recruit the wild mermaids. We have to get a picture of all this through a *man*'s perception of it, through Masahiro. You know?"

Turtleneck lady can't decide whether she's glad we have "dialogue" or whether this is a *conflict*. She's fingering the lip of her turtleneck frantically.

The teenager continues: "It strikes me you didn't have the courage to have her fully own herself underwater. We only really know her as a heroine as disabled, and constantly compromising—"

"Well, isn't that a reflection of—"

"One of the major problems with feminism"—now she is speaking to the room, not to me—"is that it is great at bitching about how hard it is to be a woman, but it fails to imagine the real fight, the real solutions, beyond, like, Beyoncé-brand leotards. I mean, I know it's fiction, but—"

As she's been speaking, I've been outwardly stable and attentive, but inwardly I've been feeling increasingly hot, lost, almost reeling. With her last words—"I know it's fiction, but"—the room falls away completely, and I imagine we are lying together on a bed or a beach, sharing a pillow, and I turn to her and say, as I'm saying now:

"Actually, it's not fiction. It's not fiction to me."

"No, I know," she says softly. Now she is not talking to the room anymore. Now she is talking only to me. "I know it's not fiction."

"There are places where it's easier to be a woman than others. A place where it's hard to be a woman is, you know, on land."

She chews her lip. Every pair of female eyeballs in this room is pinned on her, waiting for the parry, confused about who's winning. She doesn't say anything. I don't know how the room scores this, but I know her silence is a power move.

After the talk, my head buzzing a little as if I've just eaten a dozen oysters, and with the same thirst for beer, I slip outside into the bright white concrete embrace of the strip mall, the afternoon sun slicing into my eyes through cookie-cutter signage across the street. The girl is there, two doors down in front of a Starbucks, in her sensible sweater. She watches me, with little interest, as I hobble up to her.

"So you *are* actually disabled?" she asks.

"No, this is recent. I had an accident at the beach."

"Weird."

I don't want to be told I didn't deserve my own injury. I'm not giving this to her.

Fine, I'll give this to her:

"Why 'weird'?"

"Just seems like beaches are soft."

"People die at the beach all the time. Haven't you ever seen *Baywatch*?"

"I've heard of Normandy."

"Jesus Christ."

"THAT'S A JOKE," she says.

Goddammit! How did she make *me* the humorless one! I'm so chill and funny! *She's* the self-serious teenager!

She says nothing, watching me; her eyes seem to petrify, like recently molded plastic, cooling off.

"Do you want to get a drink?" I ask.

"I'm sixteen," she says.

"Oh, right." I take a pack of Camel Lights out of my bag, needing a reason to stay here. "Sorry you didn't like the book."

"It's cool. My ride will be here in a sec."

"Oh, cool, me too." I feel a cold current of fear that she will leave and I will never get to talk to her again, but I don't know why this is so important to me all of a sudden. I tend to be grateful to my readers in the collective but afraid of them in the singular. "Do you want me to come speak at your school?"

"No."

"Yeah, I guess schools don't do that kind of thing anymore."

"No, they do."

Cars pull out, coughing to life, crunching the asphalt. The parking lot, the shape of a rounded rectangular speech bubble, is emptying out. "Thank you," say several people as they pass. I want this girl to notice how polite, even obsequious, all of the other people sound when they talk to me.

"All right, well, have a good day. Thanks for coming. Thanks for your . . . comment." I'm being the bigger person.

"You should read Tolstoy," she spits back.

That's it.

"I'm a WOMAN and I'm writing from within my own experience as a woman and I'm sorry mine didn't match yours or something." My voice rises, against my will: "But I guess Tolstoy's did."

"He's just really good with psychological complexity," she says by way of explanation, calm.

"Also, don't tell me to read Tolstoy, I'm an English teacher."

"You sound like the patriarchy." I'm still fishing for a lighter, now shaking my head and rolling my eyes like a beleaguered sitcom husband with a ball-breaker feminist wife. Every move I make is wrong; this is word chess and she's taking all my pawns.

"Have you read Tolstoy's *Ten Wives for Two Brothers*?" she asks.

"Obviously."

A Subaru pulls up, driven by a thin woman in sunglasses having a full-blown conversation with her hands-free system. "JUST PICKING UP VANESSA" blares out for a few seconds when the girl opens the door, swings her backpack down, and slams it shut. The Subaru pulls away. I see a FAIR VALLEY PREPARATORY sticker on the bumper as the Subaru curls away and then turns out onto the highway.

I put the cigarette back in its box, notice the lighter was in there the whole time. I pull out my phone, Google *Ten Wives for Two Brothers*. She made it up. Goddamn teenagers. Checkmate. Do not go to war with women in a state of becoming. Their dark arts are deep and indomitable.

CHAPTER 37

EXCERPT FROM *AMERICAN MERMAID*

Eleanor Granger was afraid to let go of old habits, afraid of melting altogether.

She slid the proofed rolls into the hot oven, slammed the door, and slipped off the oven mitts. Dean was in Vágar; what would she do with forty rolls?

She set a ticking timer the shape of a tomato and slipped it into her pocket.

Dean swore that he was looking for Sylvia; that they had their best people on it and they were coordinating with the authorities. But updates were scant, and when she asked to speak with the investigators or the FBI, Dean would tell her that it would only make her upset, that it wasn't looking good; they had to prepare for the worst. She knew that Dean would do anything for her, but sometimes when she drank too much, anger would rise in her out of nowhere. *Dean knows more than he's saying. Dean's not grieving like I am. How could he leave me alone to go work at a time like this?* The wave of anger would surge and then fall in the pit of her stomach with a nauseating *crash,* and like a seasick passenger of her own body she would have to grip a countertop or a bannister.

She'd sober up, full of guilt for having entertained nasty and accusatory fantasies, and grab a bag of bread flour.

Dean's focus on his company these past few weeks must be his version of baking, she told herself. He, too, must be trying to keep the fear and panic about Sylvia's whereabouts at bay. He had gone full steam into this new CleanBeam energy thing, organizing the launch on an accelerated schedule, flying off to Vágar in a huff to finish his new underground lab, built into a cliff at the level of the seafloor.

She drank the last few drops of a bottle of Chianti and was about to take the elevator to the basement wine cellar. But she remembered it had jammed yesterday. So she grabbed her keys and pivoted to the utility staircase. Down, down, down. The stairwell was so damp it almost smelled like the woods. She had stopped going for walks outside. Contemplative environments weren't safe for her in her grief. Out in nature her imagination was liable to produce visions of Sylvia in distress, lifeless in an alley or choking in the sea.

She had the vague feeling she'd gone down one floor past the cellar. *Is there a floor below the cellar?* She felt suddenly embarrassed to be lost in her own house, like a real drunk.

She put the cellar key into the lock, but it didn't work.

"Why does everything break when Dean is away?" She sighed, leaning against the damp wall. There was another key on the keyring. She had never used that one. But she stuck it into the lock anyway.

The door opened.

Twelve minutes later, when Eleanor Granger's timer rang, she stood in the center of an abandoned laboratory, her hand resting on a full glass tank the size of a hotel pool. The room was walled with heaving gun racks and plastered with nautical maps of all the channels and inlets of Vágar, gridded and dotted with pins.

There was a control panel attached to the tank. Eleanor pushed a button at random, and the tank began to shake. It generated waves, storm-high waves, that followed one another rhythmically and then fell with a deafening noise: *crash, crash, crash.*

CHAPTER 38

A chat between me and Randy and Murphy.

    Randy: Who are you guys thinking about for EG?
    Murphy: Who's EG?
    Penelope: You mean Eleanor?
    Randy: Eleanor Granger ya
    Murphy: I don't know, Meryl Streep?
    Randy: I can't think of anyone else

CHAPTER 39

Derek radiates the generic drugstore version of Old Spice, which is even more old and spicy than the real thing. It's a revolting odor: cabinet spices and lemon and tree bark and then something sick and male and glandular, an announcement of something wrong somewhere hairy. It's not fair that it marbles the air anyplace there are men, that they get to casually broadcast a smell you should smell only if you've consented to resting your face on a dying pasha's balls. I've disliked Old Spice since I first crossed it as a kid in cabs, in supermarkets, standing too close to the teacher.

Now I have a teacher in my bed. We've done this before. We talk ourselves to sleep, our responses shortening as we go, and sometimes, when we're both almost asleep, Derek entreats me, with subtlest poetizing, to make love.

"Yo, P, should we bang?"

"No." It's not just the smell of his armpits, of benzoin and male death. I would never. I don't. With anyone.

"Cooool," he says, with a long, compressed, tubular "ooo," a million miles from all that California "coal." The exchange is oddly comforting to us both.

A few minutes of silence. Derek breathing deeply.

"Derek?"

"Mm."

"How come you never read my book?"

"I don't know."

When I first started writing the book, when all I had was little paragraphs, little descriptions of swimming or of Sylvia's aching body, I read them to Derek in his car, and he always said, "More, more—do more." "I don't know what it is," I'd say, and he'd say things like "It doesn't matter, keep going, you'll figure it out." Susie was the only other person I told when I realized it was a novel, and she called me a "noony poon" and asked if it was "all, like, duchesses." If it weren't for Derek, Sylvia would never have been realized.

"I gave you a copy," I remind him. One of the first galleys.

"Let's talk about it another time."

We fall silent again. My mind is making those pre-sleep dreams that you can still examine, and they're full of the teenager who came to my reading. She swims in a pool that my subconscious borrowed from the Instagram post of a rich girl named Alwyn whom I went to college with who is always on vacation. It was some pool in Sri Lanka, at a resort overlooking tea fields where you could see the people picking tea. Now, in my dream, this teenage girl from the reading is in the pool and I'm aware that I'll join her in the pool soon, too, and she says, "Yoo-hoo!" She starts laughing at herself for saying "Yoo-hoo," repeats it again in a mocking exaggeration. The "ooo" sound is taken from Derek's "cool." She puts her head back, her messy brown hair splaying into the water, the water reflecting a lilac sky I stole from Alwyn Berkin's lifelong vacation, from her callous, sun-soaked, three-week troll of the tea-pickers of Sri Lanka. I step toward the pool and fall into it suddenly, twitching myself awake.

"Derek."

"I'm too tired now."

"No, no. I want to find this girl."

"What?"

"The one from the reading."

"The mean one?"

"I know what school she goes to. But can you just show up at any old school?"

"Sure you can. We're teachers. We can walk into any school." He's talking into his pillow. I can't tell if he's serious.

"You can't waltz into one school because you work at another, it's not like Soho House."

"Wow, you suck now."

"Anyway, it's summer."

There's a long pause. I think he's asleep. Then he says, "I'll help you." At his first job interview, for some summer thing at a law firm, they asked him what his hobbies were and he said, "Mail bombs." It was not a job he wanted. But still. I don't know if he's my man on this one.

"Just get her info from the principal. Make something up." That's actually not bad. Or is it. I start drafting an email in my mind:

Dear Principal X. I am a high school English teacher from Connecticut. I am spending the summer in LA. I recently met a very bright student from your school at a reading and promised her I would be in touch. However, I've lost her contact information. Would you be so kind as to etc. etc.

"Why are you obsessed with this chick?"

"I don't know," I say. We are both falling asleep again, me answering the question with another dream of myself and her. She's holding my hand, and we're running through a film studio lot, painted backboards of other landscapes towering above us. "I'll show you," she says, "I know what you're capable of."

CHAPTER 40

EXCERPT FROM *AMERICAN MERMAID*

It was time to see what Sylvia could do. It was time to look at the GoPro footage.

Rain tapped gently on the windows of the rental car. Masahiro wadded up a waxy paper wrapper and tossed it into the back seat. Sylvia put her foam tray of cold fries aside.

"Okay," she said. "I'm ready."

"You sure?" asked Masahiro. He scanned her face, her downcast eyes, the little wisps of hair still sticking to her temples from the dash from the diner in the rain to the car. She wasn't dejected, he knew; she was steely. She wanted to see what was on the GoPro.

"Before we see this, remember: Lawrence came there to kill me. He might have killed us both."

Sylvia nodded. She and Masahiro had an idea of what they might find. Lawrence had been there, and then he had disappeared. Sylvia, the Sylvia they knew, had been physically dependent and frail her whole life. She had never hurt anyone. It seemed impossible, far-fetched, to think that she had bested a two-hundred-and-twenty-pound brawler. But they couldn't figure out an alternative. And they didn't know this Sylvia.

"I only remember the beginning," she said. She swallowed. "And the very end." She described coming out of the water to find Masahiro on shore, bloody and unconscious. Confused and with the pain of transition mounting, she had clawed her way up to the doctor, opened his kit, washed the sand out of his wound, and bandaged it. She found a six-inch knife near Masahiro, sticky with blood. She wiped it clean and held on to it. Exhausted but afraid—would someone follow to finish whatever violence had begun here?—she pulled herself up into the wheelchair and waited, gripping the handle of the knife.

Masahiro, now working with a heavily bandaged right hand, plugged the GoPro into his laptop and brought up the footage in a grainy rectangular window. The first image was a close-up on Masahiro's face as he released her into the water, and then darkness as she plunged, pure black with a glowing center illuminated by the GoPro beam. Debris crossed her illuminated path as she swam, first slowly and then zipping past the screen, flying in one direction and then the next. They watched for what felt like a long time.

As Sylvia watched the screen, a little smile crept onto her face. These GoPros were meant to capture dizzying dirt-biking or the view of a fjord from a glider. Sylvia's murky footage would seem to have captured precisely nothing. But she saw in the streaming specks and the streaked darkness the testimony of her speed, of her power, of her knowledge about a world that a sportsman's thrill-recorder would call empty.

Occasionally her arms crossed in front of her, but she knew she didn't need her arms to power ahead. "I'm playing," she murmured. Masahiro, transfixed, smiled, too. They both jumped and Masahiro let out a little yelp as there was a sudden scuffle in the light, a quick movement of something illuminated bright white and then gone. Then, less suddenly, from the side of the window, it reappeared: a small fishtail.

"A-HA!" said Masahiro. He looked at her proudly. "You *are* a hunter."

But now something else was happening. With a sloshy sound, the camera emerged at the top of the water, just above the surface. It turned around, searching for shore, and then slowly approached.

Masahiro was visible in the distance, sitting cross-legged on the towel. But Sylvia, instead of approaching Masahiro directly, took a circuitous route, cleaving close to shore, mostly underwater, coming up occasionally, it seemed, to spy on the doctor.

"Maybe I see you being hurt," she said, but Lawrence hadn't appeared yet. Sylvia rounded a bank of reeds, dipping underwater and coming up just above the surface to keep eyes on Masahiro as she came closer. By that point she was six or seven meters away from Masahiro on his towel. Only then did Lawrence emerge behind the doctor on the path.

"There he is," said Sylvia.

Masahiro stopped the footage. "You sure you want to see this? Should we take a break?"

She shook her head. They turned back to the screen. Masahiro pressed play. The video captured all of it—the flash of the knife in Lawrence's hand, Masahiro scrambling out from under his attacker, wounded, darting away with startling speed. And then there it was, so slow as to be nearly romantic: Lawrence, staring straight into the camera, for two, three minutes as he moved toward the water. His face came closer and closer, dark swooshes of Masahiro's blood across his Mets jacket becoming visible. But his eyes—they were like the eyes of a man coming in for a kiss, softened and overjoyed. Relaxed. This man had been a background figure in Granger's world for years, always tough, unreadable, a gun safe of selfish calculations and violent brags. Yet here, onscreen, he was a vision of quivering emotional nakedness, eyebrows angled down, eyes longing. He even walked in a completely unfamiliar way, languidly—ridiculously, if you knew Lawrence—like a dancer cueing his every muscle to the aural experience of ambient beauty.

Then he knelt down, facing the screen, until his face came in too close and disintegrated into pixelation. As Sylvia pulled away for a moment, the screen showed one last image of a man in love. It was an image, if you'd frozen it and shown it to a stranger, of a nice guy, smiling in a home video, just given a cake or a compliment, until behind his head slipped Sylvia's long arms, and then it was black again, just the glow and the debris. Occasionally a puffy, darkly clad arm crossed the screen, at first moving frantically, then not at all. Finally, after several minutes, she backed away slightly, looking down at him, and the screen gave one last image of the man, through a few feet of dirty water, an indistinct face glowing greenish-white in the GoPro's beams and the arms out on either side as if relaxing on a sun chair. Then she was racing again, into the darkness.

"You must have pulled him out into deeper water," said Masahiro. "You were calculating."

"Calculating what?" said Sylvia.

"You didn't want him to wash up right away, or right there, where we'd been. You're hiding your work."

There was a long silence, the GoPro footage still just streaming debris in the darkness.

"What are we waiting for," said Masahiro, "the credits?"

Sylvia put her head in her hands, not crying but overwhelmed by seeing the film version of an experience she couldn't remember. And what it showed—something she could never imagine herself capable of. But then little moments did start to come back to her, triggered by the film. Her own limbs stored a memory of the underwater dance of gently shoving the big body lower and lower, as it writhed and writhed and then stopped. She had barely needed to touch him, once she'd pulled him under. It made her think of her mother handwashing the polyester seat cushions and liners of her wheelchair in the bathtub once a week. Eleanor would just tap them down with the tips of her fingers from above; once waterlogged, they stopped rising. Sylvia didn't remember precisely what she'd done with the body or when she'd come back, but that gesture of tapping him down she could still feel in her fingertips.

The video left her with a new set of questions. She'd spent so long not knowing who she was, and then that night in Boston Harbor, when she swam for the first time, she'd finally had an answer: she was something strong and beautiful.

Now she was a stranger again. A killer.

"You saved both our lives, Sylvia," said Masahiro, trying to pull her back from dark thoughts. "Thank god for that song."

"What song?" said Sylvia.

"What do you mean?" said Masahiro. "Your song. Oh, you're right, it doesn't get picked up by the audio. It must be some other kind of frequency . . ."

"What—what song?" asked Sylvia again.

Masahiro looked her in the eyes, held her puzzled gaze as if he could stir her memory of the music with his own memory of it, by feeling again that feeling of—of a loved one laughing in his ear, of a private joke told through tune.

"What do you *mean*?"

"You lured Lawrence away from me with a song. I heard it, too. It was—I can't compare it to anything I've ever heard."

"When did it start?"

"I don't know," he said. "I noticed it after I stopped running from Lawrence, at the top of the path, when I realized he wasn't behind me."

Sylvia looked away, covering her mouth. "Doc. I think I remember the feeling. Oh no . . ."

"Sylvia, what is it? You can tell me."

"Think about it: What am I doing in this video?"

"It's okay, Sylvia, he was a bad man. You were protecting me, protecting yourself."

"No, think: What was I doing *before* the attack."

"You were swimming. You came back—"

"What am I doing, clinging to the shore? Popping up like that?"

"I don't know . . ."

"Doc, I'm stalking you."

Masahiro paused. It was true, she had moved stealthily toward him, keeping him in her sights like a hunter. But—"How do we know you weren't protecting me? Just watching?"

"You weren't in any danger yet. I had no reason to surveil you. Remember the blood under my fingernails after the first swim in Boston Harbor? We don't know for sure what that was. What if I was going to kill you?"

"You would never, Sylvia."

"We don't know *who I am* when I'm down there. We can't trust me."

"Whatever you become when you go under—we're just going to have to face her. Your father has found us. He knows we're alive. It's only a matter of time before he gets his hands on us. Our best chance now is to *find him first* and dismantle those machines. Did you ever wonder why your dad pushed so hard for you to study fracture mechanics? He wants you to be able to run Earth-Source with him. But your training also means you can take these machines apart, you can disable his infrastructure. And it's now or never, look." Masahiro reached into a stack of papers by his feet and tossed Sylvia the Business section of the *New York Times*: "Environmentalists Cheer as Investors Line Up." The CleanBeam launch was in two days.

"But I thought you said he needed the mermaids to staff CleanBeam. Do you think he's found them?"

"God, I hope not. Maybe it's a bluff. Or maybe he's decided he can't wait any longer. He'll fire up the machines, and when they feel their ecosystem cooking, the mermaids will come knock on his door."

"But we can't go to Vágar."

"We have to." Masahiro put the key into the ignition and turned on the windshield wipers. They squeaked and banged from side to side. "It's the only way to find the mermaids, protect them, and stop Granger."

Sylvia fell into a sort of trance, as she often did in the car. The rain fell loud on the tinny roof, the windshield wipers drummed along. As she stared at the passing strip malls and the slushing traffic, the fast-food signs and the stoplights, blurry and misted through the window, Sylvia imagined herself pulling Masahiro into the water as she had pulled Lawrence. She imagined an amoral, selfish animal hunger driving a powerful female mind. Is this what her immunity to sexual love granted her? Free of caring, free of pleasing, free to take lives.

"I wonder what she's like, the other Sylvia," said Masahiro. "I would like to meet your mermaid self." Masahiro, too, had a dreamy look on his face, as if, while Sylvia had been envisioning herself as a pitiless thief of life, he had been imagining a seaborne friend, Sylvia with salmon breath.

"Not if she kills you, you wouldn't."

He looked at Sylvia. "There are two possibilities. One: you were coming back to save me. Two: you were coming back to kill me."

"That's what I'm saying."

"I don't believe you were coming to kill me. I know you. But if you *were*—I'm okay with that."

Sylvia gave him a level glare.

"I don't want to die. You saw me fight for my life. Did you see me run away from Lawrence? It was impressive. I sprinted like it was the eighty-eight Olympics and I was full of phenylpropanolamine." A little smile crept onto her face. Only he would make a *very* niche pharmacological joke and then look at her with the big, expectant eyes of a lounge comic killing it. "But I would be okay with dying," he continued, "if it meant some kind of—I don't know. If it had to happen."

The idea of losing him was, as she'd shown the world once already, unbearable.

"It doesn't have to happen."

"Sylvia, realizing you existed changed my whole idea of the world. You think I've taught you things? Not a fraction of what you've taught me. About evolution and biology and the accidents that lead to one species owning the planet while another hides. But also about toughness, and forgiveness, and—believe it or not—love. Love that doesn't get you anything but maybe . . . survival. Helping you get back to the sea—and stopping Granger from bringing it to a boil—is worth anything. Everything."

He had become expansive, staring into the middle distance, but now he turned to her, animated. "Plus, Sylvia, you *came back*. Why go through the pain of transition, why become human again, ever? You must retain some consciousness of yourself, and a will to rejoin me, even if you can't remember it."

Sylvia nodded. He had a point. She'd come back and bandaged him. He had been vulnerable, unconscious on the beach, and she'd passed through an agonizing transition to crawl up to him, stop him from bleeding out, and protect him from further harm.

Masahiro parked in front of the hotel.

"I want to do some more training," Sylvia said. "In the pool."

Masahiro looked at his phone. "No time, we're off to Newark."

"We're going to Vágar?"

Masahiro nodded.

"Isn't that exactly what he wants?"

"Don't worry, we'll be on the island for a matter of minutes."

Sylvia thought about it. "We're renting a boat?"

Masahiro's eyebrows danced. "Aye-aye."

Masahiro stepped out of the car and came around with Sylvia's wheelchair. He lifted her into the chair, and they turned toward the hotel.

"Doc, do you know anything about boats?"

"Not a thing," said Masahiro. "What's the worst that could happen?" he asked, slamming the handicap button outside the entrance. The two doors slowly gaped open like the jaws of a whale, and Masahiro, with Sylvia's wheelchair before him, glided through. "Are we gonna drown?"

CHAPTER 41

An email from Murphy titled "SYLVIA'S FINAL DEAD DEAD DEATH SCENE" catches my eye, in bold at the top of my email inbox. He and Randy want my notes. I will have to drink extra to forget this.

I am at a party, lying on a cushioned lounger next to a dark, empty swimming pool at night. I'm still looking for Stem Hollander, who people say is here, and I'm supposed to connect with a writer named Jill Something—I forgot her last name already—who runs a show about a female superhero. But I don't know how to find anyone if I can't move. Fireworks of pain have been lighting up my coccyx today, so Danielle left me here—propped me up, put two tequila-sodas next to me, and said she'd be right back.

I hear someone say, "It's like Petrarch, ache, and archery combined." I crane my head around in disbelief, but all I see is a foursome talking a few feet away, turned in toward one another, all tanned elbows facing out as they hold their drinks and laugh. Is someone here, at this pool party in Brentwood at the house of married lesbian entertainment lawyers, talking about Petrarch?

I loved Petrarch when they made me read him in grad school. He seemed kind of lazy. He had one poem that just listed rivers: "Po, Varo, Arno, Adige." And then at the end of that list of rivers, "the breaking sea," nameless and huge, that much bigger for not needing the monument of a capital letter. "The breaking sea," unsqueezed by settlement. I've never been so startled to see the sea.

And what are the proper names of rivers and the sudden sea doing in a love poem? They're not Love rushing through him or Love big like the sea. He's deliberately ignoring Love, warding it off by writing poems about stupid wet water—poems, he writes, to "the sound of water." Petrarch, too, had sonar. He turned off his ears to sexy love and turned his sonar to the sea, seeing it do what servile rivers and self-spending lovers never will: break, break, break, unharmed in its unknowable depth.

This is my kind of love poem. He offered himself to Laura like an unsexy, sexless, useless thing. *Here I am, a guy who'd rather read an atlas than talk about your sweet lips.* If that's what love is, then won't it bind us all collectively instead of being a thing that makes two vain shitheads hump? Thrilled and stunned to hear his name here, my ally, I think I should go to the hills outside Padua and dig up Petrarch's body and tell him they are talking about him at a cool party in LA. Maybe they're making a movie of his life.

"Who's playing me?" Petrarch would ask.

"Mark Ruffalo," I would say.

"Goddammit," says Petrarch, with a rattle of his bone jaw. "I wanted Tom Hanks."

"Ruffalo's a good actor."

"Yeah, but Hanks is Hanks. Plus, I looked like Tom Hanks."

He looked like Dick Cheney, but I don't want to antagonize him.

Petrarch begs me to make them include the deathbed scene where he bequeaths his rival Boccaccio a heap of florins for a decent dressing gown. I break it to him: "Not likely; I think the movie is all about the whole forbidden love story of you and Laura." Petrarch, lifting himself up on his parched elbow in the black soil, furious, says, "But we didn't even bang! That was the whole point!"

"Try telling *them* that," I say, wise and tired from my own Hollywood adventure, now lying parallel to him in the soil, on my elbow, like we're babes on a beach towel. I'm staring over the white rim of his orbital bone into the hole where his eye lived. I'll unload about Murphy and Randy and how "you need some kind of *drive*, they tell me," and he'll say, "The flight from idolatry and lust in the face of our Lord isn't sufficient drive?" I'll say no. The skeleton slowly turns his skull side to side. But now, into my own daydream, Randy and Murphy materialize in their crisp shorts out of the blue-green cypress trees between the poet's grave and his terra-cotta villa. Randy holds up his hands in two connecting *L*s like a viewfinder through which he looks at the two of us (me and Petrarch's bones, lounging in black dirt). Murphy says, "This is perfect. Cut to you fucking."

In reality, I'm on a lounger, the lacquered slats of it rattling as I laugh alone. The group of four people near me holding drinks watch me, in total silence.

"Sorry," I say. "I was thinking about something."

"No worries," says a voice out of the quatrefoil of bodies. It adds, "What were you laughing about?"

"I was imagining fucking a skeleton."

"Ew!" says one of them.

"Of a famous person!" I add.

"Oh! Well! That's okay!" they all chime together, laughing hugely like they'll remember this someday, even though they won't. I've catapulted myself out of a zone of fatigue and anxiety into a sudden surge of fellow feeling with these tanned, glossy-voiced laughers on the white lapel of a tiled pool. After all, who am I anymore that I love these rich homes and this easy life almost enough to cover the panic of what I'm letting happen to my beloved story, to a story I *believe*? But what could be wrong in a place so flat, with hot stones underfoot and the plastic slats of the lounger clicking under me like crabs clapping their claws in applause as I giggle?

"Which famous person?" one of them asks.

"Petrarch, the poet," I say.

"Who's Petrarch?"

"Weren't you guys just talking about him?"

"Oh, is *that* who that is?"

"Is what who what is?"

"Are you talking about the guy they named 'patriarchy' after?"

I still want them to be my friends, this foursome that is game for laughing and talking to me.

"They named patriarchy after fathers."

"Whose father? The poet guy's father?"

"No, just fathers."

"Like Father's Day?"

I think I can agree with this and live with myself and be happy and live in California forever in my stucco castle where I write movies with Jill McNowhere while somewhere in the no-place of the internet Stem Hollander, like a million-thumbed Vishnu, smiles upon my every work.

"Yeah, like Father's Day."

CHAPTER 42

"Susie tells me you're a new kind of gay." I wouldn't have picked up the phone if I'd known it was my dad. He tricked me, calling from the landline, the earthy, irrelevant terrain of my mother.

"I'm not anything."

"That's exactly what she said."

"Is this why you're calling? I have an important meeting."

Derek sits against the refrigerator with a pained face, slowly putting an erect slice of long-refrigerated pizza into his mouth and chewing mechanically. He's been trying to eat his way through the stacks of it. Derek never managed to locate a shelter to which we might deliver Michelangelo's spare pizza. So every night for two weeks he's picked up six to ten boxes of unsold pizza and brought them up to the apartment.

The whole apartment has a salty-sick waft, and the entire kitchen floor and half the living room are stacked with white cardboard boxes bearing the red-printed compound lie PIZZA FRESHLY MADE FOR YOU. I've kept the cleaning woman out for five days. There's a whole pizza under the lid of the scanner, sticking out like a Muppet's tongue. But Derek can't take the boxes out of the building, because he doesn't want the guys from Michelangelo's to know he never found a homeless shelter and took all the pizza for himself, and the pizzeria is directly beside the entrance to the building. Derek is a structure made unstable by the ungiving beams of principle that run through him at inconsistent and inconvenient angles:

I believe he may eat seventy-five cold pizzas. This morning I asked him how he planned on making the pizza boxes disappear without taking them outside. He said, "Let me think!" and started eating the slices in a huff and suggesting, in the tone of a senior manager at an important strategy meeting, that weed would help. He's been on the floor for ninety minutes and conversation has been scarce.

Over the phone, my father turns wistful, his tone a distant lament. "It's become so unfashionable now to do what your mother and I did."

"What. Start hippie and go Republican? Hoard money?"

"Get married and have kids! Start a family. *Value family*."

I remember Felicia, emanating her easy vapors in Danielle's living room, describing the half naked man at the party: *Some nobody,* she had said, *someone's family*.

"I'm not interested in talking about this," I say. "We're finalizing our script for a big table read with some studio honchos and big-name celebs. I have a lot of work to do."

HONCHOS. What is a *honcho*? I've never said this word. Only the sycophant anchorettes of *Entertainment Tonight* emit the occasional "honcho" from between the squirming earthworms of their glossed lips. Derek is jumping on pizza boxes to try to collapse them into as small a size as possible. I surmise his plan is to put them in garbage bags and sneak them out like bodies in the night.

"Your mother told me a story that I found very troubling."

"Uh-huh. There will be no saltwater fish by 2050?"

He releases a slow, exasperated sigh. The sound of this particular sigh, its length and frequency, gives me the vision that he's taking his glasses off and rubbing the bridge of his nose.

"Your mother plays tennis with Denise Mortenbauer at the club. Her husband David's a bond trader at UBC. He also plays tennis at the club, but he's a very poor athlete. I think he had a bypass in his midfifties, which might have something to do with it, but he was never blue-ribbon material. I think he does fine as a bond trader."

"There's no reason I need to know this."

He continues.

"Denise and David's son Chase is some kind of TV guy in LA. He told his mother, who told your mother—I mean, I can't believe this—"

"I remember Chase." We went to high school together. He was two years older than me. He was a physics and chemistry genius with a silky bowl cut who went to Harvard. We expected him to cure cancer. He produces highly successful prank shows where, for example, three snickering dudes in a food truck sell burritos full of dog shit to hipsters at a festival. He makes gazillions of dollars.

"Well, he says you showed up to a party with a gun and started shooting it. I mean—*what the fudge*."

My face flushes as if I've done something terribly wrong and am in trouble.

"I didn't *shoot anyone*."

There's a sudden *pop* sound, and I jump. I turn around to see Derek on the ground, on his side, having thrown his body weight onto a stack of boxes.

"And I didn't bring a gun anywhere."

All of the pizza boxes Derek had previously folded have defiantly unfurled back into flat squares, barely kinked. He's rolling on a mound of them, attempting a prolonged compression. I shut myself in the bathroom for some silence and sit on the closed lid of the hateful modern square toilet that bruises my soft thighs in the night and that, because I'm on the phone with my dad, I suddenly imagine he designed.

"Chase Mortenbauer is a choad and God hates him!" What I would give to have said anything different, to have archly delivered the cool winning point of the debater. But I can't. It's a magic my father has, to effect some electrochemical shift within me in which I become blinded and rage-filled. I black out, I become a teenager, the teacher in me eclipsed by a flowing substance that in another world might be powerful but that here, in his world, only drowns my word function and makes me, to his ears, inarticulate.

"A *toad*?"

"A CHOAD!"

"A *what*? You don't make *sense*. Speak *English*. And don't you take the Lord's name in vain! I think you're losing your marbles out there, Penelope. I can't believe what we're hearing."

"I can't believe Chase Mortenbauer is tattling on me. I was a big hit at that party and met some very important people and Chase Mortenbauer is probably just threatened by a successful woman in his lane."

I have cracked the door to the toilet open to the sight of the cleaning lady standing just within the threshold of the apartment. Jaw dropped, she eyes the far edge of the pizza pile. Derek, lying on a stack of two dozen pizza boxes, one hand rubbing a circle on his tummy, tries to wave her in with a stiff pizza flag. She shakes her head vigorously.

"You know what, this meeting is starting. I've got to go. Stop believing bullshit—"

"BULLCORN."

"—from a stranger about how I'm losing it out here. I'm making all the right connections."

"With that mouth, I don't believe it."

"Different mouths for different worlds, Harold."

"Is that Penny?" My mother's voice floats in from what I can calculate based on distance and echo is the kitchen. "Hold on, don't hang up," she says. "I want to hear her voice."

CHAPTER 43

EXCERPT FROM *AMERICAN MERMAID*

"My mother never told me her experience of that day, and I never asked. I've read a thousand accounts of it now, and there are common points.

"Everyone had become used to the sound of raids and their effects. Bombs were loud, they left craters where they hit. Fire was an enemy you knew. It exploded in reliable ways, even with accelerants like magnesium and jelly gas. They had prepared for fire, cleared streets and installed firebreaks.

"This was different. A flash of light, and then nothing. Then, a massive gust of wind. Strange effects. People stunned. People burned where they were hit by light, as if a giant flash photograph had been taken of the city, and anything captured directly was, depending on proximity to the camera, incinerated or scorched. But 'burned' isn't the right word. It had nothing to do with fire. Many people describe using the word 'magic' in the minutes and hours after the flash: some terrible magic trick."

Sylvia sat next to Masahiro in the SAS jet to Copenhagen, where an oval portal to a purple sky framed the doctor's profile. She must have looked distressed, because Masahiro stalled and slipped into his most hushed tone.

"I said I would tell you how Granger could compel me to do whatever he wanted, even operate on a perfect infant and keep it a secret for over twenty years; how I—a *good* doctor, Sylvia, a caring doctor—could throw medical confidentiality out the window and report on you like you were one of Granger's fracking wells. I'm not invoking Hiroshima to horrify you for no reason: the story starts here."

They were in neither Sylvia's natural home nor Masahiro's, neither sea nor land. They traveled under assumed names, and they were now lofted up between countries, between known and unknown. The aural cocoon of white noise was like a drug. It impeded thought and made Sylvia sleepy. As realities of time and place became unthinkable, Masahiro's story unfolded like a Twilight of the Gods—it was hard to believe that what he described was historical and not cosmic. It was hard to believe people didn't talk about it every day, that we hadn't restarted the human calendar the day after.

"My mother was in a train on the way to school. That's all I know. In a window seat. I don't advise you to look at pictures. The way skin went from pink to black within hours. The way skin split or peeled off in tissue-thin wisps. You saw your friends' and neighbors' faces, pitch-black and swollen twofold, grotesque masks. Mothers and their children unrecognized by each other. For others, a single dark mark might appear on the skin. Within weeks it would become a suppurating laceration that wouldn't heal.

"With a normal bomb, you could be killed or maimed horribly, but you could tally your damage right away. What my mother experienced was more like a curse. I read of one woman reunited with her teenage son, who had been doing volunteer work just outside the city center. He had been protected by thick factory walls from the immediate rays of the blast. He returned to his village, an hour's train ride outside the city, on the other side of the mountains, sheltered from the fallout. The mother felt so lucky. But one day, her son walked into the garden with blood pouring from his eyes and fell to the ground dead midstride. Others regrew hair and regained strength only to be diagnosed with leukemia in two years or ovarian cancer in twenty. They lived in fear and anxiety, and the society in which they lived agreed they were cursed and made them outcasts. Undesirable, unmarriable, cordoned off for fear that their curse might catch.

"My mother was sixteen at the time, and a great beauty. I knew this wasn't just family lore, because it was preserved in half of her face. When I was little, if we were at the grocery store or in a park and I was standing behind her, I would see people stare at the side of her face, but I would forget which side was which. Were they staring because she was so arrestingly beautiful or because she was so disfigured? The reaction was often the same. Attempt to be discreet, attempt to linger and look longer. Fascination."

Sylvia nodded, listening. It was easy to imagine this woman, half annihilated by the ingenuity of men.

"It may seem strange that she wanted to come to America, until you know what she endured in the years after the bomb. She had at least two surgeries in Hiroshima, one a graft of skin from her thigh onto her face, the other an attempt to remove scar tissue from her arms to restore some mobility." He closed his eyes and took a deep breath. "The only anesthetic available was topical novocaine. No anesthesia."

He looked right at Sylvia now.

"I know you can imagine. I *try* to imagine. It's the least I can do for her." A ghost of Sylvia's own pain rose up in her, so that the vision of Masahiro's mother in Sylvia's mind was also a feeling in her body.

"Men who were damaged faced discrimination. But women at that time were primarily candidates for marriage and childbirth. A strong, healthy body was capital. A woman damaged by the bomb lost every prospect, whereas a man might still work, find some kind of place.

"My mother once said the bombs were named wrong. They shouldn't have been Little Boy and Fat Man. They were women, the generators of all matter, sought out and enriched, then split open. As a child, one of the first things I looked up at the library was the bomb. I remember thinking the way they had enriched the uranium first, before smashing it, was like Hansel and Gretel, how they were first fattened. Given cookies and cakes so that they'd be wobbly and loaded up with themselves, extra defenseless and combustible when the time came.

"She had planned to continue her studies in Japan but even walking to the market was both physically difficult and a gauntlet of minor cruelties on the part of neighbors and strangers—laughing schoolchildren, dirty looks. Despite the devastation that American science had just wreaked, science drew her to the US. It was the promise of superior medical treatment in America at the hands of cutting-edge doctors in the most advanced country on earth."

Masahiro's pauses elongated. At one point, he lunged out at the aisle when a flight attendant passed, and asked, desperately but inexpertly, for a drink ("a wine?"). Sometimes, it seemed he forgot Sylvia was there. But there she was, still and alert, as most other passengers shivered under thin blankets and dozed.

"Of her schoolmates," he continued, "she was one of ten survivors in a class of fifty-three. They had all been near the center, the camera."

He told her about Dr. Powell, the radiation specialist who received Masahiro's mother in the US and gave her a home. Once the publicity faded, the church group who had arranged her immigration receded, having placed her in the hands of a world-famous doctor. And when the doctor slowly drew the curtain around her, Masahiro's mother was purely a captive. No one was coming to check on her. When people were reminded of her existence—Masahiro's teachers, his friends' parents, the hospital staff who assisted in her treatment—all anyone thought was *She must be so grateful.*

"She lived in a little white house not far from the Cleveland hospital where Dr. Powell worked, and, without a checkbook, with no language skills, with no other contacts, she found herself completely isolated. The doctor came around a few times a week.

Growing up, I knew nothing else, so I wasn't suspicious when he slept over. I thought he was friendly, someone who occasionally took an interest in my grades. She had no idea what was normal in this country either. She didn't know enough to suspect that Dr. Powell had another family, a real family, in another part of town, about a twenty-five-minute drive away.

"Of course, he's my father," said Masahiro. Seiko Harada had arrived in the United States in 1950, at the age of twenty-one. In 1956, when she had her first and only child, she was twenty-seven years old, ensconced in complete isolation, most certainly what we would now understand as the victim of a crime. "I'm sure Powell told her they were in love," he said. He blinked and shook his head. "You asked me once if I'd ever been in love. How could I, when this is what I saw of it? A powerful man imprisoning a brilliant and resourceful woman in a cage of caring, in romantic assurances?" Masahiro shivered violently. "It makes me so furious."

"The crazy thing is," he continued, "I could never persuade her to leave. She *was* grateful. And also scared. Not of Powell but of what would happen without him. He alone had treated her, over and over, and truly alleviated her suffering, and restored her mobility and, ironically, some of her dignity. So I went off to med school—Powell couldn't pay for it out of his own pocket because it would tip off his real wife, so I left medical school in huge debt. I had the skills to replace your scales and reengineer your joints because of my mother, because I specialized in reconstructive surgery and skin grafting so that if her condition deteriorated, if her suffering returned, I could help."

"What happened to Powell? Did you tell the police? The FBI?"

They were up beyond the clouds now, and there was nothing outside the window but a blackening deep blue. Masahiro looked through the gap between the seats ahead and those behind. All the nearby passengers were slumped in sleep or plugged into their screens. Masahiro looked at his tray table and took a deep breath.

"I was a few years out of medical school in the summer of 1984 when I tracked Powell down to a power plant where he consulted as a burn specialist for on-site injuries. I followed him into the plant one day—flashed my medical credentials at security and said I had been called in. I confronted Powell. I told him that what he'd done to my mother was wrong. He laughed at me, he said he was the best thing that had ever happened to her. He had all her papers, he owned her house, he had her medical records. He *refused to release her*."

Sylvia, now six miles above sea level in a canned vortex of desiccated air, could not imagine killing. "How did you . . ."

"Power plants are dangerous places. I made it look like he'd slipped on a ramp and landed in a slick-water tank. That's the chemically treated water they shoot so hard at the earth, it flushes gas out of rock."

Sylvia was horrified, her mouth agape.

"You become calculating when you need to, I guess. Sometimes not calculating enough." Masahiro described how Granger had shown up at the hospital where Masahiro then worked with a videocassette in his hand—security footage from the power plant, owned by Granger. He hadn't gloated or been vulgar, Masahiro recalled icily now. "He had obviously done his research into me. He said he was so sorry for my mother's suffering, during the war and after." Granger had held the cassette in a paper sleeve labeled clearly with the date of Powell's accident. "I'll keep your secret if you can keep mine," he had said, as if foreclosing Masahiro's professional freedom and imprisoning him in his employ were consensual, buddies pricking their fingers in a tree house.

"His secret," said Masahiro, now in the dark. "His secret was you."

Sylvia tried to process two things in tandem: one, a historical fact, openly known for seventy years, and the other, a deep personal secret, the revelation of a horrible crime committed by her closest friend. The latter made her sad; that Masahiro had been driven to a degrading act of violence and then carried the guilt of it for years.

But what roiled her mind with rage was not the newly revealed secret but the long-known fact. It was Seiko's story she could not stop replaying in her mind. A blameless child cursed in a flash, robbed of comfort and connection, denatured, sent careening on a twisted path of sickness and alienation. Rational men claimed that, in the long run, the atom bomb would save lives. She grasped with a clarity born of rage that they were not two damaged creatures alone in this fight, but that all the future victims of her father's callous plan sailed with them through the black vaporous night, screaming that the numbers were wrong and begging history, like a wild river, to whip off course and leave them standing.

CHAPTER 44

"Hiroshima is *such a bummer*."

"It's literally the *worst*."

We find ourselves on the Posse Pit horseshoe sofa, facing the theatrical proscenium of the stone hearth that never holds a fire. Randy's feet are up, shoeless in ankle socks, papers on his chest. Murphy, elbows resting on a leather trunk used as an ottoman, leans into his laptop.

"Also, it turns out the A-bomb stuff is way too expensive effects-wise and the marketing department will ax it anyway," says Murphy.

"Huge point: this has to play in East Asia. So." Randy looks from Murphy to me, as if the matter's settled.

"But parts of East Asia are more vulnerable than ever to the threat of nuclear war," I inject.

Murphy wrinkles up his face as if he's been presented with a carb-y sandwich. "Yeah, double triple bummer, Penny. Also? We just don't have time."

I know I won't win this, but I haven't given them a sign yet. These are the last moments of resistance, of a fight that's left my body and lingers only in my slack face.

"Look," Murphy continues, "I get it. Kim Jung Un. Peeps are *getting nuked*. This shit is real. But that's a different movie."

"How do you explain Masahiro's specialty in reconstruction and skin grafting?" I ask. "His deep, uncommon empathy for Sylvia's suffering?"

"He's just *da man*." Randy's arms rise, face beatific.

"Yessss." Murphy nods slowly side to side. "I think an actor can do that with the right look. Let's save ourselves a bundle of money, keep Asia cool, and let this story *breathe*."

"There's plenty of drama here without the literal worst thing that's ever happened."

"We've done this a thousand times, Penny. Trust us."

I will. I have to. I'm paid to. I don't know how to write a movie. They do. From within their Western soundstage house, they write successful movies. The script is due this week and the people who will read it are not a table full of female English teachers who woke up with sore breasts because they fell asleep in sports bras that they meant to jog in before getting drunk. They are complex financial project managers. Randy and Murphy know what kind of gatekeepers' riddles we need to solve, not I. Let them take away Masahiro's past and his pain. Make him—what?—an extremely nice man.

Oh, oh, but now I bat away the little acid whisper saying they will make something I never intended of Japan. There will be tatami mats and tea, and Masahiro will have an ambient, Asian-ish wisdom. His character won't come from experience but from a gentle waft blowing off a raced face. That's what Murphy means: *the right look*.

These two skilled men have done this before, and it's always worked! They will please the *honchos*. I assumed "honcho" came from Spanish, like "poncho," that it was imported to the top floors of studio towers from the rare rancher air of the Andes, but no. American servicemen brought it back from Japan in the 1940s—*honchō*, group leader. They can't go *that* wrong, can they, Americans, sympathetic and liberal, born speaking this mixed-race language? These are capable, hardworking people. (Look at them, chewing their gum, with their matching tans and socklets, passing their annotated drafts back and forth!) I have to believe this, I have every reason to believe this. If I want to be a person here, and buy myself back, I will believe this.

CHAPTER 45

"I can't believe this is it," I say, craning my neck.

Derek double-checks the map on my phone as we roll out of the sun into the parking garage under a giant metallic office building downtown.

"This is definitely it."

"It's so . . . *corporate*. I thought we'd be someplace with palm trees and pictures of Fred Astaire."

Derek pulls into a spot and cuts the engine. The smell of gasoline is suffocating. There's an echo of voices and slamming car doors. A lock beeps somewhere.

"Dude, why are you surprised? Your studio is probably owned by the United Arab Emirates, which is owned by Disney, which is owned by the US military, et cetera et cetera."

"Disney owns the United Arab Emirates," I repeat skeptically.

"Have you seen pictures of Dubai? It's mostly waterslides."

"Okay, you're right and I agree with you, and the Gap owns Oman—"

"Well, now you're being ridiculous. Oman owns the Gap."

"Don't say this stuff at the table read."

"Look, Penny, I know this thing is important for you and you're nervous. I don't want to make you any more nervous. Do you want me to just drop you off and come back later? I can go read somewhere." Derek is *always* happy to kill time. He's lived his life so that his time is not valuable, and therefore disposing of it with careless determination (public bench, stained paperback) marks him as superior to those who wring their earthly minutes for profit. But I need him here.

"No. Come with me. I want to see your reactions. You were there with me at the beginning of this project. Plus, you never read the final book, so you'll be hearing the whole thing for the first time. Although it's different."

"Yeah." Derek inhales and opens his mouth to say something but closes it. I want to pursue whatever that was, but there's no time.

"They need bodies in the room. They want to see where you laugh, where you're bored. Come on, let's just go." We open our doors, step out, and slam them in unison.

"Cool. I'm a body." Derek makes a clown-fart noise with his beautiful mouth as we look for the exit.

"Don't do that either."

Following instructions from an email from the studio—twenty-second floor, turn right, conference room Q—we enter into a glass-walled room housing a shiny white oval table that seats about thirty. There are chairs lining the walls, many of them taken already by people turning to each other chatting, standing around swizzling coffees, kissing cheeks. There's a cold buffet brunch spread on the far narrow wall. A couple of samovars fill the room with the smell of coffee and the promise of pleasant productivity.

Danielle blows me a kiss with one hand. She's wedged in the back row with a teetering thirty-two-ounce Starbucks in her other hand. I spot Randy greeting everyone like the mother of the bride. He pauses briefly over a bank of four men and a woman in suits, and straightens up, nodding as one of them addresses him. These must be the studio people.

I don't see Murphy. My eyes scan over a young, hot, Japanese-looking guy who's seated at the table and rotated casually toward the older actress next to him. His graphic T-shirt tightens around a panel of rock-hard bauble-shaped abdominal muscles as he twists. I try to begin to compute how this man could be Masahiro but quickly recognize the softer midsection of Dick Babbot, now clothed in plaid flannel. He approaches me and puts his hands on my face: "My mermaid," he says, and kisses my right cheek. My blood goes cold with alarm at this swift intimacy, but I'm also suddenly self-conscious of my breath, my pores. I go for a second kiss because I assume that was his plan, but he stops at one. I cascade into shame because I wanted no kisses at all and now I look horny for Dick Babbot.

I'm thrilled to pivot away from him and find the minuscule frame of Jellica Nye. At first I don't think she is all that impressive. She's small and so thin you can see all the pipes in her neck. She shakes my hand firmly and looks at me with eyes whose whites are veinless boiled egg up to the fern-green iris. She describes her enthusiasm for the project with no slang, no assumed girly closeness. She folds one arm across her chest and reaches with the other one to the table, where her hand rests on a script marked with highlighter. She is here to work. I like her immensely.

Jellica introduces me around. Jellica's sister, agent, and manager are arranged behind her in a row of chairs. They look like a family on a flight: A skinny ten-year-old girl in shorts and a glittery T-shirt, bored, gnawing on a maki roll. A man and a woman, nicely dressed, tapping away at phones. Each in turn nods and shakes my hand.

I don't retain anyone's name because my mind is preoccupied with the slow but sure smashing of my defenses by something about Jellica Nye. There's no redness at the base of her nostrils, no gleam of grease or little gray sinkhole anywhere on her nose or chin or forehead. Things that moments ago I would have considered precisely human, like the colorless mole on my right eyelid, now seem like gross aberrations in light of the sandpapered organ of perfection that is Jellica Nye's face. Jellica Nye's skin, I realize as my mouth emits warmer and warmer gratitude for her willingness to participate, has no abrupt transitions of color and betrays no artifice; it's a tea candle in a farm egg and finally I realize I would rather look at her than anything else. And there's a *full* buffet in the room. With shrimp.

I rip my eyes off Jellica as she introduces me to her mother, a barrel-chested fortysomething woman with skinny legs sucked into white jeans. Loose brown skin from her armpit folds over the rim of a ruffled, one-shouldered top, showing little white cracks in her spray-tanned façade when she moves. The horror of the obvious falseness of the mother's skin, stained brown like a barn, contrasts with her daughter's unlabored perfection. Bending toward the mother in sympathy, I'm ready to do anything to prop up her sense of herself as beautiful and important, to playact the idea that she is young, or whatever she needs. The most horrible thing would be for her to know how humiliating she is to herself; we have to protect her.

The mother gauges quickly—ruthlessly, more ruthlessly than anyone in this city yet—that I'm not important and cranes her head around to catch eyes elsewhere.

Fucking hag.

A guy who looks like Matt Damon is Matt Damon.

I spot the drunk podcast girls at the far end of the room. They're nocturnal animals spotted during the day, deflated and preserving themselves for sundown. I reach Randy.

"Where's Murph?" I ask.

"Dude. He got hit by a car."

Oh my god.

"Is he okay? What happened?"

"I was there. We were jogging together, by the reservoir. We crossed an intersection, but when we got to the other side, he suddenly turned around and jumped. *Into* the intersection."

"*What?*"

Randy exhales sharply, wipes sweat from his brow with a shaking palm. "He said he heard his name, like really loud and sharp. *Mur-*

phy! Murphy! So without even thinking he pivoted back into the intersection, and he got clipped by a car. Flipped over the hood."

"Who was calling him?"

"No one. I think it must have been a dog owner."

"Murphy," I mumble. "It *is* a name for a dog."

"Yeah." Randy is shaken still. "He's at Saint Vincent's. The trauma ward."

"Is he conscious?"

"He's conscious, but he broke his arm and at least one rib and the side of his face is all fucked up."

I put my hand to my jowl. "His sort-of-beautiful face."

"I know," Randy agrees. "He's devastated. Hopefully it's just deep structural damage but nothing on the surface." I nod. Everything is wrong with this place.

"Anyway," Randy continues, "he said he might make it in later." Randy bites his lip, clicks his phone screen on, and glances down to check the time. "He was going to read the action and the slugs," the direction lines. "He was good at that stuff."

"He's not dead."

"Yeah." Randy chews his lip more. His eyes dart around the room nervously. "Penny."

"What?"

"He had his earbuds in."

"What do you mean? So what?"

"How could he hear someone calling him? He was listening to Maroon 5 so loud I could hear it."

"Maybe that's why someone tried to kill him."

I wasn't joking, and Randy doesn't smile. He's trying to suggest something—that someone called Murphy's name intimately in his ear but not from nearby, somehow cutting through the audio of his headphones. Randy searches my eyes for recognition—a recognition that would mean we both believe in something completely insane.

Mermaid song.

Derek's face arrives between us, partly obscured by a bagel heaped with smoked salmon. "Yo, can I save one of these for later or is there gonna be, like, intermission?"

"Derek." Of course. "Derek, eat quickly. We're going to need you to read."

Randy gazes out the window, too distracted to approve the choice.

The thing that I remember most is the look on Jellica Nye's face when it started to happen. She is such a good actress and a dedicated, straining young professional. She didn't know what was happening, so she just said the words even harder.

I have to admit, as the table read began—after some introductory remarks by someone from the studio I've literally never laid eyes on in my life, as if a complete stranger named Tim had shown up at my wedding to give me away—things started to get a bit wonderful. I was proud of Derek. He was good at the job we gave him, didn't space out or miss cues, even stopped eating salmon.

Like a pro, he began: "Exterior, Pier 27, Boston Harbor, night. A taxi pulls away, leaving a woman in a wheelchair on the dock. Close-up of her face, staring toward the sea, determined. Camera traces her body, beginning with her neck, her arms, her waist, her legs, and finally lingers on two shriveled gray stubs where her feet should be. Cut back to distant POV and we see the chair go over the pier into the water. Splash. Cue flooding symphonic intro music and titles: American Mermaid."

I felt at home here. I sat along a back row, watching all the people at the table flip pages at the same time, like my students. The actors jumped on their cues right away; no one ever got lost. Murphy was right, actors *can* read. They read *well! You literary snob, thinking these people, because they don't have pubic hair or debt, won't be deep and fluent animators of the printed page!* But they were! And Derek shepherded them through the action, right on time. Derek reading, as if we were back at Holy Cross and I'd left my tenth graders and popped a few doors down to Derek's juniors, and I was watching him entrance them, and them entrance him, with my words that bought me my $240 silk-blend shirt with bananas on it and that will buy me my life.

Knowing the machine was running smoothly, my mind drifted. I pictured me and Franck in the messy master bed of an expensive geometric house. There are Alps outside the sheer drapes. Franck ties his tie while kissing my face, which my imagination has reupholstered in Jellica Nye's skin. After he goes, I take up my chair at a narrow wooden desk by the window, and I set to work writing something that writes itself. Four thousand words later, I swim in a lake.

The table read ticked along for what felt like hours. (I had time to go, in my fantasies, to a Swiss village market in a halter dress carrying a basket, time for a restaurant meal with Franck and his colleagues where I made them laugh and he sat proudly in front of his espresso with a hand on my back; my dad calls and asks for a loan; my mother leaves my dad and sits in an Adirondack chair facing my lake; I turn down cake; I play tennis.)

Little familiar lines seeped into my consciousness as I daydreamed and half listened: "Sylvia, we have to know what you're capable of." I adjusted with remarkable speed to the fact of Ken Kimura as Masahiro, young and ever-so-slightly accented. Why stop this whole smooth locomotion of talent and energy and shrimp on account of my academic, poor-person politics?

Back to daydreams (on the phone, to no one: "I'm so sorry I can't make your baby shower—didn't you know? I live in Switzerland now").

And then it all broke.

"Masahiro pushes Sylvia through the glass doors of a chain hotel," said Derek.

KEN: "What's the worst that could happen? Are we going to drown?"

"No," said Jellica Nye. "That's not the worst that could happen. I'd rather drown."

KEN: "Rather drown than what?"

JELLICA: "What they're doing to me."

KEN: "Who?"

JELLICA: "Randy and Murphy."

KEN: "Who the hell is that?"

JELLICA: "The writers. They're changing our story. They're going to kill me, record it on high-resolution digital video, and sell my degradation and death to the world."

DEREK: "Tight frame on Sylvia as she puts a hand on Masahiro's face."

JELLICA: "You're going to get away. You'll live. But I'll die."

KEN: "Surely Penelope will save you. She's there, we can trust her."

My blood at this point was pumping cold, pure ice through my veins. I was frozen. I noticed people looking around at each other, as if it were their fault, as if they'd gotten on the wrong page, the wrong movie. A studio guy was scrutinizing Randy for a sign. Danielle in full quizzical face, head knocked sideways, sucking on her cheeks.

JELLICA: "We can't trust her anymore. She got greedy. She just wants to be rich."

KEN: "How can you be sure?"

I felt the bananas on my shirt burning into my skin.

JELLICA: "She used to fight for us, but now she stopped. She's deaf to us, to what we're fighting for. What *I'm* fighting for." Jellica Nye strained, acted without knowing for whom or in what direction. She became histrionic and vague. "NOT TO BE A WOMAN. TO BE SOMETHING ELSE. TO BE AN INTELLIGENCE, A BODY WITHOUT A SEX, LIKE SHE WROTE ME."

Ken: "I can't believe she would let them kill—"

JELLICA: "PENELOPE! PENELOPE!!!" Jellica now gave it her all; her throat closed a little with emotion as she raised her voice, and her eyes seemed ready to release tears down her distorted face. "PENELOPE, PLEASE DON'T LET THEM. DON'T LET THEM MAKE ME SOME. DUMB. WOMANNNNN!"

The gasps. The gasps between words. Jellica nearly out of her seat.

Derek was lost, not watching the page, and even the back-bench idiots who'd been reading their phones the whole time sensed blood in the water and were eyes-up and alert.

"PENELOP—"

"PENELOPE!" Now it wasn't Jellica's scream. It was a man's voice. We all whipped our heads toward the glass door of the conference room, where a man whose face was streaked with scabbed blood from his forehead across his cheek and down his chin, whose arm was in a sling and who slumped slightly against the wall for support, stared at me. It was Murphy. He was out of the hospital.

"Jesus," said someone.

I was about ten feet away, to his left down the row of chairs. I could smell the hospital on him, the blank vapor of long-closeted bandage. Mouths curled down at him. People wondered if he should have gotten past security. Randy tried to get up out of his seat to handle Murphy and knocked over someone's coffee and that was a separate kerfuffle.

"GET THE FUCK OUT OF HERE!" Murphy screamed at me. The room jumped. He shifted then and repackaged his anger in a business tone, which only made it more sinister, like a briefcase dripping blood. "You gotta get the fuck out of here," he said nearly under his breath, slurring a little ("you gottagetdafugoutofhere"). "You can't *invent*. You can't *make shit up*." Now he pointed to his temples. "You think your book is real? What are you, a *child*? Are you like a TRIBESWOMAN? Like you don't know we can change your words and it isn't going to hurt anyone? It's not fucking *voodoo*, you fucking *village idiot. Fuckinnnnnn'* . . ." Here he started to stir a mimed pot of some sort of stew. Or maybe the gesture of stirring a pot was meant to communicate "primitive woman." He forgot he was stirring. He kept stirring, a little hunched over still, as if around a huge cartoon pot. *"Go."* At almost a whisper now. *"Go."* He dropped his hand from around the pot, but the other hand, now in the air, threatening, held an invisible spatula that we both could see.

I looked around briefly before shoving my script in my tote bag and shimmying down the row of seats past Murphy, grisly and blood-stinking, and out the door. Every single face was a face of What the Fuck, with the exception of Jellica Nye's, which was the one that haunted me most afterward.

She didn't know what had happened. She had been immersed in the world of the script, given her voice to Sylvia, to this striving, beautiful, broken creature. And she had been pulled up out of it by force, so the words that she screamed seemed unfamiliar to her, so the voice that she used had gotten away from her. She had, in a sense, humiliated herself, been pulled up naked before the assembled group, been seen to act, purely to act, while the part had dried up around her. She had been screaming my real name, out of character, exposed, in the real air. And now she sat there, exhausted and pained, patches of red under her nectarine skin. Her eyes stayed on her script. I felt so bad for her that my last glance back, as I slipped past the glass door before it shivered shut behind me, was toward Jellica Nye. She raised her face and glared at me like she wanted me to die.

PART III

DROWNING

CHAPTER 46

EXCERPT FROM *AMERICAN MERMAID*

Down, down, down.

There were no words, there was no name for this dark expanse. Men might say "Three hundred meters deep," or give the coordinates on a map, or explain to a child that it was the depth of a hundred swimming pools. A person wanting to tell you about this place would be trapped by names—"off Vágar," or "seventy sea miles from Sørvágur"—but the names would be irrelevant, like opinions. They wouldn't tell you anything about how it felt to move in it, to shoot through it, to pulse within its dark pressures. Those names would tell you nothing of the place where now the long muscle of the mermaid's body whipped and coiled through the gyrating shelf of herring. She pivoted and snarled as she snatched at the tiniest flash of flinching prey. She emerged from the swarm with a bag across her body, bulky with bloody fish, and a last catch still twitching in her mouth. Kevin called for her pod. It was time to turn home.

Home: although it was a long swim from where they now hunted, if they had come up to the surface, they would have seen the black cliff face of their home towering in the distance, eight hundred meters high, vertically ribbed, glossy, moss-topped, and dripping. Seabirds that looked smaller than gnats soared and spiraled, often disappearing, black against black, as they crossed before the monumental rock. If you followed two of the cliff's giant, rounded ripples from the top all the way down, you might notice that they plunged into the sea like iron doors, open just a few feet. Peering between those doors, which no man had ever tried to do, you would see nothing but what you expected to see, more of the black volcanic matter belched up and laid down sixty million years ago, now a wet rock face unreached by roads, too sheer even for the nests of the storm petrel or the sea eagle.

But not everything happens as it should. Things get twisted up, even in nature. A tree splits and grows around a rock. An invisible genetic mutation leads to the preposterous event of a white tiger. And sixty million years ago, when the cold sea was home to creatures whose bones would make Victorians dream—crocodile heads on dolphin bodies; swimmers half snake, half seal—lava trickled down from the molten spout of a sea volcano and sizzled into the water. And in one particular spot it flowed down in two rivulets. And in that particular spot, for whatever reasons of wind or weight or chance, the lava that followed continued to coat and build up and flow upon those two rivulets until they formed deep rails, deeper and deeper, without filling in the space between them. So while most of the cliff's ripples folded inward only a matter of a meter or two before jutting back out, this one pair of ripples contained inside of it a long and narrow space, a sheer-walled lagoon twenty meters deep. At its innermost point was a chamber the size of a city church. This chamber was the home of Kevin's pod.

Happy with her full, blood-streaking bag, Kevin called out again to the other hunters, but a surprising picture came back to her: A boat, a rarity here, idling at the surface. A man, asleep in a chair on deck.

Some kind of idiot, thought Kevin.

Who sleeps in a chair on deck in this wind? added glinting green Max, swirling now into Kevin's view with the others.

Dumb tourist with a death wish, said Dave, big-boned and serious, picking fish from her teeth.

Well, said Kareem. Let's make his wishes come true, and then we'll go. Kareem, a new mother, wanted to get home.

I'll do it, said Dave.

The hypnotic, hollow chop of the fiberglass hull against the waves had sent Masahiro dozing, his head falling forward and bobbing up. He dreamed that Sylvia stole through Granger's laboratory, bashing switches and hammering keyboards.

At a particularly loud knock, Masahiro's head flew up and his body twitched awake. A GPS device had fallen from his bandaged hand onto the deck. The wind whipped by his ears, but inside the boat it was quiet.

"Sylvia?" he called.

She was in the hold, eating at a foldout table, storing energy for a long swim. Remembering an exotic doughnut thing he'd squirreled away earlier, Masahiro thought he'd join Sylvia. He put the GPS device on his seat and stood up, when suddenly he heard a familiar song.

Within minutes, she had pulled Masahiro into the water. She held him there gently, surprised that he seemed to be trying to *talk to* her. It was almost funny, if Dave had been the laughing type, to see the man try to make words underwater. They emerged from his lips in strands of silver bubbles.

She monitored him without pity, counting idly as if at a chore. The other four watched on, leaning toward home, ready to jet when Dave was done.

Then they became aware of her: there was a woman in the boat. They all received the sonar transmission of the same body, unable to walk. She was alone, stranded, elbowing her way up the galley steps and shouting for her companion.

She'll be fine.

Someone will find her.

In awe, they watched her wriggle her way across the deck and, without hesitating, plunge off the boat into the water just meters from them.

She'll die, they thought. Killing men was one thing, but none of them had ever killed a woman.

To their astonishment, minutes later they were all at the surface. One by one the mermaids registered that, among the fizzing commotion, in the time that this woman had wrenched the man from Dave, dragged him into the air, and breathed into his mouth, her legs had become a tail. They had never seen anything like it. They were so fixated on the miraculous tail that they had not noticed the mermaid wincing and whimpering through its transformation.

"Thank god, oh thank god," said this now-mermaid, in the normal human way, to the man she had saved.

The water was usually busy with their thoughts, but no sonar moved through it now.

When the cold adrenaline subsided from Sylvia's mind, she registered that she'd found her family. They had rotated around her like a maypole while she'd breathed life into Doc, inspecting her in disbelief. Now it was Sylvia's turn to look: four mermaids, long-haired and long-limbed, different complexions all and different through the tail—the big one gunmetal, and another green-gray, the littlest one almost pink. The waterborne tulle that protected their chests was, upon closer inspection, a careful arrangement of plastic bags, weathered and ripped.

Sylvia took a heavy breath, ready to explain, but Kevin beat her to it.

"You're the one we lost." She spoke with a calm certainty.

"We've heard about you our whole lives."

"The trouble you've caused," said Dave, who had escaped Granger's nets by a hair a few years ago.

"It's not your fault," said Kevin. "You were a baby."

"Jimmy," said little Kareem, smiling with a hand to her heart.

"Is that my name?" asked Sylvia.

"No," responded Kevin. "That's your mother." The mermaids looked at each other with a kind of solemn thrill. "She's been hoping for this the whole time."

Doc had remained in Sylvia's arms, where he now sputtered. It reminded her what they were there for. Where would she start? The surgery, her life on land, seemed irrelevant now that she was whole again, swishing her strong tail in the saline bath of the sea. But Granger: they must be told why he wanted to capture them all, how imminently he would destroy their home.

"I have to tell you so much," she said.

"*We* have to tell *you* so much," replied Kevin. She would not have to excuse her presence here, talk her way in, prove herself. This slick world awaited her, and she slid into place.

Leave him in the boat and come with us, Kevin said, not in words but in some other way that Sylvia received perfectly.

She looked at Doc. "They've found you," he said. "You can go with them. I'll be okay."

Kevin noticed the new mermaid's face wrinkling up. She was crying. And her tail, covered not in scales but in a shimmering kind of metal, spoke to Kevin of difficulty—of approximation, of strain. As Kevin looked at this creature, a lost object, repurposed and repaired, her eyes oozed seawater like the basalt face of her black cliff home.

CHAPTER 47

Email from Pschleeman to VanessaChapman:

Dear Vanessa,

I hope you don't mind this bolt from the blue. I got your email address from your principal, as I was eager to follow up with you after our discussion at the bookstore. I'm particularly interested in your dissent regarding my choices about Sylvia because I'm working on the film script and perhaps this would be an opportunity to address some of my earlier failings.

I've reread Tolstoy's *Ten Wives for Two Brothers* now as well as *The Logman's Catch, The Granary Spire,* and *Alexei's Plea.* I would love to discuss them all.

Email from VanessaChapman to Pschleeman:

omg relax Gail from HR just come to my house sometime after dinner on like Friday
　my mom will let you in, we'll be in the basement

CHAPTER 48

"Okay, so, don't freak out."

Danielle and I are at dinner, outside under a trellis. But I'm not going to shoot anything in this trellis. I'm in civilized mode. My agent has asked me to dinner. I'm wearing a new outfit. It's new to me, although it probably looks conventional to anyone else. It's an olive-green canvas skirt, below the knee like a scout instructor, with a white $185 cropped shell on top, and I'm wearing *mules*, which feel very fashion-y because they're so stupid. I pounced on the mule at a micro-moment of the spinning fashion wheel in which mules were pointy and white, so it looks like I walked into an unfurling burrito and kept walking, leaving my chalky, fissured heels exposed. Because the mules fly off with every step, I have to clench my toes against the slick leather sole to keep them on, frantically when the sole gets slicker with dampness because the mule permits no sock. This has caused cramps in my calves and hamstrings, which in turn have reinjured my back. I shuffle, tilted forward a little like I've just been punched in the womb. They were expensive and, I think, worth it.

"You're fired."

The trellis is still. Danielle suddenly appears to me like a photograph, her big skull and her blowout frozen like a headshot of a character actor who plays secretaries of state, people cast to give bad news I should have seen coming.

How can Danielle fire me? Don't I have to fire her? Fired from what? Eating embarrassing tacos, not-working in a not-hotel, fired from writing a script I already wrote based on a book I already wrote? Can they rip out our past accomplishments here? With some kind of movie magic, can they pull so hard the roots come out from last week, last month, last year?

"What am I fired from?" I ask.

"This happens all the time," she says, and then her eyes light up at the presence of a server. "Oooh, let's order."

A line cook in black clogs has just written "local surfperch" on the specials board leaning against an ivy wall. Danielle orders the fish with a gesture to the board, and a Gavi di Gavi. Even though I know she will pick up the tab, and that my politeness is in a currency that cannot be traded here and will just sit in my own pocket like a washer, I order the cheapest thing on the menu, an appetizer of bruschetta with tomatoes. (Danielle, like she's talking dirty: "I love how non-carb-phobic you are.")

"Get wine," she insists when I decline a drink. I order a glass of white.

The words seem to come out of my mouth, but I'm on autopilot, stunned.

"What do you mean, fired?"

"They just want fresh eyes. This happens on *every movie*. Don't worry. You still get paid for the final script delivery. And more when the movie goes into production. C'mere." She takes my hand across the table. "You look freaked out."

"Was it the table read?"

"You're acting like being fired is *bad*. It's not bad! Not here! It's actually great."

"Are Randy and Murphy fired?"

"I think so." As her wine is deposited, she says "score" instead of "thanks."

For some reason I feel responsible for Randy and Murphy being fired. It would never have happened if it weren't for me, and it compounds the guilt.

"I know the table read didn't go smoothly."

"Mmm-hmmm," Danielle agrees, shaking her head slowly. The wineglass attached to her lips rotates with her.

"I think some crazy shit is happening." Can I tell Danielle my darkest fears? She's an agent, the facilitator of things between the mind and the page, the page and the world. It's her job to make money off mermaid magic: but would she believe it's real? "I know it all went a bit crazy. But I'm not crazy."

"I know you're not crazy. Look, nothing you did in the past like thirty years interests me." Here she means, I assume, my MA, my PhD, the teaching. Also, doing some quick math, much of my childhood. But I get that no one with a financial adviser wants to talk about the fifteen-year-olds that I taught to use adverbs. "You're weird about money," she continues. (Don't know what you're talking about, just eating bread crust in my white sheikh's slippers.) "You obviously have issues with zoning out and not being present." She opens her eyes wide and flutters her hands in front of her face, conjuring a skill at *being present* that she has in spades. "But you're not crazy. You've never sent me a single thing late. You make every meeting, prepared. I've seen crazy, and you're not crazy. I think of you as a sane person from another world."

"Like a ghost?"

"We don't need labels," she says, swiveling her head like an expensive guru. "Whatever. That said, there's something out of control with this project. I don't know why. Chemistry with you and the boys? Something internal to the script? Issues with casting and production?" She shrugs. "But I say, you're lucky to be fired. Get out of there. Shit's getting weird. Take your paycheck, get on a new project. GET. MORE. MONEY. That's why you're here!"

"But it's *my story*."

Her big shiny head swivels again. "Not really. You sold it."

I must look dejected. Boss bitches do not experience dejection, and this sends Danielle into battle mode: "HEY. LISTEN. You need to be a BOSS about this. You need to say, 'Hey, World. I sold my project for a BUNCH of money to some dicks. Now some other dicks are gonna work on it. It's cool. BYE.' Can you say 'bye'?"

"Yeah."

"Say it. Say 'BYE-BYE, MERMAID.'"

I don't want to say it.

"Say it. You'll feel so much better. This is how you climb up into this reality. This is how you join us up here. Join us. Say it. 'BYE-BYE, MERMAID. SEE YOU AT THE MOVIES.'"

"Bye-bye, mermaid."

"Louder."

I say it a little louder.

"One last time."

"BYE-BYE, MERMAID." I feel sick. I take a deep breath of the odorless, toxic air that comes to this baroque Italianate veranda from the highway on the other side of the foliage, and I think about Petrarch dead in the soil of his villa, and I want to die with him, dreaming through the dirt about a deep sea that's never heard of the Hollywood it hammers. Danielle is still looking at me expectantly. I say it: "SEE YOU AT THE MOVIES."

"See?" Danielle says. "Don't you feel better?"

Suddenly there is a high-pitched squeal followed by a deafening pop and, a second later, a tinkling sound, a gemstone shower. Then screaming and shouting.

Everyone on the patio is frozen.

"Car crash," says Danielle.

Everyone on the patio starts to eat again.

But the shouting came from the other way, from behind a swinging door that leads to the kitchen. Liquid trickles out from behind the door over the pale cement ground, turning this way and that, leaving a dark stain as it goes. A waitress pushes the door open with her palm and looks down at her feet. Two, three surfperch, like ladies' pocketbooks in fine snakeskin, slither out the door. I can't tell if they are alive or dead, swimming or spilling.

Stepping carefully, the waitress, looking stunned, arrives at our table. A large fish tank has burst. In the kitchen.

"It wasn't a car crash?"

The waitress shakes her head. She needs to take a new order for Danielle.

"What do you mean?"

"You can't eat the surfperch. There could be broken glass in your fish."

"I'll sign a waiver."

I want to reassure the waitress that it's fine, Danielle's body will break down the glass and use it to shellac her teeth and nails, but also I want to tell her something that sounds insane but that I know to be true: It's my fault your tank broke. It's Sylvia. She's here, she's angry, and she's screaming.

CHAPTER 49

EXCERPT FROM *AMERICAN MERMAID*

The mermaid shrieked when she heard the pop, but it was too late. The needle-tipped dart had entered her chest.

"Hold her! Hold her!" Captain Horgan now sprang up from behind the gunwale. The young man who had served as lure gripped her as she thrashed. She pulled him into the water, and the two disappeared below the surface.

"Niall!" Horgan leaned over the edge of the boat. "Niall!" He waited, nervous, staring into the murky green water. A few seconds later, the young man broke the surface, paddling with one arm toward the boat, the mermaid limp in a headlock. "Good lad!" yelled Horgan, hoisting the gun in his clenched fist.

"I can't believe this," said the young man as he climbed back on board the life raft attached to the trawler, trying to catch his breath. He ran the tips of his fingers along her green-gold hips, felt the tightness and toughness of her finely wrought scales. "What do we do with her?" Horgan pointed behind him, where an older man in an expensive-looking parka stepped up, smiling ear to ear.

"I'll take over from here."

CHAPTER 50

A text from Randy: "I know who has mermaid. Call me."

I lean far onto the patchy wood bar and trace Derek's Paul Newman profile with my eyes like a hometown skyline. Since my firing, I have been escaping myself by clinging extra hard to Derek in the dark bars he has a talent for finding. I pretend I'm within the cramped borders of an East Coast state, as if someone's about to tell a routine story about hitting a doe on the parkway.

It's comforting.

I plug one ear and hold my phone up to the other ear, wincing with effort to hear Randy.

"Yeah, they fired me," he says, "but I would have quit anyway. That's how it works in this town. *Fresh eyes.* Always *fresh eyes.*"

"I want you to know I *didn't do it*. I didn't write that stuff into the script."

There's a long pause. There's a possibility Randy believes me. But if he believes me, we're together in believing a written fiction has turned on us, has melted and rearranged the black electric letters on our screens. Sylvia, what, stole my password? Sat at my desk? How?

"You know She Sells Seashells by the Seashore?"

"Your girlfriend?"

"Yeah. We're having a baby."

"Oh, cool. Are you moving out of the Rancho Diablo Posse Pit?"

"The what?"

"Are you getting your own place?"

"Yeah. It's time. Listen, maybe Dick will be really faithful to your vision."

"What do you mean, Dick?"

"Dick Babbot. *American Mermaid* is his now. That's who the studio hired."

We talk more, but my loud thumping heart blurs my ears. I gather Randy has an overall deal with one of the studios to develop "action-heavy female comedies."

"Action for heavy females?" I can't hear in here, but I've accidentally made a real Randy joke.

"Yeah," he says. "*Pie Hard*!" He's laughing, and I feel I should produce more fat-action puns, but my mouth dries up and I fill it with beer.

He tells me not to be mad at Murphy. "You know, his parents are real assholes. He financially divorced them at like eighteen. He had to come out here and make money, and he did."

Women are not the only women. Randy, always the wife to Murphy, wants to mend things in the world, pro bono. I, too, to no end, have to correct an untruth he believes, even though it doesn't matter anymore.

"I didn't get drunk and write that stuff in the script." Someone has scored in a baseball game and people are cheering. It doesn't help my case that I'm now obviously at a bar.

"I don't know *what* you did," he says. "Girl, you *crazy*." I hold the phone away from my ear. This man writes comedy? "What's your next move?" he asks.

"I'm taking meetings," I say. Derek hears me and mimes a hand job, which only plunges me into guilt, remembering the mermaid semen-harvests I let them cut when I was a big-time Hollywood screenwriter. "Taking meetings" suddenly seems like a phrase they invented to trick young women into giving things away.

I start to say good-bye, but Randy interrupts. "Penny, he said it was a woman's voice. Murphy. In his headphones. And she was singing."

CHAPTER 51

EXCERPT FROM *AMERICAN MERMAID*

"We've got to get them all. We can't leave a single one out there. I've seen good lads, good, sound young men lose their senses and walk into the sea. We're *defenseless*," said Horgan, talking more than usual in the company of an important man.

Horgan had always been intensely practical, his mind occupied with shipping forecasts and yield quotas, never distracted by superstitions or conspiracies. Witnessing a mermaid pull his lineman off a dock had ripped his sanity from him, made him a stranger to himself.

Then Dean Granger—*the* Dean Granger—had rescued him from insanity. Just when Horgan had become a laughingstock, a news clip to titter at for telling the truth about the mermaids, Granger, a *titan* of industry, had come to the rattled captain in calm tones with arms outstretched, like a peer. Granger listened to him, believed him. And now he said he wanted to go into a partnership with *him*, with Horgan! No more hauling pollock guts. Together they'd round up the mermaids. They wouldn't kill them. They'd domesticate them. Horgan had all kinds of ideas, and after their successful hunt, Granger was ready to listen to the captain. Granger had paid for his travel, put him up in luxurious guest quarters with soaps that smelled like the landlocked gardens Horgan never saw.

And he was about to go where few had been: he had shot down in a narrow lift next to Granger, who bragged of the engineering it took to put a lab inside a cliff on the ocean floor. He now trailed Granger as he spoke, both men bearing golden pools of whiskey in carved crystal tumblers, through a final pair of groaning double doors into what looked like a black stone amphitheater stacked with rows of keyboards, monitors, and other equipment Horgan didn't recognize. The banks of equipment faced a fifteen-meter-long curved-glass panel through which he saw only black. Yes, that's what this place reminded him of—something else he hadn't seen in years. A movie theater.

There was a gentle *tap, tap, tap* as Granger trotted down the shallow flagstone steps in his navy suede driving shoes. He was genial, breezy. Horgan didn't know the man from Adam, but he got the impression Granger was somehow particularly giddy. Horgan was still clutching his stomach and popping his ears after the precipitous drop in Granger's narrow elevator that had deposited them down here.

"I always suspected they existed, but I could never *find* them. What you taught me, Captain, is that I should stop looking for them and let *them* find *me*. Or your men, rather."

"I can't keep putting my men at risk, Granger. We have to find some other way to get the rest."

"We'll give 'em a call," said Granger, now reclining into a high-backed chair at a bank of monitors, picking up a handset and giving it a jiggle.

"How?"

Granger gestured to the dark glass panel that separated the lab from the bottom of the sea. As Horgan approached, it reflected him in perfect clarity as if in a black mirror.

"My secretary here will see to it," said Granger. "She's calling them right now." Granger slammed his hand down on a button, and lights went up on the other side of the glass, illuminating a black sandy stage and two main attractions. The first was a machine, some kind of hulking metal drill with a long barrel shooting up out of it like a gun shaft. And the second, so close to the glass Horgan felt he could touch her, was a mermaid, hovering in a fine net tethered to the ground. It was the last thing Horgan saw before Dean Granger shot him in the neck: a mermaid, aloft in the center of the pane, hovering like an angel. Her green scales caught the light occasionally as her tail rotated slowly beneath her. Her eyes were open but unseeing as she sent a silent scream to her sisters.

CHAPTER 52

I am in a wide basement with low ceilings strewn with soft, beaten-in furniture, each beanbag and sofa chair and papasan garnished with a teenage girl. There are six of them. One is Vanessa, the girl in the sweater from my reading.

"This is Tiff, Tiana, Gabby, Esther, and Dee."

I rename them silently based on their expressions: Smiles, Sexy, Strong, Serious, and Mean.

"Wow. Thanks for having me." This phrase, intended as a polite convention, seems to confuse them. I see a twitch go through Mean's eyebrows, and her head ducks back, like she's avoiding a bee.

"What's up?" asks Vanessa.

"I wanted to talk to you. I didn't realize you'd have so many friends over. About my book."

"These people have read your book, too."

"Oh, have you?"

Some of them smile, some of them peer out at me with searing analytic purity.

"So what are you here for? A little market testing? Want to see how the movie version will play for the youth market? We're sixteen and seventeen, but I'd say we have the taste and intelligence of the eighteen-to-twenty-five bracket."

"I'm much older," says Serious, whose hair is bleached white like

Mrs. Claus and cut close to the scalp. She points to her temple—the seat, it would seem, of her oldness.

"I'm not here to market-test things." They don't give any visible indication of believing me, of sudden, disarmed welcome. "I don't know why I'm here."

"Relax," says Smiles. She has crescent-shaped, friendly eyes and long brown hair. "You don't have to be here for a reason." She turns her smile up even further and pushes bowls of chips and guacamole toward me.

"Thanks. Sorry, I forgot your name."

"It doesn't matter right now," says Smiles, already forgiving.

I crunch into a chip. It seems inordinately loud. Six teenage girls are arrayed around me, all watching me carefully. "Sorry, I didn't mean to interrupt. What were you talking about?"

Vanessa looks around. "We were talking about the inherent racial bias of facial recognition software."

"You *were*?"

They all nod.

"Awesome."

When I was their age, all I wanted was to be thin and to buy myself baby-doll dresses made of petrochemicals at the mall. This doesn't seem like a story I should tell.

Mean levels her gaze at me. "So you're a teacher. Are you trying to teach here in LA?"

"No. I'm not. I'm not trying to become *your* teacher or anything."

Some of them nod.

"Okay," says Vanessa. "So it's not a job interview."

"No," I say, laughing (alone) at the idea that they'd have the students perform the interviews, a singularly good idea.

Maybe I'll take Smiles's advice. She's still looking at me so kindly. *Relax.* I take a deep breath and lean back. I sort of thought I was in front of a beanbag chair, but I've misremembered the room and now I'm just lying on the floor. In front of six teenagers. Like they're about to autopsy me.

"Okay," I say, closing my eyes. "What I need from you is . . . your opinion on something."

"We're listening," says Vanessa, "Okay," says another one, "Mmhmm," another. Lovely waves of assent from these smart-seeming young women. I can feel my heart folding open like a letter.

I tell them everything, from the beginning. Why I came out here, how it began. And then the script interventions, which I didn't know if I had made, and then the table read. I tell them about Jellica Nye calling out to me with the voice of my offspring, begging for protection: PENELOPE, PENELOPE, PLEASE DON'T LET THEM.

"I know it sounds insane, but I think Sylvia's here. I think she broke my back as a warning and I think she threw Murphy into traffic because he tried to kill her off. *I think she ruined my agent's lunch.* I think I cracked the book open somehow and it's leaking into real life and Sylvia's doing things, and she'll keep doing things, and maybe hurting people, until I stop it."

I'm still lying on the ground, eyes closed. Silence.

I open my eyes and prop myself up. Mean tosses a handful of dry Cinnamon Toast Crunch into her mouth, never breaking eye contact with me, and mills it loudly in her workhorse jaws. All six women are alert, concentrating on me. I must have been lying there a good while—my hips and knees crackle when I fold them back under me to sit up.

"Do you think I'm crazy?"

There's a single beat of silence. And then, on top of one another:

"No, makes total sense."

"THIS IS WITCH SHIT."

"You let some juju loose."

From beneath thick bangs, Sexy, coiled into the papasan, asks, "Did you want to kill Marky? I'm trying to understand how psychically connected you are."

"Murphy." (Here were go: *Borfa Dorset.* They can't hold on to names, they're immediately in the deep.) "No. Honestly, they're good at their jobs. They got hired to do something and they were doing it."

"What about your agent? You want her dead?"

"Absolutely not."

"But you want her pranked, teased, made a bit crazy?"

"No, I don't." But the question makes me realize that maybe I do. If Danielle just gets knocked off-balance, if a chip is made in her steel-plated confidence, will she see the world like I do? Will she see that I'd rather die than let Sylvia become a sexpot? "Sylvia does."

"The question is," interjects Serious, "who's she coming for next?"

"You?" says a baritone voice that's been silent till now. Strong, a brick shit house in a track suit.

"What do you mean?"

"Is she coming for you? Does she hold you accountable?" asks Serious, calmly, as if all I have to do is remember.

The chips are gone. I lick my finger, stick it in the salt and crumbs, and touch it to my tongue.

"Ooooh, could you not do that?" Mean pulls the bowl away. "We need to maintain our viral autonomy."

"Sorry."

God, these women are mature. Lionesses, lounging but alert, ears twitching, beautiful in their differences. I can't stop moving my eyes from one to another, drinking in their self-possession, their confidence, their full, ripe intellects poised atop their messy, lush, new bodies. They are magnificent.

"MOM!" yells Vanessa, her mouth unhinged momentarily.

Mrs. Vanessa pads halfway down the stairs.

"Could we have some more chips?"

"Sure."

"And guac."

"Sure. What do you say?"

"Please."

"Sure thing." She dashes in like a timid zookeeper, snatches the bowl, smiles at me, and dashes out.

Lionesses.

"Well, I'm not sure if Sylvia will hold me responsible. I'm fired now."

Each one of their positions changes. Vanessa's back straightens.

I hear six versions of "What?" like a chord, Strong the base note and Smiles on top.

"I was fired from the movie. I'll still get credit. When you see the credits, it will still say my name. And I still get another payment when it goes into production."

"How much?"

"Like fifty K."

"Not worth it," says Strong.

I want to ask, *How much do YOU make?* but I'm afraid to cross any of them.

"Who's taken it over?"

"This guy named Dick Babbot. He's a big-deal writer and producer. *Jasper's World, Growing Up, Open Season.*"

"Hmmm." Sexy, unimpressed, uncoils and recoils onto her other haunch.

"Fantasies of bourgeois heteronormative stability," says Vanessa.

"And he's rewriting your feminist revolution? HA." Mean almost looks gratified.

Vanessa translates: "You fucked up."

"Or *got fucked*," offers Smiles, kindly.

"I *personally* think," says Serious, "that if you walk away from this, she'll kill you. Or she'll punish you seriously."

"But would she kill her *mother*?" wonders Smiles. "Mothers have a gravitational pull on their daughters, even while they exhaust themselves with emotional labor."

The door slams above the stairwell, and Mrs. Vanessa descends with a filled bowl in each hand. No one looks at her. The women continue.

"What about that warning shot? She almost drowned you."

"I read that differently," says Smiles. "I think she wanted to remind you how similar you are. She wanted you to *feel* the pain she feels. She's worked so hard to become powerful and autonomous, through all that pain and suffering. 'Don't trivialize my pain,' she's saying, 'don't take it away from me.' She wasn't going to kill you. She wanted to bring you closer."

Hm. I hadn't thought of that. I feel like I just read an excellent paper and am proud of Smiles.

Silence. Contemplation. The beeps and chimes of phones in pockets, ignored in a stunning display of self-possession. When my parents' phones make any noise, they pat themselves down, shrieking like a grenade pin's been pulled. These women hold their eyes on me.

Vanessa stands up. Walks to the back of the room, reaches an old NordicTrak, turns around. "We need to stop this project before someone's hurt, or worse. Where does Dirk Babcot live?"

"Dick Babbot. Malibu."

CHAPTER 53

EXCERPT FROM *AMERICAN MERMAID*

Sylvia tuned her body ever more acutely to the way her sisters moved and thought together as they streamed toward Granger's lab. A little current coming off a change of direction from Kevin, who led the group by a head, nudged the other mermaids into their own slight change. And with that, the five crossed fields of boulders gripped by meaty starfish. They wound through forests of slick kelp, shot through with shafts of light. Now they dashed over beds of long, ropelike stalks topped with shaggy orange-gold pom-poms, like flying over a field of sunflowers in a sunken world. The sunflowers gave way to slappy kelp, blindingly green when the sun poured through the leaves like stained glass. Sylvia frequently caught sight of the backs of schools of little silver darting fish as they departed, always a few seconds ahead of the mermaids. Every new section of the undersea forest was like a room of a house that had just held a conversation; a busy, peopled home. Her home.

The sound of their sister calling to them from the net where Granger held her captive worked on them viscerally. They were desperate to free her. Her calls located Granger's lab for them, but it also confirmed what Sylvia had told them. The mermaid was not merely shrieking but describing in detail a machine with a giant piercer poised above the seabed, ready to plunge and fracture.

As they sped through the pennants of slippery kelp, an idea struck Sylvia from some vestigial human part of her brain. Suddenly she hollered for the mermaids to stop. They all shot forward a few more thrusts and then turned to face her, alarmed and annoyed.

We don't have to do this alone, said Sylvia, who had quickly picked up how to communicate like them, pulsing her thoughts through the water they shared. Why don't we go back and tell the authorities? Masahiro would back us up, tell everything he knows to the press, to the cops. We know who Granger is, and now *where* he is. If the FBI, the EPA, Interpol take him out, then we'll have saved everyone without risking more mermaid lives.

Kareem and Dave were impatient, but Kevin flashed her a short smile. That's the human in you thinking that there is a benevolent "authority" to trust. Our whole existence is a challenge to that authority. If we make ourselves known to people—scientists, governments, well-intentioned children who've read a lot of fairy tales—they will try to own and contain us. You must never think of calling on them, never.

Just as the last waves of Kevin's thoughts departed into the swaying light between the weeds, the group heard a loud crack and then a lasting reverberation from the ground.

Jesus Christ, yelped Sylvia.

I can see it, said Kareem. The others faced the same direction, and now Sylvia saw it, too. Their sonar couldn't penetrate the thick glass panel or the cliff wall in which Granger's lab was embedded, but they saw the drill, twirling furiously, and the ground, split and belching debris beneath it.

The group tightened and departed in unison toward the lab. Again in tune with her pod as they swam in formation, her heart racing, Sylvia felt wholly mermaid—the thought of calling on "the police" felt like someone else's idea. And, idly lavishing her attention on the mossy boulders and the patches of kelp as they swam, *Jesus Christ* echoed through her mind. She almost had no idea what *Jesus Christ* meant, but had some faint recollection that it was a hybrid creature, part human and part something else, and that men had tried to kill it, and failed.

CHAPTER 54

At around eleven this morning I lowered myself into the passenger seat of a Subaru that a sixteen-year-old girl borrowed from her mom and sped on a highway I can't name to invade the home of Dick Babbot, whose gorgeous view of a private sea once nearly gave onto my death.

When we were still in Vanessa's mom's basement, I bit my nails, but the others were on some sort of muscle relaxer of adolescent confidence, shoulders rounded, eyelids half down, snacks a priority. Smiles had voiced some concerns on an ethical level and Serious had a lot to do this weekend, but no one seemed jacked up like men with pantyhose over their faces about to storm a bank.

"You know what it's called," said Vanessa, as we filed up the stairs from the lateral, cushioned pit of her basement into the otherworldly organization of her mother's matching furniture. "It's called a *fishing expedition*."

"What is?" I said.

"When you're not looking for specific evidence, but you're just generally looking around to try to find something to implicate someone. A *fishing expedition*. They say it on every episode of *Los Angeles: Woman Murder*."

Strong boomed with melodramatic frustration, in a very convincing baritone, "YOUR HONOR, THIS IS A *FISHING EXPEDITION*."

"Righty-o, bitches," said Vanessa. "To the boats." We divided into two cars.

I thought we might get there, "case the joint," and they might give me a pep talk, and I might, who knows, talk to Babbot myself, ask him what was happening with the script while the lionesses licked their paws in their parents' cars. But I found us caught in a current of incidents that moved along so swiftly and naturally that it could not be stopped. There was nothing to be done other than to first be let into Dick Babbot's house by his own feckless daughter, and then for my pod to disperse throughout his home in a vague search for information about the status of my script.

"Penny," said Damaged Sarong Daughter when we arrived at the door, heartbreaking in her easy dupability, giving me a big hug. She was on her way out. "So great to see you," she said breathily, looking into my eyes too deeply. I told her I was working on something with her dad and he said I could swing by. She barely batted an eye, tripping lightly off the back steps toward her car as we entered, five minors and me. "Have a great time," she said, jangling her keys good-bye at us.

The house looked different with no one in it. Before, it had seemed like a beach shack, but now I noticed stately furniture, a triangular modernist chair on three peg legs (I shuddered with shame recalling the tessellated pizza puzzle at my non-hotel). There was art on the walls: a kind of sculpture made of string, some paintings hung in bursts on some walls, other walls left bright and stark. I walked around assessing his taste, which seemed at first careless and bohemian ("He doesn't really care about money," Danielle had told me that day on the way here)—beach shoes in sandy corners and hoodies tossed over rattan. But it was also deeply nourished inside its bohemian husk by oodles and oodles of money.

. . .

I warn the girls, "Nobody go swimming!" They look at me quizzically. I tell them about the riptides. I limp a few paces and point to my coccyx. They ignore me. I watch them peel off their clothes and run off the deck, through the sand, into the surf. I watch fretfully from behind the railing. They splash and bob. Sometimes they disappear and I scan the nearby waves for the one that's gone under, but she always comes up, wiping her eyes, beaming. I am hungry, ravenous like when I was teaching, but I can't leave the deck until they've left the water. I remember the feeling of being yanked suddenly, even though I, too, am a good swimmer. But something tells me these women are allies of the tide. For a moment, as I stand watchful on the deck, I imagine this is my home. I have paid for this home with words I wrote and sold to men who chopped those words up afterward. I imagine that I sponsor the joy of people I love here. I'm so glad I moved to California all those years ago to become a screenwriter. I'm delivering a script this week about a stripper who becomes a derivatives trader; about a burned-out corporate mom who falls in love with her male nanny; about a white celebrity who adopts a Black baby and comes to know the restorative beauty that is Africa. I live comfortably with all this and feed my healthy daughters, all strong swimmers.

I light a cigarette on the deck. Vanessa and the women come back in from the water, their wet underpants droopy. There's a basket of towels just inside the sliding door that leads from the deck to the living room, and I hand the towels out with one hand, holding my cigarette outside with the other. Smiles takes a towel from me and wordlessly plucks the cigarette out of my hand and tosses it over the railing into the sand. She replaces it with what looks like a black USB key and departs. *Has she found something pertaining to the script on an external drive?* I wonder for a moment, until I realize it's an e-cigarette. I examine it and suck on the end that doesn't look like a computer chip. At first it feels like a vapid scam in my throat, but my brain tingles after a few drags and I sense it pouring over my gullet like cool rapids instead of hot air. These women don't fire-smoke, they water-smoke.

Inside, I've opened the fridge and taken out some beers, but none of them want any. Clothed again, toweling hair, sitting with legs askew on couch arms and in leather chairs, they face one another, and me, in the living room.

"So what are we looking for here?" I ask. "Should we just go? What are we hoping to find? A copy of the latest version of the script, printed out? What are the chances? A contract? Pornography? Drugs?"

"We're doing drugs," Serious says, swirling a finger around the room to indicate the plenary group.

"You are?" I say. They nod slowly.

"I have summer softball training tomorrow, so I only took a little," says Strong.

"What kind of drugs?" I ask. "Can you drive us back?"

"Verrry small quantities of MDMA. Completely okay for driving."

"It makes you a better driver." Smiles smiles. "More empathic."

"Do you want some?" asks Vanessa.

"No," I say. Absolutely not. I can't be doing Molly in the middle of the day in the home of a *colleague* who doesn't know I'm there. Also, I've never done drugs. I have no idea what the consequences could be. These few weeks *matter*, don't they? These few days, even. Will I fail and fall on my face, leave LA jobless, in humiliation that I ever thought I could do something so ambitious, so world-dazzling, as make the words that movie stars say with the conviction their shimmering faces barely need? This is the time for me to be my sharpest, my keenest. Drinking at Danielle's friends' parties is different; there I lubricate the space between me and opportunity, although I've only moved through lubricated space so far without touching the other side. But this, this is pointless. Illegal, even. You are wonderful women, and I trust you know what you're doing in your young bodies and your rich, hopeful, growing minds, but you have nothing to worry about but "summer softball" and Mom's guac. My future is on the line.

"Are you sure?" asks Vanessa, plainly.

"Fine."

I hold the phone to my ear and it buzzes.

"Hello?"

"Hey."

"How are you?"

"I'm *great*. I'm so, so great."

"Oh! Good. I'm actually at work."

"I'm working, *tooooooo*."

"Fantastic. Euh—can I call you later?"

"*Definitely*. Do."

"Hey, I read your book!"

"You did?"

"Yes! You know, you should come to Switzerland. We have a statue of the little mermaid in Lake Geneva."

"I've never imagined spending any time in Switzerland."

You can lie on MDMA! I feel great. What a great idea to call Franck. Franck and I are in love.

I toss the phone onto Dick Babbot's super-king bed. It lands without a sound in the duck feather duvet. I'm parched. I step back from what I've been doing.

"Whoa," says Serious, who's popped into the master bedroom. "Is it cool to paint on someone's painting?"

I wave my sopping brush at the painting on Babbot's wall. "They're all fake! They're all digital reproductions! Worthless!"

"Where'd you get the paint?"

I got the paint from one of Dick Babbot's Damaged Kids' rooms—or maybe a damaged wife or ex-wife. When I walked into the small, sunny, top-floor room converted to a painting studio, I got the feeling of a sad mom. I sensed foiled, amateurish creativity expressed as a humiliating compulsion, an accidental parody of real "creatives." I could hear the children: "Mom, *don't*." She had made seascapes, the mom, impressionist imitations in flamingo and teal. It made me want to paint, to avenge mom-painting with paint.

Evening sun bright behind his head. It's the lifeguard again. He's back. Has he saved me again? Is he back for the sex I owe him? He's standing over me. I was sleeping. Or was I swimming? Was I swimming in my sleep?

"Mermaid," he says.

I blink a few times. It's Dick Babbot.

"Why don't you put your clothes on. Meet me downstairs."

Dick Babbot tells me there's nothing I can do. He says he's got "like thirteen thousand kids" himself, but showing up here with the fucking glee club is a little weird. "Did any of them drink?" he asks. I say no. He seems relieved. (No need to mention the Molly.) No longer lionesses, they have been shooed out like naughty kittens. They've driven home. Dick Babbot and I are alone. I want to warn him that there are powers that this process has unleashed. The script—it's been changing itself, that's for sure. It's Sylvia. I *know* this. She tried to kill Murphy when he tried to kill her, and Babbot is next in line. There's real danger. I want to tell him, but he's such a strange highball of deadly dad liquor and chill kid fizz, I can't tell whether he will believe me or think I'm cracked. Maybe he'll think it's a threat ("People will get hurt, Dick"). Or he'll buy it—heck, "*This* I gotta write," he'll probably say.

He promises he'll make it a good movie. But it's not mine anymore. "You're out," he says. "Is she gonna be a little sexier than in the version you saw? Yeah, maybe." (*Saw? Saw* in the picture house in my head? As if it was just one of many showings.) "Are some background plot things getting filed down? Yeah." *Some plot things:* Hiroshima. "And I'm sorry, but I've got to kill her off at the end, it's just too good an emotional payload. But it's still your story, okay? This whole seventy-million-dollar machine is whirring into place because of an idea you had. I think that's pretty special." Dick Babbot's cold homemade iced tea, tannic and clawing at my tongue and slapping me awake, goes down gulp after gulp. "If you pull this kind of shit, nobody will want to work with you. And it's not over. People get fired and then get rehired for the final rewrites—be gracious, be lovely, be collegial, and things will come *back* to you. Fired in LA isn't like fired from General Motors."

Everyone is reborn here. Or does porn here. Finds something. The plant never closes. We are not the men in boiler suits whose TVs get taken. Our failures evaporate in the sun and rain back down in other forms.

I must look miserable, because the victim of my own break-in puts his hand on my knee, which I can't be mad about because I came to his house, took a club drug, and fell asleep with my pants off on the heavenly cumulus of his master bed. He says, "I'll show you my notes, if that's what you want."

"What do you mean?"

"I'll tell you what I'm planning to do to the script."

Oh, *notes*. Right. Building-block baby vocabulary of LA writer life that never became intuitive. "Give me notes." I always saw in my mind a literal notepad with "Buy more Pert Plus" scribbled in thin BIC. I nod at Dick Babbot, who pats my knee again and lopes upstairs to get his notes. Maybe this is very generous—he doesn't have to do this. He could kick me out. Worse, I suppose. He could really ruin my life now. But he's sharing the state of the project with me, just to make me feel bet—

"PENELOPE!"

The hair stands up on my head. Oh shit: his painting.

CHAPTER 55

EXCERPT FROM *AMERICAN MERMAID*

There was nothing in his voice but the softness of a loving father reunited with his prodigal daughter.

"Sylvia."

Granger had never seen his daughter swim, never seen her split, until now. Only minutes ago, Granger had watched Sylvia appear on the other side of the glass pane, at first like a distant animal and then, as she got closer, taking shape as something Granger never imagined possible: Sylvia, moving through the water with a powerful tail. From her side of the glass, she had been able to look into the amphitheater, which glowed like a diorama in the dark sea. She saw Granger waiting for her in an office chair. They locked eyes, and Granger, in wonder, approached the glass. They couldn't speak, but Granger found himself clapping, silently applauding her new aquatic existence. He had made a waving motion as if to invite her in. He pointed to a pressurized portal that would permit her entry to the lab. She had consulted with the five mermaids at her side—the four who had swum there with her, and the one they released from Granger's net with knives they pulled from the back of their plastic bodices. They had all said, Go. Talk to him. We'll be here if you need us.

The interior chamber of the portal had opened and dumped Sylvia like a load of washing. Unlike the workmen in wet suits who usually stepped out, Sylvia landed on the floor where, within thirty seconds, she had split. She now sat slumped, exhausted and diminished. She could no longer hear her sisters. She had no powers. Worse, Granger had made no preparation for her: there was no wheelchair, no towel, no clothes. Embarrassed, he had thrown her a fire blanket. Stunned, face framed by stringy hair, she looked like a woman rescued from a sinking ship.

"This is what you go through?" Granger sensed there was something impolitic about hovering over the sad heap of his daughter, so he crouched down beside her. "I did not order Masahiro to do this. Your mother and I made the decision that you'd be safer, you'd lead a better, richer life, among us. Maybe you feel that we were wrong. But we never intended you to have this kind of torturous pain—that was all Masahiro."

"It's fine." Sylvia didn't like the way her father dwelled on her pain. It was hers; she'd spent years with it. She would decide what that pain meant, not her father. Besides: "I live in the water now—there will be no more pain. I've come out one last time to talk to you." Granger listened, but he was distracted by the biological spectacle of Sylvia's lower half: the fibers snapping shut over Sylvia's legs, the retraction of her fins into the stumps he had always considered an unfortunate inevitability of her conversion. Silently, he admitted to himself that Masahiro's ingenuity and skill were remarkable.

"The most important thing is that you're alive. I couldn't be happier just to see you, sweetheart." He felt that a hug would be unwelcome—his daughter seemed guarded and ashamed under the fire blanket. But he stayed crouched next to her, held her shoulder. "I need you. I need you to help me."

"*Help* you? Masahiro told me your plan. I'm not here to help you."

"I doubt he related it accurately. He couldn't have known the full scale or ambition. Did he tell you *why* I've decided to advance global warming?"

"To become more powerful—to capitalize on a disaster."

"I am worth over three billion dollars, Sylvia. I don't need more money or power. I am initiating the Great Flood for you, and for them." Sylvia followed the sweep of Granger's arm toward the glass, where the mermaids all hovered together. They stayed at the pane, pressing their hands to it, watching Sylvia as if their very attention could protect her.

"It's also the right thing to do." Granger asked her to imagine a future *without* their intervention: In the developing world, coastal regions would become unlivable and agriculture impossible. Within thirty years, five hundred million poor people would be set on paths of migration, killed by disease and violence. "There's only one way to prevent this scenario." He pointed to the machine on the seabed beyond the glass, behind the mermaids. "I'm going to put a lot of people out of their misery, quickly. It's a compassionate move. We are the only ones that can possibly survive," Granger assured her. "I know this."

Sylvia, naked, powerless, herself a migrant between worlds, felt she and her father acting out this global divide between a wretched south, benighted and doomed, and a powerful north, arid and confident, technology at his disposal. She was naked and half woman and hurt, her insides sloshing around with the compromising toxin of rage; he was the tidy man, tall, cool, and clothed, in possession of all the facts.

But Granger was inviting her to join him, to climb up into the dry seat of power. This wasn't about him, he said—he was sixty-five, he wouldn't inhabit this new world for long. This was about *her*.

"If this is all for me, then why isn't Mom involved? She loves me more than anyone." Granger was silent. "You did all this behind Mom's back. She would never sign on to this kind of destruction."

"No, she wouldn't. I had to leave her out of this. Your mother would want to save everyone, and we don't have that luxury. But *you* do, at least when it comes to your own kind. When the catastrophe comes—and make no mistake, it's coming—where will the mermaids be? Starving? Dying? At the mercy of men? Imagine, instead, we could not only save them but hand them the controls. Think about it. Instead of using their *astonishing* sonar telepathy to hide from tourists and find shrimp, they'll use their skills to build, to work. Let's unleash their abilities, let them really develop. Think of the education you've had! Do you not want to share it with them? Are they all as clever as you? Imagine the power, the ingenuity that's been rotting away in their damp domes for a million years."

"You don't know the first thing about their intelligence or how they use it."

"Then tell me! I'm dying to know. How many are there? How is society organized? What's the farthest your sonar travels? Does it transmit complex imagery or only verbal cues? *You* are the link, the only one who can help us find and incorporate the mermaids. And in so doing, save them. When the plankton's fried and the clams have shriveled, you will need access to the lab-grown proteins, the military MREs that keep people alive."

"You just want to exploit the mermaids. This isn't about saving their lives."

"You have it all wrong," said Granger. He described how at the time of their choosing—it could be tomorrow, everything was in place—Granger and Sylvia would set off the geothermal lasers, all identical to this one. Within a matter of days, the lasers, strategically positioned on the seafloor all over the world, densely beneath Greenland and the international Arctic territories, would liquefy the world's largest remaining ice holdings. Within a matter of weeks, there would be 40 percent less visible landmass. "More *sea*, Sylvia. More for you!

"EarthSource will no longer be a company. It will be more important than any single government on earth. It will hold survival in its hands." He described the pontoon systems that would protect the global north, already manufactured and ready to be sold, already shipped precisely to the locations Granger had calculated they'd be needed. Passports, nationalities, health insurance. None of it would matter. Whether you live or die would depend on EarthSource.

"You'd be a murderer."

"Another reason mermaids are my ideal staff. They are cold-hearted and efficient killers."

Sylvia shook away the memory of the GoPro footage of a man drowning at her own hands and resented her father acutely for the possibility that he may be right.

"If you want to be a hero, this is how you do it. Leave the darkness and come up into the light." Granger had been pacing, not with anxiety but with energy, with pride in all the carefully considered facets of his plan. "What I'm offering you *now*, in no uncertain terms, is to be the most powerful woman—person—on earth." His words echoed in the empty amphitheater, so cold and uninhabited compared to the sea she had just traversed.

She didn't want to be restored to a life on land, dusty, unsalted, everything detached and crumbling. But there was some angle that her mind now worked, some promise in what her father said. She looked down at her thin, wilted legs, tucked under her out of a habit of shame. *The most powerful woman in the world.* Maybe he was right that joining this project was the best way to look after the mermaids.

"You are the only person on the planet who can stand atop the final calamity and own it, manage it—profit from it. The server farms will be sitting in two feet of water, the South Asian tech assistants will be floating in rivers. There will be no infrastructure, no communications. Your mermaids will manage the pontoons, you will build and run and control the new infrastructure that humans inhabit."

Sylvia looked through the glass at the mermaids, hiding out and unknown for thousands of years. Would they want to run the human world, to own everything?

"There's one last reason I've done all this, Sylvia. A systemic ecological apocalypse is coming for everyone's sons and daughters. Its floods and hurricanes will take their homes and their savings; its freshly released pathogens will poison their blood. They will lie, cheat, bribe, and kill for clean drinking water. You're my daughter and I love you, and you can call me a madman or a cynic, but I'm also a rational actor, and I have a chance to give you an economic advantage. You will sail above this. You, and maybe your kids someday, will never have to worry. And you'll have them on your knee, and they'll be healthy and strong and educated, and you'll say, 'My dad was a complicated guy. But look what he did for us.'"

"But all those other people? Their kids?"

"Survival, like anything else, is a marketplace."

Granger saw this last sentence land badly with his daughter, who shook her head vigorously, droplets still falling from the tips of her hair. He had overestimated her grasp of economics. It was time for him to use the last persuasive device that remained to him.

"Of course, Masahiro is with us."

"With us?" Sylvia looked up, round-eyed.

"A key player in CleanBeam. He's a smart guy—you think he wants to end up sick and starving? He's seen what happens to the losing side of a great war."

The last she had seen of Masahiro, he had been leaning over the edge of the boat, his hair spiky and mussed from near death at the strong hands of a mermaid named Dave. He had given Sylvia a smile of encouragement as she dipped below the water and charged off with her sisters to find Granger. Masahiro, they agreed, would bring the boat as close to Granger's R&D station as he could and remain at the ready to treat any mermaids wounded in an eventual conflict. She had mapped him, in her mind, hundreds of feet above their heads, staring into the wind and waiting for a sign.

"He's in a boat, he's—"

"No, no. I fetched him earlier today—we've been in touch via text since his 'death.'"

"He faked his death to get away from you!"

"No, sweetheart. He faked his death to get away from the FBI.

He'd been a suspect in his father's death for years and they were finally closing in." Granger leaped up a few steps of the amphitheater to a bank of equipment where he picked up a phone and mumbled some instructions. A few seconds later, he pushed a button, and with a buzz, a door to the lab opened and Masahiro appeared.

"Doc!" Sylvia leaned toward him, but her legs remained immobile under her. She searched his eyes as he emerged into the bright lights of the amphitheater. But he was strange. He wore newer, nicer clothes in all black. As if the Masahiro she had known had been an actor, the Converse and the shaggy hair and the doctor's coat with the Twix in the pocket had been part of his "character," and here he was, cleaned up, ready to do press. He didn't run to her, as she would have expected, but walked coolly over and placed a hand on her shoulder, just as her father had done.

Sylvia turned to her father, baffled. "You tried to have him *killed*. You sent Lawrence after us."

"Lawrence was only supposed to bring you in. But he did something far more valuable, as Masahiro has informed me. He's shown us what *you* are capable of." Sylvia looked away, so filled with conflicting impulses that she was afraid her father would see some fatal vulnerability in her, would find a point of entry to poison her mind. "There's no shame in it, Sylvia. Not here. We understand. We've taken lives, and we will take more." Masahiro nodded guiltily like a parishioner listening to a hard sermon on sin. "Not everyone can survive. We have to choose. I chose you. Masahiro chooses you. What do you say?" He moved toward his daughter.

Sylvia felt disoriented. The idea that they were a hard-nosed confraternity of compassionate killers was both ridiculous and, on the facts, impossible to dismiss. Mermaids might be natural allies in the work of human triage that Granger had described—of allowing some to live at the expense of others. And if the mermaids refused to collaborate, they would need Sylvia's protection all the more. Granger kneeled next to Sylvia and swept her hair off her face.

"Join me."

Sylvia put her head on her father's shoulder, something she hadn't done in ten years.

"Will you join me?" he asked, pulling away, holding her head in his hands.

She locked eyes with him and nodded yes.

CHAPTER 56

"Just let me come meet you," I begged Derek. He had not been picking up his phone. "What bar are you at?" I was headachy from the MDMA, the ocean receding behind me through the rear view of a cab. "I'll meet you anywhere."

I assumed he was at a bar. Night had fallen, after all. My non-hotel room—our apartment—had become almost uninhabitable, the pizza-box flood not yet drained. These days we pushed open the door, kicked our way to our beds, and that was about it.

"I'm at a party," he said. "I don't know the address. I'll meet you back home."

Derek had his own parties now?

We are on the life raft of the sofa, our feet up. Derek lights a glass pipe full of weed and, choking on his breath, hands it to me.

"No, thanks," I say. "I need to be clearheaded." I pour a third of a bottle of sauvignon blanc into a pint glass of ice.

"Derek." I fall straight forward, my face landing between Derek's shoulder and the sofa, which, of course, both smell like mozzarella. "I don't know what's happening." I tell him about how we snuck into Babbot's house to try to take him down and ended up naked and humiliated. I can hear Randy and Murphy talking about it somewhere in their Posse Pit:

Babbot says Penny did Molly with children.
I thought dorks were supposed to be smart.
I told you, she has a screw loose.
Where did she find children?

I tell Derek about the painting, about Sylvia. "Sylvia's doing it," I say. "Remember how sometimes—didn't this happen to you?—when we were teaching, you would feel the book leak into your life in strange ways?"

Derek is unusually silent, his default geniality switched off. He's holding my arm. His bowl is on the table. He takes a gulp from my pint glass.

"Sylvia's here in LA," I continue. "She's doing things. You remember the reading? That wasn't me. I didn't insert those lines in the script, I swear to god. And it wasn't Randy or Murphy, and they're the only ones with the password. Sylvia. Somehow. I'm *not drunk* right now. I'm being serious. She's here. And she's mad. And I don't know what to do. I did the dumbest thing, going to Babbot's, and I failed. I didn't manage to warn Babbot. But I *know her*, I know her so well, and I know that she is capable of killing."

Just the two of us, we've been our own kind of crazy before. I don't feel stupid telling him this. He knows, he's been to the deep places in all the books with me.

"I failed to rescue her. She's stuck in this horrible script and they're carving her up, they're giving her huge terrible implants and sexual chemistry with Masahiro who's, like, a hot karate instructor now and—"

"Penelope." Derek's voice is like a stranger's. It's so executive. It belongs in this apartment he's trashed with his charity. It knows what to do with the scanner. It makes a Nespresso Fortissio in the morning and puts its cup in the dishwasher. "There's no mermaid magic. Sylvia's not here."

But she is, she is.

"It was me."

"What do you mean?" He must not understand what I'm telling him.

"I did the edits in the master script." It was for my own good. He knew this was making me miserable, he knew I didn't want to see this book I cared so much about go under the knife of these money-grubbing creeps. "I didn't know it would get to your head like this. It got out of hand. I just thought I'd help you assert yourself with these dickhead writers. I didn't think it would make you *crazy*."

For a moment he melts back into the Derek I've always known. A little rakishness animates his face, a little grin: "See? Of *course* I read the novel. I read the whole thing, before I even came out here." As if he is a great friend, after all. As if he wants me to think he's considerate because he gave me a signed Hallmark card for my birthday, but he also went to my job wearing a mask of my face and broke all the rules.

Derek's arm drops like a fishing hook behind the sofa and comes up with a triangle of pizza. After some labor-intensive chewing that strains the elasticity of his soft sofa lips, he says, words still food-choked, "I hope I didn't get you fired."

"They say that happens on every movie." *You most certainly did get me fired. But I can't say that to you, because I'm a human woman who can't bear to hurt your feelings.*

He takes my pint glass again.

"Ice in wine. Penny. *So good.*" As if *this* is why I'm a genius. This is the most brilliant thing I've ever done. He swooshes it around in his mouth to help him swallow pizza and hands me back the glass with bits of food in it. "I also have more news." *News. News ticker: Best friend and moral anchor impersonates woman at work, gets her fired.* "I got an agent."

"A what?"

"I'm doing voice-over stuff." Derek's performance at the reading impressed one of Jellica Nye's agents, who put him in touch with a voice-over agent, who hooked him up with a coach.

"How are you paying for the coaching?"

"They're doing the up-front coaching free." He drinks from the pint glass and ice rattles and pops like distant applause, an old-fashioned flash. "It's really giving me an insight into how they make ads and things. It's hilarious. Can you imagine? I'll be the guy like, 'Hey, are your tampons dry enough?'"

I flinch.

"When did you tamper with the script?"

"At night," he says cheerfully, as if this is when people with probity do things. "When you were sleeping. I must have logged in with your password."

"What do you mean you *must have*? You don't remember?"

"Hold on, let me think about it." Derek freezes a moment. He thinks hard. "Yeah. I used the ten-digit password you keep on that index card by your laptop."

"Well, I didn't expect—"

"Can you get *me* a wine tumbler? That's honestly so good."

"Sure."

"The thing I love," I hear him say from the sofa as I open the fridge, "is that I'm going to get to see capitalism *from the inside*, you know? It's fucking cool. Maybe I can even slip in subliminal messages of institutional critique."

"'Go bleach your asshole!'" I say, quoting him like he's Marx and the phrase is from *Capital*.

"Exactly! And the pay is crazy. It doesn't make any sense."

"No," I say, plopping back down on the sofa next to him and welling up. It doesn't make sense. I'm an idiot English teacher. It's the only thing I can do. Derek hugs me. "I thought Sylvia had sabotaged the fish special at a restaurant," I say through bursts of sobs, feeling tiny and ridiculous. I had no enemies here but myself.

"Yeah," Derek says smoothing my hair. "You need a break."

There's no such thing as Sylvia, only "Sylvia," contained in quotation marks, the paired joke drawing of seabirds. There are only jokes and drawings, only the things people make to delight each other that fail or succeed, but none of it saves anyone, and none of it kills.

CHAPTER 57

EXCERPT FROM *AMERICAN MERMAID*

Dead, not dead.
Dead, not dead.

This was a game Eleanor Granger played. She didn't want to play it, but it played anyway in her mind as she did anything, plucked peas from their pods, replaced books on their shelves. Not much of peas and books now. A friend had reported to Dean that Eleanor had been roaming the neighborhood disheveled, so he brought her to Vágar, where she bumped around the glossy pine mansion, walking into rooms to get something and forgetting what she needed.

Dead, not dead.

She counted measures of gin, two, three, four. *Not dead.* Her heart soared a little, bumped aloft by childish hope. Dean had told her that they found Sylvia's wheelchair by the pier, but no body yet. It looked like a suicide. In all likelihood, he told her, Sylvia was gone. *I am drunk, crazy, tired,* thought Eleanor. *I am a foolish woman. I have no evidence, but I don't believe she's dead. She's here, doing things, in this world.* Absentminded, she wandered out of the kitchen. The words began to lose their meaning and filled her head like a nursery rhyme or an elocution game: *Not dead, not dead, Sylvia is not dead.*

Eleanor found herself at the elevator to Dean's lab, a place she'd never set foot. She pushed the button and waited. Her daughter had hit rock bottom. Her daughter had needed her. She hadn't been listening. But she listened now. And she heard something. She stepped inside the elevator doors. *My husband doesn't know everything.* She remembered when they decided to keep Sylvia, the feeling of bursting, melting, becoming the sea for her new baby. She had forgotten to do it. Too busy being a wife. But she did it again now, brackish gin moving a whole torrent of blood in her—a marine ecosystem of currents and tides. She was becoming not the woman of ten, fifteen years ago, but a creature of tens, hundreds of thousands of years ago. She heard her baby's voice. Sylvia, she suddenly felt with intense conviction, was not dead. Once again, she needed to dive down.

The glass fell from her hand as the elevator doors to Granger's lab slid open and she saw them all.

CHAPTER 58

This party feels different. In contrast to the empty promises made about Dick Babbot's house, at this sleek, tiered mansion jammed into a canyon there are goats. When I arrived here (Uber—Derek had a mysterious commitment), I sought out Danielle as my immediate social anchor. I found her quickly, her stiff blazer threatening to razor bits off the ethereal maxi dresses of the two women who flanked her. I recognized one of the women as the costume supervisor Felicia from Danielle's house, a little lost, bodily, in the ruffled pinafores of a Mennonite bride, but beaming nonetheless. All three leaned against a granite-topped island. When Danielle gave me a hug and said, "Have you met the goats?" I thought she was introducing me to her friends as "Have you met the ghost?" I was stunned at how quickly my death-by-firing had been achieved.

Felicia picked a lime out of her tumbler and handed it to me. "Here," she said, "give it to the goats. They eat it, rind and all."

The other woman was a tall blond foil to Felicia's short, dark curves. She said, with a voice that was, untraceably but certainly, that of an idiot, "Goats are *suuuuper* environmental."

So before I had uttered a word, I had transformed into some combination of a dead person and a child, given a sugar cube to feed the ponies. Fine with this, Felicia's rum-soaked wedge in my hand stinking like the dentures of a drunk, I walked outside. I passed scattered groups of people until they thinned out, past an empty, undisturbed pool that only shot back, in harsher form, the strings of yellow-white bulbs that illuminated my path across the patio. The lights terminated at a tall post, after which I could make out, with the residual light from the house and the help of a big moon, an uneven but inviting slope of low shrubs and polished pebbles and cacti and flagstones. (This must be "*suuuuper environmental.*") Back farther, the shape of little beasts, and the sound of them bleating gently. They scuffed the stones with hooves that sounded soft and hollow, like baked pottery.

I walked out to the goats until, even in the dark, we were close enough that I could see them clearly, the absolute lovable ridiculousness of them, with their bone-hard faces and baby snub horns, the nervous, simple, endless lateral chewing of their narrow, girl-child mouths, and the hilarity of their human teeth. I showed a little gray-and-black one Felicia's lime and asked skeptically, "You want this?" He put a warm lip over the rind, brushing my finger, which gave me a giddy frisson of animal contact, and the lime was gone. Two more goats came over to me, collarless and similarly brindled. "I got nothing," I told them, appreciating, as they hovered near me, the white-and-black bristles of their muzzles like a fine pencil drawing. It's what I'd been wanting to tell everyone in LA since I got here, and I could finally say it, alone in the dark, to a trio of garbage-can goats: "I've got nothing for you."

Somehow relieved, and oddly, though not drunk, feeling drunk in the freedom of animal company, I pulled a cigarette out of the ass pocket of my jeans—pre-LA jeans that are horrible and give me a weird dick and widen my waist by miles. But I've stopped believing in the whispering silkish promises of whimsically overpriced shifts and shells. I lit a cigarette and took a deep drag and reached for the fence to lean against.

I found myself yelping, my arm flung back from the fence, my hand throbbing with pain. "WHAT THE FUCK!" I screamed into the night, and in the pale dregs of light, I could see that the palm of my hand was snow-white, bloodless, veinless. I heard a high electric whine in my ears. *"What the—"*

"Someone should have warned you." Too shocked to register the secondary shock of company, I tried to shake the feeling back into my dead hand.

"What the *fuck*?"

"Yeah, that's an electric fence. How do you think they keep the goats in?"

"Jesus."

"It's cool, it's like two hundred volts. It's like putting your finger in a socket. A couple sockets."

I finally looked up from my fried hand to the source of this wisdom. It was a woman with a low voice, about my height, sitting in a wheelchair.

"I'll take a cigarette," she said. I handed her one.

"What are you doing out here? Aside from not warning people?" I lit the cigarette in her closed, laughing lips.

"What are *you* doing out here?" she asked.

"Feeding the goats," I said. Her hand sailed out, palm up, as if to say *Well, there you go*. We exhaled simultaneously and took a moment to survey the strange landscape on the other side of the fence, the illuminated squares and rectangles of the houses nailed to the facing side of the canyon, their Lego-like geometry vaguely sensed in the dark against the balding slope. It was completely silent, except for the occasional peal of laughter from the party and the hiccup-cackles of the goats. "Where are all the fucking crickets?" I asked, residually annoyed by my electrocution. I brought my hand up to my face: it was still pale but now crackled with red, like the map of a state showing county lines. I dropped my hand.

This woman weighed something silently, her eyes now pinned to mine, as a smile expanded across her face. "You're not in Connecticut anymore, Penelope."

CHAPTER 59

EXCERPT FROM *AMERICAN MERMAID*

"I promise, you belong here." Dean Granger was on his knees, holding his damp child. "Masahiro—open those cases." He pointed to a stack of Dom Perignon parked in the corner of the room that he'd been saving for the CleanBeam launch.

Sylvia turned again to the mermaids. They were all pressed against the glass. Their glinting tails swirled beneath them as they peered at Sylvia, looking for a sign. Still seated, she raised herself up on shaky knees and held her hands to the screen. They gathered around her image, their hands pressed against hers, shrieking out cries that died on the glass.

"Look at that," Granger marveled. "You are their leader, Sylvia. They've stayed for you. They'll be your secret weapon at EarthSource. Your deputies. They look like they're ready for orders."

Masahiro, Granger, and Sylvia gazed together at the undulating women, who, silenced by the pane between them, were a gorgeous display.

The cork popped. Three glasses hovered. "To Sylvia," said Masahiro. "Safe and sound."

CHAPTER 60

I'm in the back seat of a stranger's tin can car going home—*home* now, for real—from the last LA party I will attend, where, to my surprise, I was electrocuted in a field of goats. I will stop at the non-hotel to pack my salt-stinking things from among the wasteland of cardboard, and then I will fly to New York. My mom will pick up the pieces. As my father, a successful person, predicted.

"You're not in Connecticut anymore, Penelope," said the wheelchair-borne woman in the scrub-brush field, and I squinted at her to make sure, but no, I had never seen her before in my life.

"How do you know my name?" I asked.

"I'm the reason you're here."

It was her. Finally. She was here. "Sylvia?"

She looked around. I could see in the moonlight that she had a brown, matte bob like me, that she was a careless user of shitty shampoo.

"*Sylvia?* Ha!"

"But—but the wheelchair!"

"Oh. I just had my varicose veins lasered. I'm not supposed to walk."

"Who *are you*? How do you know my name?"

"I'm Stem Hollander."

For all of these weeks, at all of these parties, I have looked for the chiseled puckish blond billionaire that we all know and like like like from the internet. I've held his Lancelot locks in my mind's eye as I've scanned the rooftops and the poolsides, knowing that he read me and liked me and led lots of readers to me with a momentary cast of his heavily filtered digital lamplight. And then this frizzy-haired lady in a wheelchair was upon me, telling me that the man in the Instagram pictures—the man everyone knew to be Stem Hollander—was an Argentinian himbo she paid to perform. This brought in the millions of followers and the hundreds of thousands of likes. She told me she came out here when her novel was optioned, ten years ago. "You remember *One Hot Mama*, the Cameron Diaz comedy about a teenager whose mom is an embarrassing nudist?"

Of course.

"That movie started life as my deeply serious memoir about my mother's early onset dementia."

"Jesus."

"Penny, you think you've failed."

"I know I have."

Stem Hollander dropped her cigarette butt and stamped it out. A goat trotted over and ate it.

"On the contrary. Without knowing you were doing it, you've outsmarted the whole system. You've done the only thing you can to save your book."

"What? Made an asshole of myself? Shown everyone how crazy and incompetent I am?" I figured it was just a woman giving another woman a boost, feeding me lies to restore my self-esteem. "I didn't protect her. I got greedy."

"Development, Penny. You got *American Mermaid* stuck in development."

"What do you mean?"

"Penny, you made just enough trouble that the studio needed 'fresh eyes.' They're bringing in a new team—"

"Yeah, Dick Babbot—"

She was unflappable. Nothing was new. "It doesn't matter, they could revive the corpse of Orson Welles, it would still be stuck *forever*. New executives, young dudes with tight little balls, will want to 'make their mark'; they'll veto things in the script they hit with a dart from the other side of their tiki bar. They'll think they need to suggest plot twists and character developments in order to leave their special mark—*ssssss*," she hissed with wide eyes, I think intending to invoke the sound of piss but momentarily looking like a hypnotized adder, "on the script."

I'd already seen what mark-making looked like on my work. "Masahiro will be a sex god."

"Yeah, and he'll have partial facial palsy or mild Tourette's. The dad will be a tortured war vet." That didn't make sense.

"From which war?"

"THE WAR." She rolled her eyes and waved her hands.

"The war," I repeated, as dumb as the dumb truth of it. She motioned for another cigarette. I handed her one, put one in my mouth, and lit both.

"Penny." She breathed deeply and shot the smoke out in a hard, direct stream, up into the night. "Sylvia's fine. She's swimming around, unharmed, in a big, beautiful tank, a holding tank. They can't hurt her. This movie will *never* come out."

"But *One Hot Mama* came out! They ruined *your* life, they made a joke out of your dead mother."

"She's not dead yet."

Must learn to listen better.

"You have to be like your namesake."

"Penelope Gruber, my mom's best friend from growing up? I should be an eye doctor outside of Tampa?"

"No, the original Penelope. From the *Odyssey*. Who undoes her own tapestry every night. Never finishes it. The men never get to possess her."

"Oh, sure. Penelope—Ithaca—McIthica or whatever." Electrocution is no joke.

"Let them unweave your tapestry. Never complete it. Development, always in development. That's what I learned." She pointed at me with two short, chubby fingers, like a lady's pistol in a noir. "I've sold six more scripts and learned the art that *you intuited* of having other people put them into development. 'Fresh eyes' are actually shriveled Craisins in the skull of a mummy in a wide Brioni tie in Burbank or Culver City, and they will turn to dust before reaching consensus with ten other Craisin-eyes about the story that once was yours." Another gorgeous jet of white smoke, her head back. Then she looked me dead in the eye. "I take home a ton of money."

"What's a Craisin?"

"It's a cranberry-raisin hybrid."

How did they do that? I'm incompetent. I should die.

"Why 'Stem Hollander'?"

"I'm trying to *do something* in the world, Penny. Imploding, farcical scripts pay the bills. I use Stem Hollander as a lighthouse beam, to pick out the talents I think deserve attention. Put it this way, Penny. I'm your real agent." My fairy godmother, watching me the whole time. Please, warm watcher of my waylaid summer, tell me:

"What do I do now?"

"Write more."

The only answer I was not prepared to hear. The only thing I cannot do. "I don't have any more ideas." I have looked inside me, but there is nothing. I'm still consumed with *American Mermaid,* mangled and leering in the foreground, and the rest is the factory settings: fear of poverty, loneliness, and death.

"That's not true."

"I'm telling you, I only had one story."

"Then I guess I was wrong about you."

Tired and confused, without thinking, I leaned on the electric fence.

ZZZAP.

"GODDAMMIT."

. . .

I will live at home. I have seventy-six thousand dollars in my checking account, but the restoration of Dick Babbot's John Currin painting is going to cost over fifty thousand. It was not a digital print. I painted a black sports bra over the wobbling, carnation-pink, gum-chewed breasts of a barely teenage nude, and where her hands parted her sex as if picking the pickle from a burger, I slathered black again, down to the bottom of the frame. I should have covered her face, her Mouseketeer nose and yearbook smile, but I must have fallen asleep. Thankfully I had used a water-based paint (the choice of amateur moms, just playing), which could be lifted off the oil without leaving a trace on any part of the $2.8 million painting.

I'll pay for my surgery and I'll have nothing left.

Two point eight million dollars! I should be a painter. I'll paint in my parents' guest room, like Dick Babbot's embarrassing wives.

I called Principal Pamela and asked for my job back, but she said they'd already inked a contract with a replacement. I think back to my students on Lily Bart in *House of Mirth:* "When she has nothing left to sell, DUH, she takes a thousand Tylenol." I envision myself in one of Lily Bart's dresses, dead on Lily Bart's divan.

I shrink into the back seat of the Uber. I'm embarrassed to be in LA now. If the real people of LA—the guy pulling a picnic cooler down the street, the bored lady in her banged-up white car next to us, the group of young girlfriends in loud clothes waiting to cross the street—were to turn their attention to me, they'd become fierce right away. They'd smell it on me: "You're still here? Go home!" I'm ashamed to be seen by the driver whom I called.

We stall in a long line of cars at a red light next to a strip mall and I stare absentmindedly at a big green Starbucks logo. My breath catches.

My gaze skates over the algae-green lines of the sign above my head. The Starbucks logo is a mermaid, and her tail is split down the middle, and she's holding each half up in one arm. I never noticed before—I think I thought the logo was of a deer or an owl—but it's a mermaid sawn in half. How overwhelming, how impossible was the burden to protect her, when the world excites itself and wakes and works under the sign of a mermaid razored in half, not in literature but in life. She's been in every city, on every corner, following me from the start. She *has* been here. I'm so tired, so tired, but I hear a ringing in my ears that becomes a singing in my ears. It is high-pitched, a song coming from within and without, my inner world and outer world hysterically joined by a sound like a musical saw. I am not drunk, and I find in myself a belief I can't dislodge: This is Sylvia's song.

I lean toward the driver: "I'm so sorry, but could you take me to the sea?"

"What do you mean 'the sea'?"

"I don't know, the nearest sea?" Silence. "The ocean." As if "The Ocean" is the sea's address, the name of its condo.

"I could take you to Santa Monica. It's, like, a thirty-minute drive."

"Perfect."

"Are you sure you're okay?" he asks.

"Yeah," I reassure him. "I'm meeting my boyfriend there."

Just before midnight, at the public beach, some wandering couples stroll along the boardwalk, having drifted over from the pier. The Ferris wheel is still lit up garishly against the blue-gray sky and the quiet water. I take my shoes off and curl my toes, which my ugly mules have strengthened freakishly, into the infinite sand. I leave my clothes in a pile.

There are some people in the water. I feel more connected to them, bobbing like bottles, than to anyone I know. We swimmers, we who had to be here, wet together in the dry night, we are bonded like drunks. Even the couple I see side-lit in red from the Ferris wheel, who are maybe having intercourse or maybe just straddling and bouncing with the bounce of the sea that's bouncing me, they're my kin. Once in, I feel the cold on every part of me, feel every hair zing, feel every bump plump, feel more than anything—maybe out of shock—my female biology awakened by iciness, frigidly alive like the sea itself. The cold, all-infiltrating water tells me, "You're right, you're absolutely right to forego love and its tacky transactions, its foregone conclusions of pawing and pairing off, its resemblance to buying and selling. You are more alive with your poon on ice, alone in the black bath of the sea. Welcome. We know you here. Dive down and play."

Then I meet an old acquaintance: I feel the tide wrap its fist around me and pull.

As I'm ripped down shore, the words of the script race through my ears—*what you're capable of—are we gonna drown—you are a hunter—what a waste—why aren't I normal?*

Wait. The first time. When Murphy said I'd cut that scene from the script, the horrible scene with Sylvia moaning about desire. Derek wasn't in LA yet. Derek couldn't have done it. I didn't do it and Derek didn't do it.

I dive down, where the only color is cold, the only sound is stinging, the only thought is a clattering of pebbles.

I hear the sex couple call for a lifeguard.

No more need for heroes. I feel my muscles alive as I twist and I twist, my spine suddenly a perfect rosary, free of pain. Thrashing my tail, I know I will get back.

PART IV

UP FOR AIR

CHAPTER 61

Up, up, up. I have left the black deeps where the eyeless fishes move unseen. The air gulped and held in my lungs pulls me up, as if in a straight, walled shaft.

But at the same time, I am in the lagoon with the mermaids, tails flopped over the basalt ledge, everyone gathered. My mother, my real mermaid mother, is there, quietly watching me. Kevin speaks.

You think she'll stay here? Or go back.

It's up to her, honey.

I hope she stays. That place was all wrong for her.

There's a pause.

Do you know what went wrong?

Have you read her book?

Of course.

She thought Sylvia sort of . . . exerted some kind of power in LA. Like she was there.

I bet she did! I bet she was.

No, it turned out it was her hot homeless friend pranking her.

Are you sure?

Don't know. *He* quit teaching now. So Penny's gonna get his job.

She told me. I'm so happy for her. It's what she loves.

Do you want to get, like, Seattle Bread Company?

I think I'd prefer to stay here.

Ew, no, not for us. For her. But we have to put it in a no-name bag because I think she thinks Seattle Bread Company is racist or something.

(I'm rising faster and faster.)

Well, if she doesn't want to eat Seattle Bread Company maybe we shouldn't try to sneak it into her.

Well, which is worse? That? Or this hospital Jell-O made from racehorse carcass?

The mother mermaid *ummm*s softly, her tail swishing. She looks into a bloody bag of fish.

(I'm rising so fast now that the surface is seconds away.)

I brought some homemade buns.

Oh my god. Buns. You are John Jacob Jingleheimer Schmidt. Like, you live in a shoe.

The mother mermaid laughs softly. What do you mean?

Buns!

She loves my buns. She's coming back now, I have a feeling.

Mommy, there's no such thing as buns. A bun is just a roll that a nursery rhyme calls a bun.

The mermaids laugh.

I reach the air. Cutting up through the surface, I gasp and sink back down, bobbing now. My eyes crack open. Susie and my mom are sitting to my left. To my right is a trolley stacked with machines. One beeps regularly.

My mother says, "Penny, baby. Oh, she's up. Penny. Are you okay? Are you hungry?"

"You look great, by the way. This flat-chest thing is *so you*."

My mother looks at Susie with concern.

"Trust me, she knows what I'm talking about." Susie winks at me and mouths "asexual." I'm too weak to protest.

My mother turns back to me, running her hand down the length of my legs because my upper body is too tender, tears welling in her eyes. "You're safe," she says. Without saying it aloud, she tells me that I will not die of the things that tried to kill her.

CHAPTER 62

EXCERPT FROM *AMERICAN MERMAID*

"Partnership," said Granger. "To partnership." He pointed to the mermaids and then to his daughter: "Them and us, me and you."

Masahiro slid the case of champagne from the corner of the room to Granger's feet and began to tear it open. Since he had stepped out of the shadows moments ago in the getup of a software baron, Masahiro had looked strangely lifeless and wan.

As her father began to elaborate on the schedule of their Clean-Beam detonations, Masahiro came toward Sylvia, crouched down, and handed her an empty glass. He looked at her pointedly and Sylvia saw that Masahiro's eyes were alive with a familiar sparkle, a sparkle that always seemed to coincide with moments of faith in Sylvia's hidden depths and the chaos they might contain. Her heart leaped: he *hadn't* brought her here to join Granger and rule a ruined world. But what did he expect from her now? How could she stop Granger, desiccated and weak as she was?

"There's nothing I can do," she whispered to him. "I'm just a woman."

"Not for long," said Masahiro. Sylvia was helpless. She had fully split, she had no sonar, no telepathy, no strength. For a moment, she had a premonition that this might be the last time they could talk. And if she lost Masahiro, with him would go the deepest knowledge of her body, the knowledge of a doctor who'd reached into her spine. So here, with the whole world in the balance, Sylvia nevertheless yearned to ask Masahiro, finally: *Am I immune to love?*

But there was no time.

Masahiro stood over Sylvia and turned two champagne bottles upside down, dousing her. He shook them furiously and grabbed two more. At first, she gasped while Masahiro played the jester and Dean Granger protested about the mess. Even Sylvia didn't realize what Masahiro was doing—she thought maybe he was making a distraction, but then what? Four bottles doused, then six—Sylvia heard them pop, felt them gush down her neck, splash into her lap. Had Masahiro simply lost it? Eight bottles, *glug glug*, all over Sylvia, Granger now squinting, suspicious, at the madcap doctor—what was he up to?

Suddenly Sylvia's mind filled with the awareness of her sisters' calls. She received their sonar shrieks, vibrating through the glass. It had been enough: champagne was water enough; Sylvia was soaked. Her legs began to bond. She was becoming mermaid again. Masahiro nodded at her. As if in slow motion, she saw Dean Granger redden with rage as she rose up to her knees, closed her eyes, and gave the shrillest sonar shriek she could power from her head.

A whiskey bottle, left by a keyboard, shattered. The champagne bottles exploded in Masahiro's hands and rattled the ground from within their cardboard case and leaked out in a foamy river. Dean Granger's eyeglasses crackled and fell from their frames. But when she had pressed the last air out of her lungs, the great glass wall was intact. And Dean Granger, wiping the blood from a nick on his cheek and removing the empty wire frames from his face, knew that he'd been played.

Before he could say anything, there was a muted, civil *ding*, and the elevator doors opened to reveal Eleanor Granger, dopey-faced and smiling. Her hand sailed to her heart at the sight of Sylvia. A crystal tumbler slipped from her grip and hit the floor with a delicate, decisive crunch.

"Mommy." Sylvia was stunned. Eleanor raced down to Sylvia,

landed on her knees, and gathered the soaking, stinking creature in her strong arms. She squeezed her and wailed her name. Sylvia, emitting vapors of booze herself, was unused to this smell of alcohol on her mother. And there were hints of untidiness that made Eleanor slightly alien—she was in pajamas. Her hair had grown longer than Sylvia had ever seen it. Whatever Granger's plan had been, for EarthSource, for Sylvia, for a cataclysm that this family would possess like a ruby-red scepter, it was clear her mother had had no part in it. The last thing this woman wanted was power.

Sylvia looked past her mother at Granger, head drooped and shaking slowly. "Shame, shame, shame," he said to himself. "What a waste."

Sylvia gave a little sob and a moan. She was spent. Her cry, her full-body, last-ditch rebellion, had not worked. She was useless in here. Trapped. Granger would find a way to sideline Eleanor, he always had. This was too big, and now he knew Sylvia could not be trusted. He would cage her. God knew what he would do to Masahiro, who had finally bit the hand of his master. Her sisters—she only hoped they might escape Granger still, avoid enslavement, go back into hiding, forget her.

But now Sylvia became aware of Eleanor, who had drifted away from her daughter and walked slowly, dreamily across the back row of the amphitheater whose walls were pinned with eccentric objects.

"I've never been down here before," she said. "It's amazing. Feels just like your office in Westchester. Look at all this—all these artifacts." Her hand skimmed over a circular brass shield from the seventeenth century and an oval Yoruba mask with slit eyes, and landed on a handmade VO Vapen luxury hunting rifle, a six-hundred-thousand-dollar present Granger had given himself just recently.

"This," said Eleanor, "is gorgeous." She unhooked it from the wall and turned it over in her hands. She admired the floral engraving on its walnut-root stock and chatted on, as if at a fund-raiser.

"You know, I'm trained as a scientist. Gave it up." She looked up at her husband, smiling.

"Nell, careful. That's not a toy."

"Would a toy be more suitable for me, Dean? Like my little toy charities." Her attention drifted back to the gun, which she rotated toward her face. With one eye closed, she peered into the steel barrel.

"Nell, it's not me. *I* didn't do this. Blame the fossil fuel industry, blame Big Chemical. This catastrophe is coming and I alone have come up with a way to keep Sylvia safe—safe, protected, with resources and control."

The gun was now a V-shape in her hands, the chamber hanging open. The carefree act fell away as she snapped it back together with a loud click in one swift gesture and stared at her husband for the first time since her arrival. "You told me my daughter was *dead*."

"Your daughter *is* dead, Nell. This isn't Sylvia. This is a creature who would kill us if she could." Eleanor didn't show any sign of listening. "She just tried!"

"Maybe all she needed," said Eleanor, "was a little help." Tears welled in Eleanor's eyes. To Sylvia, she said simply, "I love you." She stood ten meters from her daughter now, her back against the wall. "I've missed you *so much*." Tears poured down her quivering face. "I know"—she could barely form the words—"I know what we did was wrong. We should have told you from the start. We should have accepted the possibility that you were more than us. *More* than we knew. I'm so sorry."

Sylvia cried now because she knew exactly what her mother would do. Through telepathy or because she knew her mother's love for her had no outer limit, she could see the minutes ahead. She longed for her embrace, to curl up in it like the serene scoop of a nautilus, this person who had given her growing soul a home day after day, year after year. She forgave her everything. She saw her as if for the first time now, this consistent woman, sandy hair tucked behind the ears, bright eyes scanning for danger behind frameless glasses (they were there if you looked, the vestiges of the scientist).

"Mom," Sylvia whimpered. It hadn't been her mother's fault. Eleanor Granger had been a good wife—a great wife. She'd stood beside and supported and been deeply in love with her husband. They'd had what people considered a great marriage. Eleanor Granger did not have her daughter's immunities: she had fallen in love. The habits of home life had eroded her from a tall rock cliff to something submerged and supportive. But now Eleanor Granger melted, molten with grief for what was to come. What they saw change in her was not emotion but geology as she hardened again before their eyes. She seemed to grow taller, her arms angled under the shotgun.

"I'm so sorry," Eleanor repeated, her voice now clear and calm. "I'm going to speak for your father, to say what we should have said years ago. *Go.* Inhabit a world we don't understand. Be more than we know." Finally, as if there was no one else in the room, eyes full of tears, Eleanor Granger told her daughter, "I'm so happy for you."

She raised the rifle and aimed directly at the glass wall, above Sylvia's head, where the mermaids had congregated. "I'm a little out of practice," said Eleanor, sniffling. "But it's funny, I've always been a good shot." She closed one eye. The gun went off with a rich crack as the bullet hit the glass and ricocheted. Everyone but Eleanor and Sylvia dove for the floor. When they looked back up, the glass was intact, with just a thin web of crackles radiating out from the impact point. No one was hurt.

"We're two hundred meters deep, Eleanor! What do you think this is, a *windshield*? Drop the gun, Nell! And come with me! We're getting out of here."

Sylvia, still saturated in sweetly stinking champagne, put her hand directly on the spot from which the cracks radiated. She looked at Masahiro, who nodded at her: *Yes, now.* She remembered him, alongside her in the misty car in a diner lot, saying he would die if he had to. She had time to whimper, "No," but she could feel the skin around her tail becoming tight, itchy. There was only a matter of seconds before she split again.

"Now." Masahiro gave her permission. She could see no other way.

She lifted herself up once more on a shivering tail and slammed her hands against the center of the fracture on the pane. She took a deep breath and squeezed the powerful sound waves out of her head with all her strength. Her sisters, on the other side, did the same, their hands mirroring hers on the glass. Masahiro and Granger covered their ears and ducked instinctively at the terrifying volume. Eleanor Granger dropped the gun and, smiling a dreamy smile, blew her daughter a kiss.

The amphitheater filled with water, through to every crevice in every gear shaft, up to every corner, around every body, in a fraction of a second. It was the depth: the water didn't rush in so much as it was suddenly, simply, there. It was a storm of bubbles, debris, and bodies through which, nevertheless, Sylvia tried, as her tail fully bonded and she regained strength, to get to her mother at the back of the amphitheater. She had some vague intention to preserve a pocket of air, using something, to protect her mother and bring her up safely. But it was too late. There was no air to preserve. Her sisters' calls came to her, begging her to quit the turbulent chamber of swirling fractured glass and ripped metal. Eventually she felt Kevin's arms around her, and the next thing she knew, she was lying on the seafloor in a bed of kelp. Trivial amounts of blood leaked from nicks on her sides and arms. The dark blood seeped into the water like smoke, as if a single votive candle had just been pinched out on the site of each cut.

Sylvia knew that they were all gone. Her mother, her father, and her friend. She knew that, in time, she would forget them completely, so she tried to let the sadness sting her as she held the shape of their lives in her mind like sandcastles that would be licked away.

For now, her mind clung to one moment. She had wanted

to ask Masahiro, for the last time, about her immunity to love. She had never had the chance. Now the mermaids, hovering over her, pulled her up and embraced her. They would, they told her silently through a collective song, take her to the chamber where her real mother awaited, heal her, and help her to find her place. As they swam together, she began to forget the question that had lingered last in her mind. There was only one kind of love, communal, among these creatures. All connection here derived from the most primal love, the one that rips iron gears from their shafts and torches the bright man's best laid plans: maternal love. Mermaids weren't afraid of the way women loved. They had not gone down the human path of evolution, which constrained and repressed it. They never cut it to the shape of a doorframe or made it wave good-bye in the morning. They let it leak into the water where it did everything, hunted and killed and held them all in a warm current that would have seemed hysterically sensitive anywhere on land. There is nothing mythological about this: Have you ever seen a mother spring up from a table when her child, two floors above, has a fall? Mothers move in the dark at night, while men fumble for the lights. The mermaids knew that the love of women, on land, had been domesticated, diverted, and dammed. For women, it had become a weakness; here it was a superpower. They believed they had summoned the power from Eleanor Granger that day in the amphitheater, and who's to say that they hadn't?

In the months and years to come, every now and again, breaking the surface, taking in the lavish oxygen of the open air, Sylvia would remember this thing she used to worry about, so constant it had once burned like a phantom limb. She would occasionally remember sitting with her doctor friend in a hotel she couldn't place at the start of the adventure that had brought her home, and would remember holding back the question, "Am I capable of love?" Now she knew the question made no sense. *No,* was the answer, not if love was a link between two people, a straight line you could walk. But yes, if love was something that took you in every direction, flooded out from you in the dense molecular body of the sea. Yes, yes, she answered the question that her doctor never could: You are capable of love, great, generous, surging seas of it.

And of killing.

One mermaid did not hover over Sylvia as she lay in the kelp, stunned at the loss of her human world. Dave had tended to unfinished business. It takes a man about four minutes without oxygen to die, but it takes a man about forty seconds to come. Masahiro Harada's final minutes were spent in a dimming daze of debris and pleasure, his slowing heart soothed by a song it knew. A year after the destruction of Granger's lab, a baby was born in the mermaids' chamber, with impish humor and black hair and a huge appetite. They called her Masahiro.

CHAPTER 63

One hundred and fifty miles off the coast of Los Angeles, fifty miles past the last channel island—a pounded strip of sand where US test missiles whistled and soared in privacy—a submarine moved through dark waters at two hundred and ninety meters deep. At a radar screen in a large room filled with the low buzz of instrument noise, Seaman Jenkins chatted with his neighbor, Seaman Nuñez, who was, like himself, in his midtwenties, Southern, and affable.

"Come on, that's what everybody says, *If I hadn't torn my ACL!*" Nuñez shook his head. "I'm not buying it."

"I swear man, I'd be Drew Brees!"

"Uh-huh. Yeah, you'd be Tom Brady. Hottie wife, the whole thing."

"Damn straight!" The two chuckled.

Suddenly, Jenkins drew himself up. He peered in close to his screen. Grabbed a notepad and jotted down a few numbers. "Hold up," he said to his neighbor. "Can I show you something?"

Nuñez leaned over.

"Radar picked up very high heat activity and motion at—I mean, am I right? Eight hundred meters. That's . . . seafloor?"

"What kind of activity?"

He sectioned off a portion of the screen and zoomed in. Directly below them, a red-trimmed white patch, flickering, indicated high heat. It expanded and shrunk and expanded again.

"I think you better log it, and flag it for the LCPO."

"Yeah, you're right. Never seen anything like it."

Seaman Jenkins pulled an index card out of his drawer, held it up with one hand, and punched the ten-digit password it contained into his computer to override the default screen. Then he spent a few minutes logging the details of the incident, complete with radar screenshots, and flagged it for review by his LCPO. "All right," he said when he had finished, leaning back to stretch. "I'm gonna take a leak."

Jenkins slammed the drawer shut and trotted off.

As Nuñez returned to his work, the clicking, chatter, and machine beeps faded suddenly, and in their place, Nuñez heard the sound of blood whooshing in his own ears, softly, whooshing and whispering and finally humming a song that he couldn't name. But the song told him what to do. He moved into Jenkins's seat, opened the drawer, and pulled out the index card. Using the stolen password, he logged into Jenkins's computer and erased every trace of the note his friend had just made. Nuñez logged off and returned to his seat.

With a shiver, the room came back to him in all its chaos, and he realized he'd been daydreaming. He shook himself and reached for the water bottle at his feet. Jenkins reappeared.

"Ladies and gentlemen, quarterback Seaman Jenkins takes the field!" Nuñez cupped his hands around his mouth and breathed a stadium roar.

Jenkins's hand flew out to smack his neighbor on the biceps as he slipped in front of his monitor.

Eight hundred meters below them, Sylvia was on lookout. She had just concluded a brief but necessary bout of song. The submarine had now passed, and she had released Nuñez back to himself. The note was erased. There would be no record, in machine or human memory, of any disturbance in the deep. The mermaids could continue to dismantle the lethally damaging work of men and allow the broken seabed to heal.

Sylvia's group moved out of the desolate, krill-specked dark into the shallower coastal waters after their work was done, to find food and to rest in sheltered vegetation. As they approached land this time, at dusk, Sylvia came to the surface. Seeing the city before her, she had the strangest feeling she'd seen this place before. A white ribbon of surf gave way almost immediately to a gridded metropolis, out of which rose, a certain distance back, massive gray and black towers. Then past the towers she made out a scrabbling civilization, dust-dulled lights twinkling up the mountains. Sylvia *had* been here before. She knew what it looked like, closer in. Not through sonar but through memory, she saw flashes of its wide and roaring roads, its blue pools, still as platters, serving sunlight. She remembered a feeling of rage, one that, like a rousing song, sustained itself with intermittent harmony, with little satisfactions. She had learned things. Of course—what she had just done with the sailor in the submarine she had learned here. She had taken control of a man, a uselessly handsome man, she now recalled; she had sung his salty fingers over the keys and made him enter new words into the machine. This way she kept the machine from drilling into her, from cutting her up.

She had had a life in this city. A complex one. She couldn't remember its details as a sequence in time, only in fractured images. Houses dressed like castles, houses dressed like forts, houses dressed like other houses; the glint of varnished nails wrapped around sweating goblets of cold gold stuff; ridged footsteps printed in the dust by a reservoir dried like an artifact; and wet, wetter as she pushed him deeper down, the mossy white hairs on the brown chest of a man who, kind and confident, spoke his last words: "Dude, I gotta write this."

EPILOGUE

In *Tickets to the Gunshow,* Penelope Schleeman (*American Mermaid*) tells the story of a United Airlines flight attendant who discovers during a botched hijacking that she's a world-class sniper.

Advance Praise for *Tickets to the Gunshow*

"Schleeman's turned up the dial on female trouble with Melanie and Franck, a badass flight attendant and her (literally) killer captor, a Swiss fox you'll be *wishing* would sweep you off in his unmarked van. *American Mermaid* fans might be surprised to find Schleeman in the mood for love. With her first book, feminism learned to swim, and now it's learning to *sex*. This poolside punch is super-spiked!"

—*Cosmopolitan*

"As the novel's hijackers deploy Melanie like a weapon (recalling the helplessness of the contemporary techno-precariat), Schleeman relocates us from the dusty villages of Syria's eastern plateau to the commodity vaudeville of a Gap Outlet in Oman. Schleeman's fantasy is equal parts Marx and

Marco Polo, as a woman's talent circulates like a grenade in the pocket of global capital."

—*The London Review of Books*

"You may experience turbulence on this ride! Schleeman's heroine, a flight attendant named Melanie known for neckerchiefs and polite nods, discovers she's a one-in-a-million marksman. She trades the beverage cart for the spare cartridge, but can she escape her own lust for a Swiss arms dealer? With gritty globe-trotting and a fierce feminine lead, this story is made for a leap to the big screen!"

—*Entertainment Weekly*

Penelope Schleeman teaches eleventh-grade English at Holy Cross High School in New Haven, Connecticut.

ACKNOWLEDGMENTS

This book would not exist if Barbara Bourland hadn't found a pulse in her at twenty thousand words under the sea and said she was real. I began to believe. Mermaid magic *works*. Barbara cared about me so much that she brought this to life.

If books need believers, this one also needed full-throated laughers, she needed people to look at her perform and to enjoy her, and she also needed someone to say, still smiling warmly from the laugh, "It's okay to stop juggling mackerel for a moment and feel some feelings." I'm so grateful to my editor, Lee Boudreaux, for being all those people and also a brilliant surgeon—not the kind that breaks a creature but rather gets her scales aligned and gets her taking tighter corners than she ever knew she could.

How much further should I take this mermaid-book metaphor? Wish I could run it by my agent, Sarah Bedingfield at Levine Greenberg Rostan, whom I thank for her pivotal conviction early on and for brilliant reading and essential guidance along the way.

I want to thank the whole team at Doubleday, who put so much energy and intelligence into shaping this book and putting it into the world, including Cara Reilly, Elena Hershey, Lindsay Mandel, Emily Mahon, Kathleen Cook, and Megan Gerrity.

I owe much to my draft readers, whose messages of joy and support while reading ("the universal experience of drinking Sangria and fruit hitting your face . . . That's what literature is ABOUT") were like those packets of goo literally called GU that people slurp during marathons so they don't have to stop for burgers. That text was from Justine van der Leun, writer, woman, mother, investigator, hero, whom I thank for an important early read and for giving me Lorrie Moore when I was fifteen. I thank readers Tom Ogier, Caroline Frost, Mei Chin, Priya Swaminathan, James Tracy, Liz Riley, and Masato Hasegawa for all kinds of insights that helped this book sparkle and make sense. I'm grateful to Irene Lynch, a true fiction reader, for an enthusiastic response that meant a great deal to me. Many thanks to Andy Blomquist, who builds actual power plants, for helping me build imaginary ones. Thanks to Lang Fisher, who had no idea, during all those visits to LA when I was making her take me to the mall to buy shorts like a poor relation, that she was sowing the seeds of a story, and for telling me about plots on a train ride to Kilkenny when we had only one kid between us and had no idea just how complicated plots could get. I also thank her for a crucial late read and for giving me the line where Danielle tells Penelope to go to a meeting naked, which sounds like something we did in our twenties.

I thank Susanna Fogel for specific wisdom, general enthusiasm, and successful matchmaking, Melissa Wells for magic dust and sound advice, and Gabe Liedman (and Lang again) for helping spread the word.

Kirsti Langbein knew decades before I did that this would happen. It is hilarious now to think about all the years during which I felt embarrassed for being "garrulous," and I would have shut up if she hadn't said, "When you write your novel . . ." She was listening more deeply than anyone, and she sounded out my future and let me know there would be a place for my play.

Why do I always thank my husband at the end? He's not an afterthought, but it feels appropriate to end with him, as days do. I like to do a cruel impression of women who call their husbands their "rocks." I follow my husband around on Father's Day scream-

ACKNOWLEDGMENTS

ing, "CHAD, YOU ARE OUR ROCK," even though his name is John. But I apologize for that impression now because his unshakable belief that this speculative endeavor would come good was a bedrock on which everything else was built. So, thank you, Chad, I can hear you eating right now and I still love you.